AUSTRALIA

THE SPIRIT OF A NATION

Not as the songs of other lands
  Her song shall be
Where dim Her purple shore-line stands
  Above the sea!
As erst she stood, she stands alone;
Her inspiration is her own.
From sunlit plains to mangrove strands
Not as the songs of other lands
  Her song shall be.

From 'An Australian Symphony'
by George Essex Evans

AUSTRALIA

THE SPIRIT OF A NATION

A Bicentenary Album

MICHAEL CANNON

Picture Research
DEBBY CRAMER

VIKING O'NEIL

A Land of Gold and Strange Beings Lies to the South . . . and a Great Adventure Begins

In ancient times, men already knew that Australia must be waiting somewhere beyond the horizon. If there wasn't such a land mass to the south, they argued, the world would tip over like an unbalanced dish. Explorers should simply keep on looking, and they would assuredly find the Great South Land.

In 1271 AD, Marco Polo, a brash young Venetian merchant, accompanied his father and uncle on an expedition to the almost unknown civilisation of China. Some versions of his travels have him speaking of rich lands several hundred miles south of Java, where 'there is found greate plentye of gold'. He added that 'Vnto this Ilande there commeth very fewe Strangers, for that it ftandeth out of the way'.

Map makers took this to refer to the legendary South land, adding elephants and treasure to their fanciful descriptions of 'Terrae Australis Incognitae'—the unknown lands of Australia. In this way Australia remained a tantalising mystery. But an increasing number of people were convinced of its existence and future importance. Which of the emerging empires would reach out to grasp it, and stamp the imprint of one or other European civilisation upon those apparently virgin shores?

The Portuguese and Spanish, at the height of their world maritime power, became interested in Australia. Evidence exists that a Portuguese captain, Cristovao de Mendonca, sailed along the east coast of Australia in 1522—nearly two hundred and fifty years before Captain Cook—turning back only when his 'mahogany ship' was wrecked on the Victorian coast near present-day Warrnambool.

In 1606, Pedro de Quiros, a navigator for the Spanish fleet in the Pacific, found what he thought at first was the rumoured South land. Full of zeal to convert the natives to Roman Catholicism, he named

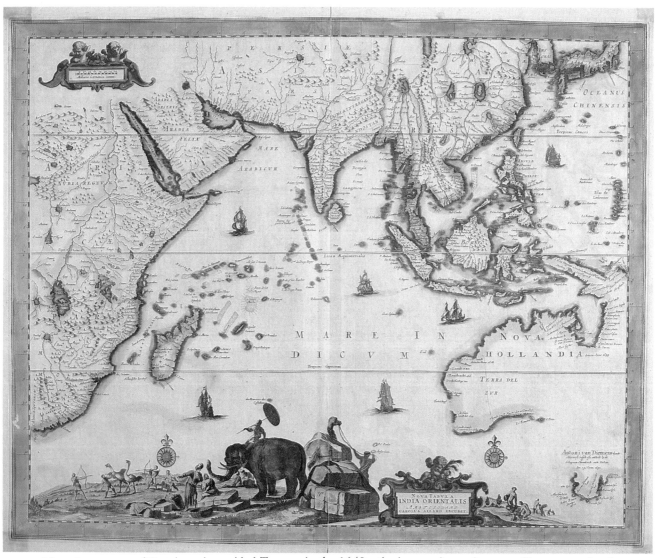

After the voyages of Dutch explorer Abel Tasman in the 1640s, the known Australian coastline appeared as in this **map by Karel Allard of Amsterdam, c. 1650.**

Tasman shows his voyages on a world globe to his wife and daughter. Painting attributed to Jacob Gerritsz Cuyp (1594–1651).

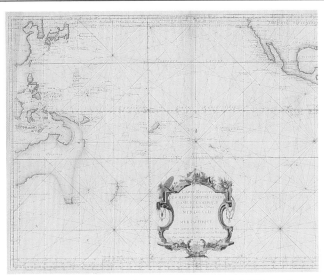

Even as late as this **French map of 1742**, explorers thought that the Spaniards' 'Espiritu Santo' (New Hebrides) was part of the Australian mainland.

it 'La Austrialia del Espiritu Santo'. In fact he had discovered the New Hebrides, about one thousand miles off the Queensland coast. One Spanish commander, Luis Vaez de Torres, disagreed with Quiros. He continued sailing westwards, discovered Torres Strait, but did not sight the Australian coastline. By only a few miles, Spain failed in the quest for the fabled continent.

In fact the Dutch became the main early European discoverers of Australia. Freed with Britain's help from Spanish occupation, Holland was soon swept by a passion for empire-building. This expansion brought the Dutch very close to the still unknown South land. After formation of the United East India Company in 1602, the Netherlands won control of Java, Sumatra, the Celebes, Timor, parts of Borneo and New Guinea, and many smaller islands. With Dutch ships everywhere, the discovery of Australia became inevitable. Willem Jansz, sent in the little *Duyfken* in 1606 to chart New Guinea, missed Torres Strait and mapped part of Cape York Peninsula instead. That was the first confirmed discovery. Ten years later another Dutchman, Dirk Hartog, made the first authenticated sighting of our western coastline.

In 1627 the south coast of Australia was discovered just as accidentally. Frans Thyssen, captain of the *Gulden Zeepaard*, was blown off course to the East Indies and limped into the Great Australian Bight instead. He got as far as the Nuyts Archipelago, nearly halfway along the South Australian coast-line, before realising his mistake and turning back.

Antonio van Diemen, Governor-General of the Dutch East Indies, commissioned Abel Tasman to explore the remaining coast. Tasman made two voyages. On the first he discovered the southernmost point, naming it Van Diemen's Land (Tasmania), then sailed on to discover New Zealand. On his second voyage two years later, Tasman mapped the Australian coastline from Carpentaria westward to Nuyts Archipelago. But the Dutch East India Company authorities were not ready for another major colonising endeavour. Tasman lost his main supporter when Van Diemen retired in 1645. That year the Directors wrote: 'It were to be wished that the said land [Australia] continued still unknown and never explored, so as not to tell foreigners the way to the Company's overthrow'.

After Tasman's arduous labours, the Dutch reaction was to suppress all knowledge of Australia! They didn't need it, at least for the moment; nor did they want anyone else to get hold of it. But within two years, a copy of Tasman's map was stolen and smuggled to London. Perfidious Albion, flexing her own muscles, was turning a thoughtful eye to those little-known regions on the opposite side of the globe.

It is impossible to conceive a Country that promises fairer from its Situation than this of Terra Australis; no longer incognita, as this Map demonstrates, but the Southern Continent Discovered. It lies Precisely in the richest Climates of the World . . . whoever perfectly discovers and settles it will become infallibly possessed of Territories as Rich, as fruitful, & as capable of Improvement, as any that have been hitherto found out, either in the East Indies, or the West.

ABEL TASMAN

Conversion Tables

Money values below show theoretical conversion rates
from sterling to decimal currency. To get a better idea of
comparative values, readers should allow for the huge
inflation of the currency which has occurred in recent decades.

CURRENCY
One halfpenny (½d) = ½ cent approx.
One penny (1d) = 1 cent approx.
One shilling (1s) = 10 cents
One pound (£1) = $2 = 200 cents

LENGTH
One inch (1 in) = 2·54 cm
One foot (1 ft) = 30·5 cm approx.
One yard (1 yd) = 0·914 metres
One mile = 1760 yards = 1·61 km

AREA
One acre = 0·405 hectares approx.
One square mile = 640 acres = 259 hectares

CAPACITY
One gallon = 8 pints = 4·55 litres
One bushel = 8 gallons = 36·4 litres

WEIGHT
One ounce (1 oz) = 28·3 grams
One pound (1 lb) = 16 oz = 0·454 kg
One hundredweight (cwt) = 112 pounds
One ton = 20 cwt = 1·02 tonnes

Viking O'Neil
Penguin Books Australia Ltd
487 Maroondah Highway, PO Box 257
Ringwood, Victoria 3134, Australia
Penguin Books Ltd
Harmondsworth, Middlesex, England
Viking Penguin Inc.
40 West 23rd Street, New York, N.Y. 10010, U.S.A.
Penguin Books Canada Ltd
2801 John Street, Markham, Ontario, Canada L3R 1B4
Penguin Books (N.Z.) Ltd
182-190 Wairau Road, Auckland 10, New Zealand

First published by Currey O'Neil Ross Pty Ltd 1985
This edition published by Penguin Books Australia Ltd 1988
Copyright © Michael Cannon, 1985

Produced by Viking O'Neil
56 Claremont Street, South Yarra, Victoria 3141, Australia
A division of Penguin Books Australia Ltd

Typeset in Australia by ProComp Productions Pty Ltd
Printed and bound in Hong Kong through Bookbuilders Ltd

National Library of Australia
Cataloguing-in-Publication data

Cannon, Michael, 1929–
    Australia, the spirit of a nation.

    Includes index.
    ISBN 0 670 90079 6.

    1. Patriotism—Australia. 2. Australia—
History. I. Cramer, Debby. II. Title.

Contents

PART I

The Heroic Struggle to Occupy a Whole Continent

The Captains

The Captains sailed from Portugal, from England, France, and Spain;
Each sought to win his country's ease, her glory and her gain;
The Captains sailed to Southern Seas, and sailed the Spanish Main;
And some sailed out beyond the world, and some sailed home again . . .

The Captains sailed to India, to China and Japan,
Received the Strangers' Welcome, met the Friendliness of Man;
The Captains sailed to southern seas, and wondrous sights they saw—
The Rights of Man in savage lands, and lands without a law.

They found fresh worlds for crowded folk from cities old and worn,
They found the new great empty lands where Nations might be born;
They found new foods, they found new wealth, and newer ways to live,
Where sons might grow in strength and health, with all that God would give.

HENRY LAWSON

1. Britain Sends a Buccaneer to Find Australia

Somehow it seems fitting that a freebooting adventurer should have been the first man to explore the Australian coastline on Britain's behalf. William Dampier, born in 1652, son of a Somerset farmer, soon decided that life as a clod-hopper was too dull for him. First he joined the Royal Navy, then in 1683 teamed up with a buccaneer on the Spanish Main. Their pirate ship *Cygnet* terrorised Spanish and Portuguese vessels from South America to the Philippines. In January 1688 they found their way to King Sound on the north-west coast of Australia, where today Derby is the main port.

Dampier's journals, published in London after his return three years later, caused a sensation. His *New Voyage Round the World* went through four editions in two years, and was quickly translated for European consumption. The British Admiralty readily forgave Dampier's dubious reputation, commissioning him to continue the exploration of Australian waters as captain of HMS *Roebuck*.

The romantic pirate-explorer **William Dampier**, painted by W. Dobson.

New Holland *is a very large tract of Land. It is not yet determined whether it is an Island or a main Continent; but I am certain that it joyns neither to* Asia, Africa, *nor* America . . . *The Land is of a dry sandy soil, destitute of Water, except you make Wells: yet producing divers sorts of Trees: but the Woods are not thick, nor the Trees very big. Most of the Trees that we saw are Dragon-trees as we supposed; and these too are the largest Trees of any there . . . The leaves are of a dark colour; the Gum distils out of the knots or cracks that are in the bodies of the Trees. We compared it with some Gum Dragon, or Dragons Blood, that was aboard; and it was of the same colour and taste . . . There was pretty long Grass growing under the Trees; but it was very thin. We saw no Trees that bore Fruit or Berries.*

We saw no sort of Animal, nor any track of Beast, but once; and that seemed to be the tread of a Beast as big as a great Mastiff-Dog. Here are a few small Land-birds, but none bigger than a Blackbird: and but a few Sea-fowls. Neither is the Sea very plentifully stored with Fish, unless you reckon the Manatee and Turtle as such.

WILLIAM DAMPIER, report after spending three months exploring the north-west coast of Australia in 1688.

2. The Amazing Voyage by James Cook

The story of Cook's discovery of the Australian east coast really begins with a British East India Company official, Alexander Dalrymple. Translating captured Spanish documents in 1762, Dalrymple found Luis de Torres's record of his passage between New Guinea and Australia, kept secret for 150 years. Dalrymple included this revelation in a book of oceanic discoveries published in London. As a result he was recommended to lead a Royal Society expedition planned for the Pacific area in 1768–69 to observe the transit of Venus over the face of the sun. Dalrymple insisted on command of the vessel, but this did not suit Admiralty officials at all. They had secret motives, and needed a naval commander who could be trusted to keep his own counsel: not a geographer who might be tempted to publish prematurely. So they appointed James Cook, a comparatively unknown 40-year-old lieutenant in the Royal Navy.

Unable to use Dalrymple, the Royal Society urged that Joseph Banks, a young botanist who had inherited considerable wealth, should be allowed to join the expedition and finance its scientific research. Clearly he would be under naval direction. So Banks boarded His Majesty's barque *Endeavour* with eight assistants and dozens of the latest scientific appliances.

Preparations by these botanists and astronomers could scarcely be concealed. But the Admiralty's underlying motives were highly confidential. Lieutenant Cook was given two sets of instructions. The first dealt openly with arrangements to sail around Cape Horn and observe the planet Venus from recently discovered Tahiti. Then . . . 'When this Service is performed, you are to put to Sea without loss of Time & carry into execution the Additional Instructions contained in the inclosed Sealed Packet'.

We can imagine the excitement with which Cook broke the seal and extracted his secret orders. These were stunning in their implications. He was instructed to discover the unknown coast of the Great South Land and take control of it for His Majesty! This was much more than a voyage of discovery. It was clearly aimed at possession and early settlement.

By August 1769 the voyagers had completed their astronomical work. Cook sailed on for New Zealand, circumnavigating and charting both islands, and proving they could not form the eastern coast of the great southern continent. His instructions were now quite clear: to sail between the latitudes of 35° and 40° S (roughly today's Jervis Bay to King Island) until he discovered land. That is exactly what he did. Yet chance again played its part. On 18 April 1770, a gale through Bass Strait forced Cook to run north of the 40th parallel. At 6 a.m. on 19 April, Lieutenant Zachary Hicks, in charge of the watch, sighted land at about 38° S. He immediately woke the captain. Cook named the low promontory Point Hicks, not yet knowing whether it was an island or part of a large land mass. What should he do now? Let his journal take up the story:

> To the Southward of this point we could see no land, and yet it was clear in that Quarter, and by our Longitude compared with that of Tasman's, the body of Van Diemen's Land ought to have bore due S. from us, and from the soon falling of the Sea after the wind abated I had reason to think it did; but as we did not see it, and finding the Coast to trend N.E. and S.W., or rather more to the Westward, makes me Doubtfull whether they are one land or no.

Already Cook suspected that Van Diemen's Land was not part of the great continent. Think about his mental processes at this point. If he continued to sail west, he might discover a passage through what we now call Bass Strait. Eventually

he must simply join up with the well-known Dutch discoveries in Western Australia. Not much glory in that. But if he turned north . . .

'We got Topgallant Yards a Cross, made all sail, and bore away along shore N.E. for the Eastermost land we had in sight', Cook recorded laconically. Next day, 'The weather being clear gave us an opportunity to View the Country, which had a very agreeable and promising aspect, diversified with hills, ridges, plains, and Valleys, with some few small lawns; but for the most part the whole was covered with wood, the hills and ridges rise with a gentle slope . . .' The fertile east coast, so long imagined by the world's navigators, had at last been discovered.

Now it was time to look for a safe harbour, to rest, find fresh water, scrape barnacles off the ship's bottom, and calculate future moves. On 29 April, the *Endeavour* sailed into what Cook at first called Stingray Bay. Banks and his scientists were so enthralled by the hundreds of unknown plants and animals which had evolved on the isolated continent that Cook soon renamed the landfall Botany Bay. The anchorage was, he wrote, 'capacious safe and commodious'.

The few Aborigines there rejected Cook's friendly approaches. The soil was disappointingly sandy and lightly timbered. On 3 May, however, Cook walked further inland: 'I found in many places a deep black soil which we thought was capable of producing any kind of grain at present it produceth besides timber as fine meadow as ever was seen . . .' He also discovered 'a very fine stream of fresh water', plentiful sandstone suitable for building, and 'a variety of very boutifull birds such as Cocatoo's, Lorryquets Parrots &c'. Every day Cook 'caused the English colours to be display'd a shore', while an inscription was cut into a tree to record the ship's name and date of arrival.

Cook finally took back to England in July 1771 the message about Australia that British expansionists most wanted to hear. What a challenge and opportunity for a vigorous maritime nation! In the seat of government, Cook's report was discussed behind closed doors but with growing excitement.

Cook's ship left Plymouth on 26 August 1768 on its great voyage of Australian and New Zealand discovery. Painting by Thomas Luny shows the **'Endeavour' leaving Whitby Harbour.**

This Eastern side is not that barren and Miserable Country that Dampier and others have described the Western side to be. We are to Consider that we see this Country in the pure state of Nature the Industry of man has had nothing to do with any part of it and yet we find all such things as nature hath bestowed upon it in a flourishing state. In this Extensive Country it can never be doubted but what most sorts of Grain, Fruits, Roots, &c of every kind would flourish here were they once brought hither, planted and cultivated by the hand of Industry.

LIEUTENANT COOK, report on the Australian east coast.

Australasia—A Poem

Illustrious Cook! Columbus of our shore,
To whom was left this unknown world t'explore,
Its untraced bounds on faithful chart to mark,
And leave a light where all before was dark:
And thou, the foremost in fair learning's ranks,
Patron of ev'ry art, departed Banks,
Who wealth disdaining, and inglorious ease,
The rocks and quicksands dared
  of unknown seas:
Immortal Pair when in yon spacious bay
Ye moor'd awhile its wonders to survey,
How little thought ye that the name from you
Its graceful shrubs, and beauteous wild
  flowers drew,
Would serve, in after times, with lasting brand
To stamp the soil, and designate the land.

W. C. WENTWORTH

James Cook's landing at Botany Bay to take possession of Australia in 1770 was imaginatively re-created in 1901 in this famous painting by the Melbourne artist E. Phillips Fox (1865–1915).

3. Revolutionary Events Force a Decision on the Settlement of Australia

'Taxation without representation is tyranny', cried American patriot James Otis. Mark that cry well, for we will hear it again when Australian colonists begin to demand a voice in their own affairs.

In December 1773, as Captain Cook turned homewards from his second voyage of discovery, thousands of miles away in Boston, Massachusetts, a group of American rebels dumped 342 chests of tea into the harbour rather than pay the hated British taxes. In April 1775 a British detachment marched to destroy rebel arms hidden at Concord. Forewarned by Paul Revere, the 'Minutemen' met them with accurate rifle fire. Other victories followed, and finally in 1781 Lord Cornwallis surrendered to a combined American and French army at Yorktown.

The impact on Australia's history was profound. Up to 1775 an average of 1000 British convicts had been transported each year to work alongside Negro slaves on American plantations. When war broke out, this economical solution to the overcrowding of British gaols was no longer feasible.

In 1779 Joseph Banks (not knowing that his friend Captain Cook had just been speared to death by Hawaiian natives) proposed to a House of Commons committee that Botany Bay would serve well as a place of banishment. It contained enough rich soil, water and timber to make a settlement self-supporting within twelve months. Eventually, said Banks, 'if the people formed among themselves a Civil Government, they would necessarily increase', thus forming an excellent market for English products.

Six years later Admiral Sir George Young revived Banks's scheme for a penal colony to receive Britain's worst unhung criminals. New South Wales was far enough away, Sir George remarked sombrely, to prevent for ever 'the facility of their return'. He found a supporter in Lord Sydney, Home Secretary, who announced on 18 August 1786 the government's decision to settle Australia.

To take charge of this far-off gaol, the government selected Captain Arthur Phillip, son of a German language teacher who had married a Royal Navy officer's widow. The young Arthur Phillip, enrolled on the 'poor boys' list at Greenwich training academy, had displayed dogged qualities which won him promotion to lieutenant in early manhood.

On 12 October 1786, Phillip, then 48, was appointed first Governor of New South Wales. His responsibility covered all the land stretching from today's Cape York Peninsula to Tasmania, and from the east coast to 135° longitude—roughly halfway through South Australia and the Northern Territory. It also included 'all the islands adjacent in the Pacific Ocean'. The discoveries made by Dutch explorers in Western Australia were excluded from Britain's claims at this stage, so that in 1786 it was still open for Australia to be subdivided among European powers.

Commanding this huge empire with tiny resources, Phillip in theory was given the total power to enforce British law and perform 'all manner of things thereunto belonging'—subject of course to further directions from his superiors. In this way began the period of autocratic rule by a supposedly all-powerful Governor.

The 'First Fleet' of eleven ships set sail from Portsmouth on 13 May 1787. On board were Phillip and his staff of nine, 443 seamen, 568 male convicts, 191 female convicts with 13 children, 211 marines, and 27 wives with their 19 children. After a voyage lasting eight months, the fleet arrived safely at Botany Bay. Phillip was unhappy with the location, and sailed a few miles further north to penetrate what we now call Sydney Heads. On 26 January 1788—now celebrated as Australia Day—the first marines and convicts landed in Sydney Cove near the Tank Stream. The Union flag was raised and toasts drunk. Captain Watkin Tench described the 'highly picturesque and amusing' scene which followed:

Sir Joseph Banks
(1743–1820), famous English naturalist who accompanied James Cook on his first voyage of discovery, and later suggested Botany Bay as a penal settlement. Painting by T. Phillips.

The several gaols and places for the confinement of felons in this kingdom being in so crowded a state that the greatest danger is to be apprehended, not only from their escape, but from infectious distempers, which may hourly be expected to break out amongst them, His Majesty, desirous of preventing by every possible means the ill consequences which might happen from either of these causes, has been pleased to signify to me his Royal commands that measures should immediately be pursued for sending out of this Kingdom such of the convicts as are under sentence or order of transportation.

His Majesty has thought it advisable to fix upon Botany Bay, situated on the coast of New South Wales, in the latitude of about 33 degrees south . . .

LORD THOMAS SYDNEY, Home Secretary, announces Britain's decision to settle Australia, 18 August 1786.

One party was cutting down the woods; a second was setting up a blacksmith's forge; a third was dragging a load of stores or provisions; here an officer was pitching his marquee, with a detachment of troops parading on one side of him, and a cook's fire blazing up on the other.

A few days later the remaining ships sailed around from Botany Bay and the female convicts were landed. According to Arthur Bowes Smyth, a ship's surgeon: 'The men convicts got to them very soon after they landed, and it is beyond my abilities to give a just description of the scene of debauchery and riot that ensued during the night'. Seamen with the fleet, who had been issued with rum, joined in the revelry.

Amid frequent disease and semi-starvation, life had to continue. In February 1788 Norfolk Island was colonised by a small party under Lieutenant Philip King, a future Governor. In March, Arthur Phillip left his hateful convict gangs for a refreshing exploration trip by longboat through Broken Bay into the Hawkesbury River. Immediately round the headland he discovered, as he wrote, 'the finest piece of water I ever saw, and which I honoured with the name of Pitt Water' (after Prime Minister William Pitt).

Despite clashes with some of his officers and a worsening shortage of food, Phillip was able to report cheerfully enough to Lord Sydney in July 1788: 'Time will remove all difficultys, and with a few familys who have been used to the cultivation of lands, this country will wear a more pleasing aspect . . .'

Two years later, when officers dining with the Governor were still being asked to bring their own bread, Phillip could report that only seventy-one of the 1030 people landed had died in these benign surroundings. 'I believe a finer or more healthy climate is not to be found in any part of the world', he added. Many

Soldiers as well as convicts in effect suffered banishment to Australia. '**The Soldiers' Farewell**', an 1803 watercolour, was probably painted by Isaac Cruikshank.

We got into Port Jackson early in the afternoon, and had the satisfaction of finding the finest harbour in the world, in which a thousand sail of the line may ride in the most perfect security.

GOVERNOR PHILLIP, report to Lord Sydney, 25 January 1788.

Captain Arthur Phillip, who had an equally humble background to James Cook, became the first Governor of New South Wales. Contemporary portrait by Francis Wheatley was painted in 1786.

emergencies lay ahead, but this potent breed of Anglo-Saxon invaders clung tenaciously to the beachhead and were now ready for expansion in all directions.

While the Sydney settlement fought for survival, the south-eastern coastline remained an enigma. But like Captain Cook, the second Governor, John Hunter, suspected that an ocean separated two lands. The question was important. Discovery of such a strait would considerably shorten voyages to and from England. As the French became more active, fresh sightings of desirable land and harbours might prompt them to settle permanently in southern Australia.

In 1797 Hunter commissioned George Bass, a 26-year-old naval surgeon whose hobby was navigation, to establish the truth of the matter. Bass set out with six men in a leaky 28-foot whaleboat built in Sydney from native timbers. Through constant storms they sailed southwards, hugging the coastline, and finding the Shoalhaven River, Twofold Bay and Wilson's Promontory. They touched on the Ninety-Mile Beach in Gippsland to become the first Europeans to land in Victoria.

The following year, in a larger sloop, Bass and Flinders circumnavigated Van Diemen's Land, discovered the Tamar River which leads to today's Launceston, and sailed up the Derwent estuary where Hobart now stands. Military forces sent from Sydney quickly occupied both sites, effectively closing the island against non-British intrusion.

A voyage, expressly undertaken for discovery in an open boat, and in which 600 miles of coast, mostly in a boisterous climate, was explored, has not perhaps its equal in the annals of maritime history.

MATTHEW FLINDERS, on the voyage by George Bass which discovered Bass Strait.

George Bass and Matthew Flinders charted Botany Bay, Port Hacking and Port Kembla in this open eight-foot dinghy called 'Tom Thumb'. Painting by Hugh Sawrey.

True Patriots All

*From distant climes o'er
  wide-spread seas we come,
Though not with much eclat
  or beat of drum,
TRUE PATRIOTS ALL; for
  be it understood,
We left our country for our
  country's good;
No private views disgrac'd
  our generous zeal,
What urg'd our travels was
  our country's weal;
And none will doubt but
  that our emigration
Has prov'd most useful to
  the British nation.*

From 'Prologue by a Gentleman of Leicester', spoken at
the opening of the first
Sydney theatre in 1796.

Norfolk Island, settled only
a few weeks after Sydney,
became feared by convicts as
a place of extreme
punishment. Painting by
George Raper, midshipman
on the *Sirius*, shows **the
settlement as it was in
April 1790.**

Visit of Hope to Sydney Cove
Near Botany Bay

*WHERE Sydney Cove her lucid bosom swells,
Courts her young navies, and the storm repels;
High on a rock amid the troubled air
HOPE stood sublime, and wav'd her golden hair;
Calm'd with her rosy smile the tossing deep,
And with sweet accents charm'd the winds to sleep;
To each wild plain she stretch'd her snowy hand,
High-waving wood, and sea-encircled strand.
'Hear me,' she cried, 'ye rising Realms! record
Time's opening scenes, and Truth's unerring word. —
There shall broad streets their stately walls extend,
The circus widen, and the crescent bend;
There, ray'd from cities o'er the cultur'd land,
Shall bright canals, and solid roads expand. —
There the proud arch, Colossus-like, bestride
Yon glittering streams, and bound the chafing tide;
Embellish'd villas crown the landscape-scene,
Farms wave with gold, and orchards blush between. —
There shall tall spires, and dome-capt towers ascend,
And piers and quays their massy structures blend;
While with each breeze approaching vessels glide,
And northern treasures dance on every tide!' —
Then ceas'd the nymph — tumultuous echoes roar,
And Joy's loud voice was heard from shore to shore —
Her graceful steps descending press'd the plain,
And PEACE, and ART, and LABOUR, join'd her train.*

DR ERASMUS DARWIN, physician-philosopher and grandfather of
Charles Darwin, in preface to Governor Phillip's journal of the
first voyage and settlement, published London 1789.

4. Despite All Difficulties, Sydney Begins to Prosper

Governor Phillip returned home to seek medical attention after less than five years in charge of Britain's new convict colony. By that time, the foundations had been laid for a peculiar class system in which free men and ex-convicts jostled for the right to participate in the settlement's economic development.

The first layer in this growing prosperity consisted of 'emancipists'—well-behaved convicts who had been released and granted 30-acre blocks of land on which they could hope for self-sufficiency. Marriage was encouraged by an additional 20-acre grant, and population growth by an extra 10 acres per child. The second layer consisted of those few free men and women who had come with the convict fleets and turned to farming or trading. The third layer in the colony's class system consisted of officers of the New South Wales Corps, raised in 1789 to replace the navy's marine force. Francis Grose, a 30-year-old major who had fought courageously in the American war, was appointed Commandant after Phillip's departure. Without warning, Grose began to overturn the principles of orderly settlement laid down in Britain.

Phillip had consistently refused to allow officers to take up farming, believing it would distract them from their proper duties. Grose promptly issued a land grant to any member of the NSW Corps who requested one. He allotted ten convicts to each officer's farm, continuing their rations at government expense. Such actions might have been justified by the results, for the colony's productivity increased steadily as officers competed to build farms and profits. But it was indefensible for Grose to allow the NSW Corps to engage in the liquor trade. They quickly monopolised imports and distribution for their own benefit, and became a force powerful enough to defy any Governor.

Captain John Hunter, RN, appointed to succeed Phillip as Governor, did his best to restore normality. He was horrified to find that his military officers were spending much of their time buying and selling rum and other imports. During one six-month period, 36,000 gallons of rum and 22,000 gallons of wine were shipped in to supply a total population of 5000 inhabitants. Hunter issued suppressive orders, but in vain. The NSW Corps, accustomed to its commercial privileges, simply failed to obey. No other power in the colony was strong enough to force them.

In 1800 Hunter was unfairly recalled, and the unmanageable colony handed over to Philip Gidley King, aged forty-two. Son of a Cornish draper, King had fought in the Royal Navy against the American rebels. A renewed burst of prosperity, partly due to good seasons, followed his appointment. The new Governor resumed land grants to emancipists. He opened a government store where they could buy or even hire their farm needs—including sheep and oxen—at low prices.

Yet the more prosperous the colony became, the more problems were caused by rapacious army officers. Captain John Macarthur suggested to his superior officer, Major William Paterson, that they should retaliate by breaking off social relations with the Governor. Paterson was outraged, challenged Macarthur to a duel, and had his right shoulder blown to pieces. Macarthur was arrested and sent to England to stand trial. This was the worst thing King could have done, for it enabled Macarthur to bring his imperious will to bear on officials in London.

While Macarthur was absent, other officers began to circulate defamatory 'pipes' or verses. King foolishly sent the verses to London with an offer to stand aside while an inquiry was conducted. The British government interpreted this as an offer to resign, and began to cast around for yet another Governor who might control this unexpectedly prosperous, unexpectedly troublesome, penal colony on the other side of the world. Little did they suspect what revolutionary forces they were about to unleash.

Instead of the rock I expected to see, I find myself surrounded with gardens that flourish and produce fruit of every description. Vegetables are here in great abundance, and I live in as good a house as I wish for.

FRANCIS GROSE, reporting to London in 1792.

Captain John Hunter, second Governor of New South Wales, who attempted to halt the rum trade. Painting by William Bennett.

Captain Philip Gidley King, third Governor, was forced to resign in the conflict with military officers. Artist unknown.

The convict town they couldn't hold back: **Sydney from the Rocks, painted in 1803** by J. W. Lancashire.

5. Two Kinds of Rebellion Shake Sydney

Stern discipline worked wonders in the Royal Navy—why wouldn't it work in New South Wales? A succession of naval Governors tried in vain to impose quarterdeck discipline on the brawling colony. On one side were now thousands of banished, restless, rebellious convicts and expirees. On the other side were their masters—often military officers who increasingly abandoned their duty to snatch at the lure of quick profits. Savagely exploited by their masters, flogged without mercy if they did not work until they dropped, many convicts came to believe that death through rebellion was preferable to this living torment.

Such attitudes were particularly common among 'United Irishmen' transported for rebellion in their homeland and in Royal Navy mutinies of 1798. By 1800 New South Wales contained 1600 Irish convicts in a total adult population of 6000 people. That year Governor Hunter reported their 'turbulent appearances' and 'improper designs'. To assist the regular troops in maintaining control, Hunter raised Australia's first armed militia, with platoons of gentlemen drilling at Sydney and Parramatta. Such precautions nipped the first uprising in the bud.

Hunter's successor Governor King pleaded with Britain not to send more Irish rebels. But Australia was too convenient as a dumping ground for the tragic results of British policy in Ireland. Late in 1802 a further 400 Irish convicts arrived. King did what he could to disperse them among free settlers, and prevent communication between their leaders. It was not enough. In March 1804 the long-expected insurrection began. Rebel leaders sent to work at Castle Hill circulated a plan to overpower the guards, capture the Hawkesbury and Parramatta settlements, enlist 'croppies' to help them, march on Sydney, shoot the officers, seize a ship and sail back to Ireland.

The plan started well: Castle Hill barracks was burned to the ground and the soldiers' weapons seized. But one man escaped on horseback, making a desperate midnight dash to Sydney. Governor King and Major George Johnston immediately mobilised the available men to march through the night.

Early the following morning, with only twenty-six troops behind him, Major

The Irish convict rebellion at Rouse Hill in 1804 is crushed by Major George Johnston and his small detachment of troops.
From a contemporary water-colour by an unknown artist.

Johnston confronted a much larger band of about two hundred and thirty Irishmen at Vinegar Hill (Rouse Hill) near Toongabbie. He demanded a parley: two of the rebel leaders walked forward and were asked what they hoped to gain. 'Death or liberty', one rebel replied. But these were not gentlemen with whom an officer might debate such matters: they were scum. 'I'll liberate you, you scoundrel!', Major Johnston cried, raising a gun. The two convict leaders were promptly taken prisoner. While they looked on in horror, the troops fired at close range into the mass of convicts, then advanced with fixed bayonets and cut them to pieces. As at Eureka fifty years later, a force of disciplined troops crushed an amateur rebellion without difficulty. Fifteen rebels were killed, others severely wounded, and the remainder fled into the bush. One leader was hanged on the spot; eight more after due process of law.

A long-term result of the rebellion was that many surviving rebels were sentenced to work underground in chains on coal deposits which had been found at the mouth of the Hunter River. In this way Newcastle was built on the scarred backs of those who had once shone the torch of freedom.

An Angry Beginning to the Battle for Constitutional Rights

Four years after the Irish convicts' rather pathetic blow for freedom that rarest of events in British public life occurred—a successful mutiny by well-fed, well-paid army officers against their own government. How did this extraordinary business come about? The answer lies in two headstrong individuals who attempted to dominate affairs in New South Wales. One was John Macarthur, officer in the NSW Corps, sheep farmer, and notorious trader in spirits. The other was William Bligh, loyal naval captain, appointed to succeed Philip King as Governor.

In earlier pages we saw how Macarthur was sent home in disgrace after wounding his superior officer in a duel. Awaiting his court-martial in London, Macarthur studied the works of noted law reformer Jeremy Bentham. He was not much impressed by Bentham's vision that politics should aim for 'the greatest happiness of the greatest number'. But a publication of 1803 entitled *A Plea for the Constitution of New South Wales* seemed useful to Macarthur's ambitions.

Bentham's pamphlet concluded that because New South Wales had been established by the King's command instead of parliamentary action, the settlement was illegal. That being so, it followed that every government action taken in Sydney was also illegal. To Captain Macarthur, the significance of this was that he had been illegally charged with fighting a duel. Never mind his opponent's smashed shoulder—the rights of Englishmen must be upheld! By propagating this curious logic, Macarthur escaped trial and was allowed to resign from the army.

While in London, Macarthur also published a scheme to develop fine wool production in Australia, to replace European supplies cut off by the Napoleonic wars. Here was the first vision of a vast commerce which was to hold Australia within the British Empire's embrace for nearly two centuries. Macarthur was permitted to buy rare Spanish merinos from the King's own flocks, granted 8500 acres of the best pasture lands outside Sydney, and given dozens of convict shepherds to watch his sheep. Macarthur returned home in June 1805, not in disgrace but in triumph.

The earlier enmity with Philip King was patched up. In 1807 Macarthur sailed his schooner through Sydney Harbour alongside HMS *Buffalo* to cry farewells to the former Governor as King left for Britain and premature penniless death at the age of fifty. No doubt the thought occurred to Macarthur that Governors come and Governors go, but the dynasties of wealthy graziers go on forever.

Certain obstacles still lay in Macarthur's path. The main problem was the new Governor, William Bligh, already installed in Government House and hatching his own plans to wipe out illicit trading by officers and their friends. Bligh had come to

The iron-willed, scheming **John Macarthur** who broke Governors and founded Australia's fine wool trade. Artist unknown.

A Plea for the Constitution of New South Wales

Jeremy Bentham, the English reformer who claimed that Governors' actions in New South Wales were illegal under the British Constitution. Painted by H. W. Pickersgill in 1829.

Sydney with a considerable reputation for courage, tenacity, and quick temper. As a lieutenant he fought bravely in naval engagements against the French. At the age of 33 he was appointed commander of HMS *Bounty*, charged with procuring breadfruit plants from Pacific islands and transplanting them as food for slaves in the West Indies.

Bligh reached Tahiti in 1788, only a few months after Phillip's First Fleet reached Sydney. Five months were spent harvesting plants and loading them carefully into the *Bounty*. During that time the seamen lived an idyllic life with Tahitian women. Rebellious grumblings began when Bligh ordered them to set sail for the West Indies.

Subsequent fiction has distorted the famous 'Mutiny on the *Bounty*' which followed. Bligh was certainly subject to bursts of anger when faced with dereliction of duty. He had men punished, but not more severely than elsewhere in the Royal Navy of those days. He had not been given even one commissioned officer to assist him. His senior mate, Fletcher Christian, was not quite the romantic symbol depicted in Hollywood films, for here is his official description:

> Fletcher Christian, mas'r mate; aged 24 years; 5 feet 9 inches high; very dark complexion; dark-brown hair; strong made; a star tatowed on his left breast; backside tatowed; a little bow-legged; he is subject to a violent perspiration in his hands, so that he soils any thing he handles.

Christian and his fellow mutineers, determined to return to their island paradise, seized Bligh and eighteen men who remained loyal, casting them adrift in a 23-foot launch with six oars. In this open boat, they completed an incredible 3600-mile voyage to arrive safely at Timor, where the Dutch helped Bligh to return to England.

This then was the iron-willed man, promoted to captain, who was sent at the age of 52 to discipline the wayward entrepreneurs of Sydney. On touring the colony, Bligh found that despite King's orders, the officers were still 'indulged with great quantities of spirituous liquors, which they disposed of at enormous prices'. The effect on ordinary people was catastrophic:

A sawyer will cut one hundred feet of timber for a bottle of spirits—value two shillings and sixpence—which he drinks in a few hours . . . Farmers are involved in debt, and either ruined by the high price of spirits, or the high price of labour, which is regulated thereby; while the unprincipled holder of spirits gets his work done at a cheap rate and amasses considerable property.

Bligh intensified government regulations and penalties, locking up all liquor imports in the official store and fixing the price at which they could be retailed. In February 1807 he banned altogether the use of rum for currency or barter. Macarthur and his associates were immediately affected. Macarthur himself had just bought 378 gallons of spirit, watered it to 447 gallons, and resold it at a mark-up of 154 per cent. Such profits were too good to lose.

Unfortunately for Bligh, his savage tongue undid much of the good he could otherwise have achieved. More foolishly still, he interfered in the internal working of the NSW Corps, making an enemy of every man from commandant to lowliest soldier. Even these difficulties might have been overcome, if the personalities of Bligh's main opponents had been moderate and amenable. But the commandant, Major George Johnston, born in Scotland in 1764, had fought just as bravely as Bligh against the French and Americans. As a lieutenant of marines with the First Fleet, he had been carried on James Ruse's back to become the first man ashore in

Attacks on Governor Bligh

I have heard much said of Bounty Bligh before I saw him, but no person could conceive that he could be such a fellow . . . He has been every day getting worse and worse, and continues so still since, and if some steps are not soon—nay, very soon—taken, this place is ruined. Caligula himself never reigned with more despotic sway than he does.

JOHN HARRIS, Government Surgeon, in a private letter.

If any person dared to object or remonstrance against the unlawful conduct of the Governor, his rage became unbounded; he lost his senses and his speech; his features became distorted; he foamed at the mouth, stamped on the ground, and shook his fist in the face of the person so presuming . . .

JOHN BLAXLAND, gentleman immigrant, to the Earl of Liverpool.

1788. He could claim to know more about the young colony's needs than most men. In earlier days Johnston too had trafficked in spirits, but charges were not pressed. His prompt suppression of the convict uprising had made him a hero with respectable people. And he was greatly influenced by the opinions of his former officer friend John Macarthur, now one of Sydney's wealthiest private citizens.

Ill-feeling between Bligh and the NSW Corps came to a head in the summer of 1807–08. Comparatively trivial incidents set light to a bushfire of emotions, impossible to extinguish. Macarthur wished to import two stills to distil his surplus peach crop into spirit for resale. Bligh angrily rejected the application, ordering the copper boilers to be seized from Macarthur's private warehouse. A few days later, when a convict managed to escape in Macarthur's schooner, Bligh 'arrested' the ship and had a warrant served on its owner. Macarthur refused to recognise the jurisdiction of a court headed by the Judge-Advocate, Richard Atkins, who owed him money. In a ringing courtroom speech, Macarthur declaimed on his 'lawful rights as an Englishman', alleging plots to deprive him of 'property, liberty, honour, and life'. Six military officers sitting on the court agreed with Macarthur, and set him free. Enraged, Bligh ordered them to appear at Government House next day to explain their 'treasonable practices'.

By coincidence, the date was 26 January 1808—exactly twenty years after the foundation of Sydney. That morning, the Judge-Advocate issued another warrant for Macarthur's arrest. Major Johnston recorded that several armed constables, mostly ex-convicts, paraded at Macarthur's door 'for the purpose of seizing his person and dragging him to gaol'. The re-arrest, he said, produced 'a very awful impression upon the minds of the inhabitants'.

Bligh had now alienated any possible support from the military. Rumours spread rapidly that the Governor would next imprison the officer members of the court. When Major Johnston arrived at the barracks, he found most of the civil and military officers excitedly discussing events, while 'the common people were also to be seen in various groups in every street murmuring and loudly complaining . . .'

Johnston decided to release Macarthur from what he believed was illegal confinement. Shortly afterwards, he was handed a letter approved by all the officers and civilians outside his office, 'imploring me instantly to put Governor Bligh in arrest, and to assume the command of the colony'. In full agreement, Johnston ordered the NSW Corps to be paraded under arms. With flags flying, and the band playing 'British Grenadiers', the rebellious officers and men marched up Bridge Street towards Government House.

As in the *Bounty* mutiny, Bligh had no idea that opposition had reached such a pitch. Betrayed by his own guards, he ran upstairs and began destroying vital documents. Soldiers found him in what Johnston claimed was 'a situation too disgraceful to be mentioned' (that is, hiding under a bed). Bligh could justly be accused of wilful stupidity, but never of cowardice.

Johnston next suspended the Governor's few remaining supporters from office. He appointed John Macarthur as unpaid Colonial Secretary to administer civil affairs until a new Governor arrived. What Bligh described as 'committees of Terror' were set up to examine witnesses and manufacture fresh evidence about Bligh's alleged tyrannies.

After keeping Bligh in confinement for more than a year, the rebels placed him on board HMS *Porpoise*, on the understanding he would sail direct to England for an official inquiry. Once on board, Bligh took command and sailed to Hobart to enlist Lieutenant-Governor David Collins's aid against the rebels. Collins refused, unwilling to allow Bligh to plunge the two colonies into civil war. Bligh's ship remained at anchor until his successor, Lachlan Macquarie, arrived.

Major Johnston returned to England to face a court-martial. He was found guilty and cashiered—a mild enough penalty, explained on the ground of 'novel and extraordinary circumstances' in the colony. Johnston returned to Sydney as an ordinary settler and died there in 1823, leaving considerable wealth.

John Macarthur, the prime instigator of the rebellion, sailed to England to support Johnston at his trial. Much was made of the right of free Englishmen to

Colonel David Collins,
Lieutenant-Governor of Van
Diemen's Land, who refused
to denounce the rebel
government in Sydney when
Bligh arrived in Hobart.
Engraving from a miniature
by I. T. Barber.

conduct trade without undue interference from meddling Governors. For legal
reasons Macarthur himself could only be charged with treason in Sydney: he left
his wife to manage the properties for eight years until the danger had passed.

The unfortunate William Bligh received routine promotion to Vice-Admiral, but was never again entrusted with executive office. The wild men of Sydney had laid him low, and demonstrated to the British government the results of disregarding the rights of free, ambitious men in what was no longer a simple penal settlement.

Our humble equivalent of the American Revolution was over. Australia would stay British to the backbone for many years to come.

Song on the New South Wales Rebellion

This dastardly Junto—disgrace to the sword
Which dangles beside them, ne'er before drawn in anger
Till the King's Captain General to them did accord
A discipline more brisk than their grog-selling languor...

From an anonymous ballad written in Bligh's defence.

The arrest of Governor Bligh in January 1808, announced to the citizens of Sydney outside Government House by Major George Johnston. Painting by Raymond Lindsay.

6. Freed Convicts Find a Friend in Lachlan Macquarie

Lachlan Macquarie did more than any other Governor of his era to assert the radical idea that all people, no matter how humble, had the right to strive for a satisfying life. In the context of the brutal times in which he lived, Macquarie was a phenomenon. How on earth could a 'jungle-wallah', a colonel of the British Army in India, become the common man's greatest friend in Australia?

The answer lies partly in Macquarie's own background. He was born in the Scottish Hebrides in 1762, of a mother who was probably illiterate and a father who was too poor even to buy stock for a small farm rented from the Duke of Argyll. Somehow Macquarie obtained elementary education, and took one of the few paths to advancement by volunteering for service with a Highland regiment. Outstanding natural ability during the American war won him a commission at the age of nineteen. In 1788, the year Australia was settled by Governor Phillip, Macquarie was promoted to captain in India, later a major, then lieutenant-colonel.

Back in Scotland in 1808, Macquarie heard that the regiment would be sent to replace the mutinous NSW Corps. All four naval Governors at 'Botany Bay' had failed in one way or another to control the seething colony. After twenty years of dissension, the British government at last decided to appoint a military Governor who was also in direct charge of his own troops. Macquarie's commanding officer did not care to go. Greatly daring, Macquarie applied for the position and was accepted. By this succession of accidents, the history of Australia was about to change direction.

Arriving in Sydney in May 1909, Macquarie followed instructions by reinstating Bligh as Governor for one day and annulling all acts and land grants of the rebel

Macquarie! candid, gen'rous,
noble, free,
All, 'neath perfection,
blended, shone in thee!
Thou, when the hapless
widow pined for bread,
Shed bounty o'er, and raised
her drooping head;
When Affluence spurned the
beggar from his door,
Cheered by thy smiles he
felt no longer poor.
CHARLES TOMPSON, son of a transportee, who became an official of the first New South Wales Parliament.

Below left. **Lachlan Macquarie**, one of Australia's most farsighted early Governors.
Below. **Macquarie's wife Elizabeth** (née Campbell), who is said to have pioneered haymaking in New South Wales. Watercolours by Richard Read, 1819.

Francis Greenway,
transported for forgery,
became the Governor's
favourite architect. Probably
a self-portrait.

administration. The NSW Corps was disbanded and sent back in disgrace to Britain. Major Johnston and John Macarthur had already sailed, and the new Governor was free to concentrate on the task ahead.

Macquarie saw that free colonists with wealth and property could look after themselves. But unless released convicts were given some hope of achieving independence, they would rapidly slide back into criminality. So disproportionate were their numbers that they would swamp the whole colony with endless depravity. Macquarie made his attitude to emancipists quite clear. As his family's personal physician he appointed Dr William Redfern, transported for supporting the Royal Navy mutineers of 1798. The new Governor even appointed two emancipists as magistrates. Those who once offended the law should now uphold it! The first was Andrew Thompson, transported from Scotland for theft, who became a prosperous farmer, ship-builder, and chief constable on the Hawkesbury River. The second was Simeon Lord, transported from Manchester for stealing ten-penn'orth of cloth, now a prominent Sydney merchant. This former sneak-thief was asked regularly to dine at Government House with Macquarie, who supported the efforts of such men to inaugurate the Bank of New South Wales (now Westpac), helping to defeat the 'shameful traffick' in high-interest private notes.

Many other such men (and one woman, Mary Reibey), who had proven their worth by fair means or foul in the cut-throat mercantile world of early Sydney, were warmly supported by this astonishing new Governor. Even today there are few government authorities who try to reform prisoners by such personal methods.

Macquarie idealistically believed that grander architecture would help to lift Sydney above its miserable origins and symbolise people's hopes for a better future. Disregarding British pleas for economy until the Napoleonic wars were over, Macquarie authorised some of the most beautiful buildings seen in Australia.

For this noble work he was fortunate to find a peppery little convict architect named Francis Greenway, transported from Bristol for forgery. Macquarie had already arranged for the free construction of Sydney Hospital in exchange for a three-year monopoly on rum imports. Greenway took over what would have been a constructional disaster and turned it into a triumph. Next he built the striking Macquarie Lighthouse at South Head. Stables for a new Government House, now the Conservatorium of Music, were completed in grandiose fashion. New convict barracks (now a colonial museum) were erected near Hyde Park, and a female 'factory' near Parramatta. Several fine churches and courthouses were built, and survive today in good order.

Macquarie's favouritism towards 'the lower classes' soon antagonised those wealthy free settlers whose prosperity depended on a docile labour force. Greatly outnumbered by convicts and ex-convicts, these settlers formed themselves into an exclusive caste whose families became known jocularly as 'pure merinos', able to trace bloodlines free of 'the convict taint'. One of their leaders was none other than John Macarthur, permitted to return to Sydney in 1817 on condition that he stay clear of political involvement. But the manipulator of earlier crises, now 50, could not help himself. Secretly he began undermining Macquarie's reforms with sarcastic letters to highly-placed friends in London.

As these pressures came into open view, a young Australian barrister named William Charles Wentworth, born of a transported convict mother, wrote angrily in London of the 'pure merinos':

> Short-sighted fools! they foresee not the consequences of their narrow machinations! They know not that they would be sowing the seeds of future discords and commotions, and that by exalting their immediate descendants, they would occasion the eventual degradation and overthrow of their posterity.

Wentworth even warned that if young Australians were, like Americans, forced into a war of independence, all of Britain's might would not be able to conquer a colonial army hidden in the mountains around Sydney. 'Of what avail would whole armies prove in these terrible defiles, which only five or six men could approach abreast?', he asked.

But political feeling in London had changed. With the end of the Napoleonic

wars, hordes of savage unemployed ex-soldiers and sailors had descended on Britain's cities. Again the old policies were propounded: again Australia must become the dumping-ground for the most recalcitrant criminals. To support its policy, the British government first conducted an inquiry into Macquarie's administration. Men can usually be found whose character is guaranteed to produce the desired result from such inquiries. In this case John Thomas Bigge, a 39-year-old judge, was selected. Son of a high sheriff, and now Chief Justice of the slave colony of Trinidad, Bigge had no experience at all of what might be required for a country like Australia.

The inquiry was further prejudiced by Lord Bathurst's instruction that transportation should be made 'an object of real terror', without foolish notions of 'ill-considered compassion for convicts'. All of this was designed to rid London of half-starved footpads, many of whom had fought bravely for Britain in her hour of need. When completed after two years, Bigge's reports formed a tissue of special pleading, aristocratic bias, and untested evidence. But they were exactly what the British government of the day wanted to hear.

All Macquarie's hopes and projects began to fall apart. He answered as best he could what he called Bigge's 'false, vindictive and malicious' recommendations. From the moment of Bigge's arrival, said Macquarie, he showed a 'strong and deep-rooted prejudice against all persons, who had had the misfortune to come out as convicts, be their merits, talents, and usefulness ever so conspicuous'. Macquarie even wrote personally to Bigge, pleading with the commissioner to 'let the Souls now in being as well as millions yet unborn, bless the day on which you landed on their shores, and gave them (when they deserve it) what you so much admire, Freedom!'.

Even the colony's remarkable material progress failed to impress Britain. Between Macquarie's arrival in 1809 and his departure in 1822, population increased from about 10,000 to 40,000 inhabitants. Customs revenue in Sydney

The Union Flag flies bravely from **the first Sydney lighthouse and signal station, designed by Francis Greenway**. Lithograph by Augustus Earle, c. 1826.

John Thomas Bigge, the Royal Commissioner who attacked Macquarie's enlightened policies. Artist unknown.

31

Whaling off Twofold Bay, shown in this dramatic painting by Oswald Brierly, was important to the struggling economy of early Australia. Until the 1820s, whale oil exports were worth more than wool.

rose from £8000 to £30,000 a year. Sheep numbers increased from 25,000 to 300,000; cattle from 10,000 to 110,000. Crops rose from 7000 to 32,000 acres. Many small factories were now making cloth, clothing and pottery. A stable currency and banking system had been instituted. All in vain! Constant rebuffs from London forced Macquarie to resign. In 1822 he and his family were fare-welled by a vast crowd gathered at Sydney Cove. Michael Robinson, ex-convict, lawyer and poet wrote in tribute:

> Our gallant Governor has gone
> Across the rolling sea,
> To tell the King on England's throne
> What merry men are we.
>
> Macquarie was a prince of men,
> Australia's pride and joy!
> We ne'er shall see his like again;
> Here's to the OLD Viceroy.

In London, the government kept Macquarie waiting until April 1824 for its decision on a pension. Nine weeks later he died, leaving his devoted wife Elizabeth practically bankrupt. Eventually she swallowed her Scottish pride and accepted a small pension. In Australia meanwhile, fortunes were being made from the prosperous colony her husband had ruled so lovingly.

7. A Wide Land Beckons

Under Macquarie's benign autocracy, men began to lift their eyes to the hills and wonder what lay beyond. Jagged ranges and dense bush seemed to enclose the Sydney area in a permanent grip. In the blue hazy distance settlers could see the mountains which few had tried to penetrate. What rich pastures, broad rivers—even inland seas—might lie hidden on the other side?

Gregory Blaxland, 35, a prosperous free settler from Kent, had special reasons for wanting to know the answer. By 1813 his stock was outbreeding even the 4800 rich acres granted to him near Sydney. The Governor refused to increase grants to such men of wealth, but gave him permission to explore the Blue Mountains.

Blaxland took William Lawson, 39, a former surveyor who owned land at Prospect, and the young William Charles Wentworth, acting Provost-Marshal of Sydney. They decided to keep to the tops of mountain ridges rather than follow the impenetrable valleys, and by this means managed to cut their way across Mount York and Mount Blaxland. From there they could see 'enough grass to support the stock of the colony for thirty years'. By 1815 the way to the fabled west was open. Stock was driven across, the town of Bathurst established, and the pastoral industry began to grow to huge proportions.

Macquarie's successor Sir Thomas Brisbane, a veteran of the war in Spain, was charged with implementing the harsh recommendations of the Bigge reports. To strike terror into the hearts of frequent offenders, places of 'secondary punishment' were planned well away from the slowly improving civilisation of Sydney.

By coincidence, Surveyor-General John Oxley, 38, discovered in 1823 that Moreton Bay was suitable for settlement. On 2 December a strong tide swept his boat up a large fresh-water inlet which he named after Governor Brisbane. The Governor took advantage of this discovery to establish Moreton Bay penal settlement. Captain Patrick Logan, 34, took control in 1825 and managed it with savage efficiency until speared to death by Aborigines five years later.

Meanwhile, a young English botanist named Allan Cunningham found his way from the Hunter Valley into the fertile Darling Downs in 1827. Cunningham discovered several important rivers *en route*, including the Namoi, Gwydir and Condamine. The way was open for squatters to take their flocks into these vast grazing areas, eventually to join up with settlements along the Brisbane River and form the nucleus of modern Queensland.

The Mysterious Lands of Port Phillip

South-west of Sydney, squatting settlement reached Yass and Lake George, near today's Canberra, by the mid-1820s. Further expansion southwards appeared to be blocked by the Great Dividing Range. But a glance at the map showed that a considerable distance remained between Yass and the southern coastline. What kind of land might lie beyond the snow-covered Alps?

In 1824 William Hovell, a 38-year-old British merchant captain, agreed to assist Hamilton Hume, a 27-year-old squatter, on a private expedition. In a four-month journey their small party skirted the worst of the southern mountains, discovered Australia's largest river, the Murray, crossed the unknown Ovens and Goulburn rivers, and traversed rich lands with 'soil everywhere good beyond description'. On 16 December they emerged at Port Phillip Bay. Unfortunately the explorers thought they had reached Westernport Bay.

On their return the Governor reported the existence of 'new and valuable country' to London. Perturbed by French maritime activity around southern

*The boundless champaign burst upon our sight
Till nearer seen the beauteous landscape grew,
Op'ning like Canaan on rapt Israel's view.*

W. C. WENTWORTH, after breaking through the Blue Mountains.

At sunset we had proceeded about 20 miles by the river; the scenery was peculiarly beautiful; the country on the banks alternately hilly and level, but not flooded; the soil of the finest description of brush woodland, on which grew timber of great magnitude, and of various species, some of which were unknown to us, among others a magnificent species of pine was in great abundance.

JOHN OXLEY, on discovering the Brisbane River.

William Hovell, British merchant captain who first travelled overland to Port Phillip with Hamilton Hume, noted in his journal upon first seeing Port Phillip Bay: 'It was one immense sheet of water . . . equal to any harbour I have seen'.

Australia, the British government authorised the permanent occupation of Westernport. In this comedy of errors, Captain Samuel Wright sailed from Sydney in 1826 with a party of convicts and soldiers to form a settlement on the sandy soil of Corinella, at the head of Westernport. Where was Hume and Hovell's soil, reported as 'good beyond description'? Hovell, who accompanied the expedition as expert adviser, was too embarrassed to admit his incompetence as a land navigator. When Captain Wright reported the 'sterile, swampy, and impenetrable nature of the country', and the French threat receded, the tiny settlement was abandoned early in 1828. For a few years more Port Phillip remained unknown to all but a few visiting sealers. But rumours continued to spread of lush pastoral lands waiting for the taking.

In 1834 the Henty family, originally farmers in Sussex, packed their 57-ton schooner *Thistle* with stock and farm requirements, and set off from Launceston to settle illegally at Portland Bay on the mainland. Shortly afterwards a private 'Port Phillip Association' was formed by leading graziers of Van Diemen's Land. In 1835 their representative John Batman, 35-year-old son of a Sydney convict, sailed into Port Phillip Bay and discovered 'as rich land as ever I saw in my life'.

The Sydney government declared all private occupation illegal, but by the time police magistrate William Lonsdale and his troops were sent down to control the invaders, Melbourne and Geelong had grown into substantial towns with a brisk import-export trade. The authorities were forced to recognise the *fait accompli*, and by 1839 to declare Port Phillip a separate district with its own superintendent.

Batman himself died almost bankrupt that year, but many of his associates were already making fortunes from squatting, trade, and land speculation. In this strange land of Australia, it seemed profitable to defy government restrictions—as long as the enterprise turned out well and assisted national development.

I purchased two large tracts of land from them—about 600,000 acres, more or less—and delivered over to them blankets, knives, looking-glasses, tomahawks, beads, scissors, flour, etc., as payment for the land, and also agreed to give them a tribute, or rent, yearly.

JOHN BATMAN

Tiny Settlements Keep the French Away from the West

A major change began to occur in British strategic thinking towards Australia after the Napoleonic wars. Previously Britain had claimed only the eastern half of the continent, as far as 135° longitude which bisects South Australia and the Northern Territory. At that time the British government seemed unconcerned whether any other nation annexed the western half. By the 1820s, however,

An early view of Fremantle. Artist unknown, possibly Nicholas Chevalier.

The Foundation of Perth, painted by G. P. Morison, shows an officer's wife blazing a tree to mark the event.

Major Edmund Lockyer, founder of Albany.

Australia had begun to prove its value in many ways. Imperial planners dreamed of a bolder plan—to annex a whole continent.

The first step was an expedition to Arnhem Land and occupation of Melville Island, named after the First Lord of the Admiralty. Soldiers and convicts sent from Sydney built Fort Dundas there in 1824, raising the flag and firing a salute to commemorate Britain's victory at Trafalgar nearly twenty years earlier.

In 1826 Britain instructed Governor Darling to continue occupation of the west by raising the flag at King George Sound, site of today's Albany. Major Edmund Lockyer, 42, was sent with forty-four soldiers and convicts, and instructed to inform any Frenchmen he found that the whole of Australia was now under British rule. Lockyer was impressed with Albany's fine harbour and whaling prospects, but recommended Swan River for its superior soil.

The following year Captain James Stirling, 36, a veteran of naval battles against the French, went to inspect Swan River. He reported enthusiastically on its soil and water, and a climate which would permit Europeans to labour there throughout the year. Stirling added a warning that 'as it is moreover favourably circumstanced for the equipment of cruizers for the annoyance of trade in those seas, some foreign power may see the advantage of taking possession, should His Majesty's Government leave it unappropriated'.

In 1829 the Admiralty sent Captain Charles Fremantle, 29, from the Cape of Good Hope in HMS *Challenger* to take formal possession of the Swan River area, 'which possession is meant to be extended to the whole of the Western Coast'. On 2 May Captain Fremantle hoisted the Union Jack on the south head of the Swan River, site of Fremantle today.

Captain Stirling meanwhile had returned to London, where he lobbied success-fully for the establishment of a free settlement with himself as Governor. A private syndicate led by a 36-year-old lawyer, Thomas Peel (cousin of the Home Secretary, Robert Peel), won approval for a land grant of one million acres in return for sending out 540 emigrants with stock and stores to support them.

Stirling chose a site further up the Swan River as capital of the new colony, proclaiming the establishment of Perth in 1829. Much land from there to Albany was pioneered under great difficulties. The soil was not generally as good as claimed in the first enthusiastic reports, rainfall was erratic, and the Aborigines aggressive. Some settlers, like the Hentys who went on to pioneer Portland, left in disgust. Others battled on to maintain a weak but sufficient grasp on the west.

Stirling himself was ultimately promoted to Rear-Admiral in charge of British naval forces in the Far East. His eldest son became commander of the Australian naval squadron in the 1870s. By that time the Australian colonists were vividly aware that only the Royal Navy lay between them and an awakening Asia.

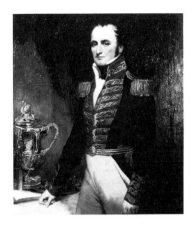

Captain James Stirling, RN, first Governor of the Swan River Settlement.

'South Australia Will be a Free Colony . . .'

The exploitation inherent in the convict system aroused disgust among reformers in England. One of the most effective of these publicists was an ambitious young lawyer-diplomat named Edward Gibbon Wakefield. He argued that the existing system of land grants in Australia forced both old and new settlers to rely on convict labour. A vicious circle emerged in which the expansion of settlement was made dependent on continued transportation of the dregs of British society.

Under Wakefield's proposals, Crown land should be sold at a price carefully regulated to attract men of substance, but high enough to exclude poor men from acquiring their own land too easily. The revenue from land sales should be used to finance the emigration of suitable families from Britain, who would provide an ample labour force of poor but honest men.

As criticism of the convict system grew louder, this apparently logical scheme became a cornerstone of British policy towards Australia. The first experiment was made with the South Australian Act of 1834. The South Australian Company, a combination of wealthy investors, paid twelve shillings an acre for 35,000 acres of land around Gulf St Vincent, a likely-looking area first surveyed by Matthew Flinders in 1802.

William Light, 50, son of an army officer and a Malayan princess, was appointed Surveyor-General. Colonel Light rejected the settlers' first choice of Kangaroo Island, selecting instead a site between Port Adelaide and Mount Lofty: 'an immense plain of level and advantageous ground for occupation', where he laid out the town of Adelaide. Sir John Hindmarsh, 51—who had conquered Mauritius in 1809 and released Matthew Flinders from French captivity—was appointed first Governor. Hindmarsh inaugurated the new colony on 28 December 1836.

Unfortunately Wakefield's scheme did not work as systematically as planned. He of all men failed to allow for human greed. Once in possession of their blocks, many colonists concentrated on land speculation rather than productive farming. Constant emergencies racked both government and company officials, and development through the depressed 1840s remained slow.

Yet the South Australians clung to their ideal that free men rather than oppressed convicts should develop the land. Their reward was a colony with a remarkably low crime rate, and a liberal inheritance which gave them some of Australia's first democratic institutions.

The ideas of **Edward Gibbon Wakefield** led to settlement of South Australia. Engraving by A. Wivell.

Sir John Hindmarsh, Rear-Admiral and first Governor of South Australia.

With the colonisation of South Australia, all the basic elements of modern Australia were in place. By one means or another, each of today's State capitals had been established. Only Darwin and Canberra remained for the future to establish as major administrative centres.

Those small settlements spotted around the continent in 1836 might seem a skeletal means of holding together such a vast area. But the gamble worked: after the 1830s no other nation seriously threatened the integrity of Australia until the Pacific war of 1941–45. The way was clear for those distinctive characteristics known as 'Australian' to be born.

8. What Lies Further On? The Inland's Mysteries Revealed

Charles Sturt was still trying to discover an inland ocean in 1845. Ivor Hele's painting 'Sturt's reluctant decision to return' shows his party trapped without water in Central Australia.

Practically all the Australian coastline was known by the 1820s; only the inland remained as a gigantic question-mark in men's minds. But they had no aeroplanes in which unknown areas could be quickly surveyed. Aerial balloons had been invented, but could not be steered. The only way to go was painfully, slowly, by foot, horseback, or rowboat where rivers existed.

Early explorers were intrigued by the fact that many rivers flowed inland instead of emptying into broad oceans. This led some to think that a delightful inland sea awaited them. Soon after the Blue Mountains were conquered in 1813–15, the inland sea legend began to take firm hold. Men simply could not believe that the western plains continued practically for ever.

Part of the mystery was solved by the epic pioneer voyage of Charles Sturt through the inland water system of the Murrumbidgee, Darling and Murray rivers. Sturt, son of an East India Company judge, and a veteran of the Peninsular War, was one of many officers sent to Australia in charge of convicts. In 1829, when Sturt was 34, he and Hamilton Hume discovered the Darling River in outback New South Wales. Sturt asked permission to return and trace the Darling towards the supposed 'inland sea'. Instead he was commissioned to investigate the Lachlan-Murrumbidgee river system.

E. J. Eyre almost perished trying to cross the Great Australian Bight. J. MacFarlane's painting shows **Eyre being rescued by Captain Rossiter** of the French whaler *Mississippi* in June 1841.

Broken Hearts of the Inland

Like echoes of dead voices, there are rills,
Dry waterways that mutter 'Sturt' and 'Eyre'.
Blue ridges sing for Stuart. On the bare
Cragged inland rock the low wind murmurs 'Wills'.
Far up and down the opened landscape thrills
To names of men who faced death and despair,
Who found no enterprise too high to dare,
And broke their hearts to conquer distant hills.

Margaret Kiek, lines from 'Centenary Ode — South Australia — 1836-1936'.

Augustus Gregory's expedition to the Northern Territory in 1855 covered 5000 miles of largely unknown territory. His official artist, Thomas Baines, painted this **scene on the Victoria River**, later the site of one of Australia's biggest cattle stations.

Early in 1830 Sturt's party embarked on the Murrumbidgee in a whaleboat they had brought overland. Within a week, powerful currents swept them to a junction with 'a broad and noble river'. Sturt did not know it, but this was the Murray River which Hume and Hovell had managed to cross upstream on their way to Port Phillip six years earlier. Further down the Murray, Sturt's party landed at its junction with the Darling River. 'I directed the Union Jack to be hoisted', he wrote, 'and giving way to our satisfaction, we all stood up in the boat, and gave three distinct cheers'.

Seventeen days later the voyagers arrived at Lake Alexandrina on the southern coast—'the grand reservoir of those waters whose course and fate had previously been involved in such obscurity . . .' After this triumph the explorers had to row back hundreds of miles against the current, reaching assistance on the day their last rations were consumed.

Sturt's epic voyage solved the mystery of the south-eastern rivers. These did not after all flow into an inland sea. But they did form, as Sturt wrote, a 'high road to connect the eastern and southern shores of a mighty continent'. Squatters and stock poured down this high road to bring white man's civilisation to yet another section of the fertile south-east.

Sturt himself was rewarded with a 5000-acre grant, and after establishment of the South Australian colony took up various government posts. Still believing that northern rivers must flow into an inland sea, he left Adelaide in 1844 with fifteen men and a boat to sail on its phantasmagorical waters. Instead the party almost perished from drought and scurvy after it passed Cooper Creek. On the return journey, the sight of the Simpson Desert finally destroyed Sturt's faith in an inland ocean. Reality about the nature of Central Australia was beginning to penetrate men's minds.

Equal disappointment awaited Edward John Eyre, son of an English vicar, who had emigrated to Australia at the age of seventeen. In 1840 Eyre, then 25, attempted to discover an overland stock route from Adelaide to Western Australia. Surely a river must emerge somewhere along that extensive coastline! After many exhausting weeks of travel around the practically waterless Great Australian Bight, two of his Aboriginal guides murdered the overseer, John Baxter, and fled with most of the party's food and firearms. Eyre was left with one faithful servant, Wylie, a native of the King George Sound tribe, whose knowledge of these harsh lands saved the explorer's life.

Several weeks later the emaciated pair sighted the French whaler *Mississippi* at Thistle Cove, near today's Esperance. The French gave them water and fresh supplies. After recovering, Eyre insisted on completing the journey overland to Albany. Even if no river existed, Eyre was determined to prove it.

For this heroic feat, Eyre was awarded the Royal Geographical Society's gold medal, reserved for extraordinary endurance and discoveries. Wylie was put on free government rations, and given a medal and £2 by Perth Agricultural Society. All that their sufferings really achieved was to prove that the Bight region, like Central Australia, was not suitable for white settlement during those times. Yet their heroism in the face of incredible odds added to what was already becoming an Australian legend.

If Central Australia was mostly barren, perhaps northern Australia might yield extensive pasture lands. Ordered by London to economise, Governor Gipps refused to send an official survey party to explore the unknown areas.

In 1844 Ludwig Leichhardt, a 31-year-old German naturalist, set out from Brisbane on a privately-backed expedition to explore the unknown north. Leaving the last outpost of Jimbour station after singing 'a full chorus of God Save the Queen', the explorers finally completed an astonishing 3000-mile journey. They discovered many important rivers and crossed huge empty areas of central Queensland and Arnhem Land, emerging near today's Darwin. Returning by ship, the explorers were greeted in Sydney as national heroes. 'No king could have been received with greater joy and more affection', wrote Leichhardt. '. . . I believed the

Australian-born **John Forrest** was one of the nation's last great explorers. As a young man he led a vain 2000-mile search for Ludwig Leichhardt. In 1870 he made a full survey of Eyre's route from Perth to Adelaide, enabling a telegraph line to be built. Later he led the first west-to-east expedition through the harsh central deserts. In 1918 Forrest was created Australia's first native-born baronet.

whole town would go mad with joy.' The public, it seems, had a shrewder insight into Australia's future than cautious official planners.

More than any other explorer, Leichhardt had shown the way by which cattlemen could take over northern lands, to spread the elements of European civilisation across vast areas of a continent easily claimed but not so easily settled. Leichhardt was lost on a further expedition in 1848. Searches for his party failed, but had the effect of expanding his discoveries in many directions.

In 1855 Augustus Gregory, a 36-year-old English surveyor, led an official search party 5000 miles across northern Australia and back. They failed to find any trace of Leichhardt, but explored many northern areas as far as the enormous Victoria River, south-west of today's Darwin. Gregory's careful maps and descriptions were basic tools for pastoralists following in his footsteps. In 1858 he turned his attention south to trace Cooper Creek, discovering a workable track around Lake Torrens to Adelaide. The new Colony of Queensland appointed Gregory as its first Commissioner of Crown Lands in 1859. He used his official powers to grant large areas of the best land to wealthy squatters. These, he felt, were the only men with sufficient resources to stand up to bad seasons.

His mission was not to destroy, nor comes he back to tell
Of fields, in which, though nobly won, our best and bravest fell;
Far higher conquests his than these—and well he knew his God
Would watch him all along the way his trusting footsteps trod.

JUSTICE SIR WILLIAM A'BECKETT on Ludwig Leichhardt.

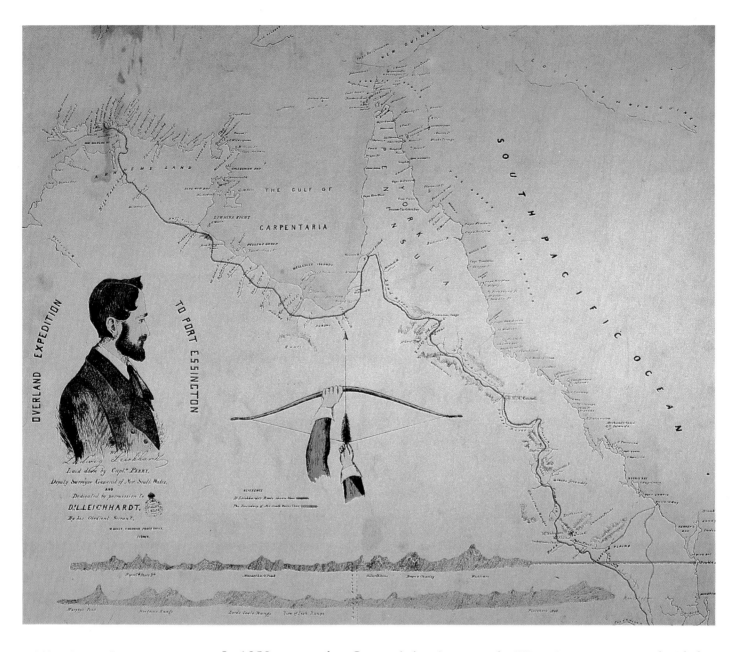

Official map showing the extraordinary journey through unknown country undertaken by Ludwig Leichhardt in 1844, which opened much of the north to cattlemen.

In 1859, a year after Gregory's last journey, the Victorian government decided to enter the exploration stakes. At that date the southern colony was rich with gold discoveries, and ambitious to extend its pastoral territories through the Riverina and western Queensland, even to the northern coastline.

To assist a dash to the north, the government imported the first camels from India. Robert O'Hara Burke, 39, an adventurous Irish-born police superintendent, was named leader. In August 1860 'the largest and best appointed expedition yet organised in the Australian colonies' left to the cheers of 15,000 loyal Victorians.

The party established a base camp at Menindee on the Darling River. Impatient to achieve the first south-north crossing of the continent, Burke left much baggage behind and quickly pushed on 500 miles to Cooper Creek. Here, the last message received from Melbourne warned him that a 45-year-old Scottish surveyor, John McDouall Stuart, had just succeeded in planting the Union Jack in the centre of the continent. 'The honour of Victoria is in your hands', the message concluded.

Burke impulsively left most of his remaining men, animals and supplies at Cooper Creek. With only the surveyor, W. J. Wills, and two other men, six camels, a horse and twelve weeks' rations, Burke made a 1000-mile lunge for the Gulf of Carpentaria, reaching it roughly where Burketown is located today. On the return trip, one exhausted man died in the Stony Desert, and the others were reduced to mere shadows.

Now occurred one of the legendary moments in Australian exploration. Late on 21 April 1861, the three starving survivors crawled back into camp at Cooper Creek. They saw a message cut into a tree which read 'Dig'. Under the sand they

The Fate of the Explorers

The tragic anti-climax to Australian exploration: **the exhausted Burke and Wills return to Cooper Creek** to find their party and supplies had left the same day. Both men starved to death. The third man, King, received help from the Aborigines and survived. Painting by Sir John Longstaff, completed 1907.

> *Let them rest where they have laboured! but, my country, mourn and moan;*
> *We must build with human sorrow grander monuments than stone.*
> *Let them rest, for oh! remember, that in long hereafter time*
> *Sons of Science oft shall wander o'er that solitary clime!*
> *Cities bright shall rise about it, Age and Beauty there shall stray,*
> *And the fathers of the people, pointing to the graves, shall say:*
> *'Here they fell, the glorious martyrs! when these plains were woodlands deep;*
> *Here a friend, a brother, laid them; here the wild men came to weep.'*
>
> HENRY KENDALL

found a longer message telling them that their party, tired of waiting, had left the very same morning for Menindee. The explorers were too weak to chase them.

Burke buried a message saying they would attempt to follow the creek towards Adelaide, but forgot to leave a new sign above ground. A relief party did not bother to look. Later expeditions discovered one survivor living with an Aboriginal tribe, but by that time Burke and Wills, rejecting native assistance, had both starved to death. Wills's diary when found reported for 26 June: 'My pulse is at 48, and very weak, and my legs and arms are nearly skin and bone'.

Alfred Howitt, who found the skeletons, wrapped them in a Union Jack and buried them near Cooper Creek. In Melbourne the lost men were eulogised as heroes. They were given Victoria's first State funeral, attended by 40,000 mourners. Charles Summers made the colony's first bronze statue, one of the largest ever cast in a single piece, which today stands in Melbourne's City Square.

In reality the expedition was a monumental fiasco, which achieved little for science, exploration or pastoral settlement. But the tragedy peculiarly entered the souls of generations of admiring Australians. What mattered in this harsh country was not necessarily to survive, but to throw oneself courageously against overwhelming odds. When that was done: 'Where is death's sting? Where, Grave, thy victory?'.

It was, in fact, the same spirit which, displayed *en masse* on the blood-soaked cliffs of Gallipoli half a century later, won the admiration of the whole world.

PART II

A Land of Convicts and Capitalists Finds Something Worth Defending

Pioneers

They came of bold and roving stock that would not fixed abide;
They were the sons of field and flock since e'er they learned to ride;
We may not hope to see such men in these degenerate years
As those explorers of the bush—the brave old pioneers.

'Twas they who rode the trackless bush in heat and storm and drought;
'Twas they that heard the master-word that called them further out;
'Twas they that followed up the trail the mountain cattle made
And pressed across the mighty range where now their bones are laid.

But now the times are dull and slow, the brave old days are dead
When hardy bushmen started out, and forced their way ahead
By tangled scrub and forests grim towards the unknown west,
And spied the far-off promised land from off the ranges' crest.

Oh! ye, that sleep in lonely graves by far-off ridge and plain,
We drink to you in silence now as Christmas comes again,
The men who fought the wilderness through rough, unsettled years—
The founders of our nation's life, the brave old pioneers.

A. B. PATERSON

1. Bush Life Produces the Legendary Australian

By the 1830s, all of the first white settlers of Australia were dead or in their dotage. A pastoral aristocracy of 'pure merinos' occupied most of the broad acres around Sydney: the ageing John Macarthur could look with satisfaction over his 60,000 acres filled with fine sheep at Camden Park, but he was growing increasingly cranky and would die insane in 1834. The Macarthur sons and other inheritors would intensify their efforts to re-create the English class system in the new land. But it was not with them that the true future of Australia lay.

Discoveries of vast new pastoral lands, coupled with the continued demand for Australian wool overseas, broke up the cosy Sydney monopoly. Hundreds of illegal squatters, including many comparatively poor men, burst through the artificial barriers which Governors and their early legislative councils tried to impose. There was no holding back the squatters. In a famous despatch to London in 1840, Governor Sir George Gipps complained that one might as well try to confine Arabs within a circle traced on the desert sands, as to 'confine the graziers or woolgrowers of New South Wales within any bounds that can possibly be assigned to them'. Lawbreaking was too profitable a way of life.

During the early golden age of squatting, wool exports grew to levels previously thought impossible. In 1830 the export of nearly two million lb was considered remarkable. By 1850 the figure had increased to 42 million lb! By the end of the century, more than 500 million lb a year were being shorn, mostly for export. Prices fluctuated according to conditions in Europe, but the money which flowed back to each Australian property was generally sufficient for the owner to pay his men reasonable wages, build a decent home, and educate his legitimate children (half-castes were usually kept on as station hands). When prices were good, what more could an honest squatter want?

This constant flow of earnings from abroad became the biggest economic factor in Australian life. Just as important to the nation's further development was the evolution of a new type of individual throughout the broad plains and bushland of pastoral Australia. Most of the people involved were British by origin, but they found conditions here utterly different to the homeland. There was no point in attempting to reproduce England's neat fields and intensive farming methods in most parts of Australia. The new continent's hot climate, tough grasses and vast areas—ideal for fine wool production—required adaptable men with fresh ideas. Cattle raising on sparse grasslands also needed huge runs and new methods. The result was the emergence of the Australian bushman, who, with his tireless stock horse and well-trained dogs, could control large mobs over enormous distances.

The rigours of pioneering life hammered these men into similar shape and outlook. Yet all retained something of their diverse social origins. Former convicts, for instance, often reacted to their years of forced labour with exaggerated independence. When the squatter Edward Curr tried to hire men on a spree in a Melbourne pub, they threatened to tear him apart. Charles James Griffith, a squatter at Werribee Vale, found that the former convicts were fond of 'trying it on'—that is, attempting to establish ever more generous terms with new-chum squatters, and despising them if they succeeded. 'The person who excites their greatest respect is the man who is alive to their attempts (or, as they express it themselves, who *drops down to their moves*), and the highest encomium they can pass on such a one is, that *there are no flies about him*.'

A different type of British export was the educated man, often the younger son of a prominent family, who had come to seek adventure and fortune in the new land. Charles Griffith described some of them:

As a body, they are a daring, energetic, hard-working class of men, with a considerable fear of infringing the law . . . They are generally well acquainted with splitting, building, fencing, and bushwork of all kinds . . . They have a pride in fulfilling their engagements; and when they undertake a piece of job-work, they generally adhere faithfully to their contract . . . They are very fond of change, wandering about the country generally in pairs, and rarely remaining more than a year in one service.

C. J. GRIFFITH, Victorian squatter, on ex-convict bushmen.

You see a pale and delicate, but resolute-looking man—he was the first who made the dangerous experiment of taking cattle overland to Adelaide; he opposite you, with a quiet expression and mild blue eye, is one of the most determined and adventurous explorers and the best bushman in the country . . .

Such men might become leaders of 'overlanding' parties, commissioned by stock-owners to drive mobs of sheep or cattle to favourite markets, sometimes hundreds of thousands of miles across unfenced land. They too added to the bushman's legend.

Probably the emergence of distinctive Australian characteristics owed more to locally-born people than to immigrants. Knowing no other way of life, the Australian-born could only be loyal to their native land. Australia, not Britain, was 'home'. Ironically called 'currency'—supposedly inferior to 'sterling'—the native-born quickly showed that they were better able to adapt to the peculiar conditions of Australia than most immigrants.

About 80 per cent of currency youths were the children of emancipists. Many of the parents were anxious that their offspring should rise to success and respect-ability which they could never have achieved in Britain. The pride of 7500 emancipist farmers shone through in a petition sent to Britain in response to the Bigge reports. Of their 6000 offspring, they claimed, 'there is not a more sober Industrious and Loyal race of Youth in any part of Your Majesty's Empire'. Even J. T. Bigge himself, prejudiced against the lower classes, was forced to admit the rough virtues of colonial youth. He reported that

The class of inhabitants that have been born in the colony affords a remarkable exception to the moral and physical character of their parents: they are generally tall in person and slender in their limbs, of fair complexion and small features. They are capable of undergoing more fatigue, and are less exhausted by labour than native Europeans; they are active in their habits but remarkably awkward in their movements. In their tempers they are quick and irascible but not vindictive . . .

Just as important as men in peopling the outback, but often overlooked, were the courageous women who accompanied their mates to live isolated lives devoted to the endless round of housekeeping and childbearing. Watercolour by George Lacy.

The 'pure merinos' of Sydney felt greater kinship with Britain than the sons and daughters of transported convicts. Yet even here the unavoidable fact of local birth was having its effect. After Charles Darwin visited the 'most English-like house' of the Macarthur family during his stay in New South Wales, he wrote, 'It sounded strange in my ears to hear very nice looking young ladies exclaim, "Oh we are Australians & know nothing about England"'.

In the end, regardless of their origins, people bound to live in the Australian countryside could not avoid becoming a distinctive type. As prosperity increased, early hardships tended to be forgotten and the joys accentuated. Charles Rowcroft, a Tasmanian settler, wrote of 'the particular sort of satisfaction' which accompanied the building of one's own dwelling on one's own extensive pasture lands:

> 'No rent to pay for you', said I; 'no taxes, that's pleasant; no poor-rates, that's a comfort; and no one can give me warning to quit, and that's another comfort; and it's my own, thank God, and that's the greatest comfort of all.' I cast my eyes on the plain before me, and saw my flock of sheep studding the plain, with my working bullocks at a little distance . . . In my rude cottage, with the bare walls of logs of trees and the shingle roof above us, all rough enough, but spacious, and a little too airy, I began to have a foretaste of that feeling of independence and security of home and subsistence which I have so many years enjoyed.

All the factors of country life finally resulted in what Francis Adams called 'the one powerful and unique type yet produced in Australia . . . the Bushman'. 'The smaller resident or squatter or manager almost always shows signs of him; sometimes is merely a slightly refined or outwardly polished form of him', Adams wrote in the 1890s. 'The selector comes nearer to him still, so near as often to seem identical, yet a fine but unmistakeable shade of difference severs him from the true Bushman, the Bushman pure and simple, the man of the nation . . .'

Wool Is Up

Earth o'erflows with
*   nectared gladness,*
All creation teems with joy;
Banished be each thought of
*   sadness,*
Life for me has no alloy.
Fill a bumper!—drain a
*   measure,*
Pewter! goblet! tankard! cup!
Testifying thus our pleasure
At the news that 'Wool is up'.

GARNET WALCH

The Women of the West

They left the vine-wreathed cottage and the mansion on the hill,
The houses in the busy streets, where life is never still,
The pleasures of the city, and the friends they cherished best:
For love they faced the wilderness—the Women of the West.

The roar, and rush, and fever of the city died away,
And the old-time joys and faces—they were gone for many a day;
In their place the lurching coach-wheel, or the creaking bullock chains,
O'er the everlasting sameness of the never-ending plains.

In the slab-built, zinc-roofed homestead of some lately-taken run,
In the tent beside the bankment of a railway just begun,
In the huts on new selections, in the camps of man's unrest,
On the frontiers of the Nation, live the Women of the West.

The red sun robs their beauty, and, in weariness and pain,
The slow years steal the nameless grace that never comes again;
And there are hours men cannot soothe, and words men cannot say—
The nearest woman's face may be a hundred miles away.

The wide Bush holds the secrets of their longings and desires,
When the white stars in reverence light their holy altar-fires,
And silence, like the touch of God, sinks deep into the breast—
Perchance He hears and understands the Women of the West.

For them no trumpet sounds the call, no poet plies his arts—
They only hear the beating of their gallant, loving hearts.
But they have sung with silent lives the song all songs above—
The holiness of sacrifice, the dignity of love.

Well have we held our fathers' creed. No call has passed us by.
We faced and fought the wilderness, we sent our sons to die.
And we have hearts to do and dare, and yet, o'er all the rest,
The hearts that made the Nation were the Women of the West.

GEORGE ESSEX EVANS

The Man from Snowy River

'Banjo' Paterson's greatly-loved poem *The Man from Snowy River*
expresses all that was daring, adventurous and devil-may-care in
the pioneering phase of Australian life.

There was movement at the station, for the word had passed around
That the colt from old Regret had got away,
And had joined the wild bush horses — he was worth a thousand pound,
So all the cracks had gathered to the fray.
All the tried and noted riders from the stations near and far
Had mustered at the homestead overnight,
For the bushmen love hard riding where the wild bush horses are,
And the stock-horse snuffs the battle with delight.

There was Harrison, who made his pile when Pardon won the Cup,
The old man with his hair as white as snow;
But few could ride beside him when his blood was fairly up —
He would go wherever horse and man could go.
And Clancy of the Overflow came down to lend a hand,
No better horseman ever held the reins;
For never horse could throw him while the saddle-girths would stand —
He learnt to ride while droving on the plains.

And one was there, a stripling on a small and weedy beast;
He was something like a racehorse undersized,
With a touch of Timor pony — three parts thoroughbred at least —
And such as are by mountain horsemen prized.
He was hard and tough and wiry — just the sort that won't say die —
There was courage in his quick impatient tread;
And he bore the badge of gameness in his bright and fiery eye,
And the proud and lofty carriage of his head.

But still so slight and weedy, one would doubt his power to stay,
And the old man said, 'That horse will never do
For a long and tiring gallop — lad, you'd better stop away,
Those hills are far too rough for such as you.'
So he waited sad and wistful — only Clancy stood his friend —
'I think we ought to let him come,' he said:
'I warrant he'll be with us when he's wanted at the end,
For both his horse and he are mountain bred.

'He hails from Snowy River, up by Kosciusko's side,
Where the hills are twice as steep and twice as rough;
Where a horse's hoofs strike firelight from the flint-stones every stride,
The man that holds his own is good enough.
And the Snowy River riders on the mountains make their home,
Where the river runs those giant hills between;
I have seen full many horsemen since I first commenced to roam,
But nowhere yet such horsemen have I seen.'

So he went; they found the horses by the big mimosa clump,
They raced away towards the mountain's brow,
And the old man gave his orders, 'Boys, go at them from the jump,
No use to try for fancy riding now.
And, Clancy, you must wheel them, try and wheel them to the right.
Ride boldly, lad, and never fear the spills,
For never yet was rider that could keep the mob in sight,
If once they gain the shelter of those hills.'

So Clancy rode to wheel them—he was racing on the wing
Where the best and boldest riders take their place,
And he raced his stock-horse past them, and he made the ranges ring
With the stockwhip, as he met them face to face.
Then they halted for a moment, while he swung the dreaded lash,
But they saw their well-loved mountain full in view,
And they charged beneath the stockwhip with a sharp and sudden dash,
And off into the mountain scrub they flew.

Then fast the horsemen followed, where the gorges deep and black
Resounded to the thunder of their tread,
And the stockwhips woke the echoes, and they fiercely answered back
From cliffs and crags that beetled overhead.
And upward, ever upward, the wild horses held their way,
Where mountain ash and kurrajong grew wide;
And the old man muttered fiercely, 'We may bid the mob good day,
No man can hold them down the other side.'

When they reached the mountain's summit, even Clancy took a pull—
It well might make the boldest hold their breath;
The wild hop scrub grew thickly, and the hidden ground was full
Of wombat holes, and any slip was death.
But the man from Snowy River let the pony have his head,
And he swung his stockwhip round and gave a cheer,
And he raced him down the mountain like a torrent down its bed,
While the others stood and watched in very fear.

He sent the flint-stones flying, but the pony kept his feet,
He cleared the fallen timber in his stride,
And the man from Snowy River never shifted in his seat—
It was grand to see that mountain horseman ride.
Through the stringybarks and saplings, on the rough and broken ground,
Down the hillside at a racing pace he went;
And he never drew the bridle till he landed safe and sound
At the bottom of that terrible descent.

He was right among the horses as they climbed the farther hill,
And the watchers on the mountain, standing mute,
Saw him ply the stockwhip fiercely; he was right among them still,
As he raced across the clearing in pursuit.
Then they lost him for a moment, where two mountain gullies met
In the ranges—but a final glimpse reveals
On a dim and distant hillside the wild horses racing yet,
With the man from Snowy River at their heels.

And he ran them single-handed till their sides were white with foam;
He followed like a bloodhound on their track,
Till they halted, cowed and beaten; then he turned their heads for home,
And alone and unassisted brought them back.
But his hardy mountain pony he could scarcely raise a trot,
He was blood from hip to shoulder from the spur;
But his pluck was still undaunted, and his courage fiery hot,
For never yet was mountain horse a cur.

And down by Kosciusko, where the pine-clad ridges raise
Their torn and rugged battlements on high,
Where the air is clear as crystal, and the white stars fairly blaze
At midnight in the cold and frosty sky,
And where around The Overflow the reed-beds sweep and sway
To the breezes, and the rolling plains are wide,
The Man from Snowy River is a household word today,
And the stockmen tell the story of his ride.

A. B. PATERSON

Overlanders

Urged on by the hope of profit, they have overcome difficulties of no ordinary kind, which have made the more timid and weak-hearted quail, and relinquish the enterprises in which they were engaged; whilst the resolute and undaunted have persevered, and the reward they have obtained is wealth, self-confidence in difficulties and dangers, and a fund of accurate information on many interesting points. Hence, almost every Overlander you meet is a remarkable man.

GEORGE GREY, explorer and Governor.

Droving into the Light.
Painting by Hans Heysen.

50

2. Bushrangers Scorn 'To Live in Slavery'

Unfortunately the convict system produced not only hardbitten bush workers, but also a number of men made so desperate by continuous or unjust punishment that they had no hope of finding their way back to normal life. Scores of these men took to the bush to avoid further floggings or execution. With little to lose, they specialised in robbing prosperous squatters and travellers. Sometimes they were assisted by poorer settlers motivated by sympathy or fear. Governor Darling was forced to report to London in 1830 that bushrangers had 'put on a more formidable appearance':

> In the earlier part of the year, they infested the Roads about Parramatta and Committed Several Acts of Outrage even in the Neighbourhood of Sydney. The Leaders of two Parties, MacNamara and Donahoe, who had been long at large, were both Shot in an encounter with the Police, and several Men have been executed.

Generally the public romanticised the bushrangers, regardless of their true nature, into an heroic part of the bush legend. The classic early example of a popular bushranger was Jack Donahoe, transported as a lad from Ireland in 1823 for mere 'intent to commit a felony'. In Australia he escaped from custody, robbed bullock drays, was twice sentenced to death, escaped both times, and was finally shot dead by police near Campbelltown. Ballads praising his defiance of cruel authority quickly circulated in Sydney pubs, despite attempts to suppress them.

Come all Australian sons with me
For a hero has been slain,
And cowardly butchered in his sleep
Upon the Lachlan Plain.
When **police shot dead the popular bushranger Ben Hall**, folk songs like the above made him into a legend. Drawing below by Nicholas Chevalier.

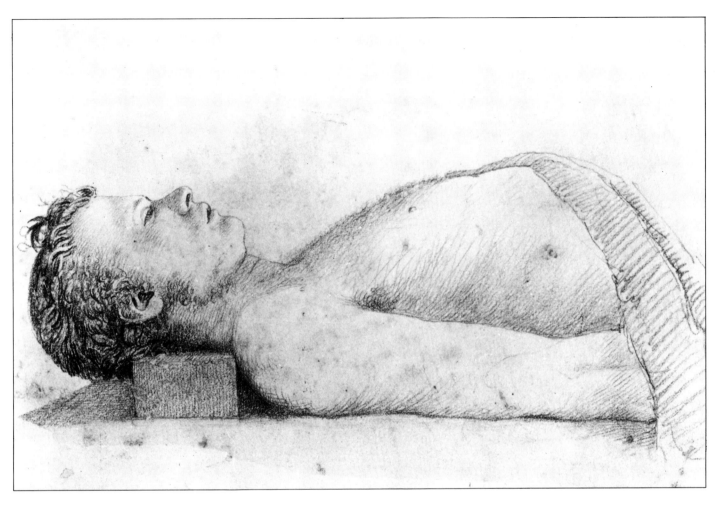

The Wild Colonial Boy

There was a wild colonial boy, Jack Donahoe by name,
Of poor but honest parents he was born in Castlemaine.
He was his father's dearest hope, his mother's pride and joy.
O, fondly did his parents love their Wild Colonial Boy.

So ride with me, my hearties, we'll cross the mountains high.
Together we will plunder, together we will die.
We'll wander through the valleys and gallop o'er the plains,
For we scorn to live in slavery, bound down with iron chains!

He was scarcely sixteen years of age when he left his father's Home,
A convict to Australia, across the seas to roam.
They put him in the Iron Gang in the Government employ,
But ne'er an iron on earth could hold the Wild Colonial Boy.

And when they sentenced him to hang to end his wild career,
With a loud shout of defiance bold Donahoe broke clear.
He robbed those wealthy squatters, their stock he did destroy,
But never a trap in the land could catch the Wild Colonial Boy.

Then one day when he was cruising near the broad Nepean's side,
From out the thick Bringelly bush the horse police did ride.
'Die or resign, Jack Donahoe!' they shouted in their joy.
'I'll fight this night with all my might!' cried the Wild Colonial Boy.

He fought six rounds with the horse police before the fatal ball,
Which pierced his heart with cruel smart, caused Donahoe to fall.
And then he closed his mournful eyes, his pistol an empty toy,
Crying! 'Parents dear, O say a prayer for the Wild Colonial Boy.'

POPULAR BALLAD

The courage of **Jack Donahoe** under fire was widely praised. After he was shot dead by troopers in 1830, the New South Wales Surveyor-General Thomas Mitchell drew this pencil sketch of his body, adding a quotation from Byron:
No matter; I have bared my brow.
Fair in Death's face—before—and now.

Sir Sidney Nolan's dramatic interpretation of the scene at **Ned Kelly's trial in 1880**. When Judge Redmond Barry, at left, sentenced the bushranger to death, Kelly replied: 'I will go a little further than that, and say I will see you there where I go'.

Even after committing his worst crimes, Ned Kelly, Australia's most famous bushranger, won the sympathy of many people who believed he had been forced into a renegade life. Ned was the eldest son of a transported Irish convict who died when the boy was eleven. To help support his mother and seven younger children, Ned began to assist gangs who stole horses and cattle from wealthier settlers in the Glenrowan district of northern Victoria. After being accused of the attempted murder of a trooper, Ned and Dan Kelly fled into the Wombat Ranges and formed their notorious bushranging gang. For two years they robbed squatters and banks with impunity, evading or shooting police sent to pursue them.

In a long letter of self-justification written at Jerilderie, Ned Kelly blamed his life on persecution of the Irish people by England: 'a flag and nation that has destroyed, massacred and murdered their forefathers by the greatest of torture'.

Cornered finally at Glenrowan, Kelly wore his renowned armour made from ploughshares, but was felled by shots in both legs. He went bravely to the scaffold, saying 'Such is life' or 'I suppose it had to come to this', and immediately entered the pantheon of Australian heroes. All attempts to break up the Kelly legend have failed: even today the greatest compliment that can be paid to an Australian is to call him 'as game as Ned Kelly'.

3. Brilliant Editors Bring Freedom to New South Wales

With the rapid growth of a free population, autocratic rule by Governors became increasingly difficult in Australia. There was simply too much happening over too large an area for one man and a few officials to control. Some free-born Australians enjoyed a wider vision. They saw that the country had already developed to the point where its residents required greater justice before the law, some form of representative parliament, and above all, an unshackled press able to speak on behalf of ordinary people.

One man, William Charles Wentworth, incorporated all these ideals within his own personality. Born two years after the first settlement of Sydney, the son of an Irish ship's surgeon and a convict mother, Wentworth as a 'currency lad' experienced the full scorn of 'pure merino' exclusion. He came to the conclusion that men should be free to rise in the world through their own qualities and achievements, not by accidents of birth. After qualifying as a barrister in England in 1822, Wentworth decided to return to Sydney with a fellow barrister, Robert Wardell, 30, editor of the *Statesman*. They brought printing plant with them, determined to fight for freedom of the press and parliamentary government.

At that time the only newspaper, the *Sydney Gazette*, was censored by officials before publication. Disdaining to ask the Governor's permission, Wentworth and Wardell set up their equipment and on 18 October 1824 began publication of the *Australian*. Governor Brisbane, a good-natured liberal, decided not to interfere. 'I considered it most expedient to try the experiment of full latitude of the freedom of the Press', he reported to London. In this benign atmosphere, the peaceful flowering of a democratic state seemed possible. Unfortunately the 'exclusive' faction could not leave well enough alone, and continually undermined the Governor through his officials and letters to London. Brisbane was unjustly recalled in 1825.

Deeper signs of conflict began to appear when the new Governor took office late in 1825. Sir Ralph Darling, 50, whose efficiency won him the high rank of Deputy Adjutant-General of the British Army, seemed the very man to replace the amiable Sir Thomas Brisbane, and set the faction-ridden community to rights.

Under Darling, official brutality fed on its own corruption. Iron discipline among convicts and guards became the order of the day. In September 1826 two soldiers, Patrick Thompson and Joseph Sudds, decided that life as convicts (with freedom after a few years) was preferable to military discipline. They entered a Sydney drapery store, tucked rolls of calico under their arms, and sauntered outside to await arrest.

Darling was appalled. He had the men clad in convict dress, two heavy spiked iron collars being locked around their necks and connected to leg-irons. In this manner they were paraded before the regiment as a grim example, solemnly drummed out of the service, and cast into prison. Sudds subsequently died.

Fury broke loose in the press and at public meetings. Wentworth openly described Darling's actions as 'murder, or at least a high misdemeanour' and demanded his recall. Such cruel autocracy, said Wentworth, could best be kept in check by an elected parliament and trial by civil juries. Darling's reply, given in his despatches to London, was that free newspapers were 'extremely dangerous' in a convict colony.

Darling then presented two Bills to his Legislative Council to restrict these 'seditious and inflammatory' newspapers. The first Bill provided for the registration of all newspapers and lodgement of a £300 recognizance to meet fines for libel. The second Bill imposed a crippling stamp duty of fourpence on every copy sold.

The convict colony happened to have as its first Chief Justice one Francis

W. C. Wentworth, a founder of the *Australian*, wrote in his first issue that 'A free press is . . . the most powerful weapon that can be employed to annihilate influence, frustrate the designs of tyranny, and restrain the arm of oppression'. Painting by Richard Buckner.

Edward Smith Hall, editor of the Sydney *Monitor*, gaoled illegally for 'libelling' Governor Darling. Painting by Gladstone Eyre.

*The services they rendered
were so great that they never
will be adequately estimated.
The name I mentioned
first—that of Mr Edward
Smith Hall—belonged to a
man of singularly pure and
heroic disposition. Even in
his old age, as I knew him,
he had an almost spiritual
purity of life about him; but
in his strong days he met the
greatest form of aggressive
power that we ever
experienced in this
country . . . I think this
country and all Australia can
never adequately thank that
singular pioneer in the cause
of civil liberty, Mr Edward
Smith Hall.*

SIR HENRY PARKES, Premier
of New South Wales, on the
achievements of early
Australian newspaper editors.

Forbes, born in Bermuda in 1784, who in his youth had been impressed with American democratic ideals. Forbes had already warned Darling that his extension of the punishment of Sudds and Thompson was illegal. The Chief Justice now concluded that the real object of imposing a stamp duty was to punish the press for its trenchant criticisms. He refused to certify the Bill, and was supported in his judgement by a more liberal ministry which had come to power in Britain.

Meanwhile, another independent newspaper called the *Monitor* commenced publication in Sydney. Its proprietor was Edward Smith Hall, a free immigrant born in London in 1786. Hall generally supported Wentworth's advanced views on political democracy, but won even greater support from the convict population through his exposures of illegal sentences by 'pure merino' magistrates. 'Many a brave man's back, through us, has been saved from the biting lash', Hall claimed. In another issue he wrote that 'Packed juries . . . and Taxation without Representation, cannot long exist in the burning radiance of a free and virtuous Press'.

To an already infuriated Governor Darling, this sounded remarkably like the seditious talk which led to the American Revolution. He withdrew four convicts assigned to assist Hall in the production of his paper. This action was declared illegal on application to the Supreme Court. Vindictively, Darling next punished Hall by withdrawing his right to graze stock on Crown land. Pressed for a reason, the Governor replied it was sufficient to state that 'you are the editor of the *Monitor*, the columns of which paper bear ample testimony to your endeavours to disturb the tranquillity of the colony . . .' Hall demanded to know whether 'the journalists of New South Wales were to be punished for their writings . . . at the caprice of the Governor'. It seemed so. In 1829 Hall was charged with several counts of publishing libels against the Governor and his officials. Military juries found him guilty in each case, and he was sentenced to three years' gaol.

Meanwhile, Robert Wardell had passed to Attwell Edwin Hayes the dangerous task of editing the *Australian*. In 1828 Hayes too was gaoled after attacking Darling's actions. Undeterred, both editors continued to write impassioned editorials from their prison cells at Parramatta. Darling retaliated with a new law imposing banishment from New South Wales of any person convicted of a second seditious libel. The British government in 1830 disallowed Darling's new Act. The Governor was forced to issue a free pardon to Hall and release him from gaol. Darling himself 'retired' the following year, and was never again employed in an official capacity. Best of all, military juries were abolished in court cases affecting the Governor or his officials, and replaced by trial before a jury of ordinary citizens. A little more than twenty years later, such a jury would refuse to convict even those men who took up arms against government forces at Eureka.

4. After Many Struggles, an End to Convictism

In Britain, the last echoes of the Napoleonic wars were dying away. The ageing Duke of Wellington, hero of those wars, but doggedly reactionary as a politician, was defeated as Tory Prime Minister in 1830. A more liberal policy was adopted towards colonial government, convict transportation, and economic expansion.

The man chosen to put this new approach into effect was Sir Richard Bourke, 54, an Irish-born relative of the statesman Edmund Burke. Soon after his arrival in Sydney, Bourke was able to extend the jury system and reduce magistrates' power to punish convicts. He ordered the irons removed from non-violent prisoners working on roads and quarries, reporting to London that 'They appear to receive with gratitude this relaxation of punishment, and their labor is said to be carried on with an alacrity unknown before'.

But many of Bourke's own officials assisted major landowners to undermine his attempts at reform. James Macarthur followed his late father's example and lobbied continually in London for the Governor's removal. Sickening at last of the battle, Bourke resigned early in 1838, departing to the sorrow and acclamation of the lower classes he had tried so hard to assist.

Yet the battle against convictism was by no means lost. While Bourke was still in power, his Whig friends in London, disturbed by scandalous treatment of the transported 'Tolpuddle Martyrs', appointed William Molesworth to investigate the convict system. Molesworth's scarifying report on the effects of transportation on the Australian colonies led the British government to abolish transportation to New South Wales in 1840. New gaols were built throughout Britain to hold her criminal population in check, but within a few years even these were overcrowded with victims of rural depopulation and urban industrialisation. In 1846 the British government proposed that transportation should be resumed to drain these ulcers. As a sop to the colonists, only those convicts would be sent who had proved by their 'good behaviour' that they were worthy of a conditional pardon and a new life in Australia.

The scheme was welcomed by many squatters. In a petition asking for more convict servants, they pointed out to the Colonial Office that increasing numbers of sheep and cattle caused severe labour shortages, which in turn meant that the price of free labour had 'increased about fifty per cent'. The only way to drive wages down again was to import convicts or coolies. W. E. Gladstone, Secretary for the Colonies, authorised the despatch of two convict ships, the *Hashemy* and *Randolph*. After some delays due to cholera, the *Hashemy* arrived in Sydney on 10 June 1849. Several thousand respectable citizens crowded Circular Quay to hear an impassioned speech by Robert Lowe (later Viscount Sherbrooke), a near-blind lawyer, then 38 years of age, who consistently fought the squatters' claims:

> The stately presence of our city, the beautiful waters of our harbour, are this day again polluted with the presence of that floating hell—a convict ship. (Immense cheers) . . . I view this attempt to inflict the worst and most degrading slavery on the colony only as a sequence of that oppressive tyranny which has confiscated the lands of the colony—for the benefit of a class . . . Let it go home that the people of New South Wales reject, indignantly reject, the inheritance of wealthy shame which Great Britain holds out to her . . . Let us send across the Pacific our emphatic declaration that we will not be slaves—that we will be free . . .

When the *Randolph* arrived at Melbourne two months later, an equally frenzied meeting took place in the Queen's Theatre. Lauchlan Mackinnon, 32, a Western District settler of Scottish birth who alone opposed other squatters demanding convict labour, told the meeting that he would resist 'even to death' the landing of

Nine Years in Van Diemen's Land

Shall fathers weep and
* mourn*
To see a lovely son
Debas'd, demoraliz'd,
* deform'd,*
By Britain's filth and scum?

Shall mothers heave the sigh,
To see a daughter fair
Debauch'd, sunk in infamy
By those imported here? . . .

Arise, then, Freemen—rise:
Secure your liberty;
Ne'er rest till Transportation
* dies;*
And Austral's isle be FREE.

J. SYME

Artist William Strutt designed this **card for the Anti-Transportation League** in Melbourne in 1851.

Sir Richard Bourke, liberal Governor of New South Wales, who tried to ameliorate the effects of transportation. Painting by M. Archer Shee.

such 'polluted cargoes'. The obnoxious policies of the Colonial Office, he cried, were 'driving a good and loyal people into open rebellion', and would make them 'wish to see these colonies separated from England. (Loud and continued cheering)'. Such barely-concealed threats caused Britain to change her plans. Most of the convicts were diverted to Moreton Bay, where little opposition could be organised.

Sir George Grey, the new Secretary for the Colonies, insisted on continuing transportation to . . . where? Some settled area had to be found. Surely Tasmania would accept these economical servants? But in Hobart and Launceston opposition blossomed anew. Help was sought from mainland towns, and the first united political policies between the eastern colonies came into being. A powerful Australasian League for the Abolition of Transportation was formed. In 1851 it adopted the first national flag, consisting of the Union Jack (for loyalty) and the Southern Cross (for independence)—remarkably similar in design to today's Australian flag.

Faced with this united front, Britain abandoned transportation to Tasmania in 1853. Unfortunately the struggling settlers of Western Australia, suffering worse shortages of labour than the east, asked for British convicts. The Colonial Office was delighted to oblige. Within a few years, convicts and their guards formed two-thirds of Western Australia's population. The result, wrote Sir Charles Dilke after a visit in the 1860s, was that Western Australia became 'a great English prison', filled with 'fiend-faced convicts' and 'scowling expirees'. Britain abandoned the last vestiges of transportation in 1868. Australian patriots had finally triumphed in one of the greatest battles of our early years.

The Anti-Transportation League even flew its own flag, remarkably similar to our national flag today.

5. Immigrants Swell the Sources of Free Labour

The Emigrant's Vision

As his bark dashed away on the night-shrouded deep,
  And out towards the South he was gazing,
First there passed o'er his spirit a darkness like sleep
  Then the light of a vision amazing!
As rises the moon, from the white waves afar
Came a goddess, it seemed, of love, wisdom, and war,
And on her bright helmet, encircling a star,
  Behold there was graven 'Australia' . . .

'O stranger!' she said, 'hast thou fled from the home
  Which thy forefathers bled for so vainly?
Does shame for its past thus induce thee to roam,
  Or despair of its future constrain thee?
In the far sunny south there's a refuge from wrong,
'Tis the Shiloh of freedom expected so long:
There genius and glory shall shout forth thy song—
  'Tis the evergreen land of Australia.'

CHARLES HARPUR

In days of slow transport, the decision to leave Britain for the other side of the world could never be taken lightly. **Abraham Solomon's painting 'Second Class— the Parting'** shows the combined sadness and hope with which emigrants sought a new life.

Caroline Chisholm, heroine
to thousands of immigrant
women, whose efforts
brought order into the chaos
of early immigration policy.
Painting by A. C. Hayter.

Up to 1830, when Australia was renowned as a prison settlement, only about ten thousand free immigrants ventured here. During the following two decades, however, great efforts were made to achieve a more balanced population. Assisted by funds raised from the sale of Crown land, thousands of immigrants, including many family units, began pouring into Australian ports. Between 1830 and 1850, more than one hundred and seventy thousand arrived. Despite scandals over their treatment on the long voyage and after arrival, they began to form a class of hardworking, fecund, optimistic people so desperately needed by the rising nation.

Even in the 'evergreen land of Australia', many perils awaited young female immigrants. Once they had arrived, governments were inclined to leave their fate to chance. Good fortune brought to Sydney a remarkable woman, Caroline Chisholm, wife of an East India Company official. Horrified by what she saw and heard, Mrs Chisholm persuaded Governor Sir George Gipps to lend her an old storeroom. She patched it up, and there sheltered and fed 'Hundreds who were wandering about Sydney without friends or protection'. Employers who wished to engage the girls were invited to interview Mrs Chisholm first, bringing with them a clergyman's letter attesting to their good character.

Migrant ships often arrived simultaneously, and the labour market became over-supplied. When that happened, Mrs Chisholm loaded her surplus girls into bullock drays, and accompanied them on long treks through the bush, searching for suitable employers and prospective husbands. During seven years she resettled 11,000 women into their new homeland, becoming revered throughout the colony as almost a saint.

6. Gold Attracts People Demanding Democratic Rights

Suddenly, with little warning, Marco Polo's ancient dream of 'great plentye of gold' came true. The gold had been there all the time in the earth and rivers of Australia, and simply needed a knowledgeable person to search for it. The official discoverer was Edward Hargraves, 35-year-old veteran of the Californian gold rush of 1849. The news, wrote Lieutenant-Governor C. J. La Trobe from Melbourne, 'unsettled the public mind of the labouring classes of all the Australian colonies'. Thousands simply downed tools, packed swags, and took the long overland trail to the diggings. Why did they go? Because it was the one chance they would have in their lifetime to free themselves from wage-slavery.

When further huge deposits of gold were discovered some months later at Buninyong and Ballarat, an even bigger rush began. Melbourne and Geelong became ghost towns, with empty ships swinging idly at anchor and every second shop closed. 'In some of the suburbs not a man is left', La Trobe wrote to London.

Within a few months the news of ever-richer discoveries reached Europe and America. The world's attention turned to the despised colonies, and one of the great migrations of human history began. Many classes and types of people decided to 'try their luck' on the Australian goldfields, ranging from eager young sons of the British aristocracy to experienced Californian diggers sporting 'wild hair, huge beards and whiskers'. These hundreds of thousands of immigrants shared common feelings of restlessness and ambition. At home they enjoyed no settled place or brilliant prospects. But they did possess sufficient energy to get up and do something about their lives. Australia beckoned like a promised land, where dreams might come true.

Working conditions in the mines speeded the development of a rawboned, hearty, democratic spirit. The diggers came looking for independence through gold, and found it through hard physical labour with the ever-present chance of high rewards. The rugged life forced each miner into a special relationship with his own group of 'mates', who helped each other through all difficulties, sharing hardships and rewards equally. Origins were not important: all that mattered was that a man should give and receive 'a fair go'. 'Although your father might have been Lord of England all-over, it goes for nothing in this equalising colony of gold and beef and mutton', wrote one observer.

Those who could not stand such equality soon returned to their homelands. Their departure only strengthened the prevailing feelings of group loyalty among those left on the diggings. 'New chums' who made an honest attempt to adapt to colonial ways were accepted as real Australians. By the end of the gold rush decade, the European population of Australia almost trebled, reaching one million in 1860. About half a million migrants came from Britain alone. Although many returned home, Australia's population remained predominantly Anglo-Saxon, youthful, and vigorous. Britain's claim to the whole continent no longer seemed so tenuous.

These population movements, and the experiences of all the thousands of individuals within them, greatly strengthened characteristics recognised as 'Australian'. Much of the old 'currency' independence remained, but most of the stigma of convictism was buried. Only a decade or so after transportation ended, every employee could believe he was as good as his master, and often superior in matters requiring practical knowledge. These were not depraved convicts or pauper immigrants: these were proud men and women who would fight for and achieve the next stage of democratic rights.

The Roaring Days

The night too quickly passes
And we are growing old,
So let us fill our glasses
And toast the Days of Gold;
When finds of wondrous
  treasure
Set all the South ablaze,
And you and I were faithful
  mates
All through the Roaring Days!

Then stately ships came
  sailing
From every harbour's mouth,
And sought the Land of
  Promise
That beaconed in the South;
Then southward streamed
  their streamers
And swelled their canvas full
To speed the wildest dreamers
E'er borne in vessel's hull.

Their shining Eldorado
Beneath the southern skies
Was day and night for ever
Before their eager eyes.
The brooding bush, awakened,
Was stirred in wild unrest,
And all the year a human
  stream
Went pouring to the West . . .

Ah, then their hearts were
  bolder,
And if Dame Fortune frowned
Their swags they'd lightly
  shoulder
And tramp to other ground.
Oh, they were lion-hearted
Who gave our country birth!
Stout sons, of stoutest
  fathers born,
From all the lands on earth!

Those golden days are vanished,
And altered is the scene;
The diggings are deserted,
The camping-grounds are
  green;
The flaunting flag of progress
Is in the West unfurled,
The mighty Bush with iron
  rails
Is tethered to the world.

HENRY LAWSON

Mr E. H. HARGRAVES.

THE GOLD DISCOVERER OF AUSTRALIA

FEB 12 1851

Returning the salute of the Gold Miners on the 5th of the ensuing May.

DRAWN & LITHOGRAPHED BY T. T. BALCOMBE.

Who Wouldn't Be a Digger?

No one out here need toil in vain
If his mind to work he's giving,
In spite of hardships, it's quite plain,
Each one may get a living;
So in Australia stay awhile,
And work away with vigour,
For many a one will make a pile
That's now a hard-up digger.

CHARLES THATCHER

ABOVE
T. T. Balcombe's version of **the discovery of gold near Bathurst by Edward Hargraves** on 12 February 1851. Hargraves later said he told his companion: 'This is a memorable day in the history of New South Wales. I shall be a baronet, and you will be knighted, and my old horse will be stuffed, put into a glass case, and sent to the British Museum'.

OPPOSITE PAGE
Above. Techniques by which poor men could extract alluvial gold from rivers are clearly shown in this watercolour painted by William Strutt at **Ballarat in 1851**.
Below. By 1854, when newly-rich diggers held this **subscription ball at Ballarat**, they enthusiastically responded to the toast 'Advance Australia'.
Watercolour by S. T. Gill.

W.S.

Gold washing. Ballaarat Diggings. Victoria. 1851.

S.T.G.

Subscription Ball Ballarat 1854
Ticket to admit Lady & Gentleman

7. Eureka 1854: The Great Rebellion Against Autocracy

When laws bear down harshly on ordinary people, they must fight back or lose their freedom. That was the position faced by 80,000 diggers on the main goldfields in the early 1850s. They chose to fight, and their decision led to the only armed rebellion by free citizens in Australia's history. The conflict stemmed from decisions by the New South Wales and Victorian governments to impose licence fees of thirty shillings a month on all people working on the diggings. In 1854, when gold was becoming scarcer, this was a ridiculous impost.

Colonial Governors, supported by squatter-dominated legislative councils, seemed determined to persecute diggers, and remove this vigorous new population from lands they had previously monopolised. Diggers with little capital who did not find much gold had no way of paying the exorbitant licence fees. Their only hope was to continue mining illegally, and rely on mates to warn them of police raids.

Ostensibly to bring 'law and order' to the diggings, a new force of 250 police troopers was approved for Victoria. Recruits came largely from depraved remnants

Digger Hunt

> *. . . suddenly the warning cries are heard on every side*
> *As, closing in around a field, a ring of troopers ride.*
> *Unlicensed diggers are the game—their class and want are sins,*
> *And so, with all its shameful scenes, the digger-hunt begins.*
> *The men are seized who are too poor the heavy tax to pay,*
> *Chained man to man as convicts were, and dragged in gangs away.*
> *Though in the eye of many a man the menace scarce was hid,*
> *The diggers' blood was slow to boil, but scalded when it did.*
>
> HENRY LAWSON, 'Eureka'.

'I'm blessed if he has'nt grabbed Harry.' **Trooper arrests a goldminer lacking a licence.** Painting by George Lacy.

of the convict system, from men who preferred petty authority to the hard labour of mining, and from those who took a perverted delight in persecuting the poor. The government piled misjudgement on top of injustice by granting this corrupt force half of all fines imposed for licence-dodging. The troopers were given a direct financial interest in perjury, bribery, and maltreatment of people whose only crime was that they had come to Australia to search for gold.

Today one can scarcely credit that governments could remain blind for so long to the evidence of their folly. Their minds were gripped by an authoritarian past, in which 'the rights of man' seemed a call to unbridled anarchy. Deputations from diggers' spokesmen were received but their pleas disregarded. A mass meeting of the Ballarat Reform League on 11 November 1854, attended by thousands of diggers, decided that the introduction of a fully elected parliament to rule the land was the only way to overcome the stupidity of imported Governors. Phrases reminiscent of the American Revolution flew through the overheated air.

The new Governor of Victoria, Sir Charles Hotham, 48, was yet another of Britain's disciplinarian naval officers sent to rule fractious colonists. He promptly prepared for civil war, borrowing soldiers from other colonies. Two field pieces and two howitzers from HMS *Electra* and *Fantome* accompanied the troops.

The diggers, growing more infuriated every day, prepared for violence more emotionally and less systematically. On 29 November, meeting on Bakery Hill at Ballarat, they hoisted a rebel flag based on the stars of the Southern Cross. Their leader, Peter Lalor, a 27-year-old Irish miner, asked them to kneel and take a solemn oath of mutual support. During the next few days the miners erected a flimsy stockade of drays and pit props around the flagpole. Men gathered arms, drilled, and asked other diggings for reinforcements.

On the fatal night, Saturday 2 December 1854, only about one hundred and fifty diggers slept in the stockade. About half were armed: many of these had only a few rounds of ammunition for their primitive weapons. Before dawn on Sunday, 276 troops in the government camp some miles away were roused and fed. They advanced quietly towards the rebel stronghold. A few Californians on guard saw the troops at about one hundred and fifty yards distance, and fired a volley which killed one private. The soldiers replied with two devastating volleys, charged with bayonets fixed and blood in their hearts, and in a ten-minute struggle overcame all resistance. Five soldiers were killed and thirteen slightly wounded. Probably thirty diggers were killed on the spot or died later from their wounds. The remainder were rounded up and taken in chains to gaol.

The brief bloody conflict apparently ended in defeat for the miners' cause. But a huge protest meeting in Melbourne three days later violently and totally condemned the government's goldfields policies. Leading newspapers supported the miners. Survivors of the rebellion charged with high treason were one after another declared innocent by juries of ordinary men. A commission of inquiry into goldfields administration reported that miners were justified in resisting the methods used to collect licence fees, and in demanding political representation.

In the end, the 150 Eureka rebels won great victories. To replace the hated monthly licence, a 'miner's right' costing only £1 a year was introduced: it granted both the right to dig for gold and to vote for the first fully elective parliament. Gold commissioners and their bullying troopers were removed from the diggings, to be replaced by a system of wardens' courts for settlement of disputes. Governor Hotham resigned office, but died in Melbourne before he could be replaced.

The immediate practical effects of Eureka were important enough. Of even deeper significance was the message that Australian colonists would not tolerate widespread injustice. As the Royal Commissioners stated: 'The tendencies to serious outbreak amongst masses of population are usually a signal that the government is at fault as well as the people'.

Despite the fears of Governors and military officers, there never was much chance of the Eureka rebellion spreading in the same way that the American Revolution exploded into full-scale national defiance. Nearly a century lay between the two events: Britain had learned that when men are willing to die for political rights, it is better to give way gracefully.

The great meeting of Ballarat diggers on 11 November 1854 resolved:
That it is the inalienable right of every citizen to have a voice in the making of the laws he is called upon to obey. That taxation without representation is tyranny . . . That it is the object of the League to place the power in the hands of responsible representatives of the people to frame wholesome laws and carry on an honest government. That it is not the wish of the League to effect an immediate separation of this Colony from the parent country, if equal laws and equal rights are dealt out to the whole free community . . . The people are the only legitimate source of all political power.

We swear by the Southern Cross to stand truly by each other, and fight to defend our rights and liberties. This was the oath sworn by miners before **Peter Lalor** (below), leader of the Eureka revolt.

**British troops attack
miners at the Eureka
stockade.** Painting by
J. B. Henderson.

Fling out the Flag

*Fling out the Flag! Let her flap and rise in the rush of
the eager air,*
*With the ring of the wild swan's wings as she soars
from the swamp and her reedy lair!*
*Fling out the Flag! and let friend and foe behold, for
gain or loss,*
*The sign of our faith and the fight we fight, the Stars
of the Southern Cross!*
*Oh! Blue's the sky that is fair for all, whoever,
wherever he be,*
*And Silver's the light that shines on all, for hope and
for liberty;*
*And that's the desire that burns in our hearts, for ever
quenchless and bright,*
*And that's the sign of our flawless faith, and the
glorious fight we fight.*

FRANCIS ADAMS

*If democracy means opposition to a tyrannical press, a
tyrannical people, or a tyrannical government, then I
have ever been, I am still, and I ever will remain a
democrat.*

PETER LALOR

*Eureka was more than an incident or a passing phase. It
was greater in significance than the short-lived revolt
against tyrannical authority would suggest. The
permanency of Eureka in its impact on our development
was that it was the first real affirmation of our
determination to be the master of our own political
destiny.*

J. B. CHIFLEY

8. Responsible Government at Last

Stern necessity will shiver to atoms the Acts of Parliament by which we have sought to fetter the colonies . . . and will give them, whether we wish it or no, the fullest powers of self-government. It only remains with us to say whether this shall be gracefully conceded, or wrested from us by tumult and violence.

THE TIMES, London, 1852.

Below: **Henry Parkes carried in triumph to his office by working-men after his first election.**
Below right: **Charles Gavan Duffy, a Victorian democrat, in an early attempt to promote Federation.**

The fight for parliamentary independence was vital to the development of Australian national feeling. As long as the basic policies of each colony were decided in London, and transmitted through Governors of varying beliefs and quality, no Australian could feel that he was truly a citizen of his own country. Britain yielded with painful slowness to Australian demands for a greater share in government. In 1829 the New South Wales Legislative Council was increased to fifteen members, adding seven settlers and merchants to its core of officials.

In 1835 an Australian Patriotic Association was formed in Sydney to agitate for greater rights. It petitioned for a representative assembly, with at least three-quarters of members to be elected by the free population. London deferred the matter until transportation to the mainland ceased. Two years later, in 1842, the first elective Legislative Councils were established in New South Wales and Van Diemen's Land. Only male property owners were permitted to vote: they had to own at least £200 in freehold property or pay rates of £20 a year. This still excluded most of each colony's free population, and ensured that control of the Councils remained with about four thousand wealthy pastoralists and merchants.

Earl Grey, Secretary for the Colonies, decided that entirely new arrangements would have to be made for governing the eastern colonies. In the Australian Colonies Government Act of 1850, Victoria won separation from New South Wales, and election of its own Legislative Council. To give wider representation, property qualifications for electors were halved in both colonies. That meant the owner of any decent-sized house could vote. Colonists were still dissatisfied, for Governors retained direct control over many matters. Finally the enormous social changes brought about by the gold rush persuaded Britain that a large degree of self-government for Australia could no longer be delayed.

In 1852 the Legislative Councils of each colony, except under-developed

"UNION IS STRENGTH."
A LESSON BETTER LEARNT LATE THAN NEVER.

Western Australia, were authorised to prepare constitutions based generally on the British system of two houses of parliament, an executive government responsible to an elected lower house, and a vice-regal establishment representing the monarch. A storm of class conflict immediately broke out. The former democrat W. C. Wentworth, who had amassed large amounts of property since his radical younger days, became leader of conservative forces attempting to construct an Australian version of the rigid British class system. Wentworth seriously proposed to elevate the squattocracy into a colonial aristocracy, intended to rule a powerful Legislative Council forever as a safeguard against 'the excesses of mob democracy'.

Wentworth's most effective opponent was Daniel Henry Deniehy, 25-year-old son of Irish parents transported for 'vagrancy'—that is, because they were paupers. Daniel, a brilliant child, received enough education to become a solicitor in Sydney. At public meetings he derided Wentworth's ideas for 'these harlequin aristocrats, these Botany Bay magnificos, these Australian mandarins'. The colonies 'were to be favoured with a bunyip aristocracy'. Deniehy's exaggerations blew Wentworth's proposed aristocracy away on gales of public ridicule.

After all this controversy, the first Legislative Assemblies were finally elected in New South Wales, Victoria and South Australia in 1856. They were not fully independent parliaments as we know them today. On strictly local matters they could pass laws, and expect them to receive royal assent almost automatically. But a long list of subjects, such as defence, foreign affairs, overseas trade and shipping, even divorce, were 'reserved' for decision by the British government. The old doctrine remained that no colonial laws were valid if they were deemed 'repugnant to the laws of England'. Each of the reserved matters was transferred from Britain to Australia very slowly and reluctantly over the next ninety years.

Victoria, with a radical tradition already established by large numbers of gold diggers in its population, quickly achieved a greater degree of self-government than New South Wales. The secret ballot, soon to be known as 'the Australian ballot', was invented by William Robinson Boothby, Sheriff of South Australia. It was first adopted by Victoria for the inaugural elections of March 1856, and later copied throughout the world.

Property qualifications for members of both Victorian houses were initially very high. However, the franchise for election of both houses was steadily widened. Miners who paid for an annual licence were given the vote as a result of Eureka. The franchise was extended to all adult males in 1857, although the effect was somewhat distorted by multiple votes granted to property owners.

In South Australia, an attempt was made by Governor Sir Henry Young to force a conservative constitution of the New South Wales type upon colonists, with an upper house of wealthy men nominated for life. George Kingston, one of the original South Australian pioneers of 1836, fought the plan bitterly after his election to the Council in 1851. Almost unanimous public support for a democratic constitution, including a monster petition to London, forced abandonment of Governor Young's scheme. After a further battle with Young's successor, the South Australians attained a high degree of self-government. Universal manhood suffrage, with no extra votes for property owners, was introduced with the first parliament of 1856. The secret ballot came into effect two weeks after Victoria.

Two years after Victoria and South Australia showed that manhood suffrage and the secret ballot did not cause instant revolution, New South Wales managed to copy the younger colonies in these matters. To achieve rights taken for granted today, crucial battles were fought by the second Premier, Charles Cowper. In 1858 he threatened to swamp the Council with additional appointments of liberal nominees. By this technique he forced the upper house to accept male suffrage, secret ballots, and redistribution.

Imperfect though these advances towards democracy were, they occurred well ahead of similar changes in Britain itself. In 1858, when Australia's eastern colonies achieved almost universal manhood suffrage, only about one-fifth of adult males in Britain could vote for the House of Commons. Not until Disraeli's Second Reform Bill of 1867 did small property owners get the vote; and not until W. E. Gladstone's further reforms of 1884 was anything like the Australian voting

Daniel Deniehy, the New South Wales democrat who scorned Wentworth's proposals for a 'bunyip aristocracy'.

We'll plant a Tree of Liberty
In the centre of the land,
And round it ranged as
* guardians be,*
A vowed and trusty band.

Charles Harpur

Charles Cowper, the New South Wales Premier who fought the Upper House to win democratic reforms.

An eyewitness sketch by William Strutt of **the opening of Victoria's first Legislative Council in 1851.**

system established. Australian colonies were also among the first in the world to introduce compulsory voting, preferential voting, public electoral rolls, and votes for women.

Queensland was separated from New South Wales in 1859, and given its own constitution based on that of the mother colony. Entrenched in an equally strong Legislative Council, the squatting interest was able to hold back much liberal and radical legislation for half a century.

During the 19th century, Tasmania and Western Australia lagged behind the rest of Australia in their democratic institutions. The many thousands of additional convicts sent to Tasmania after transportation ceased to the mainland took many years to absorb. Even in the late 1860s, convicts and emancipists formed more than one-third of Tasmania's total population. Frequent economic depressions occurred, rural magistrates retained archaic powers, and parliament remained under the domination of landowners.

Western Australia was similarly held back by under-population, and by its requests for transported convict labour in the 1860s. Only the great gold discoveries around Coolgardie in the 1890s, and the resulting massive population increase of free men from the east, enabled Western Australia to take part in the fullness of self-government by the time Federation was achieved.

The eastern democratic colonies, meanwhile, raced ahead with a good deal of important social legislation. Even before the appearance of a Labor Party, liberal forces brought in free secular universal education, factory legislation, triennial parliaments, payment of MPs, equalising tax laws, old age pensions, and other measures which gave every person the feeling that the business of government was intimately connected with their daily lives. The benefits of the parliamentary system were becoming obvious for all to see. But there were still many trials to overcome before Australians could regard themselves as a fully democratic nation.

9. Colonies Look to Their Own Defences

Sydney's earliest defences consisted of a few field guns located on headlands around the harbour. Painting by J. S. Prout shows **Dawes Battery in 1842**.

Nineteenth-century Australians, conscious of the colonies' huge undefended areas, evolved three 'stings' to warn potential enemies that any invasion attempt would meet fierce resistance. A naval screen was thrown around the continent; forts were built to protect major ports; and militia forces were recruited in each colony. In the first line of defence, colonists relied on the British navy to find and harass enemy ships before they reached Australian shores. This suited Britain's strategic purposes at the time. She could afford to keep a substantial fleet in the Indian Ocean, while detaching an 'Australian squadron' to patrol the Pacific

Governor Sir Henry Barkly reviews the Victorian Volunteer Cavalry on the Werribee Plains, c. 1860. Watercolour by William Strutt.

Australia needs no bulwarks,
No towers along the steep;
Her walls should be the
*   mountain wave,*
Her guard should be the
*   deep.*

ILLUSTRATED SYDNEY NEWS,
29 October 1853, pleading for
an Australian navy.

Ocean. But the colonists also saw the need to build their own defence forces. These, they felt, would make Australia more self-reliant and deserving of greater political independence.

On the outbreak of the Crimean War in 1854, Australia's earlier suspicions of French intentions were replaced by fears of a Russian invasion. When an emigrant ship in Port Phillip fired skyrockets to celebrate its release from quarantine, residents assumed a Russian battle fleet had arrived and called out the militia. Similar scares occurred in Australian ports in 1864, 1877, 1882, and 1885.

Victoria, especially fearful of Russian raids on her huge gold shipments, placed an order for the first warship ever built for a British colony. Her Majesty's Colonial Ship *Victoria*, a wooden 580-ton screw steamer mounting seven 32-pounder guns, arrived in Port Phillip in 1855. She was later reinforced by other ships, including the floating fortress *Cerberus* designed to lob enormous 400-lb shells on any invader. These colonial navies were assisted by a formal British-Australian Naval Agreement signed in 1887. In return for contributing £126,000 a year to the Royal Navy, Australia was guaranteed protection by five fast British armoured cruisers and two torpedo gunboats. This force could not be moved from Australian waters without colonial consent.

In case invaders were able to break through this combined naval screen, networks of powerful forts were built to protect the main seaports. By the 1880s Sydney had a complete system of forts defending Port Jackson, with heavy rifled cannon bristling from every prominent headland. A series of newly-invented electric mines (then called 'torpedoes') were submerged to keep enemy ships inside lanes swept by the big guns. In Victoria, substantial forts were built to protect the entrance to Port Phillip Bay and harbour facilities.

Meanwhile colonial armies were being recruited and trained. The number of British soldiers in Australia steadily diminished after transportation was abolished, the last troops returning to England in 1870. By the 1880s about ten thousand local volunteer infantry, artillerymen and cavalry were training in the various colonies, encouraged by 50-acre land grants given after five years' service. 'Every country town of any size has its company of infantry or rifle reserves', remarked the *Illustrated Sydney News* on 6 February 1890. There is no doubt that any invasion force which got ashore would have been faced with lengthy guerrilla actions in all rural areas.

By Federation, the number of adult volunteers had increased to nearly thirty thousand, while thousands more public schoolboys were undergoing training. Australians were obviously determined to stand on their own feet as an armed nation. Responsibility for their own defences made Australians conscious of the needs of the whole continent rather than individual colonies, and gave a powerful boost to national feeling.

Frigates of the Royal Navy's Australian Squadron join in manoeuvres in Sydney Harbour, 1881.

10. Flags of the Australian States

As each Australian colony achieved a degree of self-government, political leaders adopted flags to give their people new symbols of united endeavour. The immediate cause for the approval of individual flags was the establishment of local naval forces. Britain's Colonial Naval Defence Act of 1865 specified that all colonial warships should fly the Blue Ensign 'with a seal or badge of the colony in the fly thereof'. Even today this forms the basis of all State flags.

Since Victoria was the first colony to purchase a warship, it became the first part of Australia to have its own official flag. On 4 February 1870, Governor Sir John Manners-Sutton issued a proclamation directing that the Victorian badge would consist of 'five white stars, representing the constellation of the Southern Cross'. This flag, very similar to that of the Anti-Transportation League, was first raised on HMCS *Nelson* at Williamstown on 9 February 1870, accompanied by the firing of 21-gun salutes, cheering from the crews of every ship in the bay, and quadrilles danced on the warship's main deck. On 26 March 1877, a further proclamation added the Imperial Crown to the Victorian flag. In 1901, when Victoria became a State, St Edward's Crown was substituted, and that is how the flag remains today.

Curiously enough, the under-developed colony of Western Australia was next to adopt its own flag. In 1870, Governor Frederick Weld submitted to the Secretary for the Colonies a design showing a black swan on a yellow background. He wrote, 'This Colony at its commencement was usually known as the Swan River Settlement, and the Black Swan is represented upon its seal, and has always been considered as its special badge, or cognizance'. The flag has never been changed.

In 1875, the British Admiralty asked each of the Australian colonies to confirm their badges for insertion in a new edition of the Admiralty Flag Book. This request impelled New South Wales, Queensland and Tasmania to decide on individual symbols. The New South Wales flag, adopted on 15 February 1876, used as its badge a red cross bearing a golden lion in the centre, and an eight-pointed golden star on each arm.

Queensland at first adopted a representation of Queen Victoria's head, facing to the right, on a blue background. This was found too difficult to reproduce on fabric, and would have to be changed with each new monarch. On 29 November 1876, Queensland adopted the Imperial Crown superimposed on a blue Maltese Cross, possibly inspired by the Victoria Cross.

The Governor of Tasmania, the same Frederick Weld who had recommended the Western Australian flag in 1870, decreed on 25 September 1876 that the Tasmanian badge should consist of a red lion in a white circle. This was generally adopted, although for reasons unknown the flag was not officially proclaimed until 3 December 1975.

South Australia followed the Victorian precedent of using the Southern Cross on its flag when its first naval vessels arrived in 1872. The design was withdrawn when the Admiralty pointed out the possibility of confusion with Victorian ships. In its place, on 13 January 1904 South Australia adopted a design based on the piping shrike, or white-backed magpie, on a gold background.

The Northern Territory became largely self-governing under Commonwealth supervision on 1 July 1978. On that date a Territory flag was adopted, but it did not include a Union Jack. The flag uses the official Territory colours, black, white and red ochre. On the left are white stars of the Southern Cross on a black background. At right, superimposed on a red ochre background, appears the Territory floral emblem, Sturt's desert rose. The seven petals with a seven-pointed star in the centre symbolise the six Australian States and the Northern Territory.

Victoria, adopted in 1870.

Western Australia, adopted in 1870.

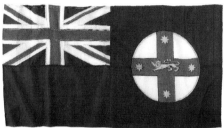

New South Wales, adopted in 1876.

Queensland, adopted in 1876.

Tasmania, adopted in 1876.

South Australia, adopted in 1904.

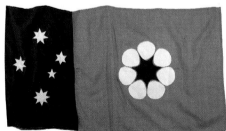

Northern Territory, adopted in 1978.

The Flag

Henry Parkes, several times Premier of New South Wales during the second half of the 19th century, wrote this poem 'The Flag' to express his hopes for Australia's continued peace and prosperity:

Fling out the flag—our virgin flag,
　Which foeman's shot has never rent,
And plant it high on mount and crag,
　O'er busy town and lonely tent.

Where commerce rears her stately halls,
　And where the miner rends the rock,
Where the sweet rain on cornfield falls,
　Where pastures feed the herd and flock.

Still let it float o'er homes of peace,
　Our starry cross—our glorious sign!
While Nature's bounteous gifts increase,
　And Freedom's glories brighter shine.

Brave hearts may beat in Labour's strife,
　They need no spur of martial pride;
High deeds may crown a gentle life,
　And spread their radiance far and wide.

Fling out the flag, and guard it well!
　Our pleasant fields the foe ne'er trod;
Long may our guardian heroes dwell
　In league with truth—in camp with God!

In other lands the patriot boasts
　His standard borne through Slaughter's flood,
Which, waving o'er infuriate hosts,
　Was consecrate in fire and blood.

A truer charm our flag endears;
　Where'er it waves, on land or sea,
It bears no stain of blood and tears—
　Its glory is its purity.

God girdled our majestic isle
　With seas far-reaching east and west,
That man might live beneath His smile,
　In peace and freedom ever blest.

HENRY PARKES

74

11. Young Australia Flexes its Muscles Abroad

Political leaders who visualised Australia supporting Britain 'to the death' were not merely orating for the sake of votes. They were expressing a fundamental feeling which ran through most of the community that they remained loyal Britons, although transplanted into strange circumstances.

The first major local test of this feeling occurred early in 1883, when the German corvette *Carola* sailed into Sydney for supplies. An alert shipping reporter learned that the vessel's destination was New Guinea. The news was received with consternation in Brisbane by the Premier, Sir Thomas McIlwraith, 48, a Scottish-born squatter who had won power on a policy of massive railway and economic expansion. McIlwraith used the new telegraph line to Thursday Island to instruct the resident police magistrate, Henry Marjoribanks Chester, to take possession of all that part of New Guinea lying closest to Queensland. Chester, an old Indian Navy officer, sailed in the armed schooner *Pearl* to plant the flag and fire salutes at Port Moresby on 4 April 1883. British diplomats, anxious to placate Germany, were aghast. Gladstone's government immediately disallowed Queensland's action — one of many indicators which persuaded Germany that Britain would not fight when she invaded Belgium in 1914.

Fury spread through the Australian colonies when Britain's reaction on New Guinea became known. Gladstone was openly called a traitor. Queensland immediately placed orders for two gunboats to cost £24,000 each. Victoria offered to bear the cost of annexing every piece of land from New Guinea through to the French convict colony of New Hebrides, in order to 'assure peace for future generations'. New South Wales offered troops and cannon to accompany an Australian battle fleet in conquest of the Pacific islands. Australia, observed the English historian James Froude, unconsciously adopted its own version of the

Sir Thomas McIlwraith, Queensland Premier who attempted to annex New Guinea. Artist unknown.

Departure of the Australian contingent for the Sudan in 1885. Painting by Arthur Collingridge.

A Passion of Patriotism

In this spontaneous act of the Australians the great Powers would see that they would have to reckon not with a small island whose relative consequence was decreasing daily, but with a mighty empire with a capacity for unbounded expansion . . . all parts of it combined in a passion of patriotism.

J. A. FROUDE

United States' Monroe Doctrine, designed to keep all rival powers well away from its shores. 'Young nations are like young men, sensitive and passionate', wrote Froude, watching events in Sydney with wry approval.

Early in the following year, 1884, Australia was proved right. Italy announced that she would acquire a slice of New Guinea to establish a penal colony. In June 1884 the German Chancellor, Otto von Bismarck, announced his rejection of Australia's claims. German forces and traders proceeded to occupy north-eastern New Guinea, renaming it Kaiser Wilhelm Land. In London, Gladstone's cabinet faced a humiliating climbdown. Not for the first or last time, German assurances proved valueless. The Admiralty instructed Captain James Erskine, RN, commodore of the Australian naval station, to sail in HMS *Miranda* to Port Moresby and again hoist the British flag. On 6 November 1884 Erskine took possession of south-eastern New Guinea (Papua) for Britain. In 1885 Britain finalised a diplomatic compromise which divided the entire island of New Guinea between herself, Germany and Holland. Nearly thirty years later, at the outbreak of World War I, Australia was left with the task of conquering the German section.

Bitterness over the New Guinea debacle did not affect the bonds between Britain and Australia. This was shown in dramatic fashion in 1885, when General Charles Gordon was trapped and killed in Khartoum by rebel forces which conquered most of the Sudan. By this time Australia had developed a direct interest in the Middle East. A company organised by French engineer Ferdinand de Lesseps opened the Suez Canal in 1869, eliminating thousands of miles from the ocean route between Britain, India and Australia. Henceforth the Suez Canal was seen as crucial to Empire strategy: thousands of Australians would die to defend it during the great anti-German conflicts of the 20th century.

In the early 1880s a poor Sudanese carpenter's son named Mohammed Ahmed proclaimed himself Mahdi (Messiah) of the Mohammedans. He won massive support for a combined nationalistic and religious uprising designed to throw off British and Egyptian influence. In less than three years his fanatical Dervishes reconquered most of the Sudan's one million square miles, finally trapping General Gordon's limited forces in the river city of Khartoum. The siege continued for 317 days. A British relief force was only two days from Khartoum when the rebels broke through, shooting Gordon dead on the palace steps.

News of the tragedy, tapped out in Morse code along the underwater cable from London to Darwin, and relayed through bush huts of the overland telegraph in Central Australia, reached Australian capitals on 11 February 1885. A wave of unconcealed grief and anger swept the nation. Acting Premier of New South Wales at the time was William Bede Dalley, 54, son of two transported convicts. His ministers immediately agreed to send an expeditionary force consisting of 500 infantry and horse artillery equipped with the colony's 16-pounder guns. Britain accepted just as promptly: Queen Victoria sent a cable expressing her gratitude.

Departure day, 3 March 1885, was proclaimed a public holiday. Special trains brought thousands of country people to Sydney. Unprecedented patriotic demonstrations took place throughout the metropolis. From Victoria Barracks to Circular Quay, a crowd estimated at 200,000 lined the route to cheer the departing 522 infantry and 212 artillerymen. Street banners bore loyal slogans; the crowd threw bouquets and roared 'Advance Australia' and 'Give it to the Mahdi!'.

The troops disembarked twenty-seven days later at Suakim, near Port Sudan in the Red Sea. On 3 April and 1 May they captured and burned two enemy villages, suffering three slight casualties. But most of their time was spent on helping to build a railway from Suakim to Berber. Britain then decided to evacuate Suakim to send troops to face a Russian danger in Afghanistan. After only seven weeks ashore, the contingent returned to Sydney, suffering six deaths from dysentery on the way. Revenge against the Mohammedans had to wait until 1898, when Sir Herbert Kitchener defeated a huge rebel army at Omdurman.

Australians cared little about the Sudan itself. They simply wanted to show that Australia, once unknown, now counted for something in the world—that it was a force, intertwined with British power, which could not be ignored by other nations seeking expansion.

The Star of Australasia

Before Federation, Australia had no way of knowing just how heavy a price
she would have to pay for intertwining herself with British interests. In a long
and curiously prophetic poem written in the peaceful days of 1895, Henry
Lawson seemed to sense what would happen.

We boast no more of our bloodless flag that rose from a
nation's slime;
Better a shred of a deep-dyed rag from the storms of the
olden time.
From grander clouds in our peaceful skies than ever were
there before
I tell you the Star of the South shall rise—in the lurid
clouds of war.
It ever must be while blood is warm and the sons of men
increase;
For ever the nations rose in storm, to rot in a deadly peace.
There'll come a point that we will not yield, no matter if
right or wrong;
And man will fight on the battle-field while passion and
pride are strong—
So long as he will not kiss the rod, and his stubborn spirit
sours—
For the scorn of Nature and curse of God are heavy on
peace like ours.

There are boys out there by the western creeks, who hurry
away from school
To climb the sides of the breezy peaks or dive in the shaded
pool,
Who'll stick to their guns when the mountains quake to the
tread of a mighty war,
And fight for Right or a Grand Mistake as men never
fought before;
When the peaks are scarred and the sea-walls crack till the
farthest hills vibrate,
And the world for a while goes rolling back in a storm of
love and hate . . .

But, oh! if the cavalry charge again as they did when the
world was wide,
'Twill be grand in the ranks of a thousand men in that
glorious race to ride,
And strike for all that is true and strong, for all that is
grand and brave,
And all that ever shall be, so long as man has a soul to save.
He must lift the saddle, and close his 'wings', and shut his
angels out,
And steel his heart for the end of things, who'd ride with a
stockman scout,
When the race they ride on the battle-track, and the waning
distance hums,
When the shelled sky shrieks, and the rifles crack like
stockwhips amongst the gums—
And the straight is reached and the field is gapped and the
hoof-torn sward grows red
With the blood of those who are handicapped with iron and
steel and lead;
And the gaps are filled, though unseen by eyes, with the
spirit and with the shades
Of the world-wide rebel dead who'll rise and rush with the
Bush Brigades . . .

'Twill be while ever our blood is hot, while ever the
world goes wrong,
The nations rise in a war, to rot in a peace that lasts too
long.
And southern Nation and southern State, aroused from
their dream of ease,
Must sign in the Book of Eternal Fate their stormy histories.

HENRY LAWSON

12. Sport Cements Imperial Ties

Australian participation in outdoor sport of all kinds arose naturally from the new country's sunny spacious conditions. Pioneering life also evoked admiration for physical achievement. Men automatically compared their prowess in all fields relying on strength, speed, stamina and skill.

In a country largely dependent on animal transport, horse-racing soon emerged as a leading sport. The Melbourne Race Club began its meetings at Batman's Hill in 1838, and the Melbourne Cup was instituted twenty-three years later. Cup Day, the first Tuesday of each November, developed into a truer expression of Australianism, nearer to a national celebration, than the official Australia Day holiday.

Establishment of Australian capital cities on fine waterways led naturally to development of rowing and yacht-racing skills, culminating in the famous America's Cup victory of 1983 and an almost unprecedented peacetime outburst of patriotic ardour.

Skill at cricket won Australians a remarkable reputation abroad. Their success probably did as much to persuade Britain of Australia's maturity as her wool trade or her military ardour. Because cricket was so deeply entrenched in the English way of life, the impact of victorious colonial teams reached right down to village level. To be beaten by *Australians* . . . That was a matter for mixed pride in colonial descendants and wonderment at the apparent deterioration of the home breed on the sports field.

Many lesser battles were fought between contenders

in most branches of sport. Each of them helped to confirm and strengthen the remarkable kinship between Britain and Australia in the years leading up to Federation.

First English Team brought to the Colony by Spiers & Pond.

International cricket began with this match in 1862, when two Melbourne restaurateurs paid the expenses of a visiting English team. On New Year's Day, more than twenty-five thousand people paid to see the match begin at the new Melbourne Cricket Ground—probably the largest audience to that date anywhere in the world. England's eleven won easily against Victoria. At Beechworth, one Englishman played against eleven locals and beat them with ease. 'They are a wonderful lot of drinking men', the Englishman conceded.

'First International Cricket Match, MCG, 1 January 1862'. Painting by Henry Burn.

13. The Age of Optimism

By the 1880s Australia was recognised as one of the wonders of the modern world. Never before had a nation arisen so rapidly from evil days of convictism, or experienced such an overwhelming rush for land and gold. Almost in the blinking of an eye, the vast land had been transformed from primeval wilderness into a bustling self-governing continent determined to leap into the vanguard of world progress. No wonder Australians became a proud, patriotic people. An age of enthusiastic optimism dawned, in which a Victorian Minister for Education, Charles Henry Pearson, could write:

> The tendency of the age is to be hopeful, and it may be admitted that a great deal in the past history of the world encourages us not to despair of the future of humanity. The best types of any given high race are demonstrably stronger, taller, healthier than their ancestors two hundred or a thousand years ago; enjoy better laws and many more comforts; are more humane, better educated, and have a larger inheritance of transmitted thought . . . the whole tendency of modern reforms is to improve the condition of the masses.

In the last decades of the 19th century an extraordinary burst of urban development took place. Australia's seaports were transformed in double-quick time from humble colonial towns into booming cities where multi-storey office buildings and mansions replaced most of the pioneers' timber structures. With the combined effects of gold rush and land boom, Melbourne outstripped Sydney to amass nearly half a million population by 1890. Even Adelaide and Brisbane reached more than one hundred thousand people each. Suburbs began to sprawl over the paddocks in all directions around these cities.

Now they had broken free from dependence on agriculture, what were people to do in the new suburbs? The role of women seemed obvious: to be housekeepers and mothers of huge families, who would grow up to continue the process of populating the country and increasing the local market for material products. Some women escaped into occupations and even universities, but the overwhelming social demand was to breed a virile race of nation-builders.

Men continued to dominate business and professional life, and most forms of manual labour. Manufacturing grew apace, impelled by the most dramatic expansion of technology since the early days of the Industrial Revolution. Steam, gas and electricity powered greatly improved machinery, and output per worker grew to unprecedented heights. By the 1880s Victoria and South Australia led the world in production of agricultural machinery. Even railway locomotives were being built in areas which fifty years earlier had not yet been discovered by white men. Clothing, metal-working, building materials and food processing industries employed many more thousands of urban workers.

As the gold rush faded, much of the miners' political radicalism was transferred to the expanding cities. The results were extraordinary. Australia, a supposedly primitive nation, appalled conservatives by achieving many social advances well ahead of older civilisations. In 1855–56, stonemasons in Sydney and Melbourne won the first eight-hour working day to be recognised anywhere in the world. This notable victory gradually spread to other trades, along with the Saturday half-holiday which did so much to encourage sporting activities.

Factory Acts sponsored by Liberal politicians—particularly the future Prime Minister Alfred Deakin—ameliorated the worst aspects of industrial conditions well before Britain and America followed suit. Trade unions were automatically accepted as an integral part of Australian society while overseas countries were still persecuting them as 'illegal conspiracies'. The Trades Hall in Melbourne,

opened on the Queen's Birthday in 1859, was the first building in the world entirely devoted to inter-union co-operation.

When workers realised that industrial action was not a universal remedy for social ills, Australian unionists also led the world in political action. Even before members of parliament were paid for their services, a Scottish-born stonemason's

Charles Jardine Don
(1820–66), Melbourne
stonemason who became the
world's first working-class
member of Parliament.

Australia's Springtime

*'Tis the Springtime of
Australia, and the dazzled
eye may see
Wondrous dreams of future
greatness—of the glories
yet to be:
Visions—not of martial
conquest—not of courage,
blood and fire—*

*But of lands by noble actions
growing greater, grander,
higher!
Of the wond'ring nations
turning—gazing with
expectant eyes,
While oppress'd and toiling
millions feel new hopes and
thoughts arise*

*In the march of human
progress as Australia leads
the van
To the world's great
Federation, and the
'parliament of Man!'*

W. L. LUMLEY

When Australia celebrated
its first 100 years of
European settlement with a
great **Centennial
Exhibition in Melbourne
in 1888**, even the Germans
erected a display saying
'Germany congratulates
Australia'.

labourer named Charles Jardine Don, 39, won election to the Victorian Parliament in 1859. He described himself as 'a new fact in the British Empire—an actual working artisan in a Legislative Assembly to speak and vote for his class'. In New South Wales another Scottish-born unionist, Angus Cameron, 27, was elected to Parliament in 1874.

Artisans found it easier to enter Parliament after plural voting was abolished and payment of members was introduced in the eastern colonies. Unionists began to concentrate more on political action. 'We are aiming now at securing an improvement by social and political reforms—and by that means alone a revolution will undoubtedly be effected in time', explained Australian Workers Union leader W. G. Spence in 1892.

By 1899 sufficient working-men had won seats in the Queensland Parliament for the world's first Labor government to be formed under Andrew Dawson, a 36-year-old Rockhampton-born miner. Although Liberals withdrew their promised support after only a few days and Dawson was forced to resign, a vital precedent had been set for Labor to take office.

The rapid growth in Australia's cities after the gold rush also created a large urban middle class. The old 'ruling class', consisting mainly of British-born governors, officials and judges, retained most of its power. But it was increasingly supplemented by Australian-born doctors, lawyers, engineers and others, who worked hard for the expansion of the first universities in Sydney and Melbourne, so that their children could be trained to follow similar professions.

In the commercial world, manufacturers, traders and bankers formed an important and generally prosperous addition to the emerging bourgeoisie. The effects of their decisions on investment in colonial industries were obvious for all to see. Products ranging from biscuits to locomotives were collected together for the whole world to admire in a series of major exhibitions held in capital cities. As all these changes took place, and society survived its periodic crises, Australia was seen as an inspiring example to the rest of the world.

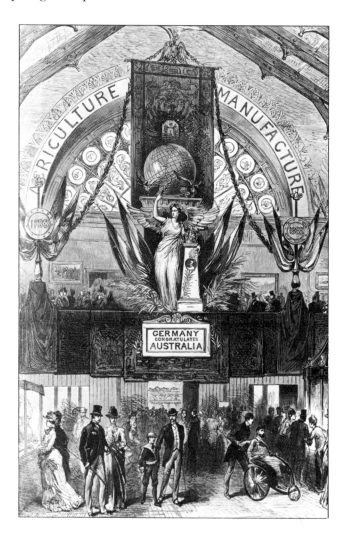

14. Selectors Bid for Independence

Many immigrants who tramped through the endless unfenced Australian countryside thought they would like to own a piece of it. As the gold petered out, those who could not find work in the towns became even more desperate for farms of their own. Diggers given the vote after the Eureka rebellion felt they could exert considerable pressure on the new legislative assemblies. Bills were drafted in each colony to 'unlock the lands' and grant small farms to the army of 'selectors' anxious to become self-sufficient. Would-be farmers were permitted to 'select' up to one square mile of Crown land (including squatters' leasehold) per year, paying for the freehold on easy terms.

Squatters and dummy applicants rushed to peg out and purchase the best parts of their runs. Nevertheless a considerable number of selectors managed to find arable land and achieve their heart's desire. By the end of the century, about one hundred thousand small farms had been successfully established in Victoria and New South Wales, and about another fifty thousand in the less populous colonies. More than one million additional cows were being milked, while production of butter, cheese and bacon increased greatly. In the forty years to 1900, the total area under crops in Australia increased by 700 per cent, reaching more than 8½ million acres. In this way the land selection laws enabled expanding town and city populations to be fed, and even provided a surplus for export.

Changes in rural life had important effects on the quality of Australian national feeling. Perhaps the most striking was the settling-down of wandering diggers into fixed places. The excitement of finding gold and then moving on was replaced by quieter domestic pleasures. Secure within his 640-acre block, the successful selector and his wife followed the national pattern of breeding a huge family. Children assisted with farm labour from an early age, until they were dragged off to school by the compulsory clauses of the new Education Acts of the 1880s.

Children and adults alike lived through the hardening processes of forcing the land to yield them a living, and enduring the frequent natural disasters of drought, flood and bushfire. Their character developed along similar lines which could soon be recognised as 'typically Australian': a wry acceptance of nature's blows, stoicism throughout suffering, and sardonic humour in the face of unpredictable events.

Selectors and their sons often assisted the family income by shearing sheep for nearby squatters. This skill enabled the sons to take up a wandering life such as their fathers had known in the golden days 'when the world was wide'. Part of the attraction of itinerant shearing, as these young men tramped or rode through the outback from one shearing-shed to the next, was the renewal of a uniquely Australian type of 'mateship'. Dependent on one another for companionship, gossip, loyalty, assistance in sickness, and inheritance of working skills, male mateship was close in some ways to conventional marriage. 'The mate that's steadfast to his mates—They call that man a "white man!"' wrote Henry Lawson.

The depression of the 1890s and defeat of shearers' strikes at first seemed to make nonsense of those ideals. But the feeling persisted that Australian society one day could operate more justly on the idea of fair shares for all.

*Then give me a hut in my own native land,
Or a tent in the bush, near the mountains so grand.
For the scenes of my childhood a joy are to me,
And the dear native girl who will share it with me.*

TRADITIONAL FOLK SONG

When wool prices fell and squatters insisted on reducing rates paid for shearing, the ideal of mateship led to formation of one of Australia's first and biggest trade unions, the Australian Workers Union. Its founder, W. G. Spence, recalled that:

Unionism came to the Australian bushman as a religion. It came bringing salvation from years of tyranny. It had in it that feeling of mateship which he understood already, and which always characterised the action of one 'white man' to another. Unionism extended the idea, so a man's character was gauged by whether he stood true to Union rules or 'scabbed' it on his fellows. The man who never went back on the Union is honored today as no other is honored or respected.

Said Hanrahan

'If we don't get three inches,
  man,
Or four to break this drought,
We'll all be rooned,' said
  Hanrahan,
'Before the year is out.'

In God's good time
  down came the rain;
And all the afternoon
On iron roof and window-
  pane
It drummed a homely tune...

And every creek a banker
  ran,
And dams filled overtop;
'We'll all be rooned,' said
  Hanrahan,
'If this rain doesn't stop.'

And stop it did, in God's
  good time:
And spring came in to fold
A mantle o'er the hills
  sublime
Of green and pink and
  gold...

'There'll be bush-fires for
  sure, me man,
There will, without a doubt;
We'll all be rooned,' said
  Hanrahan,
'Before the year is out.'

'JOHN O'BRIEN'
(P. J. Hartigan)

'Without Boundaries'.
Painting by Sali Herman.

15. Dreams of What Life Could Be

Henry Lawson

A. B. ('Banjo') Paterson

Henry Handel Richardson

Dame Nellie Melba

The last decades of the 19th century seemed to bring to full flowering the growth in Australian national pride which had been accumulating ever since the convict era ended. Plenty of people still faced misery and actual starvation, particularly during the strikes and bank crashes of the early 1890s. Yet, running a parallel course, was a strong belief that a new nation based on equality could be formed by welding together the best features of 'Australianism'. Much was wrong with society, but for the first time ordinary men and women felt that the power of remedial action lay in their hands. Poets, writers and artists seemed to receive that mass emotion as a kind of electromagnetic shock, running down their fingers and out on to paper and canvas. A national people's art, often crude but always honest, was born.

The intimate connection between mass emotions and political activism was seen best of all in the Sydney *Bulletin*. This was founded in 1880 and given its distinctive character by J. F. Archibald, a nimble-witted 24-year-old Geelong-born printer and self-trained journalist. Archibald's *Bulletin* gathered such a wide-ranging collection of contributors in all walks of life that it became a national forum for all Australians who had anything pertinent to say about current events.

New generations of poets and writers emerged to take up Australian themes where Henry Kendall and Charles Harpur left off. Pre-eminent among them were the native-born Henry Lawson and A. B. ('Banjo') Paterson, both encouraged by the *Bulletin*, and both able to write in plain but rousing terms from first-hand experience of bush life. Lawson (1867–1922) came from a poverty-stricken background; Paterson (1864–1941) from a prosperous pastoral family. Yet both these strands merged easily into a true consensus of Australianism.

Lesser lights almost too numerous to mention shone during those exciting days of Australia's approach to nationhood. T. A. Browne ('Rolf Boldrewood' who wrote *Robbery Under Arms*), Joseph Furphy ('Tom Collins' who wrote *Such Is Life*), A. H. Davis ('Steele Rudd' who wrote *On Our Selection*) and many others vividly illuminated the pattern of development in town and bush. As the century turned, talented women such as Miles Franklin, Henry Handel Richardson, Mary Gilmore and Katharine Susannah Prichard added distinctively female insights into Australian life.

Australian-born painters had less effect at the time, although we value them highly today. Artists such as Tom Roberts and Charles Conder, who broke free from formal European attitudes to painting to found a distinctive Australian school of impressionism, were grossly undervalued by the conservative art-buying public. Even if they were not very interested at the time, many Australians discovered from the impressionists how to look at their country with fresh eyes.

Singers were more quickly accepted as figures of national importance. Their performances, and the sentiments expressed in popular songs, were readily reconciled with the tradition of folk balladry, which found its place in many bourgeois drawing-rooms just as easily as in bush huts. The universal acceptance of romantic songs, bush tunes and loyal ballads provided an emotional conviction that all Australians were comrades at heart.

Australia produced many fine singers, but none as remarkable as Nellie Melba, born in Melbourne in 1861, the daughter of a Scottish builder of some of the city's finest edifices. Following an early unhappy marriage, Melba trained as an opera singer in Paris. Her 1887 debut in *Rigoletto* in Brussels brought her instant fame.

Little wonder that when the Australian Federal Parliament was completed in 1927, Melba was asked to emerge from retirement and sing the National Anthem at the opening ceremony. More than any living person at the time, this remarkable woman linked 19th-century patriotic idealisms with the 20th century's terrifying realities, and the slow rebirth of mankind's hopes for a better future.

On Kiley's Run

The roving breezes come and go
   On Kiley's Run,
The sleepy river murmurs low,
And far away one dimly sees
Beyond the stretch of forest trees—
Beyond the foothills dusk and dun—
The ranges sleeping in the sun
   On Kiley's Run.

'Tis many years since first I came
   To Kiley's Run,
More years than I would care to name
Since I, a stripling, used to ride
For miles and miles at Kiley's side,
The while in stirring tones he told
The stories of the days of old
   On Kiley's Run.

I see the old bush homestead now
   On Kiley's Run,
Just nestled down beneath the brow
Of one small ridge above the sweep
Of river flat, where willows weep
And jasmine flowers and roses bloom,
The air was laden with perfume
   On Kiley's Run.

We lived the good old station life
   On Kiley's Run,
With little thought of care or strife.
Old Kiley seldom used to roam,
He liked to make the Run his home,
The swagman never turned away
With empty hand at close of day
   From Kiley's Run.

We kept a racehorse now and then
   On Kiley's Run,
And neighb'ring stations brought their men
To meetings where the sport was free,
And dainty ladies came to see
Their champions ride; with laugh and song
The old house rang the whole night long
   On Kiley's Run.

The station hands were friends I wot
   On Kiley's Run,
A reckless, merry-hearted lot—
All splendid riders, and they knew
The 'boss' was kindness through and through.
Old Kiley always stood their friend,
And so they served him to the end
   On Kiley's Run.

But droughts and losses came apace
   To Kiley's Run,
Till ruin stared him in the face;
He toiled and toiled while lived the light,
He dreamed of overdrafts at night:
At length, because he could not pay,
His bankers took the stock away
   From Kiley's Run.

Old Kiley stood and saw them go
   From Kiley's Run.
The well-bred cattle marching slow;
His stockmen, mates for many a day,
They wrung his hand and went away.
Too old to make another start,
Old Kiley died—of broken heart,
   On Kiley's Run.

The owner lives in England now
   Of Kiley's Run.
He knows a racehorse from a cow;
But that is all he knows of stock:
His chiefest care is how to dock
Expenses, and he sends from town
To cut the shearers' wages down
   On Kiley's Run.

There are no neighbours anywhere
   Near Kiley's Run.
The hospitable homes are bare,
The gardens gone; for no pretence
Must hinder cutting down expense:
The homestead that we held so dear
Contains a half-paid overseer
   On Kiley's Run.

All life and sport and hope have died
   On Kiley's Run.
No longer there the stockmen ride;
For sour-faced boundary riders creep
On mongrel horses after sheep,
Through ranges where, at racing speed,
Old Kiley used to 'wheel the lead'
   On Kiley's Run.

There runs a lane for thirty miles
   Through Kiley's Run.
On either side the herbage smiles,
But wretched trav'lling sheep must pass
Without a drink or blade of grass
Thro' that long lane of death and shame:
The weary drovers curse the name
   Of Kiley's Run.

The name itself is changed of late
   Of Kiley's Run.
They call it 'Chandos Park Estate'.
The lonely swagman through the dark
Must hump his swag past Chandos Park.
The name is English, don't you see,
The old name sweeter sounds to me
   Of 'Kiley's Run'.

I cannot guess what fate will bring
   To Kiley's Run—
For chances come and changes ring—
I scarcely think 'twill always be
Locked up to suit an absentee;
And if he lets it out in farms
His tenants soon will carry arms
   On Kiley's Run.

A. B. PATERSON

16.   Off to the Boer War: Empire Loyalty Runs Hot

Australian patriotism was fast developing towards the foundation of a Commonwealth of Australia. Yet allegiance to Britain was in no way diminished among the bulk of the population. These dual loyalties were shown in the most dramatic way possible when the Boer War broke out in 1899. Throughout Australia, bushmen ranging from squatters' sons to station rouseabouts rode in to capital cities to reinforce existing volunteer cavalry units. They were hastily equipped to sail on the first troopships which left in November 1899.

At British insistence, the Australians were broken up and allotted to reconnaissance duties with various imperial forces—usually under the command of officers whose ideal of warfare was to advance in perfect formation directly towards enemy fire.

During December 1899, in what became known as 'Black Week', determined Boer forces managed to inflict serious defeats on the British. Commander-in-Chief Lord Frederick Roberts, affectionately known as 'Bobs' to his troops, counter-attacked. On 18 May 1900, aided by Australian troops, he succeeded in breaking the siege of Mafeking, where Major-General Robert Baden-Powell had managed to hold out against an encircling Boer army for 218 days.

Further victories followed in which Australians played a prominent part. On 12 June 1900 a British Army under Lieutenant-General Sir Ian Hamilton attacked a strong force of 4000 Boers entrenched with field guns on Diamond Hill. The Coldstream Guards were unable to advance against intensive shell fire. The New South Wales Mounted Rifles, 6th Mounted Infantry and 1st Western Australian Mounted Infantry charged on horseback with fixed bayonets. Even the brave Boers retreated in terror from this novel onslaught, leaving behind most of their guns.

One of the most courageous actions of the whole war was fought at Elands River by a combined force of 100 Queenslanders, 100 New South Welshmen, 50 Victorians and 150 Rhodesians, armed with rifles, two Maxim machine-guns, and an antique 7-pounder muzzle-loading gun. The 400 men were surrounded by several thousand Boers armed with heavy artillery and quick-firing Nordenfelt pom-pom guns. After five weeks, when nearly one hundred casualties had been suffered and practically all the defenders' 1500 horses had been killed, the Boers gave up and retreated.

By November 1900, the British had captured Johannesburg and Pretoria, and relieved the siege of Ladysmith as well as Mafeking. The elderly Lord Roberts, believing that the war was almost over, passed his command to Lord Kitchener. On departing he remarked, 'All the colonials did extremely well. They were very intelligent; and they had what I want our men to have, more individuality. They could find their way about the country far better than the British cavalryman'.

The wily Boers, defeated in pitched battles, merely changed to a form of guerrilla warfare, riding suddenly out of broken country to surprise and overwhelm small garrisons, then disappearing again before counter-attacks could be organised. Kitchener told London that new tactics and heavy reinforcements would be necessary before the Boers could be brought to heel. More imaginative than Lord 'Bobs', he realised that the Boers' own tactics could be turned against them by employing the rough, undisciplined colonial troops as highly mobile hit-and-run striking forces.

There was a dark side to the fiercer of the Australian bushmen. During one attack on a lonely Boer farmhouse, an officer was killed and his body mutilated. One of his closest friends, a horsebreaker from Australia named Lieutenant Harry Morant (who had contributed bush poems to the *Bulletin* under the name 'The Breaker') was enraged. He and other Australians pursued the Boers, took prisoners,

Celebrating the Relief of Mafeking

Old men, young men, boys, girls, matrons, men in uniform, sage bank managers, distinguished lawyers, portly aldermen, shop assistants, ran as if the fate of Empires depended upon their joining the wild throng. In three minutes there was a dense mass of roaring, cheering and singing humanity . . . Gentlemen danced like schoolboys, shook hands with grimy working men, and then, waving their hats vigorously, started marvellous versions of God Save the Queen, Rule Britannia and Soldiers of the Queen.

Melbourne AGE.

then shot them out of hand. A German missionary named C. H. D. Hesse, suspected of being a spy for the Boers, was also shot under mysterious circumstances. Three men were brought before a secret court-martial and charged with the murders. Lieutenants Morant and P. J. Handcock were executed: 'Shoot straight, you bastards!' cried Morant before he died. Lieutenant G. R. Witton was sentenced to life imprisonment. After reading press reports of the executions, the Australian government sent belated protests, and Witton was finally pardoned. The men's martyrdom made possible an increase in Australia's independence. No Australian soldier ever after was subjected to British military justice in a capital case.

The overwhelming success of colonial rough-riders eventually forced most British officers to admit their value. While Kitchener was maturing his plans to build a chain of forts across the veldt, and to gather non-combatants into concentration camps, he asked the new Australian Federal government to send more mounted troops. Prime Minister Barton, supporting the request in Federal Parliament on 14 January 1902, emphasised that 'the bond of Empire is not one only of mere patriotism . . . but also one of self-interest'. If Britain at any time lost control of the Suez Canal, the trade route via British-controlled South Africa would become all-important to Australia.

But the war was nearly over. Soon after the Australian national force went into action, on 31 May 1902 a peace treaty was signed at Pretoria, and the modern state of South Africa began to emerge.

Altogether Australia sent more than sixteen thousand men and sixteen thousand horses to the Boer War. This was twice as large as the Canadian contribution. Among the Australians, 518 men died and 882 were wounded. The Victoria Cross, instituted during the Crimean War, was awarded for the first time to six Australian soldiers in South Africa.

The military experience gained at high cost during the Boer War had a great effect on Australian military planning. Many precedents were set for World War I: most of the senior officers and instructors of the first Australian Imperial Force fought in South Africa, and learned their lessons well. Henceforth their 'Light Horse' regiments would be the fast-moving elite striking force of the Australian army, equipped not with old-fashioned cavalry swords but with the new magazine-loading .303 Lee-Enfield rifles and bayonets. 'Rule .303', Breaker Morant had called it. The world would hear much more of these hard-riding troopers before horses became irrelevant to modern warfare.

'A' Battery of the New South Wales Volunteer Artillery leaving Sydney Harbour for the Boer War in 1899. Painting by W. J. Allam.

I don't think of these men as private soldiers. They are my mates, I want them to know why I'm asking them to risk their lives.

An Australian officer, answering British objections to giving his men details of battle plans.

PART III

Nationhood Achieved Within Empire's Bonds

The Dominion of Australia

She is not yet; but he whose ear
Thrills to that finer atmosphere
  Where footfalls of appointed things,
    Reverberant of days to be,
  Are heard in forecast echoings,
    Like wave-beats from a viewless sea
Hears in the voiceful tremors of the sky
Auroral heralds whispering, 'She is nigh.'

She is not yet; but he whose sight
Foreknows the advent of the light,
  Whose soul to morning radiance turns
    Ere night her curtain hath withdrawn,
  And in its quivering folds discerns
    The mute monitions of the dawn,
With urgent sense strained onward to descry
Her distant tokens, starts to find Her nigh.

Not yet her day. How long 'not yet'? . . .
There comes the flush of violet!

And heavenward faces, all aflame
  With sanguine imminence of morn,
Wait but the sun-kiss to proclaim
  The Day of The Dominion born.
Prelusive baptism!—ere the natal hour
Named with the name and prophecy of power.

Already here to hearts intense,
A spirit-force, transcending sense,
  In heights unscaled, in deeps unstirred,
    Beneath the calm, above the storm,

She waits the incorporating word
  To bid her tremble into form.
Already, like divining-rods, men's souls
Bend down to where the unseen river rolls;—

For even as, from sight concealed,
By never flush of dawn revealed,
  Nor e'er illumed by golden noon,
    Nor sunset-streaked with crimson bar,
  Nor silver-spanned by wake of moon,
    Nor visited of any star,
Beneath these lands a river waits to bless
(So men divine) our utmost wilderness,—

Rolls dark, but yet shall know our skies,
Soon as the wisdom of the wise
  Conspires with nature to disclose
    The blessing prisoned and unseen,
  Till round our lessening wastes there glows
    A perfect zone of broadening green,—
Till all our land, Australia Felix called,
Become one continent-Isle of Emerald;

So flows beneath our good and ill
A viewless steam of common Will,
  A gathering force, a present might,
    That from its silent depths of gloom
  At Wisdom's voice shall leap to light,
    And hide our barren feuds in bloom,
Till, all our sundering lines with love o'ergrown,
Our bounds shall be the girdling seas alone.

JAMES BRUNTON STEPHENS

1. The Push Towards 'One People, One Flag, One Destiny'

It is commonly said that Australians used to have two loyalties—one to Britain and one to Australia. In truth they had *triple* loyalties, sometimes regarding themselves as Britons, sometimes as Australians, and sometimes as New South Welshmen, Victorians, or other colonial citizens.

Which loyalty was to predominate? Occasionally it seemed that colonial separatism might last for ever, and the continent might never be united into a nation whose inhabitants thought of themselves as 'Australians first and foremost'. Despite the multicultural and democratic influences of the gold rush, half a century of intense political effort was needed before the Australian Commonwealth became a reality. From the 1850s, leaders like the Rev. J. D. Lang and Charles Gavan Duffy proposed the creation of a Federal government.

National loyalties were further stimulated when a group of young Australian-born men met together in Melbourne in 1871 to found what became the Australian Natives Association. They included George Turner, 20, a future Federal Treasurer; James Purves, 28, a colourful barrister who became known as 'Emperor of the ANA'; and Samuel Winter, 28, proprietor of the Melbourne *Herald*. Annoyed by the often overbearing 'Britishness' of their elders and constant disparagement of Australian talent in all fields, these ambitious young men worked to encourage 'a vigorous and undivided Australian sentiment'.

In 1889 the ageing radical politician Henry Parkes again became Premier of New South Wales. Travelling by train along the newly-opened railway system

The great question which they had to consider was, whether the time had not now come for the creation in this Australian continent of an Australian Government, as distinct from the local Governments now in existence. (Applause.) In other words, to make himself as plain as possible, Australia had now a population of three and a half millions, and the American people numbered only between three and four millions when they formed the great commonwealth of the United States. The numbers were about the same, and surely what the Americans had done by war, the Australians could bring about in peace without breaking the ties that held them to the mother country. (Cheers.)

HENRY PARKES, at Tenterfield, 1889.

Sir Henry Parkes died shortly before Federation was achieved, but his great efforts were acknowledged in this cartoon of 1900.

The Duke of Cornwall and
York, heir to the throne,
opens the first Federal
Parliament in Melbourne
on 9 May 1901. Painting by
Tom Roberts, reproduced by
gracious permission of Her
Majesty the Queen.

We are for this Australia, for the nationality that is creeping to the verge of being, for the progressive people that is just plucking aside the curtain that veils its fate. Behind us lies the Past with its crashing empires, its falling thrones, its dotard races; before us lies the Future into which Australia is plunging, this Australia of ours that burns with the feverish energy of youth, and that is wise with the wisdom for which ten thousand generations have suffered and toiled.

WILLIAM LANE, Australian radical.

Old Henry Parkes

Coming down the street
In his out-of-date carriage,
The trot of the hoofs
In a rat-a-tat barrage,
Old Henry Parkes,
In his big top hat,
His lion-like head,
Eyes like a sword,
Blazing in a thought,
Blazing at affront,
Blazing for a word—
But, in-drawn, still, and cold
    as the ice,
As vision-held he sat, and saw
Commonwealth and Empire,
    brotherly and brother,
This State and that State, all
    linked together . . .

And Parkes was a king,
A king among men;
Men were his stubble,
Where he bound the best in
    sheaf;
And men were his sheep,
    that, line after line,
Orderly as sheep, followed
    after him—
Old Man Parkes,
The leader of them all,
Who, drawing out his fan,
Blew the chaff from the
    wheat—
Blew the chaff from the
    wheat
And gave the land the grain,
The grain that was unity,
Nationhood and pride—
Old Henry Parkes,
Driving into town,
Driving down the streets,
With the rattle of the hoofs
Rat-a-tat, rat-a-tat, like a
    barrage.

Did you say that Parkes was
    dead?
Parkes couldn't die!
Parkes couldn't go like a
    cloud in the sky,
Like a flurry in the snow,
    like a leaf that was shed,
Not while the land—
Had need of his hand—
His hand on the rein,
His foot on the thill,
His eyes like a spark,
His tongue like a whip,
His leonine head,
His hair like a mat,
And his big top hat,
Coming down the hill,
Coming down the street,
Coming into Sydney
In his old borrowed carriage!

MARY GILMORE

between Sydney and Brisbane, he stopped at the small town of Tenterfield near the Queensland border. Here he gave a speech emphasising the crucial aspect of national defence, which earned him the title 'The Father of Federation'.

With Parkes dragging New South Wales behind him, a National Australasian Convention met in Sydney in March 1891. Unfortunately Parkes, suffering from the after-effects of a leg broken in two places when his horse-cab rolled over, was forced to stay in the background. Leadership of the convention fell to Samuel Griffith, a 46-year-old Welsh-born barrister who had become Premier of Queensland and would be Australia's first Chief Justice.

Griffith evolved the scheme for Australian government which in most essentials is familiar to us today. The colonies would transfer specific powers such as defence to a bicameral Federal Parliament. The House of Representatives would be popularly elected on full adult franchise; the Senate would have an equal number of members from each colony. The colonies would become States, retaining all powers not passed to the Commonwealth. All interstate tariffs would be abolished, to be replaced by Federal tariffs levied on overseas goods. Most of the resulting revenue would be redistributed among the States to recompense them for loss of the tariff power.

The Australian Natives Association kept interest in Federation alive throughout the 1890s depression. Its president, a former immigration official named George Henry Wise, toured Australia urging that Federation had to be regarded as 'the first pulse beat of national life'. A Bendigo barrister, Dr John Quick, later to be a Federal Minister, suggested in 1893 that public interest would be stimulated by drafting a constitution and submitting it by referendum for the electors' approval. Another barrister, Sydney politician Edmund Barton, later to be Prime Minister, toured the countryside extensively, addressing 300 meetings which formed 'Federal Leagues' at grass roots level.

The new New South Wales Premier, a jocular 50-year-old Scot named George Reid (often known as 'Yes-No' Reid because he blew hot and cold on Federation), asked other colonial leaders to meet him in Hobart in January 1895 to re-examine all proposals. Success seemed near at last. The Premiers agreed to a draft Enabling Bill and summoned a second National Australasian Convention. This met in Adelaide and Sydney in 1897 and Melbourne early in 1898. Details of the proposed referendum and transfer of selected powers were worked out under Edmund Barton's chairmanship.

The most serious question considered by the Convention was the extent of power which should be enjoyed by the Senate. Everyone agreed that an equal and universal adult suffrage should apply to the House of Representatives. But the colonies with smaller populations—Queensland, South Australia, Tasmania and Western Australia—felt they would be overwhelmed by the more populous States if the Senate were elected on a population basis. New South Wales and Victoria therefore agreed that each State should elect six Senators. The Senate was to have the same powers as the Representatives, except in the case of money Bills—but these could be rejected, deferred, or sent back with suggested amendments. Thus the stage was set for the dramatic constitutional crisis of 1975.

In the context of 1898, it seemed more important not to let the chance of Federation slip away again. The eloquent 42-year-old Victorian delegate, Alfred Deakin, told the Convention that 'It is scarcely possible to imagine, and certainly not possible to propound, a more liberal constitution than this when thoroughly and carefully examined'.

Still it was too soon to celebrate. In Sydney, 'Yes-No' Reid betrayed the Convention's hard-won agreement by criticising the powers proposed for the Senate. He added that he would vote for the Bill himself, but that each elector 'should judge for himself'. When the referendum was finally held in June 1898, huge majorities turned out to vote for Federation in Victoria, South Australia and Tasmania. In New South Wales, a small majority voted in favour, but the total 'Yes' votes fell short of the 80,000 minimum deemed necessary for approval. (At that time, voting was voluntary.) Upon hearing the news, the British writer Rudyard Kipling suggested hiring German cruisers to bombard Australian capital

Alfred Deakin, the Melbourne journalist-politician who fought for Federation, and was three times Prime Minister between 1903 and 1910.

cities for a few minutes. 'There'd be a federated Australia in 24 hours', he predicted. In January 1899 another Premiers' meeting took place in Melbourne. A further referendum was proposed, with several amendments to meet various criticisms. A juicy carrot was dangled before New South Wales voters: if they approved Federation, the national capital would be established in their State, although not closer than 100 miles to Sydney. This time Queensland also agreed to join the voting. The second referendum, held at various dates in 1899, was an outstanding success. Of the half-million who voted in the eastern colonies, nearly three hundred and eighty thousand favoured Federation. This time a sufficient majority was won in each colony.

Western Australia, fearing loss of customs revenue, still hung back. The strongly-Federationist goldfields population petitioned the Queen for separate Statehood or amalgamation with South Australia. Then a new incentive was offered, in the form of a transcontinental railway financed from Federal funds. On 31 July 1900 Western Australia too voted heavily to join a completely federated Australia. 'To the world we shall be one people', rejoiced the Melbourne *Argus*.

Five Australian delegates visited London that year to help steer the Commonwealth of Australia Constitution Bill through the British Parliament. Compromises were reached on such matters as appeals to the Privy Council. The Constitution Act passed, to be signed by Queen Victoria on 9 July 1900. A Proclamation issued under her name on 17 September 1900 fixed the first day of the 20th century as the inaugural date of the Commonwealth of Australia. Alfred Deakin recalled that the Australian delegates 'seized each other's hands and danced hand in hand around the centre of the room'. Federated Australia was a fact at last. 'For the first time in history', as Edmund Barton put it, 'we have a continent for a nation and a nation for a continent'.

2. How the Constitution Works

The Australian Constitution, as approved by the British Parliament, consists of 128 sections divided into eight chapters. These set up a bicameral parliament, an executive government, and a judicature; and deal with financial arrangements, powers of the States, formation of new States, methods of altering the Constitution, and miscellaneous matters.

In theory the powers of any Federal administration are strictly limited to those listed in the Constitution. All other functions of government are supposed to be exercised by the sovereign States, acting independently as they think best. In practice, however, political power during the present century has steadily drifted to the Commonwealth. The emergencies of two world wars, the centralising tendencies of modern society, introduction of uniform taxation, and many legal and political confrontations have helped to bring about a largely unified nation, in which the powers of the States continually tend to be eroded.

As Australia took its place among nations of the world, several methods were used to increase Commonwealth powers. The first was by referendum. Under Section 128 of the Constitution, any proposed referendum must first be approved by both Houses of Parliament, then submitted to a national vote within two to six months. At the referendum, a majority of electors in a majority of States must approve the proposed change before it can be presented to the Governor-General for the monarch's assent. This system of delays, checks and balances was instituted to avoid hasty alteration of the nation's fundamental law. Partly because of this complex process, and partly through the voters' reluctance to tamper with the Constitution, few referendums have succeeded in Australia. Attempts by over-ambitious Federal governments in 1911, 1919 and 1944 to win large permanent extensions of power for the Commonwealth were soundly defeated at the polls. Obviously a majority of voters feared to place too much authority in the hands of any single government.

Further referendums saw Federal powers over social services and medical benefits confirmed in 1946. Power to make laws regarding Aborigines was won in 1967. Three technical adjustments were approved in 1977. But that was all. Since Federation, Parliament has voted on nearly one hundred constitutional proposals. Thirty-nine have been put to referendum: only those listed were approved.

High Court interpretations of ambiguous areas of the Australian Constitution, following the modern tendency towards centralisation, have done much to expand Federal powers at the expense of the States. During World War I, the High Court ruled that price-fixing of bread, even though conducted a long way from the battlefront, was a legitimate exercise of the Commonwealth's defence power.

In recent years, the doctrine of 'implied powers', first laid down in the bread price-fixing case, has been greatly extended through the Commonwealth's constitutional responsibility for external affairs. The signing of international treaties by Australia was held by the High Court to give Canberra powers over internal matters once thought to be the sole province of the States. This doctrine enabled the Commonwealth to control matters which were not even thought of when the Constitution was drafted. For example, when a Convention on Air Navigation was concluded in Paris in 1919, the Commonwealth quickly took relevant powers from the States. In 1983 the Hawke Labor government relied on Australia's signing of the World Heritage Convention for protection of the environment, to prevent the Tasmanian government from proceeding with the Franklin River hydro-electric scheme. There seems no limit to Federal acquisition of power under this doctrine.

Unlike its American equivalent, the Australian Constitution is a severely practical document. The nearest that it comes to an expression of lofty ideals is its statement that the people, *'humbly relying on the blessing of Almighty God, have agreed to unite in one indissoluble Federal Commonwealth under the Crown . . .'*

3. The Dawn of a New Century and a New Nation

As figurative head of the new Commonwealth of Australia, the British government chose a 40-year-old Scottish peer, Lord Hopetoun, eldest son of the sixth Earl of Linlithgow. Hopetoun had been lord-in-waiting to Queen Victoria, and Governor of Victoria during the 1890s, where his habit of powdering his hair amazed colonial politicians. To take up his new appointment, Hopetoun sailed from England in 1900 on HMS *Royal Arthur*, accompanied by the first contingent of imperial troops sent to Australia since convict times. Stopping briefly to visit India, he contracted typhoid fever and his wife malaria. Still a sick

Lord Hopetoun, first Governor-General of Australia, was **sworn in before a quarter of a million people**, in this elaborate plaster pavilion in Sydney's Centennial Park on 1 January 1901.

Hymn of the Commonwealth
(Sung at the Inauguration)

O latest-born nation!
  O first-born of lands!
To-day our Australia
  Triumphantly stands
'Mid world-acclamation,
  With hands grasping hands,
  From shore to shore!

O strong be this union!
  God, teach us our parts;
May love for Australia
  And peace and her arts
In holiest communion
  Bind fast all our hearts—
  This we implore!

Our Father! put from us
  All boasting and scorn;
Lord God! on Australia
  To wisdom re-born
In glory and promise,
  This Century morn,
  Thy blessings pour.

Ordain that as brothers
  We live in the sun
And light of Australia,
  With nationhood won,
Just, kind, as no others
  Before us have done,
  For evermore!

JOHN FARRELL

man when he stepped ashore at Farm Cove on 15 December 1900, Hopetoun could scarcely be blamed for naming the Tasmanian-born New South Wales Premier, Sir William Lyne, as interim Prime Minister. He was obviously unaware that Lyne had consistently opposed Federation. Every other political leader refused to serve under Lyne: Hopetoun was forced instead to appoint Edmund Barton as Prime Minister.

Barton formed a cabinet overnight, and the Federation celebrations were able to proceed as scheduled for 1 January 1901. In Sydney, the New Year's Eve ushering in the new century was remembered as the rowdiest ever celebrated. Nearly twenty thousand additional electric light globes had been festooned around public buildings; while a gigantic fireworks display including crests, crowns and rockets enthralled harbour viewers. Alfred Deakin wrote:

Invitation to the Commonwealth's Inaugural Celebrations on 1 January 1901, which enabled the bearer to sit near the official pavilion. The boat bearing six figures representing the Australian States flies one version of the still undecided national flag.

Invitation to celebrate the first Federal Parliament on 9 May 1901 joins Britannia at left with the young Australian Commonwealth at right.

Never was a moonlit night in Sydney marked by a wilder, more prolonged, or generally more discordant welcome than was December 31, 1900. Hymns in the churches, patriotic songs in the theatres, glees in the homes, and convivial choruses at the clubs were extensively sung. Outside these places, however, all music was lost in the tremendous uproar of the streets, where whistles, bells, gongs, accordions, rattles and clanging cutlery utensils yielded unearthly sounds.

By early morning on Tuesday, 1 January 1901, more than a quarter-million people were again strolling the city streets. Men, women and children gazed with delight at the Federation decorations—flags, lanterns and crowns—as well as massive triumphal arches built of crushed Queensland sugar cane, and erected at main intersections. They watched with pride as the official procession, led by thirty mounted shearers, appeared in Macquarie Street. The horsemen were followed by other representative working-men, community leaders, local military forces, imperial troops, and finally the Governor-General himself. All moved towards Centennial Park, which had been opened in 1888 to celebrate the first century of British settlement.

In the park an open septangular white plaster pavilion had been erected for the swearing-in ceremony. Officials, perspiring freely in English uniforms so unsuitable for the Australian climate, listened as the Queen's proclamation establishing the Commonwealth was read, the Governor-General and his ministers were sworn in, and massed choirs gave voice to the Federal Hymn.

When all this excitement was over, politicians began preparing for the first Federal election. The interim Prime Minister, Edmund Barton, opened his campaign with a policy speech on 17 January 1901. His promises laid down the general course of Federal policy through the years up to World War I, including: preservation of 'White Australia', creation of national defence forces, protection of the States' financial interests, light taxation and economical government, low federal tariffs on protected industries, introduction of old-age pensions, arbitration in national disputes, and railways to Perth and Broken Hill. Today, with the benefit of hindsight, we know that all these policies would not last for ever, nor were they necessarily wise. At the time, however, they united and enthused people and politicians into an enthralling mood of national consensus.

The elections on 29–30 March 1901 confirmed Barton as Prime Minister and leader of the Liberal Protectionists, although in both Houses he had to rely on a strong grouping of Labor members to allow passage of many of his measures against the opposition of conservative Free Traders.

The first Federal Parliament opened in Melbourne's gigantic Exhibition Building on 9 May 1901. The building itself was outlined with 10,000 electric globes. For weeks beforehand the city's streets were decorated with nine timber and plaster arches, some covered with plush and velvet; and Venetian masts fluttering with all kinds of flags. The young Duke of Cornwall and York (later King George V) had been invited to open the Parliament. On 9 May, invited guests crammed into the Exhibition Building to hear fanfares of trumpets and watch the Duke declare Parliament duly in session. James Smith, an *Argus* journalist, wrote:

> It was the 'psychological moment', full of deep significance, and calculated to impress the minds of the most frivolous and thoughtless persons in that vast assemblage with a deep and abiding sense of the momentous issues hanging upon this simple incident. In the presence of the whole of Australia, represented by the foremost citizens of every State, the heir to the throne, speaking as the mouthpiece of King Edward the Seventh, had proclaimed . . . that a new nation had just commenced its Parliamentary existence.

Up to this point the proceedings were solemn. Then the Duke read out a cabled message from his father, the new King Edward VII, saying: 'My thoughts are with you on the day of this important ceremony. Most fervently do I wish Australia prosperity and great happiness'. The 14,000 guests burst into a storm of cheering, while tears ran down many loyal cheeks. The Governor-General administered the oath of allegiance to members of both Houses of Parliament, and they retired to choose their Speaker and President, while Musgrove's Opera Company entertained the guests with the 'Hallelujah Chorus' and 'Rule Britannia'.

Federation does not necessarily bring better men to the front. It does not necessarily increase the intellectual status of the Legislature, but it gives us greater issues; it ensures discussion from different standpoints; it bestows upon us the great gift of a national rather than a provincial life.

Melbourne ARGUS, 9 May 1901.

In order to bring the celebrations before the whole population of Melbourne, two days later an immense procession wended its way through the transformed streets. In the lead were 200 mounted stockmen brought from remote parts of Victoria, who as they rode cracked their stockwhips 'like the rattle of a Maxim gun'. Behind them marched 14,000 troops from every State and several overseas countries. Trade unions dusted off their Eight Hours banners to take part. The farriers' float was halted opposite the Royal marquee at Parliament House long enough for the blacksmith, John O'Shea of Collingwood, to make a horseshoe on his anvil. A curious display of democratic loyalty followed: 'A sudden inspiration struck the man, who snatched a silvered horseshoe decorating the lorry and threw it towards the stand. It fell clanging on the steps, and was taken to the Duchess, who held it high and bowed her acknowledgements'.

The Commonwealth Parliament had arranged to meet in Victoria's Parliament House while the location of a Federal capital was being decided. After one thing and another, including delays imposed by World War I, twenty-six years passed before the Victorians could reclaim their building. During all that time, however, Australia was learning to view itself as a nation.

Pioneer Feminists Win Equal Voting Rights

Some radicals viewed Federation as a means of achieving greater national unity of males and females, through the adoption of equal voting. The parliaments of two Australian colonies—South Australia and Western Australia—had been among the first in the world to give votes to women during the 1890s. At Federation, however, the remaining State governments, like Britain itself, were still divided on the question. In 1900 Vida Goldstein's suffragette journal *The Australian Woman's Sphere* urged the laggards on with a rousing ditty:

> Fear not the coming woman, brother!
> Owning herself, she giveth all the more!
> She shall be better woman, wife and mother
> Than man hath known before!

Perhaps the voters listened. In the first Commonwealth Parliament, members who supported women's suffrage outnumbered anti-suffrage members by four to one.

To enable as many women as possible to vote in Federal elections, without offending backward States, the Constitution-makers adopted an ingenious compromise. Sections 8 and 30 provided that the qualification of electors should be that 'prescribed by the law of the State as the qualification of electors of the more numerous House of Parliament of the State . . .' In other words, where women were allowed to vote in State elections, they would also be allowed to vote in Federal elections. Enabling legislation was passed by Federal Parliament in 1902. Sir William Lyne, introducing the measure, thought that by extending the franchise:

> We shall induce women to take a lively interest in all questions that are being publicly considered, with the result that their discussion at the hearth between husband and wife and brother and sister will enable husband and brother to know more than they have ever known before of questions in which they should take a great interest . . .

The lagging States soon found themselves impelled to follow suit. For an allegedly chauvinist frontier society such as Australia, the victory was remarkably painless. In the homeland, Britain, women were not given the vote until the end of World War I: even then the suffrage was limited to women over 30 years of age.

Vida Goldstein (1869–1949), Victorian suffragette who in 1903 became one of the first women in the British Empire to stand for election to a national parliament. Painting by Phyl Waterhouse.

Rose Scott (1847–1925), daughter of David Scott Mitchell, whose efforts for women's suffrage were accepted by the New South Wales Parliament in 1902. Painting by Sir John Longstaff.

Notable Australian women were honoured by a special issue of stamps for International Women's Year in 1975. From left: **Truganini** was one of the last full-blood Aboriginal women left in Tasmania. **Catherine Spence** was a prominent fighter for women's rights in South Australia. **Louisa Lawson,** mother of Henry Lawson, published a women's journal, *The Dawn.* **Constance Stone** was the first woman doctor to win registration in Australia. **Edith Cowan** was the first woman member of any Australian parliament. **Henry Handel Richardson** was the noted author of *The Fortunes of Richard Mahony.*

4. Symbols of Nationhood

Every nation needs symbols—a flag, coat of arms, national song—to sum up its common ideals and purposes. Shortly before the first Federal Parliament opened in 1901, a contest was held to produce ideas for a distinctively Australian flag. Five similar designs were selected as equal winners from more than thirty-two thousand entries. The flag made up from the winning designs has a dark blue field with the Union Jack occupying the upper hoist, to symbolise British settlement of Australia. A large white star appears in the lower hoist, with points representing the six States (altered in 1908 to seven points, to include Federal Territories). Five

From the perpetual summer of New Guinea to the spring in Ballarat, now in its blossom, and to Hobart, where the buds are scarcely beginning to break, from the place where I speak to you tonight to Perth, where the sun has not yet set, the Commonwealth flag flies over it all . . . A continent of 3,000,000 square miles, containing nearly 4,000,000 of people scattered in a fringe upon its outer rim—a country whose increase in the matter of population is extremely small; a country whose birth rate at present is low; a country which we hold, but of which we only occupy a fraction . . . these are fundamental facts to be burnt into our memories and maintained there for the purpose of interpreting what the Commonwealth is, and suggesting what Australia ought to be.

ALFRED DEAKIN at Ballarat, 1903.

Australia's first national coat of arms, shown at left, was granted by royal warrant on 7 May 1908. It depicted a central shield with the cross of St George, bearing the five stars of the Southern Cross and six chevrons representing the States. The familiar kangaroo and emu appeared at left and right sides. A seven-pointed star was included above the shield, and below it a banner with the words 'Advance Australia'. After wide criticism, King George V approved a new design on 19 September 1912, showing the two animals in a more natural posture against a background of wattle.

103

Our Own Flag

When Australians were called on to volunteer for the Boer War, 'Banjo' Paterson wondered whether they should fight only under the British flag. In these verses written in 1900, he forecast accurately that in future conflicts Australians would carry their own national flag.

They mustered us up with a royal din,
In wearisome weeks of drought,
Ere ever the half of the crops were in,
Or the half of the sheds cut out.

'Twas down with saddle and spurs and whip
The swagman dropped his swag,
And we hurried us off to an outbound ship
To fight for the English flag.

The English flag—it is ours in sooth
We stand by it wrong or right.
But deep in our hearts is the honest truth
We fought for the sake of a fight.

And the English flag may flutter and wave
Where the World-wide Oceans toss,
But the flag the Australian dies to save
Is the flag of the Southern Cross.

If ever they want us to stand the brunt
Of a hard-fought, grim campaign,
We will carry our own flag up to the front
When we go to the wars again.

white stars appear in the fly, representing the Southern Cross. The same design, but with a red field, is flown by ships registered in Australia. King Edward VII approved the designs for both flags early in 1903.

For many years the use of the Australian flag was restricted to government establishments, including schools. While R. G. Menzies was Prime Minister during the early months of World War II, he directed that all restrictions on flying the flag should be lifted. Politicians of all parliamentary parties were unanimous in favouring the widest possible display of the flag: the direction by Menzies was confirmed by Labor Prime Minister J. B. Chifley after the war ended. The various Australian flags are now known officially as: Australian National Flag (the blue ensign); Australian Red Ensign (for merchant shipping registered here); Australian White Ensign (for the Royal Australian Navy); and Royal Australian Air Force Ensign.

The Australian National Flag, when flown or paraded, takes precedence in this country over all other national flags. Detailed rules for displaying flags are given in a booklet entitled *The Australian National Flag*, produced by the Australian Government Publishing Service in 1982.

In recent years, as the British component of the Australian population has diminished, pressure has increased to eliminate the Union Jack and adopt a purely Australian design for the flag. Most proposals have been based on the Eureka flag, alternative versions of the Southern Cross, kangaroos, and the Australian colours of green and gold declared official in April 1984. At the time of writing, government approval for changes to the flag has been considered potentially divisive instead of unifying, and has been deferred for future consideration.

The Long Search for a National Anthem

Britain was the first world power to adopt a national anthem, although the authorship of 'God Save the King' has often been disputed. After it was sung at Drury Lane Theatre in London during the Jacobite rebellion of 1745, and 'encored with repeated huzzas', it was immediately approved as the national anthem. The song was brought to Australia by the first British settlers, and remained the predominant anthem until recent times. It is still the sole salute used on regal occasions. During the reign of a female monarch, of course, the words are changed to 'God Save the Queen'.

Steady growth of Australian national sentiment encouraged attempts to develop a local anthem which would find wide acceptance among the people. In 1859 the Gawler (South Australia) Mechanics Institute offered a prize of 25 guineas for the best attempt. Eighty entries were received. The prize was won by Mrs Caroline Carleton (1820–79), who had emigrated from London to South Australia in 1843 with her doctor husband. After his death she conducted private schools in Adelaide, where she wrote the words for her winning entry, 'The Song of Australia'.

The anthem was set to music by Carl Linger (1810–62), a Berlin-born musician and composer who migrated to Adelaide in 1849. Words and music became extremely popular: in 1880 the South Australian government ordered it to be sung regularly in schools. 'It is fully recognised as the hymn of the people', said Sydney's *Town and Country Journal* in 1887. At the time of Federation, however, loyalty to Britain was so pronounced that no official attempt was made to displace the British National Anthem.

A more widely-favoured contender for acceptance as Australia's anthem was 'Advance Australia Fair'. This was written by Peter Dodds McCormick, who emigrated from Glasgow in 1855. Words and music were first performed in Sydney on St Andrew's Day, 1878. During World War II, the Australian Broadcasting Commission played the music to introduce news bulletins. Many people find the song pedestrian and uninspired. Nevertheless it has over the years attracted great public support. Opinion polls in 1973 and 1983 favoured it as

The Song of Australia

There is a land where summer skies
Are gleaming with a thousand dyes,
Blending in witching harmonies,
*   in harmonies:*
And grassy knoll and forest height,
Are flushing in the rosy light,
And all above is azure bright
Australia Australia Australia.

There is a land where honey flows,
Where laughing corn luxuriant grows
Land of the myrtle and the rose,
*   land of the rose:*
On hill and plain the clustering vine,
Is gushing out with purple wine,
And cups are quaffed to thee and thine
Australia Australia Australia.

There is a land where treasures shine
Deep in the dark unfathomed mine,
For worshippers at mammon's shrine,
*   at mammon's shrine:*

Where gold lies hid, and rubies gleam,
And fabled wealth no more doth seem,
The idle fancy of a dream
Australia Australia Australia.

There is a land where homesteads peep
From sunny plain and woodland steep.
And love and joy bright vigils keep,
*   bright vigils keep:*
Where the glad voice of childish glee,
Is mingled with the melody,
Of nature's hidden minstrelsy
Australia Australia Australia.

There is a land where floating free,
From mountain top to girdling sea,
A proud flag waves exultingly, exultingly:
And Freedom's sons the banner bear,
No shackled slave can breathe the air,
Fairest of Britain's daughters fair
Australia Australia Australia.

CAROLINE CARLETON

Mrs **Caroline Carleton**, who migrated to South Australia in 1843, wrote one of our most accomplished anthems with 'The Song of Australia'.

national anthem above all contenders, including 'God Save the Queen'. After widely-based government polls in 1974 and 1977, 'Advance Australia Fair' was adopted as our 'National Tune', to be played on official occasions but not to be sung. Nor could it be used as incidental music or a regimental march.

In April 1984 the Hawke Labor government moved cautiously to adapt the words of McCormick's composition, which was then out of copyright, to suit the modern age. The first line was changed from 'Australia's sons, let us rejoice' to 'Australians all let us rejoice', making it obvious that females were included in the song's spirit. The second verse was eliminated entirely. This referred to gallant Cook sailing from Albion with true British courage to raise Old England's flag and prove that 'Britannia rules the wave'. This verse is today partly misleading, and meaningless to many immigrants. In the third verse, for similar reasons, the sentiment of 'loyal sons beyond the seas' was changed to read 'those who've come across the seas'. The revised version was officially adopted as the Australian National Anthem.

The third contender for national song is the rousing 'Waltzing Matilda', the words of which are probably best known of all to Australians. The song had its origin when 'Banjo' Paterson was holidaying at Dagworth Station in Central Queensland in 1895. He heard the tune 'Craigielea' played, and wrote a ballad in vernacular terms, based on local events.

The title 'Waltzing Matilda' means carrying a 'swag'—that is, a rolled blanket containing personal possessions. A 'swagman' is an itinerant worker, or a vagabond. A 'billabong' is a river bend which has been cut off by a change in the watercourse. A 'billy' is a tin with lid and handle used for boiling tea. A 'jumbuck' is a sheep.

The song has retained its popularity partly because of its clever use of Australian slang, partly as a reminder of bush life, and partly because it expresses the contempt of old bushmen for organised authority. It will never be accepted as an official anthem, but seems likely to keep its place in the hearts of the people. The original words are reproduced on the following page.

Advance Australia Fair

Australians all let us rejoice,
For we are young and free;
We've golden soil and wealth
*   for toil;*
Our home is girt by sea;
Our land abounds in nature's
*   gifts*
Of beauty rich and rare;
In history's page, let every
*   stage*
Advance Australia Fair.
In joyful strains then let us
*   sing,*
Advance Australia Fair.

Beneath our radiant
*   Southern Cross*
We'll toil with hearts and
*   hands;*
To make this Commonwealth
*   of ours*
Renowned of all the lands;
For those who've come
*   across the seas*
We've boundless plains to
*   share*
With courage let us all
*   combine*
To Advance Australia Fair.
In joyful strains then let us
*   sing,*
Advance Australia Fair.

PETER DODDS MCCORMICK. Version approved in 1984 as the Australian National Anthem.

105

Waltzing Matilda

Oh, there once was a swagman camped in a billabong,
Under the shade of a Coolibah tree;
And he sang as he looked at his old billy boiling,
'Who'll come a-waltzing Matilda with me?'

Who'll come a-waltzing Matilda, my darling?
Who'll come a-waltzing Matilda with me?
Waltzing Matilda and leading a water-bag,
Who'll come a-waltzing Matilda with me?

Down came a jumbuck to drink at the waterhole,
Up jumped the swagman and grabbed him with glee;
And he sang as he stowed him away in his tucker-bag,
'You'll come a-waltzing Matilda with me.'

Down came the Squatter a-riding his thoroughbred;
Down came Policemen—one, two and three.
'Whose is the jumbuck you've got in the tucker-bag?
You'll come a-waltzing Matilda with me.'

But the swagman he up and he jumped in the waterhole,
Drowning himself by the Coolibah tree;
And his ghost may be heard as it sings in the billabong,
'Who'll come a-waltzing Matilda with me?'

A. B. PATERSON, original version.

Queensland

New South Wales

Victoria

Tasmania

Canberra

South Australia

Western Australia

Northern Territory

Coats of Arms of the States and Territories

The Australian States and Territories retain individual coats of arms for formal governmental use. The first was granted to Queensland by Queen Victoria in 1893. Supporters at each side were added by Queen Elizabeth II during her Jubilee visit in 1977. The red deer symbolises links with the old world; the brolga is indigenous to Queensland. The motto translates as 'Bold, aye, but faithful too'.

New South Wales was granted its coat of arms by King Edward VII in 1906. The motto translates as 'Newly risen, how bright thou shinest'.

Victoria was granted its coat of arms by King George V in 1910. Beneath a kangaroo holding a crown, and the Southern Cross, the motto is 'Peace and prosperity'.

Tasmania was granted its coat of arms by King George V in 1917. The supporters are Tasmanian Tigers, now possibly extinct. The motto translates as 'Productiveness and faithfulness'.

Canberra was granted its coat of arms by King George V in 1928. It contains several symbols of sovereignty, authority and justice. The supporters, a black and white swan, symbolise Aboriginal and European races.

South Australia was granted its coat of arms by King George V in 1936, when the State celebrated its Centennial. The motto is 'Faith and courage'.

Western Australia has used its black swan as an unofficial coat of arms since early settlement. It was given official sanction by Queen Elizabeth II in 1969.

The Northern Territory was granted its coat of arms by Queen Elizabeth II when it achieved self-government in 1978. It includes red kangaroos as supporters, a wedge-tail eagle as crest, and Aboriginal motifs.

5. World's First Labor Governments Hailed as Democracy in Action

The sudden rise in Australia of the world's first governments representing working-men stunned observers. Equality was obviously more than a dream or an idle boast — Australian voters and politicians were actually doing something to achieve it.

Albert Métin, a French student visiting Australia, believed in 1901 that the country was on the way to becoming a 'workers' paradise'. He attributed this partly to the fact that no great gap existed between the working class and the middle class, both exhibiting 'a most unequivocal attachment to the monarchy, and the deepest reverence for the sovereign and the royal family'. Outside working hours, wrote Métin,

> The Australian worker has become a 'gentleman'. He dresses himself after his work, he is housed, and he behaves like a person of good society. If he has to attend a meeting, he will appear clean, freshly shaved, will be careful of his behaviour, will not speak out of turn, and will respect the authority of the chairman.

The political result of these attitudes was that, apart from a few extremists, the middle class generally accepted moderate Labor policies and viewed the election of Labor governments without great alarm. 'White Australia', for example, which was originally intended to defend working conditions and wages achieved by white unionists, rapidly became a bilateral policy accepted by practically the whole community. The same basic agreement was achieved with the introduction of social services; similarly with arbitration and conciliation procedures.

The world's first although short-lived Labor government had been elected in Queensland in 1899. This was followed in the Federal sphere in 1904 by the establishment of the world's first national Labor government. At its head was John Christian Watson, a 37-year-old compositor who gained his political experience in the New South Wales Parliament when the Labor Party first emerged during the 1890s. As Prime Minister, Watson attempted in 1904 to introduce job preference to members of trade unions which agreed to be bound by decisions of the proposed Arbitration Court. Opposition parties considered this an extreme measure, and combined to defeat the Labor administration after only four months.

However, establishment of the Arbitration Court itself was an agreed bilateral policy. The Reid-McLean coalition government, a temporary alliance of Free Traders and some Protectionists, amended Watson's Bill to inaugurate what was later enthusiastically described as 'a new province for law and order'.

The Court was the world's first compulsory federal system of dealing with industrial disputes extending over more than one State. It seemed to many people yet another example from a united Australia to the rest of mankind, showing how the problems of industrial capitalism could be solved or ameliorated. Matters did not quite turn out that way, for Australia's record of strikes remained nearly as bad as any in the world. But the good intentions of all political parties were obvious.

The early Arbitration Court system yielded another world 'first' — the concept of a fair and reasonable minimum wage for a worker and family. This success arose from a policy called 'New Protection', which a Liberal government led by Alfred Deakin introduced after its election in 1905. The New Protection laws specified that tariff protection would be given only to manufacturers who allowed reasonable wages and conditions to their employees.

In 1907 Hugh Victor McKay, a 42-year-old Victorian farmer who had invented the successful Sunshine combine harvester and established factories to manufacture it in Melbourne and Ballarat, applied to the Arbitration Court for exemption from the New Protection legislation, on the ground that six shillings a day (thirty-six shillings a week) was a fair wage. In court his evidence was examined by Judge Henry Bournes Higgins, a 51-year-old Irish-born lawyer who had been Attorney-General in the first Federal Labor government. Higgins concluded that the wages paid by McKay's firm were *not* 'fair and reasonable'. His judgement fixing forty-two shillings per week, as the minimum necessary for a family to live in frugal comfort, remains one of the great landmarks in Australian history. It raised factory wages by more than sixteen per cent, and established the idea that working conditions could be protected by high tariffs, regardless of their long-term effect on the competitive ability of Australian industry.

Henry Bournes Higgins

Despite the general rise in wages, manufacturers took advantage of protectionist policies to expand the number of factories from 11,000 in 1901 to 15,500 in 1914. Employment in factories grew from 200,000 to 330,000 workers over the same period. By the outbreak of World War I, secondary industry was comparatively well advanced, making Australia self-sufficient in many products previously imported from Britain.

Further bilateral action followed the basic wage. Urged on by Labor members, Alfred Deakin's Liberal government in 1908 brought the Commonwealth directly into the field of social services for the first time, by legislating for non-contributory old-age pensions to be paid to the needy. The move had become increasingly urgent. In 1880 the average Australian was decrepit at 45 years of age; most people died before they reached 50 years. By 1900, following improvements in sanitation, males could expect to live to 55 years and females to 60 years. Many exceptional people survived long after these average ages, but often suffered severe hardship because no jobs were available for them.

Germany was the first country to solve this problem, with a system of compulsory national insurance. The element of compulsion was not favoured by freedom-loving Australians, who preferred means-tested pensions paid from taxes. In 1901, the two wealthiest colonies, Victoria and New South Wales, introduced old-age pensions of ten shillings a week for 'deserving persons' who had lived here for at least twenty-five years. Outside Germany, only Denmark and New Zealand could boast of similar payments to the aged.

In Australia, 'The benefits of the pension were apparent immediately', observed the Rev. Francis Boyce. 'There was at once a marked diminution in the number of street beggars, and thousands of aged people were lifted from a condition of dependent wretchedness to a state of independence and of frugal comfort.'

The Commonwealth took up the scheme on a national basis in 1908. Littleton Ernest Groom, 41, son of a transported convict, now Attorney-General in Deakin's government, said that 'the man or party who solved the question of preventing a man who had worked hard all his life—who had maintained a family, and been a good citizen—from going in his old age to the workhouse, would deserve more glory than that to be gained by winning great victories in the battlefield'.

The scheme was approved with the same bipartisan acclamation as other progressive measures. About six per cent of the population applied for the pension in its first year. Today, with expectation of life increased to 70 years for men and 78 years for women, the number of old-age pensioners has risen to about one and a half million, or ten per cent of the whole population, absorbing one-ninth of the total Federal budget each year.

In 1907 Andrew Fisher, a 45-year-old Scottish coalminer who had emigrated to Queensland, was elected leader of the Federal Labor Party. Labor candidates were now rapidly increasing their share of the popular vote. They spoke 'magnificently strong and war-like' while in Opposition, according to Alfred Buchanan, but during brief periods in power were careful not to outrage the electorate: 'Not only has there been nothing revolutionary accomplished, but nothing revolutionary has been even tried'.

By keeping to fairly moderate policies, Fisher swept to victory over Deakin's 'Fusionists' in the elections of April 1910. For the first time in Australian Federal politics, a single party won outright majorities in both Houses. 'What we are

Surely the State, in stipulating for fair and reasonable remuneration for employees, means that the wages shall be sufficient to provide these things, and clothing, and condition of frugal comfort estimated by current human standards.

JUDGE H. B. HIGGINS, fixing the world's first basic wage.

Good government can do much to level the disparity of classes. It cannot make all men equal, but it can give to all equal opportunities as far as the sphere of government extends . . . And this without thwarting enterprise or hampering real progress.

BULLETIN, 1900.

John Christian Watson, a newspaper compositor who became first leader of the Federal Labor Party. Painting by Sir John Longstaff.

Above right. Andrew Fisher, Scottish coal miner who was three times Labor Prime Minister between 1908 and 1915. Painting by E. Phillips Fox.

Australianism was encouraged in new designs which replaced colonial postage stamps. In 1911 the Fisher government approved the first Australian postage stamps, shown below. The complete range of kangaroo stamps from halfpenny to £2 served Australia for many years.

seeing today', commented the Adelaide *Advertiser*, 'is . . . a popular movement away from State institutions towards the wider and freer field of Federal government . . . In the Federation the people have an instrument of government and legislation which is completely under their control. Hopes are more and more centred on this organ of the national will. Popular causes are looking towards it for the means of their final triumph'.

Several important events during Fisher's first years in office reinforced the Commonwealth's powers and intensified national loyalty. In 1910 legislation was passed transferring control of the Northern Territory from South Australia to the Commonwealth. In all the years of South Australian control, the Territory's total white population had grown to only 3300, including 500 families. The Commonwealth, it was generally felt, could not do worse, might improve our northern defences, and might even build a railway to connect Alice Springs to Darwin.

A further expression of nationalism came with parliamentary approval in 1911 for the construction of Australia House in London. A site on the Strand was acquired and a massive five-storey building (often criticised architecturally) was erected for a total cost of £830,000. A singular reminder of Australia occurred when King George V laid the foundation stone in July 1913: the Australians present, reported the press, 'burst into their strange echoing cooees', which reverberated through streets once prowled by so many of their convict forebears.

Defence preparations were beginning to dominate Federal affairs. Despite this, the Fisher Labor government moved swiftly to establish what it called a people's bank: 'belonging to the people, and directly managed by the people's own agents'.

Memories of the great smash of private banks in 1893 after the land boom were still clear and horrific in the public mind. 'It is of no use denying', said Fisher when

introducing the new legislation, 'that banks have played an important part in the development of Australia, and we want to give them full credit for all they have done. It must be freely admitted that they have made mistakes, and that, stern old seasoned financiers as those in charge of them were, they were in the late '80s and early '90s swept into the current of—shall I say imbecility?—like ordinary folk'.

In 1905 the Labor Party adopted as part of its platform the establishment of a Commonwealth Bank of deposit and issue. To more radical members, this did not seem an adequate solution to the social problems caused by uncontrolled private banking practices. 'We are simply stepping into the market again in the good old conservative game of borrow, boom and burst', said one member, King O'Malley.

In August 1910 Fisher legislated to introduce the first Australian government banknotes and coinage, to be controlled by the Federal Treasury. It was now obligatory for the note issue to be backed by sufficient holdings of gold in the Treasury, making it impossible to invoke expansionary programmes quickly during hard times. Nevertheless the benefits of a standard national currency were considerable, and private banknotes soon disappeared from circulation.

A Bill to establish the Commonwealth Bank was pushed through Parliament in 1911. Although formed on cautious lines, it was able to conduct both savings and mortgage business under the one roof—a unique combination at that time. And although its founders could not know it, an instrument was now available to help finance the massive expenditure of World War I.

King O'Malley, eccentric Labor Minister for Home Affairs, who attempted to form a Federal bank capable of expansionary economics in hard times. Painting by Aileen Dent.

6. A United Nation Plans its Defences

One Hour — To Arm!

*Along the frontier of our
North
The yellow lightning
shudders forth;
But we have shut our eyes.
Yet in the tropic stillness
warm
We hear the mutter of the
storm
That all too soon must rise!
After the flash the thunder
comes,
And now the menace of the
drums
Wakens this pregnant calm.
Prolong this hush of
warning, Lord,
That we have time to clutch
the sword:*
Grant us one hour — to arm!

ARTHUR H. ADAMS

*Our self-respect required the
building of this fleet. There
is no way known to the
ingenuity of man whereby
we may preserve our
civilisation without
preparing to fight for it if the
dread necessity should arise.
Every day we see nations
being battered, bruised, and
defaced — almost
denationalised . . . These
huge preparative
expenditures are better than
being bled white and
humiliated . . . For 100 years
our boats have gone out of
the Heads yonder and never
a shot has had to be fired in
their defence . . . Through
this 100 years and more the
Imperial Navy has kept
watch and ward over us,
while we have slept, and
while we have worked and
built up the prosperity of
which Australia today is so
proud.*

JOSEPH COOK, Prime Minister
of Australia, 1913.

'A nation's first duty is to defend itself.' Members of all Australian parliamentary parties agreed with that dictum in 1901, and they agree with it today. At Federation, the nationalistic ardour of most Australians was innocent of any first-hand experience of European wars. So it was curious, observed Sir Frank Fox, for Europeans to see 'the warlike spirit of the Australian peoples'. Aiming to build a working-man's paradise, Australians believed at the same time that 'safety and independence must be paid for with strength, and not with abjectness'.

The military worth of colonial troops had already been shown in the Boer War. In March 1901 a Federal Ministry of Defence was formed with Sir John Forrest as Minister to take control of the 29,000 men enrolled in various colonial forces. Deakin's Defence Act of 1903 laid down the principle that in time of war all men aged between 18 and 60 years could be compelled to defend their homeland.

Because of cost factors, and Labor objections to the militaristic spirit encouraged by large standing armies, a full-time force of only 1300 men was established for peacetime duties. These were supplemented by 'citizen forces' of three kinds: a part-time militia, who were paid; volunteers, who were unpaid; and members of rifle clubs acting as a reserve force. Overall command was vested in Major-General Sir Edward Hutton, a 55-year-old reform-minded British officer who had served in several African wars, specialising in the use of mounted infantry.

One of Hutton's first moves in command was to transform the colonial mounted infantry into an integrated force known as the Light Horse. He abolished the colourful colonial uniforms which made such good targets for snipers, substituting khaki which blended into the Australian bush, and adopting the slouch hat to give extra shade. The hat was adorned with a dull metal 'Rising Sun' badge of radiating bayonets bearing a crown and the single word 'Australia'.

Establishment of an Australian navy was a more contentious and drawn-out process, involving British world strategy to a much greater degree than the army. Australian Prime Ministers attended a series of Imperial Conferences held every couple of years in London, at which the overall interests of the Empire were stressed. The first conference in 1902 was dominated by the alarming knowledge that Germany was embarking on a massive rearmament programme designed to make its navy the equal of Britain's. Thus the strength of the British North Sea Fleet remained the dominant consideration. As far as the distant Pacific was concerned, the old 'Blue Water' policy was continued whereby the Royal Navy provided an Australian squadron from its large naval base being constructed at Singapore. Australia's annual contribution was increased to £200,000, on the understanding that the squadron would be upgraded to nine cruisers and partly manned by Australians serving under British officers. But ships could be withdrawn from the Australian area at any time to meet emergencies elsewhere.

Australia's naval planning received its rudest shock with the smashing victories of Japan over Russia in 1905. Britain hastened to renew her treaties of friendship with this potent new power in the Pacific. But Australians were not reassured. Sir Frank Fox felt that the Anglo-Japanese alliance 'brought the only real peril this continent has to face so much nearer' to the day when the Australian would 'be a slave to the Asiatic'. The *Sydney Morning Herald*, previously a firm adherent to British imperial policy, now believed that 'the yellow has taught the white man a lesson that Australians can neglect only at their peril'.

There was only one thing for it. Australia had to break free from British naval domination, and form its own strong navy under Federal government control. 'The sea is Australia's best means of defence; it is her only means of attack', Charles Bean pointed out.

At the 1907 Imperial Conference, Alfred Deakin demanded that an Australian flotilla consisting mainly of torpedo-firing submarines and destroyers should be permitted by the British authorities. He finally won his way, although the Admiralty required that Australian warships should remain closely associated with the British Pacific Fleet in training, docking facilities, and manoeuvres.

Shortly after a dazzling visit by the American Fleet in 1908, Deakin lost power when Labor withdrew its support on other matters. Nevertheless the naval programme continued without pause during successive changes of government, spurred on by the 'dreadnought crisis' of 1909 when Germany announced the building of thirteen new battleships to be completed within three years.

To inaugurate Australia's navy, the Fisher Labor government ordered three turbine-powered destroyers from British shipyards, where Australian workmen were to be taught advanced construction techniques while working on our own ships. The first two vessels of what was then called the Commonwealth Navy, HMAS *Parramatta* and *Yarra*, reached Australia late in 1910. By 1914 they were joined by a flagship, the dreadnought *Australia* firing eight 12-inch guns; three light cruisers, the *Sydney*, *Melbourne*, and HMS *Encounter* (soon replaced by HMAS *Brisbane*); a third destroyer called *Warrego*; and two submarines. Three more destroyers were being built in Sydney by the workmen trained in Britain. All ships were largely manned by Australian volunteers trained by the Royal Navy. Naval colleges, at first headed by RN officers, were established at Geelong and Jervis Bay to train Australian officers.

While these naval preparations were proceeding, the Australian army was also gathering its strength. Sir Edward Hutton's reforms of 1903 had created a useful home defence force. But the massive military resurgence of Germany and Japan demanded greater efforts yet. All political parties combined to support compulsory peacetime training intended to produce a large reservoir of trained soldiers.

In 1908, Alfred Deakin's government introduced a bill which would have seen all males between 12 and 26 years receiving some form of military training. Overseas, only the Swiss had gone so far in peacetime. Supporting the measure on behalf of most Labor politicians, W. M. Hughes called universal training 'our plain duty'. Again Deakin's government fell, but a similar general policy was planned by Fisher's Labor government in 1909. Field-Marshal Kitchener was invited to visit and give his guidance on the best form of land defences for Australia. The Field-Marshal proposed an army of 80,000 men, half of whom would provide a static force to defend the main seaports, and the other half a mobile strike force to dash by rail and horse to reinforce any area actually attacked. Under universal training, boys would rise through junior cadets (12–14 years) to senior cadets (14–18 years); then to recruits (18–20 years) and fully trained soldiers (20–26 years).

When Labor returned to power, Fisher did not hesitate to follow Kitchener's recommendations. Thus Australia became the first English-speaking country to introduce peacetime conscription. Compulsory drill commenced in 1911, the same year in which training of professional officers began at Duntroon. Soon camps all over Australia were filled with adolescents and young men acquiring the techniques of marksmanship and bayonet charges. By 1914 Australia had trained a substantial army of 42,000 citizen soldiers, who were organised into twenty-eight Light Horse regiments, fifty-six batteries of field artillery, and ninety-two battalions of infantry. In addition, there were 50,000 trained reservists in rifle clubs, 87,000 senior cadets, and 48,000 junior cadets.

The navy was also fully operational by 1914; while the first training school for what would soon become the Australian Flying Corps, and later the Royal Australian Air Force, had been opened at Point Cook.

Defence expenditure rose dramatically from £1·5 million in 1909–10 to £4·7 million in 1913–14 (and would leap to £18·2 million in the first year of war). Even the peacetime expenditure was equivalent to about twenty-four shillings per inhabitant each year—a figure well ahead of any other country in the world except Britain and France, who were trying to catch up with Germany's rearmament.

Before August 1914, Australians imagined that their great defence efforts were mainly aimed at protecting their own under-populated nation. The tragedy lying in the unknowable near future was that Australia was about to suffer the decimation of its finest young men in a Great War which it did nothing to cause.

The **visit of the American 'Great White Fleet' to Sydney and Melbourne in August–September 1908** aroused extraordinary patriotic enthusiasm for the building of an Australian fleet. Rear-Admiral Charles Sperry, commanding the American Fleet, reported home that Australia's 'astounding demonstrations' and 'hysterical heartiness' were based on 'popular sentiment looking for us to take sides against Asia'. This postcard shows something of the fervour aroused.

PART IV
Through World Cataclysms, Australia Proves Itself to the World

Australia Will Be There

(Marching song of the 1st AIF)

Rally round the banner of your country,
Take the field with brothers o'er the foam,
On land or sea, wherever you be,
Keep your eye on Germany.
But England home and beauty
Have no cause to fear,
Should auld acquaintance be forgot?—
No! No! No! No! No!
Australia will be there,
Australia will be there.

W. W. FRANCIS

1. Labor Pledges 'The Last Man and the Last Shilling'

The great efflorescence of Australian nationalism came with the outbreak of World War I on 4 August 1914. Three days earlier, Labor leader Andrew Fisher gave an election speech at the Victorian Western District town of Colac, in which he used phrases destined to echo through history. Fisher asked the electors to express their 'kindest feelings' towards Britain in the critical European situation, and continued: 'Should the worst happen after everything has been done that honour will permit, Australians will stand beside our own to help and defend her to our last man and our last shilling'.

Everyone knew in their hearts that war with Germany was not far away. That powerful federation of Central European Teutonic states had long been eager to expand her empire to rival those of Britain, France and Russia. Germany had already taken the rich Alsace-Lorraine province after defeating the French in 1871, besides acquiring her first colonies in Africa and the Pacific. Now her vast army recruitment and dreadnought building programmes brought her into a state of readiness to force new demands on the older imperial powers.

Britain and France had established their empires long ago against comparatively weak opposition. Modern armaments now multiplied the potential devastation of war a thousand times. Yet Germany seemed mesmerised by the idea of another quick dash upon Paris, and another early peace settlement which would yield the additional colonies she desired. A pretext for the war was found in the murder by a Serbian student of the Archduke Ferdinand, heir to the Austro-Hungarian throne and hence Germany's closest ally. On 23 July 1914 Austria-Hungary used the assassination as the basis for an ultimatum to Serbia to surrender her independence. Russia backed her Slav ally Serbia, and began to mobilise her forces. Germany threatened to mobilise too unless Russia stopped within hours—an impossible task.

When German mobilisation began, world war became imminent. Her plans were based on a series of feints against France's central and southern borders, and the secret massing of overwhelming forces in the north which would sweep through Belgium and straight on to Paris. Once set in motion, the German forces could not turn back.

On 27 July 1914, Winston Churchill, then First Lord of the Admiralty, ordered the Royal Navy not to disperse after manoeuvres off Portland. The navy was thus able, in less than three weeks, to convoy safely a British Expeditionary Force to help defend Belgium and northern France. On 31 July the British Foreign Secretary, Sir Edward Grey, warned the German Ambassador that 'if France and Germany become involved in war, we should be drawn into it'. Two days later German troops invaded France at several points.

On 3 August Germany demanded that Belgium allow the unhindered passage of German troops into France. King Albert I and the Belgian government refused, rallied their tiny army, and begged France and Britain to come to their aid. The following day German troops began their advance through Belgium at high speed and with considerable barbarity delayed only by the desperate resistance of forts at Liége. Britain sped troops to the rescue on 16 August, but these were forced to fall back to the Marne River as the French retreated in the south. After vigorous fast-moving battles, the front lines stabilised in a roughly north-south direction from Ypres and Armentières, running some six hundred miles from the North Sea to Switzerland, and the long bitter years of trench warfare began.

In a constitutional sense, Australia was automatically at war immediately Britain declared hostilities. But there was much more to it than that. Australians were aroused into an unprecedented outburst of patriotic fervour, coupled with pity for little Belgium and deep hatred for Germany.

Scenes of wild enthusiasm were witnessed outside the newspaper offices last night. All day long and throughout the early part of the evening there was always a crowd extending out on to the roadway reading the cables as they were posted up, but as the hour grew late, so the crowd grew denser and spread right across Collins Street. It needed only a single voice to give the opening bars of a patriotic song and thousands of throats took it up, hats and coats were waved and those who were lucky enough to possess even the smallest of Union Jacks were the heroes of the moment and were raised shoulder high as the crowd surged hither and thither. Rule Britannia, Soldiers of the King and Sons of the Sea were sung again and again.

Melbourne AGE, 3 August 1914, as war became imminent.

All Australians rejoiced when HMAS *Sydney* cornered the German raider *Emden* on 9 November 1914 and forced it to run aground on the Cocos Islands. The heavily-armed *Emden* had sunk or captured twenty-seven Allied ships in the Pacific, bombarded an Indian port, and was attempting to destroy underwater communications between Britain and Australia.

Early on 9 November the *Emden* anchored off North Cocos Island and sent a party ashore to destroy the cable station. Distress signals from the station were picked up by warships convoying the 1st AIF to Egypt. HMAS *Sydney* left the convoy at full speed, caught the *Emden* while it was attempting to flee from Cocos, and poured its heavy shells into the raider.

Eighty minutes later, only one of the *Emden*'s guns was still operational, its internal communications inoperable and its steering gear wrecked. A few minutes later it ran aground. The *Sydney* raced away to sink its accompanying collier, and returned to capture *Emden*'s crew.

Today the Cocos Islands are part of the Australian Commonwealth, after an overwhelming vote by its Malay residents in 1984.

Australia's first major naval victory: **'Emden', beached and done for**, painted by Arthur Burgess.

As soon as war was declared, Britain asked Australia to perform the 'great and urgent' task of seizing German radio transmitters which had been erected at Rabaul, Yap and Nauru. Units known as the Australian Naval and Military Expeditionary Force were quickly formed, sailing in HMAS *Australia* and three destroyers. Within a few weeks all German settlements in the South Pacific were occupied, and German New Guinea neutralised. HMAS *Melbourne* bombarded and destroyed the transmitter on Nauru.

Meanwhile, evidence of German atrocities against Belgian civilians (some inseparable from modern warfare, some genuine enough) aroused even greater hatred. The Sydney poet Christopher Brennan wrote savagely in 'A Chant of Doom':

> Chime his fame and chime his name;
> Rhyme his title, rhyme his shame;
> German faith and German trust;
> German hate and German lust:
> Bury the Beast unto the dust.

In working-man's language of the time, C. J. Dennis wrote angrily in 'The Moods of Ginger Mick':

> I tells 'im wot I read about the 'Uns,
>   An' wot they done in Beljum an' in France,
> Wiv drivin' Janes an' kids before their guns,
>   An' never givin' blokes a stray dawg's chance;
> An' 'ow they think they've got the whole world beat.
> Sez 'e, 'I'll crack the first Dutch* cow I meet!'

The Federal government decided to raise an Australian Imperial Force (AIF) of 20,000 volunteers for overseas service. Although physical standards were set at an extremely high level, the ranks filled within three weeks. Men came from all over Australia, some riding hundreds of miles from remote areas, others walking out of factories, offices and universities to join what they saw as an adventure or crusade. By the end of 1914 a further 30,000 enlisted. Nearly eighty per cent were Australian-born. The ageing Henry Lawson exclaimed in 'The Recruits' that 'the Star of Australasia/Is high in the Heavens now'.

The first volunteers from Australia and New Zealand sailed in thirty-eight transport ships to King George Sound (Western Australia), where a century before the French had planned to establish a colony. Escorted by HMAS *Sydney* and *Melbourne*, the British cruiser *Minotaur*, and a Japanese dreadnought named *Ibuki*, they steamed into the Indian Ocean on 1 November 1914. Eight days later HMAS *Sydney* was diverted to chase and sink the German raider *Emden*.

The volunteer soldiers aboard the transports spent most of their time gambling and grousing. Landed to their disgust early in December in Egypt instead of Europe, they soon demonstrated the peculiar combination of insolence, independent spirit, and individual initiative which made them an army like no other in the world. Many of these volunteers regarded the army as just another employer, and themselves as working men with a job to do, but with inalienable rights as free Australians. They strongly objected to saluting officers or addressing them as 'Sir', except in cases where leaders won their respect by outstanding courage and ability. Wrote Private R. E. Lording: 'If I salute an officer I like to feel that we are exchanging man-to-man compliments'. Charged with failing to salute a British officer, another Australian replied, 'Was I to touch my hat to him? Was I his bloomin' dog?'.

Other so-called military crimes became common as the men wearied of endless drill in the desert. They often went absent without leave from their camps near the Pyramids. Hundreds disappeared on Christmas Day 1914: on Boxing Day the 2nd Battalion could not appear on parade because few of the drunken men could be found or roused. Brothels in the notorious Haret el Wasser area of Cairo were twice burned down by Australians incensed by the disease, drugged alcohol, theft

* 'Dutch' was a common adjective for 'German' at the time.

'The Call of Humanity' was painted by Norman Lindsay in 1914 for a pamphlet issued by the Director-General of Recruiting.

Australia in the Vanguard

*What time the nations
  slumbered,
Their war-thoughts put
  away,
A creeping, crouching
  Monster
Made ready for the fray.*

*He sprang: a war-horn
  sounding
Aroused them from their
  rest;
They saw the avid Monster—
His claws in Belgium's
  breast.*

*Their veins ran red with
  anger,
They rose with souls aglow;
And lit with glorious
  purpose
Made onset on the foe.*

*For Belgium, Home and
  Honour,
While this foul Monster
  lives,
Our Empire gives her life-
  blood,
Nor cares how much she
  gives.*

*The sunshine on their faces,
The fine light in their eyes,
Spurred on by splendid
  manhood,
The young Dominions rise.*

*They rise, a shining legion,
To scale far glory-heights—
Australia in their vanguard
With deathless valour fights.*

RODERIC QUINN

and stabbings common in the district. When the fire brigade arrived, soldiers cut the hoses. A number of men who contracted venereal disease were sent back to Australia in disgrace. Yet the remainder of this undisciplined rag-tag army was soon to become famed throughout the world for its incomparable bravery and stoicism in battle.

In London, the War Cabinet accepted Winston Churchill's plan for breaking the stalemate on the Western Front by attacking through the back door. Churchill's strategy was based on sending a strong force through the Aegean Sea to seize the Gallipoli Peninsula from the Turks. This would open the narrow Dardanelles Straits to Allied shipping. Istanbul (Constantinople) could then be bombarded, Turkey forced out of the war, and Russia supplied from her Black Sea ports. Allied forces might then advance through the Balkan states to attack the 'soft underbelly' of Austria-Hungary, opening yet another front against Germany. This brilliant theory depended on the ability of a combined British, French, Australian and New Zealand force to conquer Gallipoli in the first place. God knows they tried hard enough. Yet they were betrayed by lack of ability or even commonsense on the part of senior British officers. Churchill never again fully trusted his generals.

The Bugles of England

The fate of Belgium alone does not explain the fervour of Australia's first reactions to what was once called 'the Great War'. In 1914 about ninety-eight per cent of the Australian population could claim British birth or origin: whatever happened to Britain seemed to be happening also to Australians. James Drummond Burns, born at Geelong just before Federation and killed on Gallipoli in 1915, could write as he enlisted:

> The bugles of England were blowing o'er the sea,
> As they had called a thousand years, calling now to me;
> They woke me from dreaming in the dawning of the day,
> The bugles of England—and how could I stay?
>
> The banners of England, unfurled across the sea,
> Floating out upon the wind, were beckoning to me;
> Storm-rent and battle-torn, smoke-stained and grey,
> The banners of England—and how could I stay?
>
> O England, I heard the cry of those that died for thee,
> Sounding like an organ-voice across the winter sea;
> They lived and died for England and gladly went their way,
> England, O England—how could I stay?

2.   Imperishable Glory of the Gallipoli Defeat

Anzac Cove

There's a lonely stretch of
  hillocks:
There's a beach asleep and
  drear:
There's a battered broken
  fort beside the sea.
There are sunken trampled
  graves:
And a little rotting pier:
And winding paths that wind
  unceasingly.

There's a torn and silent
  valley:
There's a tiny rivulet
With some blood upon the
  stones beside its mouth.
There are lines of buried
  bones:
There's an unpaid waiting
  debt:
There's a sound of gentle
  sobbing in the South.

Leon Gellert

Soldier, by Sir Sidney Nolan.

Before dawn on 25 April 1915, the 3rd Brigade of the Australian and New Zealand Army Corps—the Anzacs—climbed into ships' boats for the first mass assault against a defended coastline to be undertaken in modern military history. They carried rifles with bayonets fixed, but the magazines were empty, in case a stray shot warned the defenders. Ammunition was carried in bandoliers and packs.

Queenslanders of the 9th Battalion were first to scramble ashore in the half-light of early dawn. But the Turks had been roused, and intense fire met the attackers. Something else had gone seriously wrong. Instead of landing on the open plain they had expected, the Anzacs were faced with a series of twisting scrubby gullies and steeply rising sandstone ridges. The boats had beached a mile north of the spot thought best for the attack!

Undaunted by the sight of men falling all around them, the 3rd Brigade charged the Turks and forced them to abandon the first trenches within several hundred yards of the beach. A few Australians raced on to the nearest heights, but had to retreat as Turkish reinforcements arrived. Two thousand of the 16,000 Anzacs landed were killed or wounded on the first day. Finally the whole invading force was compelled to dig into its small beachhead around what became known as Anzac Cove, clinging on desperately against constant artillery and machine-gun and snipers' fire from the heights above.

A British correspondent, Ellis Ashmead-Bartlett, sent back the first news to the Australian public. 'There has been no finer feat in this war than this sudden landing in the dark and storming the heights', he reported. The 'raw colonial troops', he wrote, had proved themselves worthy to fight alongside the heroes of the Western Front. Back in Australia, 'Banjo' Paterson reflected that 'Each native-born Australian son stands straighter up today'. The English poet John Masefield waxed lyrical over the Anzacs as 'the finest body of young men ever brought together in modern times'.

Anzac

*And Anzac now is an
  enchanted shore;
A tragic splendour, and a
  holy name;
A deed eternity will still
  acclaim;
A loss that crowns the
  victories of yore;
A glittering golden dome for
  evermore
Shining above the minarets
  of fame.*

BARTLETT ADAMSON

The impossible task facing the Australians on Gallipoli is shown in this painting '**Anzac—the landing**', by George Lambert.

John Simpson Kirkpatrick (1892–1915), better known as 'the man with the donkey', became a legend on Gallipoli for rescuing hundreds of wounded Anzacs under heavy fire. Kirkpatrick was originally an immigrant canecutter and miner in the Australian outback. He enlisted in the first month of the war, and was shot dead by the Turks four weeks after landing on Gallipoli. Bronze by Leslie Bowles.

For physical beauty and nobility of bearing they surpassed any men I have ever seen; they walked and looked like the kings in old poems, and reminded me of the line in Shakespeare: 'Baited like eagles having lately bathed'.

JOHN MASEFIELD on the Anzacs.

Their pluck was titanic. They were not men, but gods, demons infuriated. We saw them fall by the score. But what of that? Not for one breath did the great line waver or break . . . A seasoned staff officer watching choked with his own admiration. Our men tore off their helmets and waved them, and poured cheer after cheer after those wonderful Anzacs.

A British officer watching the Australians advance up the bare slopes towards Krithia Heights.

An incredible series of attempts to break out of the beachheads and conquer the peninsula took place during the stifling heat of an Aegean summer. On 8 May 1915, the 2nd Australian Brigade and the New Zealand Infantry Brigade were sent to assist British and French forces fighting at Cape Helles on the tip of the peninsula. Late that day Sir Ian Hamilton, British general in command, ordered the Anzacs to advance immediately across two miles of open ground and attack strong Turkish positions on Krithia Heights, which the British and French had failed to take. The Australian commander, Colonel James McCay, protested in vain against the stupidity of such an order. In the carnage that followed all the courage, all the deaths, were useless. The Australians too had to retreat, showing that frontal assaults against strongly-prepared positions were not the way to win wars.

Soon after Krithia, Australian Light Horsemen from Egypt, who had demanded to be allowed to fight dismounted, began to arrive at Anzac Cove. The Turks staged a massive counter-attack to try to push the Anzacs back into the sea. For nearly nine hours Turkish soldiers charged with foolhardiness equal to the Australians, but were forced to retreat after 3000 of their men were shot or bayoneted. An armistice was arranged to bury the dead, but this did not stop disease from sweeping the entrenched forces.

Australians at home, following every despatch with enthusiasm, heard little of the disgusting realities of such warfare. At this stage they were content to bask in the reflected heroism of their men.

Sir Ian Hamilton next evolved a plan under which a surprise offensive would be mounted by Anzacs and Gurkhas in the even more rugged country north of Anzac Cove. Supporting attacks were made on 6 August 1915 when the British landed at Suvla Bay further to the north, and other Australians advanced to the south at Lone Pine. Some success was achieved on each front, but only at the cost of enormous casualties. To take the Turkish trenches at Lone Pine, the Australians suffered more than two thousand three hundred casualties in four days of savage hand-to-hand fighting. Of the nine Victoria Crosses awarded to Australians at Gallipoli, seven were won in this battle alone. Charles Bean, the Australian official war correspondent who saw it all, wrote: 'The dead lay so thick that the only respect which could be paid to them was to avoid treading on their faces'.

On the second day of these mass offensives, more than five hundred Light Horsemen were ordered to attack in broad daylight at the Nek, a narrow sloping plateau north-east of Anzac Cove. There was room only for 150 men at a time to advance in line towards the Turkish guns. The first 150 men scrambled from their trenches to face what Charles Bean described as 'a sudden roar of musketry and machine-gun fire'. Practically the whole line fell dead or wounded within the first ten yards. Then the second 150 men charged, and met the same fate. The third wave, knowing they were facing certain death, also charged. Their colonel was in front: he managed to get fifty yards before being shot. Of eighteen officers, only two survived.

Everywhere else, too, the British offensive failed. A week later, Sir Ian Hamilton cabled to Lord Kitchener that he needed a further 100,000 men to overcome the dogged determination of the Turks to hold their ground. Perhaps additional forces would have finally cracked the enemy lines and opened the way for Churchill's grand strategy. Perhaps the reinforcements would have been uselessly slaughtered as well. We will never know, for Hamilton was about to be brought down by that remarkable invention of democracy, a free press.

The Murdoch Report Halts Further Sacrifice

On 3 September 1915 there arrived on Gallipoli an eager 29-year-old Australian journalist named Keith Arthur Murdoch. Son of a Presbyterian minister who emigrated from Aberdeenshire to Melbourne, Murdoch had sufficiently overcome a severe adolescent stammer to win an appointment as London editor for the Australian newspaper cable service. The Fisher Labor government commissioned the young journalist to inquire into postal services for the troops on his way through Egypt.

Once in Cairo, Murdoch wrote to Sir Ian Hamilton asking for permission to visit 'the sacred shores of Gallipoli'. He undertook to 'record censored impressions in the London and Australian newspapers I represent, but any conditions you impose I should, of course, faithfully observe'. Hamilton agreed, and Murdoch signed the usual undertaking of those days 'not to attempt to correspond by any other route or by any other means than that officially sanctioned'.

Murdoch was astounded and shaken by his four-day tour of Gallipoli. Scores of interviews with troops and officers convinced him that the invasion had been bungled from the start, and success was now almost impossible. When Murdoch returned to the war correspondents' camp, Ellis Ashmead-Bartlett, the British correspondent, asked him whether he would deliver, on his arrival in London, a sealed letter addressed to Herbert Asquith, the British Prime Minister. In it the famous correspondent gave details of army decisions which had been censored from his despatches. After some hesitation Murdoch agreed, arguing that by law every person had the right to communicate privately with a member of Parliament. But British Intelligence was tipped off by a rival correspondent. When Murdoch's ship docked, he was forced to hand over Ashmead-Bartlett's letter and his own report to the Australian government. Neither document was seen again.

Arriving in London, Murdoch wrote a much fuller report to Australian Prime Minister Fisher on 23 September 1915. Although perhaps exaggerated, some of his most telling phrases struck hard at the amateurish direction of the Gallipoli campaign. Murdoch felt sure that 'if there is really military necessity for this awful ordeal, then I am sure the Australian troops will face it'. They were temporarily dispirited, he said, but 'they are game to the end'.

It is undoubtedly one of the most terrible chapters in our history . . . the work of the General Staff in Gallipoli has been deplorable . . . This lack of confidence in the authorities arises principally from the fact that every man knows that the last operations were grossly bungled . . . For the General Staff, and I fear for Hamilton, officers and men have nothing but contempt . . . What I want to say to you now very seriously is that the continuous and ghastly bungling over the Dardanelles enterprise was to be expected from such a General Staff as the British Army possesses . . . What can you expect of men who have never worked seriously, who have lived for their appearance and for social distinction and self-satisfaction, and who are now called on to conduct a gigantic war? . . .

I could pour into your ears so much truth about the grandeur of our Australian army, and the wonderful affection of these fine young soldiers for each other and their homeland, that your Australianism would become a more powerful sentiment than before. It is stirring to see them, magnificent manhood, swinging their fine limbs as they walk about Anzac. They have the noble faces of men who have endured. Oh, if you could picture Anzac as I have seen it, you would find that to be an Australian is the greatest privilege the world has to offer.

KEITH MURDOCH, Australian correspondent.

War correspondent Keith Murdoch, later a Melbourne newspaper magnate, with Prime Minister Billy Hughes in France, 1918.

Murdoch's anger so impressed the editor of *The Times*, Geoffrey Dawson, that he arranged private interviews for the young Australian with members of the British Cabinet. Murdoch's letter to Andrew Fisher was circulated as a confidential State paper, and a secret Royal Commission instituted. Sir Ian Hamilton was quickly dismissed. The new commander recommended early evacuation of Gallipoli, despite estimates that up to half the remaining troops could be lost if the Turks discovered the withdrawal and attacked while men were still trying to reach the ships.

Fortunately the evacuation was much better planned than the invasion. From 8 to 20 December 1915, groups of men with boots wrapped in sacking stole quietly at night along blanket-covered jetties into small craft which rowed them out to waiting transports. Rifles and mines rigged to explode at intervals fooled the Turks into believing that strong forces still remained in the empty trenches. More than one hundred thousand troops were evacuated without loss of life.

In those comparatively innocent days, the toll of Gallipoli seemed almost beyond belief. At home, Australians now could not pick up a newspaper without dreading the appearance of endless lists of killed and wounded. Total British casualties exceeded one hundred and twenty thousand. Nearly thirty-five thousand members of the Anzac force alone had fallen in eight months of fighting. Of these, 7600 Australians were killed and 19,500 wounded. Less than one hundred Anzacs surrendered to become Turkish prisoners. Of the dead men, only one-third lay in known graves. Appalling though these facts seemed at the time, the Australian sacrifice in World War I had just begun. Keith Murdoch's intervention, for better or worse, led inevitably to the transfer of most of the 1st AIF to the Western Front. A further 52,000 young Australians were to die, and hundreds of thousands to suffer wounds and disease, before the long agony was over.

Yet the expenditure of life and health on Gallipoli became transmuted into a special legend of courage and sacrifice. People at home could not believe that their sons had suffered in vain. When the first Anzac Day was celebrated on 25 April 1916, the new Labor Prime Minister, William Morris Hughes, exclaimed: 'Soldiers, your deeds have won you a place in the Temple of the Immortals. The world has hailed you as heroes'.

In Sydney the *Freemason's Journal* reflected that 'The price of nationhood must be paid in blood and tears'; while the *Sydney Morning Herald* forecast that Anzac Day would 'go down to posterity' as the day on which Australians achieved man's estate. Thus a military disaster was idealised into an epic tale of pride and honour—magically converted into an admirable struggle to the death against impossible odds.

The death-defying charge of the Light Horse Brigade at the Nek on Gallipoli. One of the few officers who survived wrote home that 'the roll call after was the saddest, just fancy only 47 answered their names out of close on 550 men. When I heard what the result was I simply cried like a child'.

'No one expected the flow of wounded that poured out after the Gallipoli landing, and the Army showed little realism', wrote Dame Mabel Brookes, assisting the Red Cross in Egypt. Thousands of seriously wounded men had to be kept on Lemnos and in Cairo. Others were shipped to London. George Coates's painting shows **the arrival of the first Australian wounded from Gallipoli at Wandsworth Hospital, London, in 1915.**

3. As Desert Warriors, the Anzacs Have No Equal

In the summer of 1916 an amazing campaign began to unfold on the historic sands of the Middle East. While their infantry comrades from Gallipoli were being shipped to the unsuspected horrors of the Western Front, volunteers of the Australian Light Horse returned to Egypt. There they regrouped to avenge themselves on the Turks by attacking through Sinai, Palestine and Syria.

A few months of training under harsh desert conditions turned the Light Horse into a formidable, highly mobile striking force. Their field commander was Harry George Chauvel, a squatter's son from Tabulam on the Upper Clarence River in New South Wales. As an officer in the Queensland Mounted Infantry, Chauvel had helped to break the great shearers' strike of 1891, but by 1916 this was no longer held against him. Chauvel's horsemen delighted in hunting wild emus across the plains at high speed: when they returned from the Boer War, the government allowed them to sport an emu plume in their slouch hats as the distinguishing emblem of the Light Horse. These were Australia's elite troops.

Promoted to Lieutenant-Colonel, Chauvel led the dismounted units in some of the worst fighting on Gallipoli, where he attacted attention for his nonchalance under heavy fire and willingness to share the same hardships as his men.

The Turkish victory on Gallipoli greatly increased the threat to the Suez Canal. Chauvel, now aged 51, but still a tireless horseman, was promoted to Major-General and put in charge of the Anzac Mounted Division, popularly known as 'the Desert Column'. Here he was able to complete the task of welding his wild bushmen into an effective disciplined whole. 'To my mind', he wrote, 'there is only one way of instilling discipline into the Australian and that is by appealing to his common sense and creating an Esprit de Corps and appealing to *that* when trouble comes . . .'

By mid-1916, conditions in the desert stunned even those used to searing Australian summers. Temperatures in the shade ranged up to 126° Fahrenheit. But the British commander-in-chief, General A. J. Murray, assured Chauvel that his horsemen seemed to possess 'a genius for this desert life', and that no other troops could have trained in such weather. Ion Idriess, a 27-year-old trooper in the 5th Light Horse Regiment, noted in his diary that even the men's boot leather was shrinking in the blazing sand. Nevertheless, he wrote,

> We are a crack regiment now—ceaseless training has made us so. A crack regiment of Australian Light Horse possesses a terrible fighting-power—and instant mobility adds to our regiment the strength of two. Out in the open desert our mounted regiment could defeat two thousand Turkish infantry . . .

Such bravado was soon put to the test. In August 1916, the Light Horse advanced on Romani, a large fortified oasis area about forty miles north-east of the Suez Canal. Their tough horses—'walers' from New South Wales—went two days without water, and even the men carried only one quart bottle each. Yet on arriving near the oasis, men who should have been exhausted were still laughing and joking as they fixed bayonets. Wrote Idriess:

> We held the horses in so as to have their strength in the last great clash. But they were getting excited; the men were getting excited; we rode knee to knee; right and left were excited faces and flashing steel; and our bodies felt the massed heat of the horses that tugged and strained as the squadrons broke into a swift canter. Then a horse reared high as it screamed and we were into a mad gallop, the horses' mouths open and their great eyes staring as the squadrons thundered on.

The result was a smashing success—the first decisive British victory of the entire war. Some thirteen thousand Turks were killed or taken prisoner for the loss of 200 Australians killed and 900 wounded. King George V sent his congratulations, and General E. T. Hutton wrote to Chauvel: 'You and your men are establishing Australia as a nation'. More astonishing to Turkish wounded was the way in which Australians loaded them on to their own horses and walked them in gently for medical assistance. *That* was something new in the land of the Crusades.

Four months later Chauvel's forces streamed along the coastal road towards Gaza, destroying the Turkish garrisons at Magdhaba and Rafah. The 1st Australian Flying Corps Squadron took aerial photographs and used radio for the first time in battle to direct artillery accurately: Captain Ross Smith, later famous for establishing England-Australia aerial records, was one of the observers.

Charger and Groom.
Pencil sketch by
George Lambert.

Several major battles took place before the elaborate fortifications of Gaza—fabled city of Samson and Delilah—fell to the desert forces. Typically, the Australians first conducted a 'Spring Race Meeting' on Rafah battlefield on 21 March 1917, the prize cup being donated by Chauvel himself. Four days later these wild raiders were killing Turks outside Gaza. Trooper Idriess described in his diary how it felt to stab men to death:

> ... man after man tore through the cactus to be met by the bayonets of the Turks, six to one. It was just beserk slaughter. A man sprang at the closest Turk and thrust and sprang aside and thrust again and again—some men howled as they rushed, others cursed to the shivery feel of steel on steel—the grunting breaths, the gritting teeth and the staring eyes of the lunging Turk, the sobbing scream as a bayonet ripped home. The Turkish battalion simply melted away: it was all over in minutes. Men lay horribly bloody and dead; others writhed on the stained grass, while all through the cactus lanes our men were chasing demented Turks.

The first two assaults on Gaza itself failed, and the British commander-in-chief was recalled. General Sir Edmund ('Bull') Allenby took overall command of the campaign, reorganising the Desert Column into the Desert Mounted Corps. Chauvel was promoted again—over protests from British cavalrymen—to become the first Lieutenant-General of an Australian army, and the first Australian to lead an army corps into battle. Under him were about forty thousand men organised into nine mounted brigades, five of them Anzac—the largest body of mounted troops ever placed under a single field command in modern times.

Allenby decided to keep Turkish attention directed towards Gaza, with continuous attacks by British infantry and artillery, while secretly concentrating his mounted forces for a dash against the desert town of Beersheba. The conquest of Beersheba presented unique tactical difficulties. Some thirty miles inland from Gaza, it was surrounded by almost waterless regions which Chauvel's army would have to cross at considerable speed. The approaches to the town consisted mainly of open ground dominated by deep trench systems and artillery in protected positions. German aeroplanes constantly patrolled the surroundings in daylight to warn of any movement. Yet this fortified town had to be conquered in one day, and the wells seized by the end of that day to provide water for huge numbers of exhausted men and horses.

Chauvel met these difficulties by crossing the desert on the night of 30 October 1917. At dawn, fierce attacks began at several places around the perimeter, but were held back by Turkish artillery and German aerial bombing. In the fading afternoon light Chauvel made an agonising decision—to send the 4th Light Horse Brigade at the gallop against the town's south-eastern trenches. Thus began the last and greatest mass cavalry charge of this century. Trooper Idriess, on observation duty on a nearby hill, enjoyed a grandstand view. When hope was nearly gone of capturing the wells that day:

> Then someone shouted, pointing through the sunset towards invisible headquarters. There, at the steady trot, was regiment after regiment, squadron after squadron, coming, coming, coming! It was just half-light, they were distinct yet indistinct. The Turkish guns blazed at those hazy horsemen but they came steadily on. At two miles distant they emerged from clouds of dust, squadrons of men and horses taking shape. All the Turkish guns around Beersheba must have been directed at the menace then. Captured Turkish and German officers have told us that even then they never dreamed

The last and greatest cavalry charge of this century: **the 4th Light Horse Brigade overwhelms the Turkish and German defenders of Beersheba, 31 October 1917.** Painting by George Lambert.

that mounted troops would be madmen enough to attempt rushing infantry redoubts protected by machine-guns and artillery. At a mile distant their thousand hooves were stuttering thunder, coming at a rate that frightened a man—they were an awe-inspiring sight, galloping through the red haze—knee to knee and horse to horse—the dying sun glinting on bayonet-points. Machine-guns and rifle fire just roared but the 4th Brigade galloped on. We heard shouts among the thundering hooves, saw balls of flame amongst those hooves—horse after horse crashed, but the massed squadrons thundered on . . .

The last half-mile was a berserk gallop with the squadrons in magnificent line, a heart-throbbing sight as they plunged up the slope, the horses leaping the redoubt trenches—my glasses showed me the Turkish bayonets thrusting up for the bellies of the horses—one regiment flung themselves from the saddle—we heard the mad shouts as the men jumped down into the trenches, a following regiment thundered over another redoubt, and to a triumphant roar of voices and hooves was galloping down the half-mile slope right into the town. Then came a whirlwind of movement from all over the field, galloping batteries—dense dust from mounting regiments—a rush as troops poured for the opening in the gathering dark—mad, mad excitement—terrific explosions from down in the town.

Beersheba had fallen, with the loss of only thirty-one Australians killed and thirty-two wounded in that last great charge. 'They are not soldiers at all; they are madmen!', exclaimed a captured German officer.

Gaza, Jerusalem and Jericho fell in succession during the following weeks. Allenby's forces were then greatly reduced to supply reinforcements desperately needed on European fronts. Reverses were suffered in the first Jordan Valley battles, but on 21 September 1918 Chauvel captured Nazareth with a lightning dash which nearly trapped the German commander-in-chief. Two Turkish armies were completely routed: tens of thousands were captured in battles which raged around the Sea of Galilee.

The new Australian Flying Corps played a notable part in the desert war. This painting by H. Septimus Power shows **a dramatic incident in which Lieutenant Frank McNamara, a former schoolteacher, won the air force's first Victoria Cross.** Although wounded by a bomb which had exploded prematurely, McNamara landed in enemy territory to rescue another Australian pilot who had been forced to land. They took off with Turkish cavalry in hot pursuit. McNamara became an Air Vice-Marshal before retiring in 1946.

Contrary to popular legend, Australian Light Horsemen captured Damascus well before 'Lawrence of Arabia' arrived with his Bedouin supporters. '**Into Damascus**', by H. Septimus Power, shows the **Australians riding into the Turkish-occupied city with swords drawn.**

129

Desert Mounted Corps
statue on Anzac Parade,
Canberra, by Ray Ewers.

Now began the famous dash to the north-east to take Damascus, capital of Syria. Henry Gullett, a 40-year-old journalist who enlisted as a gunner but later became an official war historian, described the race to the ancient city:

> Unshaven and dusty, thin from the ordeal of the Jordan and with eyes bloodshot from lack of sleep, they rode with the bursting excitement of a throng of schoolboys ... With swords flashing in the early sunrise, little parties of three and four men raced shouting on bodies of Turks ten and twenty times their number.

At dawn on 1 October 1918, the vanguard of the 10th Light Horse Regiment galloped into Damascus with swords drawn. Most of the Turks and Germans had fled: the remainder quietly laid down their arms. About twelve thousand prisoners were taken for the loss of ninety-two Light Horsemen. As the Australians trotted through the streets, wrote Lieutenant-Colonel A. C. N. Olden,

> The march now assumed the aspect of a triumphal procession, the dense masses of the people rapidly becoming hysterical in their manifestations of joy. They clung to the horses' necks, they kissed our men's stirrups; they showered confetti and rosewater over them; they shouted, laughed, cried, sang and clapped hands.

The British Army's Lieutenant-Colonel T. E. Lawrence ('Lawrence of Arabia') soon arrived with his Bedouin supporters, who were generally hated and despised by the Australians. Chauvel found Lawrence wearing 'a magnificent Arab costume', and secretly planning for Prince Feisal to take control of government instead of the British and French. Chauvel promptly occupied the Turkish Governor's headquarters, and placed two Australian Light Horse regiments on police duties to quieten the riotous streets and clean up a horrifying mess at Turkish army hospitals. When Allenby entered in triumph, Lawrence agreed to return quietly to Britain without causing further difficulties.

Other elements of the victorious army pushed the Turks out of Aleppo, chief city near the Turkish border. Before their country could be invaded, the Turkish government surrendered unconditionally on 30 October 1918. The desert war was over. All told, the British-Australian armies had captured more than seventy-five thousand Turks in the final six weeks, for a total of 5600 casualties. Only about six hundred of these were Light Horsemen, who had led the whole daring enterprise. Yet each of those fallen men had known unique friendships hammered out under terrible trials. The last word of the campaign lies with Trooper Idriess:

> But the dearest memory, the memory that will linger until I die, is the comradeship of my mates, these thousands of men who laugh so harshly at their own hardships and sufferings, but whose smile is so tenderly sympathetic to others in pain.

The Anzacs (Light Horse
memorial group). Bronze
by George Lambert.

4. Australian Shock Troops Break Through on the Western Front

Now the Anzacs had to be plunged into the man-eating quagmire of the Western Front. The veterans of Gallipoli were regrouped into two army corps commanded by British generals, Sir William Birdwood and Sir Alexander Godley. The thinned-out ranks were filled by enthusiastic volunteers fresh from home. These newcomers quickly picked up the same habits of wry self-mockery and disregard of authority.

Much of this cockiness disappeared in the appalling conditions of trench warfare north and south of the Somme, a river which rises near Mont St Quentin and finally emerges via Amiens into the English Channel. On 1 July 1916, the British commander-in-chief, General Douglas Haig, attempting to relieve German pressure on Verdun, ordered a massive bombardment of the German lines, followed by an equally massive infantry advance. The entire offensive was a disaster. Preliminary shelling had failed to knock out nests of German machine-guns, which were used with devastating effect. Tens of thousands of attackers fell as they climbed out of the trenches. Total British casualties on that dreadful first day amounted to 60,000 killed and wounded.

The six Australian battalions taking part at Fromelles suffered 5133 casualties within sixteen hours, while another 400 men were taken prisoner. In the 60th Battalion, only 107 men survived from nearly nine hundred. Charles Bean, who sped to the scene next day, wrote that 'The scene in the Australian trenches, packed with wounded and dying, was unexampled in the history of the A.I.F.'.

Three weeks after Fromelles, an even worse disaster for the Australians began at Pozières, a village on a slight rise about five miles north of a bend in the Somme. In seven weeks of ear-splitting artillery duels and courageous but doomed charges, 6842 Australians were killed and 17,513 wounded or gassed—just to win a few hundred yards of scorched earth. No battle before or since has resulted in such a huge proportion of casualties.

Pozières shattered the last vestiges of the belief that war could be a romantic adventure. Lieutenant John Alexander Raws, former parliamentary reporter of the Melbourne *Argus*, wrote home just before he died: 'I saw strong men who had been through Gallipoli sobbing and trembling as with ague—men who had never turned a hair before'. After the initial attack, Raws wrote to a friend:

> We are lousy, stinking, ragged, unshaven, sleepless. I have one puttee, a dead man's helmet, another dead man's gas protector, a dead man's bayonet. My tunic is rotten with other men's blood, and partly splattered with a comrade's brains. It is horrible, but why should you people at home not know? Several of my friends are raving mad. I met three officers out in No Man's Land the other night, all rambling and mad.

Lieutenant E. J. Rule of Cobar (New South Wales), newly arrived at Pozières, watched the Australians who had taken the town march by:

> They looked like men who had been in hell. Almost without exception each man looked drawn and haggard, and so dazed that they appeared to be walking in a dream, and their eyes looked glassy and starey. Quite a few were silly, and these were the only noisy ones in the crowd . . . In all my experience I've never seen men so shaken up as these.

Australia Votes for Voluntary Enlistment

So fearful were the Australian losses around Pozières that the AIF almost ceased to exist as an aggressive fighting force. Back in Australia, the humanitarian Andrew Fisher buckled under the mental strain of what he had so patriotically begun. He handed over the Prime Ministership to William Morris Hughes, a fiery, wizened little 54-year-old who endured great poverty in the outback and Sydney suburbs before rising as one of Labor's political stars.

Britain had introduced military conscription for the first time in its history in February 1916, to replace huge losses of men at Ypres and Loos in the previous two years. Similarly, W. M. Hughes came to believe that conscription of able-bodied young men was essential to fill the depleted ranks of the AIF, to help put a quick end to the war before all nations bled to death.

Under the Commonwealth's all-embracing wartime powers, conscription could have been introduced by simple Act of Parliament. Some left-wing Labor members would probably have crossed the floor against such a measure, but Liberal support would have ensured its passage. Hughes decided to go direct to the people by means of a compulsory referendum, in the hope that an overwhelming public mandate would pull all waverers into line. His philosophy was best expressed in these extracts from a 'manifesto' circulated to every voter:

> Though Europe has been drenched with blood, innocent non-combatants foully murdered or subjected to unspeakable outrages, millions of helpless men, women and little children driven from their homes, their beloved country ravaged by fire and sword, not the faintest breath of such horrors has touched these favoured shores. Though many of our brave soldiers have died on the battle field, this nation in its own home has pursued its peaceful way as though war did not exist, secure and prosperous. *But we, too, must now face the dread realities of war* . . .
>
> Our great enemy, Germany, is as yet undefeated, her mighty military power yet unbroken. Victory can only be achieved by a tremendous effort on the part of the Allies. And that effort must be made *now* . . .
>
> This is a war to the death—a fight to the finish. The future of Australia and the hopes of Australian democracy hang upon victory . . . We must supply the men asked for. It is the price we are asked to pay for our national existence and our liberties . . .
>
> The supreme duty which a democrat owes to his country is to fight for it. Others may fight for dynasties and despots, but Australians fight for Australia; for democracy against tyranny, liberty against oppression. Unless a nation fights for its liberties, it can neither earn nor deserve them.

To the astonishment of most politicians and newspapers, the referendum was lost. Men already in the armed forces voted 72,399 to 58,894 in favour of conscription. But people at home voted 1,160,033 to 1,087,557 against conscription. Three States, New South Wales, Queensland and South Australia, gave convincing 'No' votes. The Labor Party split regardless, with Hughes deciding to take many pro-conscription members with him to form a new Nationalist Party. Still Prime Minister, Hughes held a second conscription referendum at the end of 1917, after further huge slaughter of Australian troops had been suffered on the Western Front. Again he was defeated, this time by an increased proportion of votes, and with Victoria also turning against him.

Why did the electorate reject Hughes's impassioned appeals? Many reasons have been put forward, including the sheer magnitude of casualties already suffered, antagonism to Britain by Australia's large Irish population, and the reluctance of women voters to send men to death against their will. We may add a positive factor: many Australians believed in the basic principle of voluntary service—that citizens should fight only in a cause for which they believed strongly enough to sacrifice their lives. By the war's end, the AIF was unique among all the world's armies in that it suffered the highest proportion of casualties pro rata to population, while remaining composed of men who had made their own decision to enlist.

The Climactic Battles of 1917 and 1918

When would this terrible world disaster come to an end? In 1917 both sides continued to believe that with just one more gargantuan effort they could break through the enemy's defences and force their opponent to sue for peace. Back and forth on that tortured Western Front the vast offensives rocked, then ground to a halt in mud and indescribable agony.

Battle Passes

From westward, streaming down the hill,
Shot-ravaged, thinned, but urgent still,
The brown, fierce, blooded Anzacs sweep,
And Hell leaps up. The lilies weep
Strange crimson tears. Tight-lipped and mute,
The grim, gaunt soldiers stab and shoot.

TED DYSON

'Over the top'.
Bronze by
C. Web Gilbert.

WOMEN OF QUEENSLAND!

REMEMBER HOW WOMEN AND CHILDREN OF FRANCE AND BELGIUM WERE TREATED

DO YOU REALISE THAT YOUR TREATMENT WOULD ·BE· WORSE

SEND A MAN TO-DAY TO FIGHT FOR YOU

JOIN TOGETHER TRAIN TOGETHER EMBARK TOGETHER FIGHT TOGETHER

LIEUT. JACKA V.C

Enlist in the Sportsmen's Thousand

SHOW THE ENEMY WHAT AUSTRALIAN SPORTING MEN CAN DO.

Allegations of war atrocities committed against civilian populations aroused special horror during World War I, and fears that the same might one day happen in Australia. This Queensland poster by J. S. Watkins asked women to influence men into enlisting.

The TRUMPET CALLS

When casualty lists grew large in 1915–16, Donald Mackinnon, Director-General of Recruiting, proposed that Australian sporting enthusiasts should enlist *en masse*. One famous volunteer was Melbourne gambling king John Wren. **Albert Jacka**, shown on the poster, was the first Australian to win the Victoria Cross in World War I, for most conspicuous bravery at Courtney's Post on Gallipoli. He later became mayor of St Kilda (Victoria).

Australian-born artist Norman Lindsay painted many striking posters in aid of the war effort. His younger brother Daryl enlisted in the Army Service Corps and painted several wartime scenes.

In April and May 1917, the Australians were ordered to attack a strong section of the Hindenburg line around the village of Bullecourt. To help overcome the defence's 100-yard width of barbed wire and machine-gun emplacements, the British promised mass artillery support and use of the new caterpillar-track tanks. The bombardment never came, and every tank broke down. Nevertheless the Australians achieved what had been thought impossible: in the face of murderous fire they threaded their way through the wire and occupied parts of the Hindenburg line without artillery or tank support. But the two major battles of Bullecourt cost the Australians another 10,000 casualties.

In June and July 1917 fresh troops were thrown into the British offensives at Messines and Ypres. Here a further 7000 Australians were killed or wounded. The attacks were partly successful, but became mud-bound after unrelenting rain. When the weather cleared in September, the Anzacs and Canadians advanced side by side at Passchendaele, finally occupying the ruined village in November, despite intensive German use of mustard gas. About seven miles of ground were won at the cost of another 38,000 Australian casualties. Since July, nearly sixty per cent of the AIF in France had been killed or wounded.

Fresh volunteers were still trickling through from Australia. Under pressure from W. M. Hughes, the British government reluctantly agreed to form a separate Australian Corps under General Birdwood. Survivors were rested while the five Australian divisions in France filled up with the new arrivals.

In March 1918 came a long-expected crisis. Germany was heavily reinforced by troops from the Eastern Front, where Russia had collapsed into revolution and withdrawn from the war. The newly-confident Germans launched a huge onslaught at the point where the British and French armies joined, threatening to take the key city of Amiens. If the attack succeeded in splitting the Allied armies, the war on the Western Front might still be won by Germany after all.

Haig had no British reserves left to meet this grave threat. Only the refreshed Australian divisions—a mere handful of men in the overall picture—were available to defend Amiens. The Anzacs met the triumphant Germans at Dernancourt and Villers-Bretonneux, two villages south-west of Pozières, straddling the last open road to Amiens. Despite heavy casualties and great suffering from mustard gas, the thin Australian line held against continuous assaults. They were not interested in retreating. On the spot as always, Charles Bean noted in his diary: 'Our Australians have been holding nearly half the British battle line. I wonder if the British people will ever realise this?'.

The now-wearied Australians handed over defence of Villers-Bretonneux to a British relief force. The Germans immediately attacked and retook the town. Two Australian brigades, brought forward on Anzac Day, counter-attacked with such a stunning blow that the over-extended Germans abandoned their whole offensive. But it cost another 15,000 Australian casualties to turn the enemy back.

In May 1918 General Sir Hubert Gough was dismissed as a scapegoat for 'Butcher' Haig. Birdwood took Gough's place, leaving operational command of the AIF vacant. To the horror of professional soldiers, the successful contender was a mere citizen soldier, Lieutenant-General Sir John Monash, a 53-year-old Jewish Melbourne-born civil engineer who had pioneered reinforced-concrete construction work in peacetime. Monash's appointment meant that for the first time, the AIF's field commanders were all Australian-born. A master of careful planning, Monash soon showed what could be done by continual small 'cutting-out' patrols at night in the enemy trenches, followed by major attacks combining infantry, artillery, tanks and aircraft against a nervous enemy. After the Australians used these methods to capture several strategic points, Haig decided to copy them for his general offensive.

With Canadian assistance, Monash's Australian divisions formed the spearhead of this last great attack. On 8 August 1918, a day which German commander-in-chief Erich von Ludendorff described as 'the black day of the German Army in this war', the AIF advanced seven miles south of the Somme to take Hamel and some ten thousand prisoners.

Three weeks later, a small force of Australians advanced on Mont St Quentin, a heavily-fortified elevated town just north of the Somme, which was believed by

Memory, Valour and Blood

So long as Memory, Valour and Faith endure
Let these Stones witness through the years to come,
How once there was a people fenced secure
Behind great waters, girdling a far home.

Their own and their land's youth ran side by side
Heedless and headlong as their unyoked seas—
Lavish o'er all, and set in stubborn pride
Of judgment nurtured by accepted peace.

Thus, suddenly, war took them—seas and skies
Joined with the earth for slaughter in a breath
They, scoffing at all talk of sacrifice,
Gave themselves without idle words to death.

Thronging as cities throng to watch a game,
Or their own herds move southward with the year,
Secretly, swiftly, from their ports they came,
So that before half earth has heard their name
Half earth had learned to speak of them with fear;

Because of certain men who strove to reach
Through the red surf the crest no man might hold,

And gave their name forever to a beach,
Which shall outlive Troy's tale when Time is old;

Because of horsemen, gathered apart and hid—
Merciless riders whom Megiddo sent forth
When the out flanking hour struck and bid
Them close and bare the drove-roads to the North;

And those who, when men feared the last March flood
Of Western War had risen beyond recall,
Stormed through the night from Amiens and made good,
At their glad cost, the breach that perilled all.

Then they returned to their desired land—
The kindly cities and plains where they were bred—
Having revealed their Nation in earth's sight
So long as Sacrifice and Honour stand,
And their own Sun at the hushed hour shall light
The Shrine of these their Dead!

RUDYARD KIPLING, dedicatory ode cast in bronze at the
Shrine of Remembrance, Melbourne.

Men of the AIF 2nd
Division coming out of the
front line in 1917.

'**The Drover**', painting by George Benson in 1918, shows **a lone Australian mustering his prisoners.**

Sir John Monash, the brilliant Australian-born civil engineer who rose from command of a brigade on Gallipoli to full command of the Australian Army Corps in France. Painting by Sir John Longstaff.

the British to be impregnable to infantry attack. On Monash's orders the men were issued with rum before instead of after the battle. In darkness they crept up the slopes and through the barbed wire, fixed their bayonets, then charged the startled Germans shouting 'like a lot of bushrangers'. Within a few hours the town had fallen and its elite force of Prussian Guards taken prisoner. To many, the conquest of Mont St Quentin seemed the most brilliant feat of the war. When Monash phoned the British High Command with the news, they at first refused to believe it. When confirmed, the victory did wonders for Allied morale.

Scenting complete ascendancy over the now demoralised Germans, the Australians—assisted by two raw American divisions—raced to attack the main section of the Hindenburg line. On 3 October 1918 they broke through the three elaborate lines of German trenches and pillboxes. Two days later, they fought the last Australian battle of the war to capture Montbrehain. By this time the surviving Australians were totally exhausted. 'Their faded, earth-stained uniforms hung loosely from bodies which had lost as much as two stone in as many months', wrote Lieutenant H. R. Williams. 'Sheer determination and wonderful *esprit de corps* had enabled these gallant fellows to work when physically they were done.'

The Australian achievement had been incredible. Since Villers-Bretonneux seven months earlier, they had not lost a single battle. They had taken nearly thirty thousand prisoners and advanced forty miles, to help break the stalemate on the Western Front and be recognised as a major factor in ending the war. While they were still advancing, Germany began seeking a truce, and on 11 November 1918 an armistice was signed.

The dreadful struggle was over. But at what cost! Of the 330,000 Australians

The Husband

Yes, I have slain, and taken moving life
From bodies. Yea! And laughed upon the taking;
And, having slain, have whetted still the knife
For more and more, and heeded not the making
Of things that I was killing. Such 'twas then!
But now the thirst so hideous has left me.
I live within a coolness, among calm men,
And yet am strange. A something has bereft me
Of a seeing, and strangely love returns;
And old desires half-known, and hanging sorrows.
I seem agaze with wonder. Memory burns.
I see a thousand vague and sad to-morrows.
None sees my sadness. No one understands
How I must touch her hair with bloody hands.

LEON GELLERT

Russell Drysdale's painting **War Memorial** conveys the eerie presence in postwar towns and cities of young men who would never return in the flesh—who would never grow old, 'as we that are left grow old'.

who enlisted for overseas service, two out of every three were killed or wounded. Nearly sixty thousand Australian dead lay in foreign graves. No other nation had sacrificed so freely or voluntarily its vigorous young men. When people said that the flower of a whole generation had perished, they spoke the literal truth. The nation's memories began to fade as successive years brought new crises. But not one of the battle-hardened survivors of the Great War was left unscarred.

5. 'I Speak for 60,000 Dead': W. M. Hughes to Woodrow Wilson

W. M. Hughes, 'the little digger', painted by Augustus John.

The official Labor Party never forgave W. M. Hughes for the deep political split caused by his two conscription referendums. But there was no questioning the Prime Minister's motives in wanting the world to recognise the men of the AIF. After several visits by Hughes to the front lines, most diggers realised that this was not just another politician, but one who meant what he said about trying to rally Australia behind their efforts. They began to idolise him as 'the little digger'—who, as well as being their national leader, seemed also a kind of indomitable mascot.

Some of the diggers also appreciated the complex nature of the political battles which Hughes had to fight. The little man was insistent that Australia's remarkable war effort should be acknowledged by Britain and the world. In 1917 he persuaded the British government that after the war there should be 'full recognition of the Dominions as autonomous nations of an Imperial Commonwealth'. Each unit should have 'an adequate voice in foreign policy and foreign relations', with 'continuous consultation in all important matters of common Imperial concern'.

Yet when the Allied Supreme War Council met just before the war ended, it privately arranged, without even the pretence of consultation with Dominion Prime Ministers, to base the armistice on American President Woodrow Wilson's idealistic 'Fourteen Points'. Germany had already secretly agreed to Wilson's proposals while hostilities were still in progress.

Hughes was enraged when he discovered the truth. He told British Prime Minister David Lloyd George that the Australian government was 'surprised and indignant that conditions of peace should have been decided without Australia being consulted'. This was regarded as 'a painful and serious breach of faith'. Australia could never accept President Wilson's attitudes on lower tariffs, racial exclusion, and German colonies in the Pacific, all of which would seriously affect Australia's right to decide its own future. As Lloyd George wrote later:

> The Imperial Cabinet was much impressed with the critical power of the Hughes speech. It was their first explanation of the reason why this man of frail physique, defective hearing and eccentric gesticulations had obtained such a position of dominant influence in the Australian Commonwealth. It was a fine specimen of ruthless and pungent analysis of President Wilson's claim to dictate to the countries that had borne the brunt of the fighting.

Even France and America gave way before the fierce little man's onslaught. Georges Clemenceau, the French 'tiger' who brought his tortured country through the war, developed an admiration for Hughes, describing him in his memoirs as 'the noble delegate from Australia', who spoke 'symphonies of good sense'. In January 1919, as the Versailles Peace Conference began, the major Allied powers finally agreed that the British Empire delegation should be expanded to include two representatives each for Australia and the other Dominions.

Hughes made full use of Australia's first participation in a major world settlement. According to one delegate, he was the only member who could leave Woodrow Wilson speechless. When Wilson tried to object to Australian scorn for his beloved Fourteen Points, Hughes replied, 'Mr President, I speak for 60,000 dead. How many do you speak for?'. Wilson had no answer.

Hughes's main objective was to ensure that the islands to Australia's north were not occupied by any potential enemy who could 'pounce on us on the mainland'. At first he attempted to obtain full sovereignty over German possessions in the South Pacific—mainly New Guinea and the phosphate-rich island of Nauru. A compromise was reached with the creation of special 'mandated territories', in which Australia governed according to her own laws, but was responsible to the newly-created League of Nations for welfare of the native races. Many years later, when the Japanese advance of World War II was halted in New Guinea, Australia reaped the benefit of Hughes's foresight and pertinacity.

At Versailles meanwhile, the Japanese, Britain's supposed allies who had stood by while other nations bled almost to death, lobbied continuously for insertion of a clause guaranteeing 'equal and just treatment in every respect' of all races and nationalities. Woodrow Wilson liked the sound of that, perhaps forgetting the harsh treatment still being handed out to Negroes in America. To Hughes it was a direct attack on the White Australia Policy, involving the prospect of mass Japanese infiltration into Australia. Addressing the Japanese delegate, he said, 'Your ideals, your institutions, your standards, are not ours. We do not say that ours are greater or better than yours; we only say they are different'. Hughes won this confrontation as well.

On 28 June 1919 the peace treaty was finally signed. Hughes arrived back in Australia two months later to a tumultuous reception led by returned Anzacs. Newspapers reported that 'the idol of the masses' took more than an hour to make his way from the station to Melbourne Town Hall: 'but if his progress was slow, it was as triumphant as that of an old-time general returning to Rome'. The Little Digger was perched high on a motor car, 'though returned soldiers clustered so thickly upon it that it was invisible'. Hughes was captured by the diggers as soon as he stepped off the train, and his car dragged through the streets by forty enthusiastic men: 'Their devotion to Mr Hughes is as unreserved as it is remarkable'.

We believe in our race and in ourselves, and in our capacity to achieve our great destiny, which is to hold this vast continent in trust for those of our race who come after us.

W. M. HUGHES, 1919.

What has been won? If the fruits of victory are to be measured by national safety and liberty, and the high ideals for which these boys died, the sacrifice has not been in vain. They died for the safety of Australia. Australia is safe. They died for liberty, and liberty is now assured to us and to all men. They have made for themselves and their country a name that will not die . . .

Industrially, socially, politically, we cannot, any more than other nations, escape the consequences of the war. The whole world lies bleeding and exhausted from the frightful struggle . . . There is hope for this free Australia of ours only if we put aside our differences, strive to emulate the deeds of those who by their valour and sacrifice have given us liberty and safety, and resolve to be worthy of them and the cause for which they fought.

W. M. HUGHES to Federal Parliament, 10 September 1919.

6. Experience of War Stimulates Heroic Aviation Deeds

'**Archaeopteryx**', by official RAAF war artist Eric Thake, symbolises how humanity broke free from its earthbound state.

BELOW
Top. Eric Thake's design for a five-cent stamp commemorating the pioneering flight from England to Australia in 1919.
Middle. Charles Kingsford Smith's amazing flights were commemorated in one of Australia's first pictorial stamps, issued in 1931.
Bottom. Development of Australia's own international airline was commemorated in this 1970 stamp.

A new generation arose in the 1920s to whom 'the Great War' was already a somewhat legendary event in the making of a nation. New optimism bloomed with the new era: to young people of the 1920s, one of the most profound results of the war was the enormous stimulus given to aviation development. Australians, still scattered thinly over great distances, were ready to take to the air.

The first epic postwar adventure began in 1919 when Prime Minister W. M. Hughes offered a £10,000 prize to the first Australians to fly a British-made aircraft from London to Australia in less than thirty days. Six Australian crews entered the contest and left Britain in a wide assortment of warplanes during late October and early November 1919. One crashed soon after take-off; one fell into the Mediterranean; one crashed in Crete; one came down in Bali; and two managed to reach Darwin.

Outright winner was a Vickers Vimy bomber, which landed at Darwin in the then-astonishing flying time of 136 hours, spread over twenty-eight days. Its pilots were two brothers, Ross and Keith Smith, aged 27 and 29 years respectively, both Adelaide-born, and both renowned as war pilots. Their large twin-engined machine, developed in the last year of the war, had a cruising range of 2400 miles. After several close brushes with disaster *en route*, they touched down at Darwin on 10 December 1919, then continued through Queensland to Sydney and Melbourne like conquering heroes.

The nation's first regular air service began in Western Australia late in 1921, when Major Norman Brearley won the first airmail contract, a once-a-week flight of 1200 miles between Geraldton and Derby on the north-west coast. Brearley,

144

holder of a Distinguished Service Order and Military Cross from his days with the Australian Flying Corps, formed Western Australian Airways, later extending the service to Perth and Adelaide.

On the other side of Australia, Queensland & Northern Territory Aerial Services (Qantas) had been formed in 1920 to provide joy-rides and charter flights. Its founders were two more AFC officers, Wilmot Hudson Fysh, DFC, and Patrick McGinness, financed by a group of Queensland graziers. Squatters had once financed Leichhardt's explorations: now they backed the pioneer ventures of Qantas over the same territory.

In 1922 Qantas won the first airmail contract to cover the 580 miles between Charleville and Cloncurry, using converted Armstrong-Whitworth warplanes. Within six years the company expanded to operate the nation's first daily air service between Brisbane and Toowoomba. In 1934 Qantas won the first major airmail contract between Australia and Britain. In partnership with British Imperial Airways, it formed Qantas Empire Airways with Hudson Fysh as its chief.

A leisurely but comfortable Empire flying boat passenger service to England began in 1938. After World War II the Chifley Labor government nationalised the company, but Fysh remained as chairman. Although now in his fifties and a civil servant, Fysh was determined to keep Qantas in the vanguard of world aviation. In 1958 he bought two of the new Super Constellations and began Australia's first round-the-world service, taking the flying kangaroo to many more parts of the globe. The following year, Boeing agreed to deliver its modern giant jet-liners to Qantas ahead of every airline outside the United States.

Today's flights to America still keep fairly closely to the trail blazed by Australians in the first trans-Pacific flight of 1928. Two adventurous war veterans, Queenslander Charles Kingsford Smith, 31, and Victorian Charles Ulm, 30, were certain that the enormous reaches of the Pacific Ocean—6400 miles—could be crossed safely by air. To arouse interest, they flew an old Bristol plane around Australia in ten days, cutting the previous record in half. Urged on by the Returned Services League, New South Wales Labor Premier J. T. Lang granted £3500 to the trans-Pacific scheme. With this the airmen bought a damaged three-engine Fokker monoplane which Sir Hubert Wilkins had used in polar exploration. Further donations from Melbourne retailer Sidney Myer, Vacuum Oil, American bankers, Australian newspapers and other private sources paid for three new Wright Whirlwind motors.

The patched-together plane became the famous *Southern Cross*, in which Kingsford Smith, Charles Ulm and two American navigators flew safely from California to Honolulu, Fiji and Brisbane. The 36-hour stage from Honolulu to Fiji established a new world record for the longest time aloft. Australia and the world spoke of nothing else as radio stations stayed open all night to broadcast shortwave messages direct from the plane. When the aviators landed at Brisbane, a crowd of 10,000 who had waited through the night swarmed through the barriers and mobbed the pilots in 'an ecstasy of enthusiasm'.

Kingsford Smith and Ulm continued to break records throughout the world for the next few years. Then fate ordained that they should die young, like Anzacs at the height of their courage and audacity. Ulm disappeared on a flight from America in 1934 and was never found. The following year Kingsford Smith also disappeared, probably in a tropical storm off the coast of Burma, while flying the *Lady Southern Cross* home from England. Australians felt they had lost their greatest hero—the man who had conquered aerial routes and records too difficult for anyone else.

By the time of the memorable London to Melbourne Sesquicentennial air race of 1934, the winning De Havilland Comet monoplane was able to cover the 12,000 miles in just under three days. Compare this with only a century before, when convict and immigrant vessels beat their way over the seas. The average time taken for that journey was 120 days. Conquest of the air, with its forty-fold reduction in time, meant that Australia's isolation from the rest of the world was fast disappearing. World War II, which would end that isolation forever, was now only five years away.

During the 1920s the **Rev. Dr John Flynn**, a Presbyterian missionary, used Alfred Traeger's invention of the pedal wireless to begin the world's first radio-controlled Flying Doctor service for the inland. Qantas provided a De Havilland 50 aircraft based at Cloncurry (Queensland). **One of the first flying doctors, George Simpson, is shown at left with his wife.**

7. 'Men, Money, Markets'— Rallying Cries of the 1920s

As the armed forces were demobilised, Federal and State governments combined to finance 'Farms for heroes'. Mass settlement of returned soldiers on the land was seen as a fitting reward for their efforts, and a way of increasing Australia's prosperity. But the best land was left practically untouched. Of the 30 million acres selected for soldier settlement up to 1930, only one-fifth was acquired from private owners. Most soldiers' blocks consisted of dry and dusty Crown land on the margin of existing settlement. Huge expenditure was incurred in clearing and bringing water to these blocks. Here, remote from public view, men back from the Western Front 'soldiered on' to raise families in heartbreaking poverty comparable with anything undergone by 19th-century selectors.

Few of the States dared produce statistics of the results. It was known that in New South Wales, nearly four thousand of the 10,000 soldier settlers forfeited their blocks and presumably drifted to the cities. In Western Australia, the Agricultural Bank still held mortgages ten years later over 70 per cent of the 5200 blocks allotted. Throughout Australia, more than £23 million of public money was never recovered from loans to soldier settlers.

In Federal Parliament, meanwhile, W. M. Hughes lost leadership of the ruling Nationalist Party early in 1923 when he was unable to hold continuous support from the new Country Party. As often happens, a popular wartime leader was considered no longer effective for the different demands of peacetime.

The incoming Prime Minister, Stanley Melbourne Bruce, at first sight seemed an unlikely choice for the Australian democracy. Son of a wealthy softgoods

The **first Federal Parliament building** was finally ready in 1927. Inside the new building, W. B. McInnes was commissioned to paint the **official opening by the Duke of York**, later King George VI.

H. Septimus Power was commissioned to paint the scene as dignitaries arrived at the **first Federal Parliament building**.

importer, educated at Melbourne Grammar and Cambridge University, always faultlessly dressed even to the wearing of spats, Bruce was the antithesis of the popular Australian image. A background like his sometimes produced fine, highly-competitive individuals, but they were not generally noted for practical sympathy towards the underdogs of society. But as a British officer Bruce had also fought and been wounded on Gallipoli. This made his upper-class background and accent more acceptable to voters of the early 1920s.

Viewing the international scene, Bruce could not perceive any early strategic threat to Australia. He allowed defence forces to run down to the lowest proportion known in peacetime, concentrating government expenditure instead on what he summed up as 'Men, Money and Markets'. All three factors were linked in a grand design to increase Australia's population and economic strength.

During most of the 1920s, Bruce's policies seemed to work well. The 'Men' or population part of his programme was expected to come from both natural increase during prosperous times and an expanded immigration scheme. And Australia's population did rise, from 5·4 million at the census of 1921 to 6·4 million when

Australian industries had regained some of their prosperity when Russell Drysdale painted '**Industrial Landscape 1937**'.

147

The Big Brother Movement brought 12,000 young migrants from Britain to Australia after its formation in 1925. In 1983, the Hawke Labor government withdrew preferential treatment from the movement.

S. M. Bruce created the Commonwealth Police Force in 1925 and immediately won an election on the well-known issue of 'Law and Order'. Bruce also strove to increase British migration and trade.

Bruce lost power in 1929. Of this increase, about one-quarter was due to immigration from Britain. Under an agreement concluded in 1925, Britain and Australia shared two-thirds of the cost of sending approved migrants to Australia. As in the previous century, Britain was happy to lose some of her surplus population, while retaining them as part of her market in an Australia happy to see her own population boosted.

The 'Money' part of Bruce's expansionary programme came from a unique agreement signed by Britain and Australia, under which £34 million would be loaned to State governments at only 2 per cent interest for the construction of public works and expansion of rural settlement. Each immigrant accepted by a State meant an additional loan of £75 to that State. The money was spent largely on water conservation schemes, roads, afforestation, construction of butter and sugar factories, and other rural works. Such was the price paid by Bruce to the Country Party for supporting him in power. Yet the scheme was basically unsound. Of the 22,400 assisted migrants who arrived in 1928, less than one-fifth found rural occupations. The remainder settled in the cities as factory and shop workers. That was where the jobs were, and the schools, and continuous union attention to working conditions, and the best prospects for advancement. The rural loans remained as a charge on the public purse.

The question of 'Markets' was even more contentious. Australian factories had boomed since their sudden expansion during the pressures of World War I. To protect them from cheap imports, while not antagonising British exporters, Bruce preserved Hughes's ingenious Customs Tariff Act of 1921. This provided for a General Tariff, an Intermediate Tariff, and a British Preferential Tariff. Overall, any goods which could be made in Australia in 'plants of sufficient magnitude to constitute an economic unit' were heavily protected against foreign competition. However, goods made in Britain and other white-dominated parts of the Empire could be imported into Australia at lower tariff rates, averaging 32 per cent instead of the general rate of 46 per cent. A four-member Tariff Board formed in 1921 was kept busy allotting thousands of different items into their correct categories, and hearing appeals from manufacturers and importers.

The total effect was to strengthen Empire commerce, while limiting imports of goods made by despised 'coloured labour'. The policy amounted to an attempt to manipulate world trading patterns and maintain Australia's dependence on Britain, while retaining the economic basis of the White Australia Policy against increasing restiveness in the Pacific region. Under this restrictive trade system, Australian manufacturing production increased from £320 million to £420 million during the 1920s, and factory employment from 337,000 to four hundred and fifty thousand. Urbanisation continued apace.

Whatever his success in temporarily boosting the economy, the patrician Bruce seemed less interested in questions of social justice affecting ordinary people. During nearly seven years in power he introduced not a single basic measure of wealth redistribution or assistance for those in need. Only in Queensland and New South Wales, under the Theodore and Lang State Labor governments, were the first laws introduced to pay pensions to widows, and child endowment of five shillings per child each week to parents.

Indeed, Bruce seemed to go out of his way to attack the rights so painfully built up by Australian workers. In March 1929 he refused leave to prosecute John Brown, a New South Wales colliery owner, for breaching the Arbitration Act by locking out his employees. Six months later, under the pretext of returning the Commonwealth's constitutional powers on compulsory arbitration to the States, Bruce introduced a Bill to abolish the Arbitration Court altogether.

With the support of other dissentients, W. M. Hughes managed to bring down Bruce's government. At the election of October 1929, the public voted overwhelmingly against the Nationalists. Six cabinet ministers lost their seats. Even in the previously conservative Victorian electorate of Flinders, Bruce himself was defeated—the only Prime Minister in Australian history to lose his seat at an election. The people had spoken: whatever the faults of the national arbitration system, politicians must not attempt to do away with it.

8. James Scullin Forces Appointment of First Australian-Born Governor-General

James Scullin, heading Labor forces which routed S. M. Bruce's Nationalist government just before the Wall Street crash of 1929, was a type of idealistic leader we shall not see again. The son of Irish gold-rush immigrants, Scullin received little formal schooling. As a lad he was forced to work in Ballarat stamping batteries to help support the family. Who could forecast that this frail, ragged waif would rise to become Prime Minister and successfully defy the world's greatest monarch?

In 1921, when the Australian Labor Party adopted its policy of nationalising the means of production, distribution and exchange, Scullin joined Labor's Council of Action which would 'direct the socialisation of industry' after Labor regained power. In some unexplained way, the objective was to be achieved by strictly constitutional means. Then the millenium would dawn as control of each industry was handed over to elected workers' councils.

In 1928, when another Ballarat-born ex-miner named Matthew Charlton retired as Federal Labor leader, Scullin won the position with ease. He began to criticise Bruce's policy of large overseas borrowings which were financing the programme of 'Men, Money and Markets', warning that it might lead to a depression. In 1929, as unemployment began to increase and Bruce continued his assault on the arbitration system, Scullin was elected to power with a record majority in the lower house. This was the first Federal Labor victory since the split during World War I, and Scullin was Australia's first Catholic Prime Minister.

With economic conditions continuing to worsen, but with Labor still enjoying wide public support, Scullin sailed to London in 1930 to attend an Imperial Conference of Prime Ministers. He gladly went along with the British view that since war seemed 'very unlikely during the next ten years', it would be safe to defer completion of the Singapore naval base. Even after visiting Sheffield and watching armour-piercing shells being manufactured for sale to Japan, Scullin agreed that 'Japan in particular is unlikely to disturb the peace'.

Scullin had gone to London with quite a different interest: to reinforce Australian independence and nationalism by winning approval for a Governor-General born in Australia, not imported from Britain. First he obtained agreement from the British Lord Chancellor, the Labor peer Baron John Sankey, that in the selection of all new Governors-General, the King should accept the advice of Dominion Prime Ministers, after informal talks.

Scullin then put forward the name of Sir Isaac Isaacs, Chief Justice of the High Court. Isaacs had long been a special hero to Scullin. Born in Melbourne in 1855, son of a humble Polish tailor, the brilliant young Jew became a leading barrister, and in 1893 was appointed Victorian Solicitor-General. In 1906 he was appointed to the High Court, joining Justice H. B. Higgins in many radical interpretations of the Constitution.

At a private interview on 29 November 1930, King George V told Scullin, 'It is now thirty years since I opened the Commonwealth Parliament in Australia. Since then we have sent many Governors, Commonwealth and State, and I hope they have not all been failures?'. Scullin agreed they had not, but insisted on his policy. The King replied, 'I have been for twenty years a monarch and I hope I have always been a constitutional one, and being a constitutional monarch I must, Mr Scullin, accept your advice'.

The question of the Governor-Generalship was practically the only victory enjoyed by Scullin during the terrible years of economic depression engulfing Australia and the world. In every other respect Scullin has to be remembered as

Justice and Humanity demand interference whenever the weak are being crushed by the strong.

Inscription on the grave of James Henry Scullin (1876–1953).

James Scullin, Labor Prime Minister when the Great Depression began. Painting by W. B. McInnes.

Above right. **Sir Isaac Isaacs,** first Australian-born Governor-General. Painting by Sir John Longstaff.

We were asked to indicate the class of candidate we would like and we nominated one whom we knew was an Australian, who understood the Australian people, and the nomination, judged by standards of integrity and culture, training and public service, excelled any of the Governors-General who had ever been sent to Australia.

JAMES SCULLIN

'Unlucky Jim'. No matter which way he turned, a succession of obstacles blocked his best efforts to relieve the suffering of millions of ordinary people suddenly faced with destitution.

Sir Robert Gibson, 66-year-old Scottish-born manufacturer appointed by S. M. Bruce as chairman of a board of businessmen to supervise the Commonwealth Bank, soon asked to see the Prime Minister. Gibson gave figures to Scullin showing that a huge adverse trade balance against Australia had been accumulating since 1925. Much of the country's gold reserves had been lost in trying to bridge the gap. Now wool and wheat prices were dropping fast as overseas demand slackened. One of the last acts of Bruce's government had been to float £5 million in Treasury bills on the London market: these fell due for repayment in less than a year. 'I was staggered', said Scullin. 'Those obligations had to be met at a time when prices had tumbled and the volume of exports had fallen'.

The Bank of England urged that its chief financial director, Sir Otto Niemeyer, should lead a team of experts to investigate Australia's position. After a short tour, Niemeyer warned the Premiers' Conference in August 1930 that Australian living standards had been pushed too high in relation to productivity. Australian workers were 'enjoying a champagne standard on a small beer income'. Faced with the unanimous if conservative opinion of bankers, Commonwealth and States agreed to cut all government expenditure drastically in an attempt to balance their budgets. The Australian pound was depreciated in relation to sterling. The basic wage was cut by 10 per cent to match the fall in prices. Civil servants' salaries and pensions were cut by an average of 20 per cent. After an appeal to the patriotism of holders of maturing government bonds, 97 per cent agreed to convert their holdings voluntarily to lower rates of interest. Scullin called this 'one of the great achievements in Australia's history', although it has since been forgotten.

Scullin's brave attempts to ensure 'equality of sacrifice' could not stem the flood of misery sweeping over Australia. During 1931 and 1932 one breadwinner in every three fell unemployed, becoming totally dependent on charity and government food tickets to keep his or her family alive. Thousands who could not pay rent were evicted into the streets, to build bag humpies on the outskirts of cities. Ugly riots occurred in many areas: in Adelaide a mob demanding extra assistance stormed the State Treasury. Other men left their families to tramp from town to town as itinerant beggars. Immigration and many public works were halted, while the birth rate plummeted to the lowest level known since early convict days. And this in a land which, as W. M. Hughes pointed out, was still producing enough wheat to feed 30 million people and enough wool to clothe 100 million.

Mainly because of its dependence on export prices, Australia's unemployment rose to the second-highest rate in the world. Only Germany, shattered by World War I and huge reparations payments, suffered more. There the depression ensured the rise of Hitler's Nazi Party and Europe's swift descent into World War II. In Australia, with its different national characteristics, most people simply gritted their teeth and battled on. Essentially they clung to democratic ways even though the experience nearly killed them.

Scullin, now white-haired and grey with worry, made a final attempt to invigorate the collapsing economic system. In conjunction with his Treasurer, the brilliant but controversial E. G. ('Red Ted') Theodore, Scullin helped to guide a Fiduciary Notes Bill through Labor caucus and the House of Representatives. Basically the Bill was an attempt to circumvent the conservatism of bankers by printing a further £18 million in Commonwealth bank notes, without gold backing, to add to the £50 million in notes already issued. The extra money would finance unemployment relief works and assist small wheat farmers facing ruin.

This imaginative scheme, first of its kind in the world, would undoubtedly have helped to counter the intense deflationary tendencies of the depression. But Scullin met the last of his great problems: implacable opposition from a Senate still controlled by conservatives. Elected on a different time schedule from the House of Representatives, the Senate had not suffered the same landslide vote which tumbled S. M. Bruce from power. When Opposition Senators rejected the Fiduciary Notes Bill, Scullin commented bitterly: 'History will record that they have been guilty of a crime against humanity'.

At first the effects of the depression were most obvious in New South Wales,

If the problem of unemployment were tackled on scientific lines the public works policy of the Commonwealth as a whole would be formulated so that during times of general industrial depression there would be an impetus to work of this character, with a corresponding curtailment during times of general industrial prosperity.

JAMES SCULLIN in 1929.

The one God-given, inalienable right of man is the right to live. If a man or woman is denied the right to work, he and she still retain the right to live. The Government which fails to realise this has forfeited the right to exist.

J. T. LANG

J. T. Lang, Labor Premier of New South Wales, dismissed by the Governor for refusing to pay interest payments to bondholders during the Depression. Painting by Fred Leist.

William Joseph Duggan, a plumber and champion boxer, became first president of the newly-formed Australian Council of Trade Unions in 1927. In September 1930 the ACTU resolved that the Niemeyer Plan should be rejected. This was a direct encouragement to J. T. Lang to repudiate interest payments to British bondholders.

I proposed that we should fund our debt as Britain had funded her war debt to America. Firstly, America had agreed to suspend all interest payments for three years. Then Mr Baldwin had persuaded the Americans to reduce interest charges from 5 per cent to 3 per cent, rising to 3½ per cent, with payments spread over 62 years . . .

Many Australian unemployed had soldiered in France. They had made sacrifices on the battlefield. Now they were repeating them in Australia. Why should they face another ten years of misery and privation? There would have been no hardship and suffering had Australia not gone to Britain's aid. Should the men who had done the fighting now go without the necessities of life in order that the international money ring should have its pound of flesh?

J. T. LANG

hit hardest by a huge drop in commodity prices after the Wall Street crash. The reaction of the Nationalist Premier, 56-year-old barrister Thomas Bavin, was to cut wages and public works, and abolish the 44-hour week. At the State election of October 1930, Bavin lost power in landslide voting for the Labor Party, led by the 54-year-old Catholic John Thomas Lang, a relation by marriage of the poet Henry Lawson. Lang was one of the most remarkable characters thrown up by the perennial struggle within the Labor Party to achieve positions of power. He survived the 1890s depression to become a successful real estate agent in the Sydney working-class suburb of Auburn. From that strong base he was able to enter New South Wales politics and dominate it through changing fortunes for many years. During the depression Lang's overwhelming desire was to use all the resources of government to preserve employment and create new jobs. Nothing else mattered. Constitutional practice, contractual obligations, long-term plans, could all be sacrificed to the immediate need to succour the unemployed.

When he came to power in 1930, Lang found that Bavin had left him with a current account deficit of £5 million. Loan funds for public works had been exhausted. A further deficit of £3 million burdened the railways account, partly due to expenditure on the new Sydney Harbour Bridge. Lang's new government set to work undismayed. In rapid succession it passed Acts to restore the 44-hour week, prevent seizure of personal possessions of evicted tenants, and extend the period of mortgage agreements for three years. These measures ameliorated some hardships. But the great need was to expand works to create new employment.

Lang soon came to the conclusion that there was no way to finance new public works and continue to pay large interest bills on the public debt at the same time. On 27 March 1931 Lang notified Scullin officially that the New South Wales government could not and would not meet interest payments due to London bondholders. Federal Labor in turn repudiated the Lang government, expelling all its members from the official Labor Party. Fearful depositors in the New South Wales Government Savings Bank rushed to withdraw their cash, forcing the bank to close its doors on 23 April.

Towards the end of 1931, Sir Philip Game, the British-born Governor of New South Wales, began to play an important role in the crisis. After the Legislative Council rejected seven government Bills in two days, Game agreed on 20 November 1931 to swamp the upper house by nominating twenty-five new members.

Lang, temporarily triumphant, continued to refuse interest payments to bondholders—now amounting to the huge sum, for those days, of £7 million. In order to preserve what was left of Australia's credit rating, the new Lyons United Australia Party government in Canberra paid the interest and sued Lang for reimbursement. By proclamation of the Governor-General, all taxes due in New South Wales were ordered to be paid direct to the Commonwealth until the amount had been made up. Banks were instructed not to honour State cheques. At one stage no State government employees, from teachers to Government House gardeners, received their fortnightly pay.

On 22 April 1932, the High Court decided by a small majority (Chief Justice Sir Frank Gavan Duffy and Justice H. V. Evatt dissenting) that the Commonwealth proclamation was valid. Lang promptly instructed his departmental chiefs to continue refusing to pay State funds to Federal authorities. In a final desperate bid, on 11 May Lang introduced a new Bill taxing all mortgages registered in New South Wales to a total of £7 million, payable within a fortnight. This near-confiscation might have enabled him to pay the Commonwealth, but already the jig was up. The following day Sir Philip Game warned Lang that he must obey the High Court decision forthwith. 'I cannot possibly allow the Crown to be placed in the position of breaking the law of the land', he wrote to the Premier. Lang still refused to back down, claiming that his primary duty was to maintain 'the essential and social services of the State'.

On 13 May 1932 Game withdrew Lang's commission, and the Lang government came to a sudden end. At the election which followed in June, Lang Labor candidates were decimated—exactly as happened to candidates of the Whitlam Labor government in somewhat similar circumstances nearly half a century later.

9. Harbour Bridge and Australia Day: Symbols of National Recovery

The Sydney Harbour Bridge soared skywards and northwards during the good times of the 1920s and the bad times of the early 1930s. During the boom, the mighty structure provided a symbol of confidence and expansionism; during the depression, as people tightened their belts, it represented the hope that prosperity would return. Surprisingly, there was little interstate jealousy of this great scheme for joining Sydney's south and north shores: rather 'the Bridge' became revered as a national symbol second only to the Australian flag.

A bridge to span the half mile of deep water was first suggested in 1815 by the convict architect Francis Greenway. Several alternative proposals emerged during the 19th century, but lack of finance and engineering skill defeated each one. During World War I, John Bradfield, a Queensland-born civil engineer, perfected plans for a high single-arch bridge which he felt could cross the harbour while allowing room for ships to pass underneath. Overseas contractors confirmed that it could be built using new types of steel. In 1922 the New South Wales government passed a Harbour Bridge Act. Total cost was estimated at £5.75 million, to be financed by the Railways Department and an improvement tax on North Shore land values. By the time of completion, expenditure had nearly doubled. The Lang government introduced a toll of one shilling per vehicle to finance the extra cost.

At the official opening on 19 March 1932, an extreme right-wing organisation known as the New Guard decided to prevent Premier Lang from claiming credit for the bridge. One of its members, Captain F. E. de Groot, rode forward and slashed the ribbon with his sword, shouting 'On behalf of decent and loyal citizens of New South Wales, I now declare this bridge open'. Acting Police Commissioner W. J. MacKay seized de Groot by the leg, lifted him clean out of the saddle, and threw him on the ground. Next day the New Guardsman was fined five pounds.

The incident was treated by the huge celebrating crowd on the bridge as one more reason for jollification. As night fell, they remained outdoors to watch a dazzling fireworks display over the harbour, complementing the illuminated outlines of bridge, ships and pleasure craft.

Coincidentally, the worst aspects of the depression at last began to ease. In 1933 the number of unemployed fell for the first time since 1929. By 1938 unemployment had fallen to the normal rate of the preceding decade, and both State and Federal budgets were being balanced. Rural industry also gradually recovered, increasing exports and enabling Australia to meet her overseas debts. Manufacturing, particularly in the steel and motor industries, grew substantially under tariff protection. By 1939 an additional 100,000 workers were employed in Australian factories, compared with ten years earlier.

Across Sydney Harbour has been thrown the greatest arch bridge of the age, a commanding structure with stately towers that stand like the Pillars of Hercules bestriding the tide . . . It is the heaviest, the widest and the greatest single span arch yet constructed by man . . . Its vast sweeping curves, from wherever one may view it, give a sense of rhythm and harmony, of strength combined with lightness and grace:

SYDNEY MORNING HERALD, 20 March 1932.

Ironworkers who built the Sydney Harbour Bridge gather at the end of the giant construction on its completion in 1932.

The Sydney Harbour Bridge under construction, painted in 1929 by Frances Derham.

'The Land, Boys, We Live In'

Most nations set aside special days to commemorate their foundation or other turning points in their history. In Australia the practice of celebrating the date of Governor Arthur Phillip's landing at Sydney Cove—26 January 1788—began sixteen years later, when a sufficient number of free residents realised that Australia would be their permanent home. On the thirtieth anniversary in 1818, Governor Macquarie declared an annual public holiday for 26 January. Each year a salute boomed out over Sydney Harbour, the number of shots being increased according to the number of years since 1788. As they counted the shots, residents of Sydney began to feel some sense of tradition and achievement.

In 1825, the 80-year-old ex-convict poet Michael Massey Robinson, who had been transported for threatening to publish libellous verses, proposed his famous toast at the annual celebration: 'The land, boys, we live in'.

For many years Foundation Day was not as popular in other parts of the continent. The younger colonies did not particularly wish to celebrate the landing of convicts in Sydney Cove. Not until the Centennial celebrations of 1888 did these attitudes begin to change. For the first time, all Australian colonies celebrated 26 January 1888 as a public holiday. But the tendency of Australians was always to refuse to take the anniversary too seriously. They preferred to use it as a day for enjoyment. Regattas, picnics, sporting events, and other outdoor amusements were always more popular than formal celebrations. By the early years of this century it had become customary to tack the holiday on to the first weekend after 26 January, giving a three-day break which was greatly appreciated by all during the heat of Australian summers.

In 1984 a massive attempt began to convince people that they should take 26 January more seriously. Millions of dollars were spent by government and business sponsors to stage public events throughout the nation. The Governor-General, State Governors and armed forces took part in various official ceremonies, and sporting heroes were singled out for special praise.

A growing school of thought believes that a more suitable date should be found to celebrate Australia Day. The anniversary of the founding of the Australian Commonwealth—1 January 1901—seems more appropriate. It also gives a better opportunity for national leaders to survey the years past and the years ahead. The three-day holiday at the end of January could remain exactly what it is—a midsummer festival needing no other justification.

Australia Day was commemorated by this special stamp issue in 1978.

10. Films Help to Create Australian Legends

Love of country lies deep in people's hearts, and is often best expressed through emotional reactions to films, art, theatre and music. In a brief look at the history of film-making in Australia, we find that the most successful films have been those which made a genuine attempt to explore the feelings, interests, sufferings and strivings of ordinary people and their folk heroes.

The outbreak of World War I brought a flood of directly patriotic films. W. F. Barrett made 'Australia's Peril', in which troops rushed to defend Sydney against invasion. A similar warning was conveyed in the film 'If the Huns came to Melbourne'. Other heart-stoppers made during the war included 'A Hero of the Dardanelles', 'Australia at War', 'Murphy of Anzac', and the first version of 'The Fate of the *Emden*'.

During the 1920s, an American-controlled distribution cartel prevented the growth of a large Australian production industry. People wanted escapist fantasy, and Hollywood was by far the most efficient manufacturer of dreams. The few Australian producers returned to bush epics such as 'The Breaking of the Drought' and the first version of 'The Man from Snowy River'. Perhaps the outstanding film was a full-length version of 'The Exploits of the *Emden*', released in Sydney with Hollywood-style promotion in 1928. Originally a German production, this was taken over by Ken G. Hall and expanded into two parts to depict more fully the *Emden's* destruction by HMAS *Sydney*.

In 1933 a 36-year-old director named Charles Chauvel began making a number of successful films based on heroic episodes in Australia's past. His first sound production, 'In the Wake of the *Bounty*', starred Errol Flynn as the mutinous Fletcher Christian. Despite the Commonwealth censor's action in deleting documentary sequences of uninhibited native dancing in Tahiti and Pitcairn Island, the film did well.

In 1940, after three years' hard work, Chauvel released 'Forty Thousand Horsemen', one of the finest action films ever made. Photographed in the then-deserted sandhills of Cronulla near Sydney, it depicted the great charge of the Light Horse against Turkish guns at Beersheba. The film's effect on public morale in the dispiriting early years of World War II was enormous. Chauvel's final contributions to the national legend included 'The Rats of Tobruk' (1944), 'Sons of Matthew' (1949), and Australia's first colour feature, the Aboriginal story 'Jedda' (1955).

Immediately after World War II, British directors from Ealing Studios dominated Australian production with films like 'The Overlanders' (1946), 'Eureka Stockade' (1949), and 'Bitter Springs' (1950). American studios were also active with workmanlike versions of 'Smithy' (produced by Ken Hall for Columbia in 1946), 'Summer of the Seventeenth Doll' (1959), and 'The Sundowners' (1960). Although the last two films featured overseas stars, they relied heavily on the uniqueness of Australian settings and stories for their appeal.

From 1969 onwards, the local film industry began to receive considerable government assistance in the form of direct subsidies and tax allowances. Although the aid was often controversial in its application, a renaissance began which has led to reasonably continuous production of fine films during the last fifteen years. From the mid-1970s came a procession of world class features. Among the best remembered are 'Sunday Too Far Away', 'Picnic at Hanging Rock', 'Don's Party', 'Storm Boy', 'The Getting of Wisdom' and 'Newsfront'. All of these had specific Australian settings, but the themes were of such universal significance that the films were also acclaimed overseas. A large number of publicly and commercially funded series of television dramas and documentaries have also helped to interpret the Australian experience.

More recently, private enterpreneurs have poured large amounts of money into such lavish productions as 'Gallipoli', 'The Man from Snowy River', 'Phar Lap', and other intensely Australian stories which have proved phenomenally popular in other countries. Such films have probably done more to express the underlying spirit of Australia than decades of expensive immigration propaganda. But they could not have been made unless generations of battlers had gone through the real-life experiences now idealised on the magic screen.

11. Sport: Australia Faces the World

Like people everywhere, Australians gain pleasureable excitement from watching experts doing their best in any field of high endeavour. The performers provide an ideal for onlookers of the heights of strength, co-ordination, intelligence and will to win, which all human beings might one day achieve.

The first national sporting hero of this century was Norman Brookes, the lanky left-handed son of a Melbourne paper manufacturer. In 1907, although already 30 years old, Brookes became the first overseas visitor to win the world singles title at Wimbledon. In partnership with New Zealander Anthony Wilding, he went on to win the world doubles. Later that year Brookes and Wilding took the Davis Cup from Britain, then managed to retain it until 1911. After Brookes's retirement, Australia had little success in world tennis until 1939.

Andrew 'Boy' Charlton, 'the Manly Flying Fish', won many world swimming records for Australia in the 1920s.

In many other sports before World War II, Australians showed their fighting spirit to everyone. Fred Lane, a 23-year-old Sydney swimmer, now practically forgotten, won Australia's first Olympic gold medal in Paris in 1900. Fanny Durack, another 23-year-old Sydney swimmer, in 1912 became the first Australian woman to win a gold medal, at the Olympic Games in Stockholm.

Andrew 'Boy' Charlton, also nicknamed 'the Manly Flying Fish', emerged during the 1920s to set a succession of world records for long-distance swimming. Aged 17, he won three gold medals at the Paris Olympics in 1924, and returned to Australia to find himself a national hero. Charlton rarely bothered to train for competition, preferring to enjoy himself in the surf at Manly.

Horse-racing increased its traditional popularity between the wars. The attendance of 118,877 spectators at the 1926 Melbourne Cup has never been equalled. The public's favourite racehorse was the legendary Phar Lap, which won the Melbourne Cup in 1930. His time was by no means a record, but during 1931 he scored eight wins in a row. When taken to America in 1932, he won his first major race there, before dying in strange circumstances.

The most dramatic sporting sensation of all occurred when the English test cricket team of 1932–33 toured Australia. National reputations were at stake. During the period 1900 to 1914, before World War I interrupted test matches, England had stayed comfortably ahead of Australia by winning forty matches to thirty-five. However, during the period 1919–32, the Australians leaped ahead to win fifty matches to forty-seven.

One of the factors in the Australian triumph was the remarkable batsman Don Bradman. He rose rapidly through interstate Sheffield Shield matches to join, at the age of 22, the Australian team which toured Britain in 1930. Here he established record after record.

Britain's answer for the 1932–33 test series was to send out a devastating Yorkshire fast bowler, Harold Larwood. In Adelaide, English captain Douglas Jardine instructed Larwood to bowl short-pitched on the Australians' leg stump. On the first day of the Adelaide match, Australian captain W. M. Woodfull was hit over the heart by the speeding ball. Back in the dressing room, Woodfull refused to accept an apology from the English manager. During the second innings, Bert Oldfield was felled when a ball from Larwood smashed into his head. He suffered concussion and had to withdraw from the series. As the crowds gave vent to their fury, the Australian Board of Control cabled to the English cricket authorities that bodyline bowling was causing 'intensely bitter feeling between the players'.

Eventually even the British authorities realised the depth of feeling. Jardine was never again selected to lead play against Australia. In 1934 the rules of cricket were altered to allow umpires to stop bodyline bowling, after a preliminary warning to the bowler. Bradman also came back into his own. He captained

Sir Donald Bradman, the greatest batsman of all time, painted by Alan Fearnley.

Australia in the five test series played against England between 1936 and 1948—and won them all. In his last triumphant tour before retirement in 1948, the 40-year-old Bradman scored 508 runs, including two centuries. In his last appearance he needed only four runs to achieve an exact average of 100 per test innings. According to cricketing legend he was so affected by the English crowd's huge ovation as he walked on to the ground that tears dimmed his eyes—and Eric Hollies bowled him out for a duck. Such is life.

12. From Appeasement to Rearmament

Throughout the escapist days of the 1920s and 1930s, Australia shared with all Western-style democracies the illusion that major wars had vanished from the face of the earth. Desiring nothing more than the chance to rebuild her shattered population, Australia accepted Woodrow Wilson's idealistic lead and got rid of her expensive armaments. Under the Washington Agreement of 1922, Britain, the United States and Japan agreed to limit their capital ships, aircraft carriers and land fortifications. The pride of our own fleet, HMAS *Australia*, was taken outside Sydney Heads and scuttled in deep water. 'Strong men were wet-eyed; many cursed; it was a tragic blunder', thought Rear-Admiral H. J. Feakes.

White Australians happily celebrated their 150th anniversary in 1938, refusing to recognise that another world war was about to overwhelm them. **The 'Australian Women's Weekly', the country's most popular magazine, looked back to the achievements of pioneer women**, who had turned 'outposts into homes, the rough camps into townships, the straggling selections into civilised farming communities'.

The army too was slashed to only 1700 regular soldiers, and a revolving conscript force of youngsters trained for ten days each year. No money was allotted for artillery, tanks, or even the proper care of equipment left over from World War I. Only horse transport was available: no attempt at mechanisation was made. As for the air force, in 1924 Wing-Commander Stanley Goble (who that year became the first man to fly around the Australian coastline) reported that it possessed a total of two aircraft fit for war.

Although Australia could scarcely have defended itself against a band of pirates, in 1929 the strongly pacifist Scullin Labor government announced that the ten days compulsory military training would be abolished forthwith. Voluntary soldiering was reintroduced, and officer training colleges at Duntroon and Jervis Bay closed down. Severe economies continued as Scullin fell and the new Lyons United Australia Party government came to power. Ominous events overseas were ignored. The triumph of Hitler's aggressive Nazi Party in Germany, and Japan's invasion of Manchuria in 1931 followed by its contemptuous withdrawal from the League of Nations, were viewed as irrelevant to Australia's security.

Even more seriously for Australia, Japan had repudiated the Washington Agreement of 1922 and begun a vast naval construction programme. By 1935 the Japanese outgunned British naval forces in the Pacific by a huge margin. Japan now had nine battleships (Britain 0), four aircraft carriers (Britain 1), sixteen cruisers (Britain 4), 102 destroyers (Britain 10), and sixty-five submarines (Britain 15). Only the powerful American Fleet based on Pearl Harbour kept a semblance of power balance in the Pacific.

In 1938 ordinary workers sometimes seemed more conscious than national leaders of the need to stand up to international aggression. That summer, members of the Waterside Workers Federation at Port Kembla (New South Wales) refused to continue loading pig-iron which had been sold by BHP to Japan, on the ground that the iron could be used for attacks on China and perhaps other nations including Australia. Their move was courageous, for 1000 people were still living in bag humpies around Port Kembla in the aftermath of depression.

The Federal Attorney-General, R. G. Menzies, ordered the men to resume loading: when they refused, he imposed a licensing system described as 'the Dog-Collar Act', preventing strikers from obtaining any work at all on the wharves. For the remainder of his career Menzies was known to his enemies as 'Pig-Iron Bob'.

I marvel that men of British stock should deem themselves unequal to a task which their ancestors through the ages regarded as the first duty of free men! The Empire has been built up by men of courage, or daring, whom no odds could daunt; who had confidence in themselves and abiding faith in the destiny of their race; who believed that the ideals which they cherished were worth working, and if need be, fighting and dying for.

W. M. HUGHES on the need for rearmament, 1935.

Hitler continued his expansion. When German forces marched into Austria in March 1938 to 'unify' the two countries—an action forbidden by the Versailles Treaty—even the hollow men of the West realised that time was running out fast. Britain tried to speed up production of its remarkable new Spitfire fighter plane and to get its navy and army back into fighting shape. In Australia, Joseph Lyons announced on 24 March 1938 a huge increase in defence expenditure, to pay for two new heavy cruisers of the *Sydney* type, 100 new warplanes to be based at Darwin, large munitions expansion, improved coastal defences, and other measures which W. M. Hughes had been demanding for years.

Appeasement continued, but it now had a different aim. Democratic leaders desperately tried to win a little more time to make up for the years of neglect. Lyons encouraged Neville Chamberlain's attempts to calm Hitler down and compromise with his demands. During the Czech crisis of September 1938, Australia supported Chamberlain's intention to visit Hitler at Berchtesgaden to persuade him to see reason. 'Your latest projected personal course excites our warmest admiration', Lyons cabled to the British Prime Minister.

Even in August 1939, a fortnight before Hitler's fatal invasion of Poland, R. G. Menzies, now Australian Prime Minister, cabled Chamberlain asking for efforts to make Poland adopt 'a reasonable and restrained attitude' towards German demands for slices of her territory. S. M. Bruce, now High Commissioner in London, cabled to Menzies on 30 August that he had urged Britain 'to induce the Poles to make reasonable concessions' and thus avoid war. The very next day, as though to mock these Australian appeasers, Hitler marched on Poland as he had long planned to do.

I believe that Port Kembla with its studied but peaceful and altogether disinterested attitude of the men concerned, will find a place in our history beside the Eureka Stockade as a noble stand against executive dictatorship and against an attack on Australian democracy.

SIR ISAAC ISAACS, former Governor-General, on the pig-iron dispute.

Waterside workers like this group painted by Horace Brodzky in the 1930s refused to load consignments of Australian pig-iron for shipment to Japan.

13. With Sad Memories, the Nation Again Girds Itself for War

It was like a recurring nightmare. After Austria, Czechoslovakia. After Czechoslovakia, Poland. On 25 August 1939, as German forces gathered on Polish borders, Australian Prime Minister R. G. Menzies, while privately attempting further appeasement, also broadcast a warning to the Australian public to begin preparing for the worst:

> The absorption of Poland would lead to attacks upon other smaller European countries, upon one ground or another, until a vast domination of force has been established. Realising that in the long run, the happiness and well-being of every nation in the world depends upon a peaceful and civilised means of determining differences, the British and French governments have given their pledge to Poland and to several other European countries . . . We in Australia are involved, because the destruction or defeat of Great Britain would be the destruction or defeat of the British Empire, and leave us with a precarious tenure of our own independence.

Believing that the effete democracies would back down yet again, Hitler attacked Poland on 1 September 1939. On that Friday in Australia, Menzies was due to attend a meeting at the Victorian town of Colac, where a quarter-century before Andrew Fisher had pledged 'the last man and the last shilling'. A policeman stopped Menzies's car and handed him an urgent cable from S. M. Bruce advising that Germany was again on the march. It read:

> MOST IMMEDIATE. Clear the line. For immediate transmission to the Prime Minister. No official information through diplomatic sources received, but German official wireless at noon reported that troops had crossed all Polish frontiers in order to resist attacks. Air and fleet actions were also being taken.

When Hitler refused to withdraw from Poland, Britain and France kept their pledge and declared war on 3 September 1939. In Melbourne on that Sunday night, Menzies broadcast the grim declaration:

> Fellow Australians. It is my melancholy duty to inform you officially that, in consequence of the persistence by Germany in her invasion of Poland, Great Britain has declared war upon her, and that, as a result, Australia is also at war.
>
> No harder task can fall to the lot of a democratic leader than to make such an announcement. Great Britain and France, with the co-operation of the British Dominions, have struggled to avoid this tragedy . . .
>
> The history of recent months in Europe has been one of ruthlessness, indifference and inhumanity, which the darkest centuries can scarcely parallel . . . It may be taken that Hitler's ambition is not to unite all the German people under one rule, but to bring under that rule as many countries as can be subdued by force. If this is to go on, there can be no security in Europe and no peace for the world.
>
> A halt has been called. Force has had to be resorted to, to check force. The right of independent people to live their own lives, honest dealing, the peaceful settlement of differences, the honoring of international obligations—all these things are at stake.

The parallels with past years were too blatant for anyone to ignore. For the third time since 1870, Germany had plunged Europe into a murderous conflict. For the second time, Australia had been dragged into a European maelstrom not in any way of her making. Despite the sufferings previously endured, there was remarkably little dissent. Grimly, sadly, but in determined fashion, the bulk of the Australian people gathered their strength to fight against international banditry.

Only a few months before, important sections of the Labor Party had been saying that Australian troops would never again fight overseas. When it came to the test, they too promised support for Britain. Federal Labor leader John Curtin announced:

R. G. Menzies, Prime Minister on the outbreak of war. Painting by William Dobell.

In this crisis, facing the reality of war, the Labor Party stands for its platform. That platform is clear. We stand for the maintenance of Australia as an integral part of the British Commonwealth of Nations. The party will do all that is possible to safeguard Australia, and at the same time, having regard to its platform, will do its utmost to maintain the integrity of the British Commonwealth.

Compulsory military training was reintroduced for home defence, including Papua New Guinea. Single men who reached 21 years of age were conscripted, and the militia quickly reached a strength of nearly eighty thousand men. Once again, a voluntary Australian Imperial Force was recruited for service overseas. Enlisting commenced for the 6th Division—its name chosen to follow the five divisions of the 1st AIF. There was little difficulty in finding the initial 20,000 men required. Newspaper cartoonists showed the Anzac torch being handed on by old diggers to the new. As the 6th Division marched through Sydney early in January 1940, a vast crowd of half a million people turned out to cheer them on, wave flags, and throw confetti and streamers.

As in the first war, the men were sent to Palestine to complete their training while defending the Middle East. In Britain, the inspired new Prime Minister, Winston Churchill, wrote that 'The transportation of the Australian division is an historic episode in Imperial history'. Fortunately there was not to be another Gallipoli: this time Turkey stayed neutral. But there were certainly many other disasters, partly due to Churchill's enthusiasm for aggressive action with insufficient resources, before the tide was turned.

During the period of 'phoney war', while the Germans rested after absorbing Poland, and the French fed their illusions of safety behind the Maginot line, recruitment for the AIF slackened. Only another 15,000 men had enlisted by mid-1940, when the German panzers suddenly struck their devastating blow against France through Holland and Belgium. This time the full might of aerial bombing and armoured columns was unleashed against civil and military targets alike: German frightfulness had returned to slaughter innocent populations.

To Young Soldiers

*Young soldiers who go out to
  die in battle,
The boisterous and tinted
  winds of Spring
Have woven wisps of cloud
  for garlanding
Of Donna Buang above the
  Yarra Valley.*

*The hill's fat cheek beneath a
  fringe of bush
Is mantled with an apple
  orchard's blush
Where bees contend to rape
  each virgin blossom.*

*Green now are the fenced
  paddocks that will mellow
To summer's stubble and the
  brittle yellow
Of grasses dried beneath a
  sky of glass.*

*And soon will show in
  autumn's elegy
Summer's dun death,
  winter's austerity,
Echo of spring, the last and
  that to come.*

*Young soldiers who go out to
  die in battle,
Children of yours though not
  by you begotten
Will live on here and this
  your native land
Will be yours yet though you
  be all forgotten.*

LEONARD MANN

Volunteers of the 2nd AIF leave in high spirits in 1940.

Unlike World War I, the services of women were eagerly sought for all but the most direct combatant duties. The Women's Auxiliary Air Force was formed in February 1941, the Women's Royal Australian Naval Service in April 1941, and the Australian Women's Army Service in August 1941. More than fifty-two thousand women enlisted in these forces. Thousands more joined the nursing services, the Women's Land Army, and munitions factories.

OPPOSITE PAGE
This famous 'Women's Weekly' cover, painted by Virgil Reilly just after the outbreak of World War II, inspired a series of pictorial stamps (right) used throughout the war.

THE AUSTRALIAN
WOMEN'S WEEKLY

Over 400,000 Copies Sold Every Week

FREE NOVEL

October 21, 1939   Registered in Australia for transmission by post as a newspaper.   Published in Every State   PRICE

"*Sons of Australia, steady and strong*"

Painting by VIRGIL

Australians were outraged anew: in the three months June to August 1940, more than one hundred thousand men rushed to join the AIF, and new divisions rapidly formed. Attracted by the apparent glamour of aviation, a further 80,000 men volunteered for the Royal Australian Air Force, although only a tenth of that number could be accepted until training schemes expanded. Many thousands of women were enrolled in auxiliary forces to help free fighting men in each service.

On 20 June 1940 Prime Minister Menzies asked Federal Parliament to vote unanimously for complete wartime control of Australia's resources and manpower to be transferred to the Commonwealth. 'This is, beyond all question, the greatest emergency in our history', he said. 'It is for us to fight a battle that will determine the future of the world, the future of Australia.' A vast munitions programme employing nearly one hundred thousand women and 50,000 men was inaugurated under Essington Lewis, managing director of the Broken Hill Proprietary.

Despite his brave words, Menzies (like Chamberlain in Britain) was not felt to be determined enough as a leader to see Australia through the war. People remembered his earlier attempts at appeasement, and believed that his reorganisation for war was a case of too little too late. Even a section of his own party saw him as ineffectual. They forced him into resignation, soon to be followed by election of a Labor government under 56-year-old John Curtin.

Here! YOU CAN'T DO THAT TO AN AUSTRALIAN

The Rats of Tobruk, the men who fought at El Alamein and at Greece and Crete before that . . . at Gallipoli and Villers Bret., too . . . these men made history. The Aussies have won the distinction of being tough.

It's breed that makes for fighting qualities; in its absence, military technique accomplishes no more than fertiliser on the desert sand.

These men are our husbands, fathers, brothers. We who remain at home are no less of the same breed as they . . . the Aussies the enemy has learnt to respect.

In the cause of liberty, we can endure much. We can see our privileges taken from us one by one. We can work long hours, we can devote our savings to helping the war effort. We can put up with rationing and treat it with a smile. We can do without much, make shift with very little—strong in the knowledge that in so doing we are building for a brighter future.

War-time restrictions are right in war-time, even though our minds look forward to the coming of peace and the re-instatement of individual independence in all things.

DAVID JONES'
for Service since 1838

This striking wartime advertisement by Sydney retailer David Jones called on Australians to endure everything in the cause of liberty—to work long hours, put up with rationing, and donate savings to the war effort—'even though our minds look forward to the coming of peace and the reinstatement of individual independence in all things'. Design by Douglas Annand.

14. The Battle to Hold Rampaging Nazi and Fascist Forces

In the total world conflict, Australians could play only a subsidiary although still significant role. Britain was fighting desperately for her own survival after the fall of France and evacuation of British troops from the beaches of Dunkirk. For some time, defence of the British Isles had to take absolute priority over other theatres of war.

As a prelude to invasion, the Germans concentrated 3000 aircraft for the purpose of destroying British air and naval power. Instead, in what became known as 'the Battle of Britain', the numerically weaker Spitfires and Hurricanes of the Royal Air Force practically knocked the Germans out of the sky. Nearly one thousand Australians served with RAF Fighter Command. These and individual RAAF fighter squadrons built up a superb record of daring and endurance.

As their long-term contribution to the air war, Australians eagerly took part in the remarkable Empire Air Training Scheme suggested by S. M. Bruce and announced in October 1939. This was the greatest air crew training plan ever known: the Dominions agreed to pool their resources and supply 50,000 fully trained men each year. Australia's part was to train 15,000 gunners, observers and wireless operators; while another 10,000 Australian pilots would receive advanced training in Canada. Prime Minister Menzies announced in a radio broadcast:

> I have no hesitation in saying that this great scheme is not only the most spectacular demonstration of Empire co-operation that the war has produced, it is an announcement which really sounds the death knell of German ambition in the war . . . Completion of the scheme will make the British Empire just as surely the leading air power as Great Britain has been the leading sea power for many generations.

The full fruits of the scheme became apparent from 1942 onwards. More than six and a half thousand Australians served with RAF squadrons as they began massive bombing raids on German territory. Five separate RAAF squadrons flew

That young Australians would make superb fighter-pilots could have been foreseen. But in fact most of them served in heavy bombers; and the reputation they earned was the opposite of what had been expected, at any rate by the British—who seem to have imagined that Australians would be irresponsible dare-devils, reckless, careless and slap-dash. Yet actually those Australian pilots and navigators won an outstanding name—for what? For care and thoroughness, for meticulous attention to detail, for their passion for getting everything just exactly right. They became recognised as being among the most trustworthy, the most conscientious, the most responsible of navigators and pilots.

A. E. MANDER, in *The Making of the Australians.*

RAAF volunteers of 1940 boarding ship to complete their training overseas.

Halifax and Lancaster bombers in thousands of dangerous missions over Europe. During the three years until war ended, more than seven thousand Australian airmen lost their lives in these raids.

Meanwhile the six cruisers and five destroyers of the Royal Australian Navy had been playing a full part in the global manoeuvres by which the Admiralty attempted to retain control of British sea routes. Of immediate battle importance was the central Mediterranean area. Italy entered the war alongside Germany immediately Mussolini scented the imminent fall of France. He knew that unless Italy could seize naval control of the Mediterranean, its land forces in North Africa would be cut off from their homeland.

In the first naval battles in June 1940, HMAS *Sydney* sank the Italian destroyer *Espero*. When the Italian fleet ventured forth a month later, the *Sydney*, assisted by five British destroyers, sank the cruiser *Bartolomeo Colleoni*. The remaining Italian ships fled for home. The following March, in the Indian Ocean, HMAS *Canberra* sank two German raiders, the *Coburg* and *Ketty Brovig*. But when HMAS *Sydney* returned to home waters and sank the raider *Kormoran* off the Western Australian coast in November 1941, it was so badly hit that it sank as well, with the loss of its entire crew.

Australia's first great naval victory of World War II—HMAS 'Sydney' sinks the Italian cruiser 'Bartolomeo Colleoni' on 19 July 1940. Painting by Frank Norton.

OPPOSITE PAGE
Bomb Dive, by Dennis Adams.

Men of the 2nd AIF, Like Their Fathers, Prove Themselves in the Desert

Australian diggers on patrol in the Western Desert during World War II.

With the fall of France and entry of Italy into the war in June 1940, protection of the Suez route and Middle East oil supplies became paramount considerations. By December 1940 the eight divisions of the Italian army in Libya had advanced from Cyrenaica as far as Sidi Barrani in Egypt, some two hundred and fifty miles west of Alexandria. English and Indian troops counter-attacked, driving the Italians back to the heavily-fortified town of Bardia. There the Australians took over.

On 3 January 1941, men of the 6th Division—although outnumbered two to one—fought their way through the Italian defences, withstood a determined tank attack, and took the fortress the following day. More than forty thousand Italians fell prisoner for a cost of 130 Australians killed.

The victorious Australians quickly pushed on another sixty miles along the African coast to subdue the fortress of Tobruk. In a one-day battle on 21 January 1941, a further 25,000 Italian troops were captured for a loss of forty-eight Australian dead. Again the 6th Division pressed on tirelessly, with British armoured support inland. Much of the remaining Italian army was trapped, and on 6 February the Australians took Benghazi.

With the virtual collapse of Italian strength in Africa, in February 1941 Hitler sent the heavily armoured Afrika Corps under General Erwin Rommel to prevent the fall of Tripoli. Simultaneously, Churchill decided that Greece, as the cradle of democracy, must be defended at all costs against a strong German army advancing through Yugoslavia. The battle-hardened 6th Division was sent to assist British forces in Greece, being replaced in Africa by the newly-arrived 9th Division.

Rommel drove forward to recapture Benghazi, and confidently expected to subdue Tobruk as well. But the 9th Division had dug themselves in to stay. Rommel contemptuously dismissed these raw troops as 'the Rats of Tobruk', a label they seized upon with delight and converted into a synonym for enduring courage. On 11 April 1941 the Germans completely surrounded Tobruk, expecting its surrender within days after heavy barrages and tank attacks. But for 194 days the Australians hung on, assisted by British artillery regiments and seaborne support. More than any other factor, the obstinacy of the men of Tobruk prevented Rommel from a blitzkrieg advance on Alexandria and the Suez Canal.

Meanwhile, during June and July 1941 a hard fighting campaign by the raw 7th Division and other forces routed Vichy French (pro-German) armies twice their strength, in Syria and Lebanon. This important victory prevented German bombers from acquiring bases near the vital Middle East oilfields. It was won just in time, for Japan was now preparing to attack in the Pacific, and most of the Australian forces would be needed to defend their homeland.

Rommel again attacked in the African desert, this time overwhelming the British relief garrison at Tobruk in June 1942 and advancing as far as El Alamein. Here his progress was again stopped by the refreshed 9th Australian Division and British forces. Battles swayed back and forth then lapsed into a stalemate. The British command was changed, and Generals Alexander and Montgomery began building up their strength for the last great battles with Rommel.

The 9th Division played a central role in the crucial onslaught at El Alamein late in October 1942. For much of the intense eight-day artillery and infantry duel, the main pressure of the Germans fell upon Australian troops. The cost was nearly six thousand Australians killed, wounded or taken prisoner. Superior British armour finally broke through, and pursued the fleeing Germans back towards Tunisia, where they surrendered in May 1943.

One Man's Decision on Crete

Heavy losses of German paratroops during the invasion of Crete convinced Hitler that it would be useless to use the same tactics elsewhere. But Crete remained a severe defeat for its British and Australasian defenders. In this extract from 'The Tomb of Lt. John Learmonth, A.I.F.', John Manifold showed that one Australian who took to the hills to fight to the end, armed only with a revolver, was fulfilling an heroic Australian tradition:

Say Crete, and there is little
more to tell
Of muddle tall as treachery,
despair
And black defeat resounding
like a bell;

But bring the magnifying
focus near
And in contempt of muddle
and defeat
The old heroic virtues still
appear . . .

Swagman and bushranger
die hard, die game,
Die fighting, like that wild
colonial boy
Jack Dowling, says the
ballad, was his name.

He also spun his pistol like a
toy,
Turned to the hills like wolf
or kangaroo,
And faced destruction with a
bitter joy.

His freedom gave him
nothing else to do
But set his back against his
family tree
And fight the better for the
fact he knew

He was as good as dead.
Because the sea
Was closed and the air dark
and the land lost,
'They'll never capture me
alive', said he.

Driver E. H. Mackey hoists his slouch hat on the flagpole at Tobruk to celebrate its seizure from the Italians. Mackey later was captured and sent to Germany.

One of many fierce hand-to-hand battles in the Western Desert: **Australian troops attack Rommel's forces at Bulimba.** Painting by Ivor Hele.

15. The Japanese Race South, and the Australian Continent is Threatened

On 7 December 1941—'a day which will live in infamy', said United States President F. D. Roosevelt—a Japanese carrier-borne air force without warning attacked and sank much of the American Pacific Fleet anchored at Pearl Harbour.

Suddenly the whole shape of the war changed. To Australians, Europe and the Middle East immediately lost much of their importance. For the first time since white colonisation began, their own continent was in grave danger. The new Labor Prime Minister, John Curtin, had taken office only a month before, declaring that 'Labor will devote itself with singleness of purpose to achieving the desire of the whole Australian people—a maximum war effort, with distribution of the inevitable burdens of the war as fairly as possible over the whole community'. That was the kind of leadership Australians were looking for.

Now the true test of nationhood had arrived. Under pressure, the frail Curtin emerged as a man of vision. He did not wait for Britain to act, but promptly declared war on Japan. That power, he said in a broadcast, had struck 'like an assassin in the night'. As the nation began to rally behind Curtin, further disasters followed like hammer blows. On 10 December 1941 Japanese aircraft sank HMS *Prince of Wales* and *Repulse*, the only two capital ships Britain had been able to spare for the Pacific. The Royal Navy, for so long considered Australia's impregnable shield, disappeared in effect at one stroke!

Curtin kept a brave face in public, although he scarcely slept a full night from that time on. In private he was well aware that Australia's defences had been left in an appalling state. According to a secret American report of the time, only three of Australia's eleven divisions were in combat condition, and all of these were overseas. The militia possessed little equipment or training. The navy had no aircraft carrier to meet a Japanese invasion force. The home air force consisted of 'a few battered planes and combat-weary men'.

Curtin acted with speed and determination. The 8th Division, all the experts agreed, would be sufficient to assist British forces in holding Malaya and Singapore. Despite delaying tactics from Churchill, Curtin insisted that the 6th and 7th Divisions must return to defend their homeland. And on 27 December 1941 he issued an historic appeal to the United States to come to Australia's aid:

> We look for a solid and impregnable barrier of the democracies against the three Axis powers, and we refuse to accept the dictum that the Pacific struggle must be treated as a subordinate segment of the general conflict . . .
>
> The Australian Government, therefore, regards the Pacific struggle as primarily one in which the United States and Australia must have the fullest say in the direction of the democracies' fighting plan.
>
> Without inhibitions of any kind, I make it quite clear that Australia looks to America, free of any pangs as to our traditional links or kinship with the United Kingdom.
>
> We know the problems that the United Kingdom faces. We know the constant threat of invasion. We know the dangers of dispersal of strength, but we know, too, that Australia can go and Britain can still hold on.
>
> We are, therefore, determined that Australia shall not go, and we shall exert all our energies towards the shaping of a plan, with the United States as its keystone, which will give to our country some confidence of being able to hold out until the tide of battle swings against the enemy.

Further catastrophes followed early in 1942. During January the Japanese pushed irresistibly through Malaya, scattering the inept British defenders. In mid-

February they arrived at the shore opposite the supposedly impregnable fortress of Singapore. There they found with delight that no permanent fortifications opposed their passage across the narrow stretch of water. One of the gravest blunders ever made by British strategists had been to install all the heavy guns on the opposite side of the island, in anticipation of a seaborne invasion.

Churchill and Curtin urged the British commander, General A. E. Percival, to hold on as long as possible and win time for Australia. But the victorious Japanese, although outnumbered three to one, swept on. To avoid a complete massacre of his demoralised troops and civilian population, Percival ordered a surrender of his 140,000 British and Indian forces. It was the worst disaster ever suffered by British arms. As far as Australia was concerned, the 8th Division was obliterated. It suffered 3000 casualties during the swift 70-day campaign, and nearly 15,400 men now fell prisoner. They might as well have fought to the death: while General Percival saw out the war in comparative luxury, one-third of the Australian prisoners died from starvation and brutality in forced labour projects such as the Burma death railway.

The Japanese continued their conquests at high speed: the Philippines, Burma and the vital oil resources of the Dutch East Indies (Indonesia) fell under their sway. On 20 January 1942, eight obsolete RAAF Wirraway training planes sent to defend Rabaul were all shot down within a few minutes by superior Japanese Zero fighters. When enemy troops landed, they tied up 150 Australians who had surrendered and bayoneted them to death.

On 19 February 1942, nearly two hundred carrier-based Japanese planes—a force similar in power to that which had savaged Pearl Harbour—flew towards Darwin. A missionary on Bathurst Island, Father John McGrath, saw the huge flight overhead and radioed the RAAF control room at Darwin. His warning was received but ignored. Practically every American and Australian plane was caught on the ground and destroyed. Eight ships were sunk and thirteen damaged. Darwin itself was heavily bombed, causing 240 deaths and several hundred woundings.

Fearing an imminent Japanese invasion, much of the civilian population fled into the bush, being joined there by army and air force personnel who had also fled. Four days later, when a muster was held, nearly three hundred RAAF personnel were still missing. One deserter actually reached Melbourne a fortnight later. A Royal Commission into these disgraceful events, suppressed for thirty years, blamed the chaos on inefficient leadership.

Fortunately Darwin was the last occasion on which Australians were found wanting. Most of the nation rallied to Curtin's lead and began preparing for further raids. Slit trenches were dug in every populated area, especially near schools. Vital buildings were sandbagged or bricked up. Blackouts were enforced. Rationing of clothing, food and petrol was organised. Evacuation of children and invalids began from city to inland areas. As fears of invasion grew, Robert S. Byrnes wrote verses which he called 'Remembering Henry Lawson's "Star of Australasia"':

> By the lovely land they saved for us, by the cities down the east—
> For all the days of our freedom's peace, we shall pay, both great and least:
> And this is the price that she asks of us—pass on if you think it high—
> You shall live and toil for Australia, and if need be, you shall die!

Voluntary bands of guerrilla fighters formed spontaneously to carry on the struggle if all else failed. Ion Idriess, Light Horse trooper in World War I, formed a 'People's Army' which drilled men and women (armed mostly with broomsticks) in the scrub on Sydney's North Shore.

At the official level, surviving diggers of the Great War were recruited into an 80,000-strong Volunteer Defence Corps. Many old diggers possessed their own rifles and ammunition, particularly in rural areas. They also helped to man anti-aircraft guns and to lay barbed wire around the coastline. In the event of invasion, they would also have helped to carry out a scorched earth policy, intended to deny food, water and petrol to an enemy attempting to traverse Australia's vast distances. Many road signs were in fact removed to help slow down the enemy.

Japanese field commanders proposed several plans for invasion. Admiral

Prime Minister John Curtin makes one of his impassioned wartime appeals.

Our honeymoon is finished. It is now work or fight as we have never worked or fought before . . . What the Battle for Britain required, so the Battle for Australia demands.

JOHN CURTIN, in a broadcast on 16 February 1942.

The disastrous Japanese air raid on Darwin on 19 February 1942, which sank many ships, destroyed practically every Allied plane, and caused several hundred casualties. Painting by K. Swain.

Yamamoto, the Japanese hero of Pearl Harbour, suggested an invasion through ravaged Darwin and southwards to Adelaide. General Yamashita, who had conquered Malaya, proposed a landing on the east coast in order to subdue Sydney as rapidly as possible. This move would be protected by Japanese conquests in New Guinea. Yet another plan was to make a feint at Darwin while the main invasion force attacked Perth and established a base there. All three proposals were deferred by the Japanese High Command, on the ground that Burma should be conquered first, while sufficient shipping transport strength was being built up to launch the assault on Australia. The delay was fatal to Japanese prospects. By the time Burma fell, the Americans had arrived in such strength that Australia was safe.

America had not been slow in answering Curtin's anguished plea for United States aid in defending Australia. Considerable numbers of American troops began arriving in February 1942. On 18 March Curtin broadcast the first official news to the nation:

> It is gratifying to be able to announce that there are very substantial American forces in Australia. These forces are not only most heartening in their actuality, but in their expression of the spirit of fighting shoulder to shoulder that will give to the democracies the decisive strength in the struggle in the Pacific . . . Our visitors speak like us, think like us, and fight like us, and therefore we can find a community of interest and comradeship with them that will be a firm basis when the supreme test of battle comes.

Japanese sketch map of one scheme for the invasion of Australia, with English translations added.

Four days later General Douglas MacArthur, who had escaped from the Japanese attack on the Philippines, and been appointed Supreme Commander in the South-West Pacific, arrived in Melbourne. He announced his newly-coined slogan, 'I

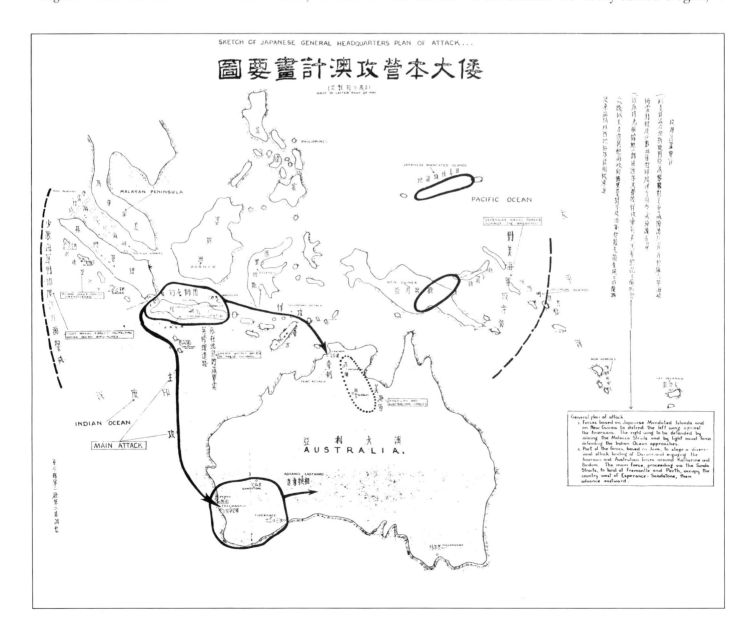

shall return', and added he was glad to be 'in immediate co-operation with the Australian soldier' whose prowess he knew from World War I. Australian General Sir Thomas Blamey was appointed Commander of Allied Land Forces, with the immediate task of planning the New Guinea campaign.

American troops continued to pour into Australia, particularly around Brisbane where MacArthur established his headquarters. By June 1942 about ninety thousand Americans had arrived. Six months later nearly a quarter-million United States troops and vast quantities of supplies were stationed in the eastern States. For all practical purposes Australia had become an American armed camp: a staging post for huge offensives to be launched against the still-potent Japanese. 'The hustle with which the Americans got things done amazed the easy-going Australians', wrote war correspondent Noel Monks.

Australians generally welcomed their new protectors. According to one newspaper 'The Americans have been staggered by the warmth of the welcome and the volume of hospitality extended to them'. Naturally there was considerable envy on the part of homecoming Australian troops who had already fought long and bravely, but were poorly paid, badly uniformed, and rather uncouth in comparison with the glamorous visitors. Serious street riots took place between the two forces in Brisbane, Melbourne and Perth. But to this day, realistic Australians have not

We shall win or we shall die. To this end I pledge you the full resources and all the mighty power, all the blood of my countrymen.

GENERAL DOUGLAS
MACARTHUR to the
Australian War Cabinet,
March 1942.

The morning after Darwin was bombed, Japanese invasion forces attacked Dutch and Australian troops defending Timor, a vital air base *en route* to Java. Most of the Allied troops were killed or captured, but the 2/2nd Australian Commando unit escaped to the hills and harassed the Japanese for twelve months until rescued. Painting by Charles Bush shows a group of these **guerrilla fighters**.

The hazards of war allowed for no respite. William Dobell painted '**Emergency landing at night**' while in Perth as an official war artist.

forgotten that when they stood alone and practically helpless, America unhesitatingly answered their cry for help.

Because of the direct Japanese threat to Australia, the need for conscription of all able-bodied men did not split the nation as it had in World War I. The fine performance of most conscript militiamen in New Guinea disproved the jeering description of them as 'chocos' (chocolate soldiers). Although the Labor Party refused to amalgamate the two armies, Curtin persuaded the Party to extend the area for service as far as the Equator and the Solomons, where conscripts fought with equal distinction to AIF volunteers.

The first real turning point in the war against Japan came with the Battle of the Coral Sea, fought off Queensland's north-eastern coast from 4 to 8 May 1942. A large Japanese troop convoy was located and attacked by American carrier-based planes. One Japanese aircraft carrier was sunk and another severely damaged, forcing the Japanese to turn back.

Arthur Calwell, Australian Information Minister, later claimed that 'Had the Americans not won the Coral Sea battle, the 27 Japanese transports would have landed at Port Moresby, Townsville, New Caledonia, Sydney and Melbourne, and the Australian loss of life would have been too horrible to contemplate'. In fact the Japanese had decided to concentrate on the conquest of New Guinea and isolation of Australia from outside help. But Australia's gratitude to the Americans was boundless. For many years the celebration of 'Coral Sea Week' was an important annual event throughout Australia.

The American Fleet scored an even greater victory at Midway on 4 June, when four Japanese carriers and five other warships were sunk. The myth of Japanese maritime invincibility was shattered. The immediate threat to Australia was over, although submarine warfare continued along the east coast. Thirty Allied ships were torpedoed, including the *Centaur* which was clearly marked as a hospital ship; three midget submarines launched attacks in Sydney Harbour; and Sydney and Newcastle were lightly shelled by larger submarines. Little damage was caused: the raids were probably counter-productive, for they kept Australia's defence effort at a high pitch.

By the time of their first two naval defeats, the Japanese had already occupied

Something of the hellish nature of the New Guinea war is shown in Ivor Hele's painting '**Taking old Vickers position, Bobduli Ridge, 28 July 1943**'.

Regarded by many as Australia's best wartime General, **Sir Thomas Blamey** commanded the 6th AIF Division in the Middle East, and was then appointed Commander of Allied Land Forces in the South-West Pacific under General MacArthur. Painting by Sir William Dargie.

In a demonstration of wartime unity, **Australian and American troops march together through Sydney streets**.

much of New Guinea, and key points in the Bismarck Archipelago and Solomon Islands. MacArthur's basic strategy was to use Australian troops to defend and then recapture New Guinea, and Americans to subdue Guadalcanal and New Britain before island-hopping back to the Philippines.

The Australians won the first important land victory of the Pacific war. On 25 August 1942, a Japanese convoy landed strong forces including tanks at Milne Bay, an area with excellent landing beaches and airfields at the eastern tip of Papua New Guinea. The only defence consisted of the 18th AIF Brigade and the 7th Militia Brigade, outnumbered at least two to one by the invaders. But by superb fighting, the Australians destroyed the Japanese force by 6 September, preventing it from establishing an air base which could have pounded Port Moresby and all Allied shipping. In his poem 'New Guinea Campaign', Ian Mudie evoked the spirit of traditional Australian heroism:

> Are you there, Peter Lalor, are you there,
> ghost with gold-dust in your hair;
> and lean Stuart do you ride
> to seek your northern tide
> where in greens they're slowly swinging
> through the mud, too tired for singing,
> where the poison of New Guinea fills the air?
>
> Are you there, untiring Eyre, are you there,
> with your heart beyond compare;
> are you there, you brave wild Kellys
> where heroes on their bellies
> through the jungle now are creeping

—may their women have no weeping—
where snipers from their tree-tops coldly stare?

You ghosts that walk beside
them, do you watch them now with pride
as through green hell and glory
they carry on your story
where in mud their feet are sinking
and in dreams they're always thinking
of their homes and of the cobbers that have died?

Meanwhile a separate Japanese force had battled its way up the precipitous Kokoda Trail across the 13,000-foot Owen Stanley Range to within 30 miles of Port Moresby. Curtin's action in bringing home much of the AIF now began to pay full dividends. On 23 September 1942, the AIF 7th Division decided it was time to stop the retreat. Breaking up into small groups, they began to inch their way forward through appalling jungle and mountain terrain, fighting all the way. Under the field command of the greatly-admired Major-General George Vasey, 47, they used the enemy's tactics of sliding silently through the jungle to attack where least expected.

War correspondent Allan Dawes described the Australians in New Guinea as 'Men in green—in faded, sweaty, mud-stained green—their bodies yellowed under the tan, lean and hard and muscular, their long trousers bagging over the tops of cut-down laced American gaiters, packs up, rifle or Owen gun slung and ready—they are Australian soldiers, flitting in phantom silence athwart a landscape of misty jungle, its every leaf and vine steaming in the sun. One . . . two . . . three . . . a dozen men, over a fallen tree trunk they slip across the stream. The curtain of the jungle closes behind them. Silence like the dead of night broods over the place, though it is high noon. Suddenly the crackle of machine-gun fire explodes like thunder in your ears . . .'

The inland village of Kokoda was captured on 2 November 1942, and the Japanese forced to retreat to the north-eastern beachhead positions of Buna and Gona. On 28 November 1942 the final battle began to drive the enemy out of north-eastern New Guinea. The Japanese had constructed hundreds of pillboxes and dugouts, many protected by steel sheets, concrete and timber ramparts. After ten weeks of desperate fighting in the knee-deep slime of 'Bloody Buna' and Gona, and uncounted deeds of heroism equivalent to anything seen in World War I, the Australians and Americans forced the surviving Japanese to surrender.

All told the New Guinea campaign to this point had cost the Australians nearly 5700 and the Americans 2800 casualties. Of the 17,000 Japanese involved in the fighting, some ten thousand died rather than surrender. When the Japanese High Command attempted to ship reinforcements from Rabaul in March 1943, air attack sank most of their shipping and killed a further 3000 men. Continued Allied assaults during 1943 and 1944 cleaned up most of New Guinea and nearby islands. MacArthur was able to keep his promise and return to the Philippines on 20 October 1944.

The Road to Kokoda

Dear God: What men are these
That we have bred,
Who bravely tread
The way to hell
Along the road that leads
To dark Kokoda?

Are these our husbands,
Brothers, sons, our friends
That once we knew—
These heroes
Who, fever-stricken,
drenched with rain,
Through jungle swamp and
endless pain
Tread the road that leads
To dark Kokoda?

GWEN BESSELL-BROWNE

He has no great love for war, or its subsequent regimentation. Bully beef, mosquitoes and chlorinated water don't appeal to him either, but he laughs, fights, swears, grumbles and gambles, saying what he thinks and rubbing shoulders with all and sundry as he goes along. Be he young and raw or veteran tried and wise, he carries his country's splendid gifts, a stout heart, courage and initiative, making him the Australian Digger—a great fighting man and a prince of comrades.

SERGEANT JAMES WIENEKE
of the 6th AIF Division.

16. Victory in the Pacific

In Europe, the now-mighty war machines of Britain and America advancing from the west, combined with Soviet Russia's massive offensive from the east, smashed the German empire which Hitler had boasted would last a thousand years.

Australia had played a notable part in preventing the Nazi pestilence from permanently infecting Europe. But 'V.E. Day' (Victory in Europe) was celebrated in Australia on 9 May 1945 in curiously muted fashion. A public holiday was declared, and churches were filled for thanksgiving services, but little wild enthusiasm was demonstrated. Europe and its troubles now seemed so far away—and never again would they seem so important to Australians. We now had perils much closer to home: Australians were still dying in Borneo and elsewhere, and the Japanese kept on fighting with such fanaticism that a great deal of sacrifice still seemed to lie ahead.

John Curtin, who had unified the nation with his calm and firm leadership, lay gravely ill in hospital: he died on 5 July 1945 from sheer exhaustion, without knowing that the war against Japan was in reality nearly over. 'The captain has been stricken within sight of the shore', said Acting Prime Minister Frank Forde.

Not one person in Australia knew that an Anglo-American team of scientists, working in profound secrecy, had solved the problem of building bombs which

Australia's last-ditch defence against a Japanese invasion was the Volunteer Defence Corps, recruited from World War I veterans and younger men in reserved occupations. In 1942 it reached a strength of 80,000 and was beginning to be properly armed. Russell Drysdale's painting of 1943 shows 'Local V.D.C. Parade'.

could utilise the power of atomic fission to cause explosions of incredible force. A new American President, Harry S. Truman, made the dire decision to test the bombs against two Japanese cities. His hope was to save the estimated one million lives of Allied troops which could be expended in conquering Japan.

The first atomic bomb was dropped on Hiroshima on 6 August 1945, and the second on Nagasaki on 9 August. Both cities were virtually obliterated in an instant; about one hundred thousand men, women and children suffered instantaneous death; and many survivors incurred lingering radiation poisoning. Australian-born Wilfred Burchett, the first journalist to see the destruction, wrote: 'Hiroshima does not look like a bombed city. It looks as if a monster steamroller had passed over it and squashed it out of existence'.

Australians, like the whole world, were stunned by the news. But for the moment, the great thing was that the Pacific war was over. This time chaos broke loose in every Australian town and city. On 15 August the largest crowds ever seen (estimated at one million in Sydney) thronged the main streets to shout, cheer, dance, wave and kiss. Total strangers hugged one another, their eyes shining. The Melbourne *Age* described that city's revellers as 'Wistful, joyous, sad, exuberant, perplexed, sorrowful, delirious, wild . . . in a celebration of strange, confusing, violent, emotional import that will long be remembered'.

Later the human cost to Australia had to be reckoned. Throughout World War II, 33,826 Australians were killed, one-third of them airmen. More than one hundred and eighty thousand were wounded; and 23,000 fell prisoner. The casualties were actually smaller than those caused by the frontal assaults of World War I, and considerably smaller as a proportion of the total population. All the same, each of the dead gave their lives for Australia just as those of the first war had done, leaving the same tragic gaps in many Australian homes. The main difference was that the nature of war had changed, relying far more on mechanisation than on human flesh. Now, with the ultimate triumph of nuclear technology, the world had entered a new era whose shape could only be dimly perceived in 1945.

As though to balance the inhuman nature of the weapon which had suddenly ended the war, the Australian soldier who survived to take part in victory marches seemed so very human and normal. 'That is something you have to understand', wrote John Hetherington. 'The Australian Soldier is not one man but tens of thousands of men. He is the man who in peacetime cashed the cheque you handed through the teller's grille at the bank, who delivered your bread at the back door, who tried to sell you a vacuum cleaner . . .' To Sergeant James Wieneke of the 6th Division, the typical Australian who went to war was 'a cheerful, adventurous, somewhat careless chap . . . sincerely hoping something will eventually work out—enabling him to live and work in peace, security and independence'.

Anzac Day 1983: old soldiers remember World War I and World War II.

No Foe Shall Gather Our Harvest

Sons of the mountains of Scotland,
Clansmen from correi and kyle,
Bred of the moors of England,
Children of Erin's green isle,
We stand four-square to the tempest,
Whatever the battering hail—
No foe shall gather our harvest,
Or sit on our stockyard rail.

Our women shall walk in honor,
Our children shall know no chain,
This land that is ours forever
The invader shall strike at in vain.
Anzac! . . . Bapaume! . . . and the Marne! . . .
Could ever the old blood fail?
No foe shall gather our harvest,
Or sit on our stockyard rail.

So hail-fellow-met we muster,
And hail-fellow-met fall in,
Wherever the guns may thunder,
Or the rocketing 'air mail' spin!
Born of the soil and the whirlwind,
Though death itself be the gale—
No foe shall gather our harvest,
Or sit on our stockyard rail.

We are the sons of Australia,
Of the men who fashioned the land,
We are the sons of the women
Who walked with them, hand in hand;
And we swear by the dead who bore us,
By the heroes who blazed the trail,
No foe shall gather our harvest,
Or sit on our stockyard rail.

MARY GILMORE

Australian poet and author **Mary Gilmore** was appointed a Dame Commander of the British Empire in 1937. Painting by William Dobell.

PART V

The Long Road to Freedom

Australia

World has no better land than this gigantic island
so little stained with blood, where many
    migrants come
still come, this long journey, longing for a peace
a past not drowned in horror and in blame
as countries left behind. Peace travels on these roads
these gradual pastures, rich with sluggish stock
    and grain
where bitter soldiers never ploughed the
    sleeping homes
sowing the seeds of hate across the smoking plain.

Peace lives in slow perpetual forests of the ranges
the changeless gumtrees stable through the
    sunny years,
and ice and snow so seldom that the winter never dies;
scarcely known the tangles of the jungles or the fears
of living creatures; or earth treacherous, the alps
launching swift invasions of their tides or avalanche,
or earthquake swallowing cities. Most favoured
    countryside
only the screaming wind and thunder tears at root
    and branch.

Cities and towns thrive along the scattered waters—
this great immensity astride the southern sea.
No terrible drama of siege or armies are remembered
to tell to frighten the heart of child at mother's knee.
The echoes of Carthage and Rome and Troy not
    to be heard
nor countless towns and villages of other lands
wrecked in the shadows of time; never a loot
    nor burning
has brought the cities to arms with wild
    fanatical hands.

Quiet is the silent heart of the vast sun-stricken desert
new frontiers still are summoned from its somnolent
    waste,
its dry expanses brought from living death with hope
as dragged those first explorers through the dread
    they faced.
Hope has had a million flames from that first fleet
setting the candle of dismay and desperation
on our shores, all oblivious through their tears
their ragged harvest was our prosperous nation.

Hope was the brand on men from war corroded
    Europe
upon their hands to turn new acres never tamed
they abdicated from beloved pasts and ways
for hope of children, leaving all but one name—
Australian. The scorn and pride of children
    gentle those
who linger choked with old vendettas of their clans
till every wind of anger from old hatred dies
and vengeance leaves no hampering shroud
    upon their plans.

My island, hold them all and weave their
    many strands
from hedgerows, olive groves or hungry throes
    of towns,
create one living family from their many tribes
across the world from alps or steppe or
    English downs.
Despite their many voice, one common thought
    be held
woe to any man who lifts a murderous hand,
for peace should rest a benediction on our land,
and citizens in one allegiance loyal stand.

AMY CUMPSTON

1.   The Imperative Need to Populate—or Perish

The Pacific war brought home to every Australian exactly what it was like to live in imminent fear of invasion by powerful neighbours. As the great conflict drew to its close, every section of society wholeheartedly supported renewed efforts to develop and populate the continent. For once, the nation was unanimous in seeing mass immigration as the answer to future threats.

When the gravel-voiced 60-year-old former engine-driver Joseph Benedict Chifley became Prime Minister on 13 July 1945, Australia's population numbered only 7·5 millions, and these were concentrated mostly around the nation's south-eastern rim.

Planners recognised that mere numbers were not enough. Sound schemes for general economic development were also needed. It was an exciting, almost visionary time of national reorganisation. The huge Snowy Mountains hydro-electric scheme was inaugurated to almost double power generation in the eastern States. Publicly-owned airlines were developed to increase and cheapen interstate and overseas travel. Co-operative joint boards helped to supervise troubled industries and market their products on a planned basis. A major Commonwealth-State effort was undertaken to boost construction of new homes and schools. Stimulus was given to the search for minerals, particularly oil. A local car manufacturing industry began with American assistance. Other urban industries which would employ much of the hoped-for migrant population expanded greatly.

While attempting to direct the growing postwar boom, Labor was also determined to ensure that a proportion of its fruits should be harvested by ordinary people. Even while the war was still in progress, Chifley as Federal Treasurer succeeded in finding the money to introduce unemployment, sickness and hospital benefits, and Federal pensions for widows. Such advances were accepted by all parties, and expanded into other areas of social need by succeeding Liberal governments, making Australia even more attractive to migrants.

When planning his vast immigration scheme at the war's end, Arthur Calwell attempted to avoid controversy by limiting the scheme initially to white British citizens. Free and assisted passages were granted to what he described as 'the best possible immigrant types from the United Kingdom'—people who would assimilate into the homogeneous population which was still 98 per cent British in origin.

However, for the first time in our history, Calwell also foreshadowed government-sponsored immigration of non-English-speaking people from war-ravaged Europe. Two types were to be invited: tragic refugees from 'Europe's army of displaced and persecuted people' who had lost everything, and young immigrants such as tradesmen looking for a fresh start in a new land.

In July 1947 Calwell signed an agreement with the International Refugee Organisation to take the first shiploads of 'displaced persons' from European holding camps. Within two years, 50,000 refugees had been successfully absorbed into Australian life. Calwell faced up to inevitable criticism from a few insensitive conservatives who would have preferred to accept only British immigrants. He appealed to Australians to abandon derogatory terms such as 'Reffo' and 'Dago', and to call the settlers 'New Australians' instead.

The general success of this programme cleared the way for unprecedented immigration of young healthy Europeans. Large numbers of Italians, Greeks, Dutch, Germans and others came to Australia, most of them settling into the community with surprisingly little conflict. Today most of their children and grandchildren can only be distinguished from other Australians by their surnames.

The total result of immigration programmes between 1947 and 1985 has been the arrival of some 4·3 million people. About 1·3 million of these decided they

We cannot continue to hold our island continent for ourselves and our descendants unless we greatly increase our numbers . . . We may have only the next 25 years in which to make the best possible use of our second chance to survive.

ARTHUR CALWELL, Minister for Immigration in the Chifley government, August 1945.

We have a great objective—the light on the hill—which we aim to reach by working for the betterment of mankind not only here but anywhere we may give a helping hand. If it were not for that, the Labor movement would not be worth fighting for. If the movement can make someone more comfortable, give to some father or mother a greater feeling of security for their children, a feeling that if a depression comes there will be work, that the government is striving its hardest to do its best, then the Labor movement will be completely justified.

PRIME MINISTER BEN CHIFLEY, 12 June 1949.

Bill Pidgeon's delightful cover for the **Federation Jubilee** issue of the 'Australian Women's Weekly' in 1951 showed immigrants from many countries dancing hand in hand with 'dinkum Aussies'.

would be happier elsewhere and re-emigrated, leaving us with a net gain of three million permanent residents. Thus about one in five of today's Australians were born in another country, but made the conscious decision that this was the best place for them to live and bring up their children.

More than half of the permanent immigrants we have won are non-British. This, combined with the scars of World War II, has led to a significant dilution of the previously overwhelming pro-British feeling in the community. To an increasing proportion of young Australians, Britain is now just another country in Europe, with which we preserve a few historical links. There is only one direction for the loyalty of such people, and that is towards Australia itself.

Arthur Calwell rigidly upheld the White Australia Policy while he remained in office. He believed strongly in its effectiveness for Australian conditions of the time. Calwell could quip to journalists that 'Two Wongs don't make a White', but in more thoughtful moments he could also say:

> I respect Asiatic people. I do not regard them as inferiors, but they have a different culture and history, different living standards and different religions from our own.

Prime Minister Chifley (with pipe) **and Immigration Minister Calwell** (centre) welcome the first British migrant tradesmen to arrive in Canberra in the late 1940s.

This policy was generally accepted in the aftermath of world war. It caused little difficulty to the External Affairs Minister, Dr H. V. Evatt, when he was elected President of the United Nations Assembly in Paris in 1948. Only when European colonial powers began to withdraw from Asia, leaving Australia as the sole white nation on the southern rim of the Pacific Ocean, did the White Australia Policy begin to appear an offensive relic of earlier times.

The first signs of change came when Labor lost power in 1949 after an ill-advised attempt to nationalise the private banking system. Under the farsighted Colombo Plan of 1950, a new Liberal government led by 56-year-old R. G. Menzies agreed to assist the emerging nations of Asia with basic development and training schemes. For the first time, large numbers of Asian students began to appear in Australian universities. After initial surprise, most Australians accepted them as part of everyday life. Several thousand highly-qualified non-Europeans were also granted permanent residence because their skills were needed here.

Without fanfare or formal announcement, the White Australia Policy gradually came to an end. It is now nearly two decades since the first cautious announcement. During those years about 450,000 Asians have emigrated to Australia. Their 'retention rate' is by far the highest of any racial group: only about one in eight have re-emigrated. Some suburbs are now crammed with Asians struggling to make their way, and many inner suburban schools are awash with their bilingual children, just as Italian and Greek children once flooded into urban facilities.

Even during periods of high unemployment there has been comparatively little backlash from the Australian community, whose general racial harmony can only be described as remarkable.

In a series of thoughtful statements during 1984, the noted historian Geoffrey Blainey warned that the Hawke Labor government was risking this national consensus by discriminating against European migrants and devoting up to 40 per cent of the annual intake to Asians. 'The poorer people in the cities are the real sufferers', Blainey noted. Although many of his fellow academics deplored such unaccustomed candour, the government took note and altered current immigration patterns to less provocative levels.

It remains a great triumph for new-found Australian racial tolerance that the nation has been able to accept any Asian immigration at all. With reasonably good fortune, the half-million Asians in our midst will ultimately merge into a new kind of Australian population, just as every previous wave of migration has managed to do, subtly altering our national characteristics while drawing new strength from the unique Australian environment.

Applications for entry by well-qualified people wishing to settle in Australia will be considered on the basis of their suitability as settlers, their ability to integrate readily, and their possession of qualifications which are in fact positively useful to Australia.

HUBERT OPPERMAN, Liberal Minister for Immigration, announces non-racial criteria for acceptance of migrants, March 1966.

2. Britain Withdraws from the Pacific, but Royal Tours Maintain our Links

In saving the world from Nazism, Britain lost forever her predominant role in global affairs. Almost exhausted by that supreme effort, she sank into decline while the new superpowers, America and Russia, contended for world supremacy.

As far as the Pacific was concerned, Japan's initial wartime victories meant the end of old-style European colonial domination. Surging local nationalism forced the Dutch out of Indonesia; the British out of India, Burma and Malaya; and ultimately the French and Americans out of Indo-China.

The reality of Britain's decline as a world power had been obvious to Australians ever since Singapore fell. Sentimental attachments to 'the old country' lingered on, particularly among British migrants in Australia, but by the 1950s our attention was increasingly concentrated on the Pacific area.

R. G. Menzies, the longest-serving Prime Minister in Australian history, shrewdly used the public arena to monopolise the pro-British vote while in power from 1949 to 1966. But recently released secret documents show that even Menzies was not willing to commit Australian forces to any new conflict involving Britain in Europe or the Middle East.

When a Middle East crisis did erupt in 1956 with Egyptian President Nasser's nationalisation of the Suez Canal, Britain and France launched an abortive invasion attempt without military support from the Dominions. World opinion was so adverse that the two former colonial powers were forced into humiliating retreat.

By 1968 Britain's interest in the Pacific had diminished to the point where Harold Wilson's Labor government decided to withdraw practically all British forces 'east of Suez'. A few troops remained in Hong Kong, scattered naval units continued to co-operate in exercises with Malaysia and Singapore, but the old days of high British commitment had gone for ever. By 1975 Britain was spending almost her entire military budget in the NATO area.

An even more far-reaching parting of the ways came with Britain's persistent negotiations to join the European Economic Community. Ever since the convict years Australia had maintained the closest trade links with Britain. Even if these usually operated in Britain's favour, at least Australia had a guaranteed mass market for her primary products. For Britain to abandon this historic relationship and wring whatever advantage she could out of the European Common Market seemed to Empire loyalists a betrayal of the bloodstained past: the greater their loyalty to those vanishing years, the greater the betrayal.

As Australia's economic and defence ties with Britain faded into memory, important new forces were at work in the Pacific. After her wartime humiliation Japan abandoned all thought of military conquest, and devoted her abundant energies to economic expansion. Within a few years of the war's end she had become the most technologically advanced nation in Asia: a vast consumer of primary materials and a vast exporter of finished products.

Australians too learned to suppress the bitter experiences of war in the rush to build new patterns of trade and prosperity. A general agreement was signed in 1957 to regulate trade between Australia and Japan, later replaced by a series of commitments which facilitated the export of Australian raw materials to Japan and the entry of Japanese manufactures into Australia.

The remarkable thirty-year-long economic boom which followed World War II was in large part due to Australia's good fortune in being able to supply wool, wheat, sugar and minerals to the predominant power in the Pacific. Without that trade, Australia could not have financed her extensive immigration and internal development programmes, and would be in a much weaker position today.

All kinds of subsidiary effects followed the decline of the British-Australian relationship. In 1970 appeals from the High Court of Australia to the Privy Council in London were abolished. The Labor governments of E. G. Whitlam (1972–75) and R. J. Hawke (1983–   ) were especially active in cutting ties with Britain. The words 'British subject' were dropped from Australian passports; 'God Save the Queen' gave way to an Australian National Anthem; and immigrants being naturalised were required to swear allegiance to the Australian nation instead of to the monarchy.

During this period of adjustment in our attitude to the world, many citizens began to favour a change from an hereditary monarchy to an elected republican form of government. Young people and migrants in particular seemed to favour a President elected on the American system as Head of State. Public opinion polls showed a steady decline in approval of the monarchy from 77 per cent in 1953 to 53 per cent twenty years later. Over the same period, those favouring a republic rose from 15 per cent to 40 per cent. The events of November 1975, when the Governor-General used the vice-regal reserve powers to dismiss the Whitlam Labor government from office, intensified republican feeling for a time.

Nevertheless, in the face of all these postwar changes, a good deal of attachment to the monarchy seems to remain in Australian hearts. The British heritage is still meaningful to many people, while an indefinable air of romance continues to surround the long history of English royalty. Many voters prefer the idea of a detached, hereditary monarchy to the turmoil of presidential-style elections. The corrupt nature of certain elected presidencies, such as Nixon's in America, contrasts sharply with the incorruptible royal family. Voters, especially Australian voters, remain generally sceptical about the true motives of many elected politicians, and prefer to maintain counterbalancing elements of power not dependent on sudden political passions.

These feelings come into sharp focus every few years when members of the royal family visit Australia. In 1954 Queen Elizabeth II made the first-ever tour of Australia by a reigning monarch, and was greeted everywhere with extraordinary enthusiasm. A public opinion poll which asked two years later 'Should royal visits continue?' was answered with an overwhelming 92 per cent 'Yes'. The royal couple returned for a further tour in 1963, when Prime Minister Menzies remarked in an after-dinner speech, somewhat to the Queen's embarrassment: 'I did but see her passing by, and yet I'll love her till I die'. In the emotion of the moment, the remark expressed what lay in many people's hearts. Later Menzies was admitted to the select Most Noble Order of the Thistle, and appointed Lord Warden of the Cinque Ports.

In 1970, Queen Elizabeth returned again to commemorate Captain Cook's discovery of the east coast of Australia 200 years before. Three years later she came back to open the Sydney Opera House. Her tour of 1977 was slightly marred by demonstrators protesting against the dismissal of the Whitlam government.

By 1984, public opinion polls showed a slight swing back to favouring a monarchy against a republic. Among the cross-section of those surveyed, only about one in three wanted a republic, while opinion in favour of the monarchy edged upwards to more than 60 per cent.

The figures indicate that even some migrants brought up under republican forms of government may have been converted to the continuation of an hereditary monarchy for Australia. Followed through into constitutional practice, this means the continuation of Governors-General recommended by the Prime Minister but approved by the monarch. It also makes fundamental constitutional change rather more difficult for the foreseeable future.

A substantial majority of Australians seem to have decided that their national pride is not affected in the slightest degree by continuation of the royalist tradition.

For 25 years the Queen has performed her constitutional duties with grace and dedication, secure in the loyalty and affection of her subjects. It is true that her visits to Australia have been field days for strutting conservative politicians, odious social climbers, flag-waving sycophants, professional loyalists and poseurs of every description. But they have never managed to spoil the pleasure that ordinary Australians take in welcoming their Head of State.

GOUGH WHITLAM, former Prime Minister, on the Queen's tour in 1977.

Bristol-born **Field-Marshal Sir William Slim** (1891–1970) was warmly welcomed by Australians as Governor-General because of his outstanding war record on Gallipoli and in Burma. In 1965, five years after his term expired, appointment of British-born Governors-General was abandoned. Painting by Sir William Dargie.

Queen Elizabeth II, shown here with Prime Minister Menzies, received a tumultuous welcome throughout Australia on her tour in 1954.

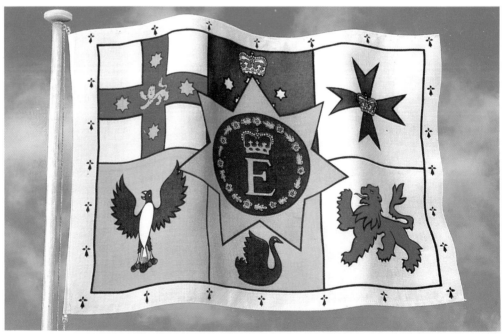

The Queen's Personal Flag in Australia. Reproduced by gracious permission of Her Majesty the Queen.

3. The Battle Against Communist Expansion

The end of World War II brought not everlasting peace and security but division of the world into bitterly-opposed, heavily-armed blocs. Although the war had originally been undertaken to free the weaker nations of Europe, Russia refused to remove her troops from Poland, Czechoslovakia and elsewhere. What Winston Churchill called 'an iron curtain' descended between all Soviet-occupied lands and the West.

World War II also opened a new era in the Pacific area. In 1948, irresistible Chinese communist forces enjoying wide popular support overthrew the brutal regime of Chiang Kai-shek, forcing him to retreat to the island of Formosa (Taiwan). The threat to Australia seemed real and urgent, combining fear of 'the yellow peril' with hatred of the totalitarianism implicit in communist rule.

Yet most Australians, democratic to the last, did not agree with the use of authoritarian methods to fight communism at home. A majority felt that if free societies were truly superior, they could prove it by allowing free speech even to those whose aim was to overthrow democracy by subversion or force.

In April 1950, R. G. Menzies as Prime Minister introduced a parliamentary Bill to suppress the Communist Party in Australia and remove communists as union officials. He outlined his view that 'communism is an international conspiracy against the democracies, organised as a prelude to war and operating as a fifth column in advance of hostilities'.

Most Liberal and many Labor politicians supported the proposed ban. However, when challenged in the High Court, it was declared invalid, on the ground that the Federal government did not possess constitutional power to legislate on such questions in peacetime. Menzies put the Act to a referendum, but was again defeated. Constitutional procedures had preserved free speech: communists could openly attempt to persuade Australians that Marxism offered a better way of life.

Externally, the battle against communist expansion led Australia into severe new commitments. These included participation in the Korean War, the Malayan civil war and the Vietnam War. Each emergency drew Australia more and more into the worldwide activities by which the United States was attempting to draw a cordon around Russia, China, and their satellites.

On 25 June 1950, without warning, the communist-controlled state of North Korea invaded the independent state of South Korea. The United Nations Security Council, voting in the absence of the Russian delegate, resolved to support South Korea with armed force. General Douglas MacArthur was appointed United Nations Commander-in-Chief: Australia became the first nation after the United States to offer units from each of its armed services.

The United Nations forces quickly conquered the capital of North Korea, but were forced back by massive Chinese intervention. After more than a year of intense fighting, the battle lines stabilised around the original border at the 38th parallel. This was accepted by an armistice two years later as the permanent division between North and South Korea. The total cost of halting this example of communist aggression was more than 73,000 United Nations soldiers killed. Australian units suffered 1538 casualties, including 281 killed and missing.

Australia's participation in the Korean War led directly to the vital ANZUS Treaty of 1951. Our first defence treaty to be concluded directly with a foreign country, ANZUS set the pattern for military co-operation between Australia and the United States down to the present day. A further pact known as SEATO (South-East Asia Treaty Organisation) signed in Manila in 1954 bound Australia, the United States, New Zealand, Britain, France, Pakistan, the Philippines and Thailand jointly to resist communist penetration anywhere in the area. The arrangement led Australia to involvement in a disastrous war on the Asian mainland.

Taking the Australian wounded from Korea to Japan. Painting by Ivor Hele.

Bitter Years of the Vietnam Defeat

The Australian-American alliance came under its harshest test when communist-led nationalist rebels began to triumph in Indo-China (Vietnam). The major battle of Dienbienphu in 1954 shattered the century-old French colonial control of northern Vietnam. At peace talks held in Geneva later that year, the country was split into two parts at the 17th parallel.

At first this division seemed an exact duplication of the position in Korea. The Americans began pouring 'advisers', arms and civil aid into South Vietnam to bolster up a regime which in theory aimed at extending Western ideas of religious, economic and political freedom. In fact the south was ruled by military cliques determined to preserve the exploitative power of wealthy landlords and bankers.

As rebellion spread, the Americans bore by far the worst of the fighting and suffered 58,000 killed. Australia was one of the few Western countries which allowed itself to become involved. Acting under the delusion that Australia's security would be enhanced by 'forward defence' in Vietnam's paddy-fields and foetid jungles, Menzies agreed in 1962 to provide a token force of Australian 'advisers' to help train South Vietnamese troops. Public opinion polls of the time showed up to 70 per cent of Australians in favour of the move. By 1965 the conflict had expanded to the point where Menzies, at America's request, committed the 1st Battalion of the Royal Australian Regiment to action with United States airborne troops at Bien Hoa.

At home, Menzies bit the bullet and introduced a scheme of compulsory military training. Australian males reaching twenty years of age were chosen by ballot to spend two full years in the army, and three years in the part-time reserve forces. For the first time in Australia's history, these 'lottery conscripts' could be sent to fight anywhere in the world. So deep was public fear of communist expansion at the time that abandonment of the Australian tradition of voluntary overseas service was accepted with remarkably little debate. To ensure that controversy would not affect the scheme, Menzies refused to risk referendums on the question such as W. M. Hughes had ordered during World War I. Between 1965 and 1972 nearly sixty-four thousand young men were conscripted: of these, 15,500 were sent to Vietnam.

Early in 1966, the ageing Menzies handed over the Prime Ministership to Harold ('Puss') Holt, a likeable 58-year-old Victorian solicitor with long parliamentary experience. A few weeks after taking office, Holt agreed with an American request to treble Australian forces in Vietnam, in a push to 'clean out' the rebels once and for all.

Australia's commitment to Asia was now far bigger than at any period of the Korean War. To fulfill it, conscripts had to be included in two new battalions, 5 RAR and 6 RAR. These were sent to Nui Dat in Phuoc Tuy province south-east of Saigon, where they helped to prevent a 'final offensive' planned by the rebels for 1966–67. Hard fighting was also necessary to help break up the enemy's major Tet Offensive of 1968. Yet the more the West intervened with fearful weapons of destruction, including mass bombing and chemical defoliation, the sterner became the rebel forces' resolve.

By the time Harold Holt came to contest a half-Senate election in November 1967, Australian support for the war had already diminished to the point where the government lost control of the Senate. On 19 December, Holt went swimming in heavy surf near Portsea, Victoria, and drowned: his body was never found.

The new Prime Minister who inherited the mess in Vietnam was John Grey Gorton, a 57-year-old former fighter pilot of World War II. Gorton, a rangy, rather

To exhaust our resources in the bottomless pit of jungle warfare, in a war in which we have not even defined our purpose honestly, or explained what we would accept as victory, is the very height of folly and the very depths of despair.

ARTHUR CALWELL, May 1965.

Below left. **Harold Holt**, Liberal Prime Minister during the Vietnam War, who disappeared off Portsea late in 1967. Painting by Clifton Pugh.
Below. **John Grey Gorton**, World War II pilot who succeeded Harold Holt as Prime Minister. Painting by June Mendoza.

Boy 1967. Linocut by
Noel Counihan.

domineering personality with a face deeply scarred by a wartime plane crash, was popular with many voters for his occasional larrikinism and genuine feeling for Australian nationalism. But what policies were in Australia's best interests? Election results showed that a growing proportion of the electorate was uneasy about Australia's continued involvement in Vietnam. The Liberal Party began to fall apart, and Gorton was deposed by his own former supporters in March 1971.

During these latter years, for the first time in our history, Australian troops fighting overseas were not supported by a clear and undeniable public mandate. Youthful demonstrators, resenting the 'death lottery' which might conscript them to kill peasants in Vietnam, fought police in bloody street riots. Some went to gaol rather than join the army, while thousands more evaded arrest.

The protest movement steadily spread among the general public, culminating in huge 'moratorium' marches which paralysed capital cities on selected days in 1969 and 1970. Democracies cannot fight any war without majority public support for their aims and methods. The new McMahon Liberal government reluctantly withdrew most Australian forces from Vietnam during 1972, pretending that the military situation had stabilised to the point where control could safely be handed over to South Vietnamese troops.

When the soldiers came home, there were no ticker-tape parades, no swell of national pride. Survivors of the Gallipoli defeat in World War I were still regarded as special heroes, but survivors of the Vietnam defeat—no matter how courageously they had fought against a tenacious enemy—were regarded as little better than takers of innocent lives. That was the kind of war it was. No brave legends emerged from Vietnam into public consciousness, even though Australians who served there suffered 2793 casualties, of whom nearly half were conscripts.

Continuation of the American Alliance

Even the Vietnam debacle did not shake Australia's faith in her special relationship with America. Every Federal government, no matter how conservative or radical, has continued to support the evolutionary arrangements under which America and Australia develop their 'collective capacity to resist armed attack'.

Australia's assumption is that if her territory were ever invaded, America would come to her aid as promptly as in World War II. If this is so, Australia is protected against large-scale armed incursions of the kind she has always feared—certainly sufficiently to make any potential invader think carefully before taking on the Australian-American partnership.

Australia pays a heavy price for this kind of security. When the Americans planned their worldwide defence against communist expansionism, they needed a network of communications bases to transmit military information and instructions. Australia seemed the perfect site for installations which could cover much of the hemisphere. But the establishment of United States bases here would automatically make Australia a primary target in the event of nuclear world war.

In 1963 the Menzies government granted the United States exclusive use until 1988 of 28 square miles of land at North-West Cape, a remote area on Exmouth Gulf, Western Australia, for a submarine and space communications base.

During the 1970s, several further United States bases began to rise in remote areas of Australia. The first was at Pine Gap, 25 kilometres south-west of Alice Springs. This is used mainly for communicating with United States space vehicles, and probably with spy satellites passing over Asia and Russia. The second main base is at Nurrungar, near the old British-Australian rocket testing area at Woomera, west of Lake Torrens, South Australia. Nurrungar appears to be part of the early-warning satellite system designed to detect infra-red emissions and sound the first alarm in any launch of Russian missiles.

Continuation of support for American use of Australian facilities springs from the belief that the nuclear arms race has so far served to prevent another world war. The existence of 'mutually assured destruction' has meant that neither side is willing to risk its own obliteration by being the first to launch a nuclear strike.

All wars have the same end,
We make our conquered
* enemies friends,*
And distrust our friends into
* our enemies.*
Only an invading army can
* simplify*
The need to shoot another
* man.*
Even so, I am not ashamed
Of having joined up to shoot
* our friends,*
The Germans and the
* Japanese.*
But conscripts, those of you
* still alive,*
What will you tell your sons
* of Vietnam?*
'I was sent, I did not ask to go.
I was taught to kill, to fear,
* and to believe*
That one man's health is
* another man's disease,*
That all men, and women
* too, are enemies.'*

GEOFFREY DUTTON

4. Whitlam Years Encourage a New Nationalism

With a series of inspiring speeches, Edward Gough Whitlam, a former RAAF navigator, took the Labor Party back into power on 2 December 1972. Impressed by the great orator's vision, and disgusted with the Liberal Party's indecision on vital issues, voters gave a considerable majority to the first Federal Labor government since J. B. Chifley's defeat in 1949.

Immediately he won power, Whitlam used the Prime Minister's prerogative to take a more forthright stand towards Britain, the United States, and other countries. In a series of swift moves he pulled the last Australian troops out of Vietnam. He extended formal recognition to communist China and exchanged ambassadors. He initiated attempts to stop France from conducting nuclear tests in the Pacific. His government changed the Queen's style and titles in Australia, deleting reference to the United Kingdom and describing her as 'Queen of Australia'.

An immense programme of social reform was also undertaken. Despite opposition from the medical profession, the Whitlam government evolved a successful 'Medibank' scheme. It laid the basis for development of decentralised growth areas. It heavily subsidised cultural activities and education on a needs basis. It formally abandoned racial origin as a test for new immigrants, and spent large sums on Aboriginal welfare. In areas of social morality, it introduced radical no-fault divorce laws, legalised homosexuality in Federal territories, and practically abolished censorship of books and films. Whitlam later summed up: 'Certainly mine was the greatest reform government that Australia has had'.

From that point on, Labor's 'light on the hill' began to fade. Probably the electorate wanted a breathing space to absorb the bewildering number of reforms already made. Economic misfortune struck when the OPEC oil crisis of 1974 led to high inflation and rising unemployment in all nations dependent on petroleum. Yet little sense of economic reality seemed to penetrate Labor's governing circles.

Late in 1974 Rex Connor, the elderly Minister for Minerals and Energy, began secret negotiations to obtain a loan of $4000 million from oil-rich Arab sheiks. This huge sum was intended for new development projects, including a national gas pipeline, purchase of six oil tankers, extension of port facilities, and extensive railway development, all intended to stimulate the sale of Australian resources.

Malcolm Fraser, a 44-year-old Victorian grazier who led the Liberal-Country Party coalition, promised in 1974 that the Opposition would not in future use its Senate majority to refuse Supply, except in 'extraordinary and reprehensible circumstances'. Those circumstances seemed to have arrived.

On 16 October 1975 the Senate voted by a narrow majority to defer two appropriation Bills, declaring that they would not be considered until the government agreed to hold a general election, thus enabling the people to voice their opinion of the Loans affair.

Whitlam, knowing that substantial numbers of voters had turned against the government, refused to resign. He decided, in his own memorable phrase, to 'tough it out', hoping that public reaction to denial of Supply would swing votes back to Labor. Meanwhile his government attempted to raise sufficient cash through the banking system and other sources to carry on.

By early November 1975 many government-financed bodies had run out of money. Some Federal departments would exhaust funds available to pay public servants' salaries after pay-day on 13 November. Medibank payments, student allowances and certain remittances to the States would stop in December. Australia faced a crisis of unimaginable proportions over the Christmas period. Yet neither Fraser nor Whitlam would back down.

During the tense period of 'toughing it out', Governor-General Sir John Kerr made several attempts to persuade Fraser and Whitlam separately to modify their

There are moments in history when the whole fate and future of nations can be decided by a single decision. For Australia, this is such a time. It's time for a new team, a new programme, a new drive for equality of opportunities: it's time to create new opportunities for Australians, time for a new vision of what we can achieve in this generation for our nation and the region in which we live . . . We will put Australians back into the business of running Australia and owning Australia.

GOUGH WHITLAM, policy speech in 1972.

Edward Gough Whitlam,
Prime Minister, painted by
Clifton Pugh in 1972.

positions. When these failed, on 10 November 1975 Kerr consulted Sir Garfield Barwick, Chief Justice of the High Court.

Barwick confirmed that under the Constitution, the Senate had undoubted power to refuse Supply if it chose to do so. A Prime Minister who could not ensure Supply to the Crown must either advise a general election or resign his post. Should he refuse to take either course, the Governor-General had authority under the Constitution to dismiss his government.

Kerr summoned Whitlam to Government House the following morning, and asked him whether he would call a general election. When Whitlam refused, Kerr handed him a letter dismissing his government from office. An astounded Whitlam returned to Parliament House to inform his colleagues that they were no longer Ministers of the Crown. Kerr meanwhile summoned Fraser and appointed him to form a caretaker government, pledged to obtain immediate Supply and call an early general election.

These events at first stunned the nation, then gave rise to the fiercest political controversy known for many years. Its ripples have still not died away. The public had assumed that once they elected a government for the House of Representatives, it would stay in office until the following election in three years or less. Now they were brought face to face with the reality: that their decision on election of Senators could be just as important as votes for the lower house; and that in a deadlock the non-elected Governor-General possessed reserve powers far beyond the ceremonial functions which he usually fulfilled.

The election for both houses took place on 13 December 1975. The result was the greatest landslide seen in Australian federal history. Fraser's forces won 91 seats in the lower house, while Labor was reduced to a rump of 36 seats.

The tragedy of 1975 was that each of the key figures involved was convinced he was acting in Australia's best interests. In their own way, all were true patriots. Nor did the turmoil produce a long-term solution. The same constitutional position remains: the same circumstances could one day occur again to tear the nation asunder. Yet voters remain so wary of changes to the Constitution that the Senate seems likely to retain for many years its power to evict elected governments.

Sir John Kerr, Governor-General, painted by Clifton Pugh in 1975.

5. Sporting Triumphs on the World Scene

Australia's international sporting reputation stands at an historically high level. During recent decades our sportsmen and women have continued to challenge the world's champions, and often beat them. They have made Australia one of the top nations in tennis, water sports, cricket, athletics and a host of other activities.

After World War II Australian tennis players became as well known in the United States as at home, battling to retain or win back the Davis Cup. During the 1950s, under the remorseless coaching of Harry Hopman, Australia won eight out of ten Cup finals; and during the 1960s, seven out of ten. After a bad spell in the 1970s, Australia again triumphed to take the Cup in December 1983.

Women tennis players also hit top form. In 1965 Margaret Court (b. 1942) became the first Australian woman to win at Wimbledon. She went on to win practically every women's world championship during the late 1960s. The first famous Aboriginal tennis player, Evonne Goolagong (b. 1951), defeated Margaret Court to win Wimbledon in 1971.

Great achievements continued in swimming. In the late 1940s John Marshall (b. 1930) broke nearly every world freestyle record before dying in a car smash. Superb Australian women swimmers dominated the sport from the 1950s onwards. In 1953 Judy Joy Davies (b. 1927) set a world freestyle record for one mile. While training for the 1956 Melbourne Olympics, Lorraine Crapp (b. 1938) broke sixteen world records. Dawn Fraser (b. 1937) became the world's only swimmer to win gold medals at three successive Olympics, in 1956, 1960 and 1964. Murray Rose (b. 1939), John Konrads (b. 1942) and others set many world records for distance men's events in the 1950s and 1960s. Shane Gould, aged 15, established world records for every freestyle distance in 1972, and was later voted the best-ever women's freestyle champion. The following year a 13-year-old, Jenny Turrell, became the youngest record-holder known when she beat all previous times for 1500 metres freestyle. In 1978 two 15-year-olds, Michelle Ford and Tracey Wickham, set new records for 400, 800 and 1500 metres freestyle.

Cricket matches between Australia and England went into decline for some

Below right. Australia's tennis renaissance began in 1983 when it regained the Davis Cup. (Left to right) **Pat Cash, Mark Edmondson, Neale Fraser, Paul McNamee and John Fitzgerald.**
Below. **Robert de Castella,** who held the world marathon championship for two years.

years after Don Bradman's retirement in 1948. The sport suddenly came back to life in 1977 when Kerry Packer's television network signed many of the world's best players to appear in a speeded-up form of the game called World Series Cricket. Night cricket was particularly successful.

Australia's extraordinary record in athletics began in 1954 when John Landy (b. 1930) broke Roger Bannister's time for the mile, clocking 3 mins 58 secs in Finland. Landy was followed by Herb Elliott (b. 1938), generally recognised as the greatest-ever mile and 1500 metres runner, who at the age of 20 reduced the record for the mile to 3 mins 54·5 secs. During the 1960s, Ron Clarke (b. 1937) set seventeen new records for distance events, at one point holding every world record from three miles to one hour's running.

Sir Jack Brabham, three times world champion, in 1966 became the first racing driver ever to win the world title in a car designed and built by himself.

Australian women athletes also began to achieve world fame. In 1952 Shirley Strickland (b. 1925) won our first gold medal for the 80 metres hurdles at the Helsinki Olympics. At the 1956 Melbourne Olympics she won more gold medals, setting new world records in sprint and hurdles events. Meanwhile Marjorie Jackson (b. 1931), equally well-known as 'the Lithgow Flyer', won practically all her sprint events at Olympic and Commonwealth Games during the 1950s, and broke ten individual world records. Betty Cuthbert (b. 1938), the original 'Golden Girl' of athletics, kept up these remarkable victories by winning three gold medals at the 1956 Olympics, another at the 1964 Olympics, and setting sixteen world records for sprint and relay events.

The year 1983 brought the greatest string of all-round sporting triumphs Australia has ever known. During the first week in January, Australian test cricketers won back the Ashes from England. Throughout the year, Australia's national men's hockey team beat every other country against which it competed. Cyclist Steele Bishop won the 4000 metres pursuit championship in Europe. The women's netball team won the world championship in Singapore. In April 1983, 26-year-old Robert de Castella broke the world record for the marathon, repeating his victory at the world athletic championships in August. Sue Cook of Melbourne (b. 1958) continued to dominate long-distance walk events with nine world records. In August 1983, 31-year-old Jan Stephenson of Sydney won the United States Women's Open Golf championship.

Sue Cook, Australian world walk champion.

Dominating all of these victories was Australia's sensational snatching of the America's Cup yachting trophy from the United States in September 1983. Britain and other countries had tried in vain for more than a century to win the famous 12-metre yacht series. Australian-designed yachts had failed in 1962, 1967, 1970, 1974, 1977 and 1980. In 1983 a Perth-based team entered their new yacht *Australia II*, which had a unique 'winged keel' giving it remarkable manoeuvrability, in the series of five races traditionally held off Newport, Rhode Island. They lost the first two races, but fought back magnificently to win the last three.

An intense wave of national pride swept all parts of Australia. Prime Minister Bob Hawke revelled in the victory, describing it as 'out of this world . . . fantastic . . . a great moment in Australian history'.

Australia's reasonable performance at the 1984 Los Angeles Olympics seems likely to be bettered on future occasions, particularly since the Hawke government announced huge financial support in its 1984–85 Budget for the Australian Institute of Sport, and defence of the America's Cup in 1987.

Climax of the 1983 America's Cup: Australia II narrowly takes the last race, the first time in 132 years that the United States had lost the series.

Australia's impressive postwar sporting record has been accompanied by heightened interest in personal fitness among the general public. Much greater numbers of adults now participate regularly in sport or disciplined exercise, while constant attempts are made by governments to persuade the less-fit to drop harmful habits such as smoking and take part in some healthy outdoors activity.

With this kind of social encouragement, athletic youngsters are now more impelled than ever to take up a wide variety of sports. From this pool of talent we can expect more world record-breakers to emerge. Meanwhile the sometimes exaggerated image of Australia as a nation with small numbers but a high proportion of athletic heroes is becoming more and more true. In a wider sense, interest in sport helps to fulfill the ideal of a healthy democracy which also strives for high achievement.

6. Civilian Honours and Awards

Below. **Order of Australia Awards.**

Knight   Companion

Officer   Member

Medal   National Medal

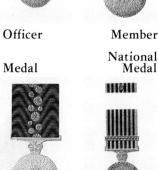

In the days when loyalty to Britain was all that mattered, the imperial honours system satisfied most Australians as a method of recognising lengthy or unusual public service. Large numbers of awards ranging from British Empire Medals to knighthoods—even the occasional baronetcy—were traditionally announced on New Year's Day and the Queen's birthday. The British hegemony seemed complete and indestructible.

Yet throughout Australian history ran a concurrent stream of protest against attempts to impose British patronage upon the Australian democracy. Many nationalists who were offered a 'gong' refused any such link with the Crown, agreeing with Thomas Paine's acid comment in *The Rights of Man* that 'it marks a sort of foppery in the human character, which degrades it . . . It talks about its fine blue ribbon like a girl, and shows its new garter like a child'.

Among prominent Australians who consistently refused knighthoods were George Higinbotham, Alfred Deakin, Deakin's son-in-law Herbert Brookes, Charles Bean, Essington Lewis, Dr H. C. Coombs, and Justice Lionel Murphy.

The Whitlam government instituted the first home-grown honours system in 1975. Known as the Order of Australia, the new honours were intended to recognise 'outstanding merit or achievement or for service in any field of endeavour in Australian life'.

At present the Australian honours system consists of three main sections. The first, the *Order of Australia*, comprises two divisions, general and military. The general division has five grades: Knights and Dames (AK or AD); Companions (AC); Officers (AO); Members (AM); Medal of the Order (OAM). The second section, the *Australian Bravery Decorations*, incorporate four awards: the Cross of Valour, for 'most conspicuous courage in circumstances of extreme peril'; the Star of Courage, for 'conspicuous courage in circumstances of great peril'; the Bravery Medal, for 'acts of bravery in hazardous circumstances'; the Commendation for Brave Conduct, for 'acts of bravery considered worthy of recognition'.

Long Service Awards make up the third section and include: the National Medal, awarded for fifteen years' service in police, ambulance or fire services; and Defence Force Service Awards that comprise the Defence Force Service Medal, the Reserve Force Decoration, and the Reserve Force Medal.

Certain traditional awards have not been damaged by any association with political preferment, and can be accepted with pride by Australians.

One of the foremost is the Order of Merit, inaugurated by King Edward VII in 1902. Limited to twenty-four living members, it is awarded solely by the monarch's choice. Although it carries no title, the Order is considered by many to be the most outstanding and exclusive peacetime distinction in the entire honours system.

Six Australians have been chosen as recipients at various times. The first was Samuel Alexander (1859–1938), a Sydney-born philosopher who became the first practising Jew to win fellowships at Oxford and Cambridge. After publication of his major work on speculative metaphysics, entitled *Space, Time and Deity*, Alexander was appointed to the Order of Merit by King George V in 1930.

The next appointee was George Gilbert Murray, born in Sydney in 1866, son of Sir Terence Murray who founded Yarralumla property where Government House now stands. George Murray became a widely-published Professor of Greek at Oxford University, and chairman of the League of Nations Union. King George VI appointed him to the Order in 1941.

In 1958, Queen Elizabeth II appointed Sir MacFarlane Burnet to the Order. Born in 1899 at Traralgon, Victoria, Burnet had a long and distinguished career in microbiological research which also won him a shared Nobel Prize in 1960.

The next appointee was Sir Owen Dixon (1886–1972), born at Hawthorn,

Victoria. After a remarkable career as a barrister, Dixon became a High Court judge in 1929, Australian Minister to Washington in 1942, and Chief Justice of Australia in 1952. His Order of Merit was announced in 1963.

In 1965 the Queen appointed to the Order Howard Walter Florey, Baron of Adelaide and Marston (1898–1968). Florey, born in Adelaide, achieved immortality for his part in developing penicillin, sharing the Nobel Prize for medicine in 1945.

The most recent recipient of the Order of Merit, in 1983, was Sir Sidney Nolan, born in Carlton, Victoria, in 1917, and famous for his unique Australian paintings. Many of his most valuable works have been donated to the nation.

Five Australians besides Sir MacFarlane Burnet and Lord Florey have won Nobel Prizes. These rich awards of $80,000 each are granted annually in Stockholm for the most important work in science, literature and world peace.

The first Australian winners were a father and son team of physicists. The father, Sir William Bragg (1862–1942) was born in England, but spent much of his working life in Adelaide exploring the new sciences of radioactivity and ionisation. He was appointed to the Order of Merit in 1931. The son, Sir Lawrence Bragg (1890–1971) was born in Adelaide, and shared the Nobel Prize with his father in 1915 for founding the science of X-ray analysis of crystals.

Sir John Eccles, a neurophysiologist, born in Melbourne in 1903, shared the Nobel Prize for medicine in 1963 for his pioneering work on nerve cells.

In 1973 the remarkable Australian novelist Patrick White won the Nobel Prize for literature. White was born in London in 1912 into a wealthy Australian family of graziers, and educated in Sydney. His books are probably more widely-read overseas than in Australia, revealing to discriminating readers the complexity below the surface of Australian life.

The last Australian to win the Nobel Prize was Professor John Cornforth. Born in Sydney in 1917, Cornforth shared the 1975 Nobel Prize in chemistry for his work showing how enzymes are affected by their three-dimensional structure.

Cross of Valour   Star of Courage

Bravery Medal

Above. **Australian Bravery Medals.**

SVENSKA AKADEMIEN

har vid sitt sammanträde den 18 oktober 1973

i överensstämmelse med föreskrifterna

i det av

ALFRED NOBEL

den 27 november 1895 upprättade testamente

beslutat att tilldela

PATRICK WHITE

1973 års nobelpris i litteratur

för en episk och psykologisk berättarkonst

som infört en ny världsdel

i litteraturen.

Stockholm den 10 december 1973

Seven Australians have won the Nobel Prize. Watercolour by G. Brusewiz is depicted on **Patrick White's Nobel Prize for Literature.**

Patrick White, winner of the 1973 Nobel Prize for Literature. Painting by Desmond Digby.

7. The Search for Aboriginal Pride

Let Us Not Be Bitter

Away with bitterness, my
* own dark people*
Come stand with me,
* look forward, not back,*
For a new time has come
* for us.*
Now we must change, my
* people. For so long*
Time for us stood still; now
* we know*
Life is change, life is
* progress,*
Life is learning things, life
* is onward.*
White men had to learn
* civilized ways,*
Now it is our turn.
Away with bitterness and
* the bitter past;*
Let us try to understand the
* white man's ways*
And accept them as they
* accept us;*
Let us judge white people by
* the best of their race.*
The prejudiced ones are less
* than we,*
We want them no more than
* they want us.*
Let us not be bitter, that is
* an empty thing,*
A maggot in the mind.
The past is gone like our
* childhood days of old,*
The future comes like dawn
* after the dark,*
Bringing fulfilment.

KATH WALKER

A century ago few white Australians had much time for Aborigines. They were generally despised as peculiar survivals from the Stone Age, who had apparently ceased to evolve while European man was emerging into the technological triumphs of the modern age.

A few humanitarians, appalled by the disappearance of a unique race, helped to herd the tribal remnants into reserves. Here, despite individual injustices and substandard living conditions (which were still an improvement on mia-mias), Aborigines began to stabilise in numbers and slowly percolate into white society. They did not die out as anticipated.

Many scandals and injustices remain today. By and large, however, Aborigines are up and running. In the long view of history, they managed to survive a staggering biological challenge. Many are now beginning to merge successfully into the technology-rich society which once threatened to obliterate them.

Much of the apparent turmoil in Aboriginal affairs today is due to short-term judgements by people who have forgotten how much worse things used to be, or are ignorant of the huge change which has occurred in majority attitudes, or are understandably impatient to achieve in a few years what took European man many centuries to achieve.

One of the first actions of Harold Holt after his election as Liberal Prime Minister in 1966 was to order a referendum on the question of granting superior powers to the Commonwealth over the States in dealing with Aboriginal affairs.

An overwhelming 90 per cent of electors agreed with Holt's move: for the first time in any Australian referendum, every electorate in the nation voted 'Yes'. A new era in Aboriginal questions had dawned, and we are still seeing the generally beneficial results.

Many Aborigines proved themselves excellent stockmen, able to compete on white men's terms.

In 1972 Prime Minister Whitlam announced that his government's objective was to restore to Aborigines 'their lost power of self-determination in economic, social and political affairs'. Aborigines who had already proved themselves as stockmen would be given at least an equal chance to prove themselves as station owners, competing with white cattlemen and selling their products to traditional markets for beef and hides.

An Aboriginal Land Rights Commission was established under Mr Justice Woodward. Its first decision was to purchase a 440,000-acre cattle station, Panter Downs, north-east of Derby in the Kimberley region of Western Australia.

This process continued apace. By the end of 1982 the freehold of nearly 29 per cent of Crown land in the Northern Territory not already held under leasehold had passed into Aboriginal hands. It comprised mainly a large slice of Arnhem Land, and a huge area west of Alice Springs as far as the Western Australian border.

Another 18 per cent of the total area of the Northern Territory is still under claim by Aborigines, much of it around Tennant Creek and Katherine, traditional centres for white settlement. If these claims are finalised, about two-thirds of the Territory's 30,000 Aborigines will be living on their own freehold land, comprising nearly half the total area of the Northern Territory.

This revolutionary change has taken place within a remarkably short time. It aroused severe reactions among most white residents, who are now attempting to stabilise the situation so that little or no further productive land controlled by whites passes to Aboriginal control.

The white majority in Australia is today remarkably tolerant in racial affairs. Most people are now willing to accept into the general society any person—white, black, yellow or brown—who shows himself to be courteous, clean, sober, honest, reasonably intelligent, moderately ambitious and hardworking.

These are universal virtues which those who really wish to help Aborigines should be impressing upon their clients. Instead, many white activists are merely spreading fraudulent 'solutions' based on their own resentment of the dominant social structure.

Their theory of preservation of the tribes in isolation from the rest of Australia represents massive escapism into an imagined golden age which never existed—an escapism which does not hesitate to take maximum advantage of white society's

Above. **Stephen Hawke,** son of the then ACTU president Bob Hawke, assisted the Yungngora tribe in Western Australia to preserve its land from test drilling by oil companies. Above left. **Aboriginal children studying in primary school in the north**—intelligence is not lacking, but social motivation for higher education often is.

Accomplished Aboriginal artist **Albert Namatjira**, once martyred for illegal purchase of alcohol, now honoured by display of his work in Alice Springs Art Gallery. Painting by Sir William Dargie.

'**The Family, 1965**', by Russell Drysdale, makes its own comment on happy mixing of the races.

productive work, but forgets the cruelty, hardship, low expectation of life, and frequent killings which disfigured tribal life until only a few decades ago.

The true success stories among Aborigines come not from the isolationism of the outback, but from those educated, urbanised Aborigines who have striven for the best of what the white man's system has to offer.

Even Aborigines who are not personally ambitious can succeed in this way through their offspring. Often enough, interbreeding with the more acquisitive European races has produced mixed-blood children whose success in competitive occupations has been rewarding to themselves and inspiring to others on the way up.

Fortunately the old idea that Aborigines are necessarily inferior in intelligence has practically died out. Enough of the luckier and brighter ones have now fought their way up through the system to show that they belong to the same breed of *homo erectus* which millions of years ago began the task of bending the world to their will.

For the sake of future racial harmony, it is important that all whites should realise that, given a fair chance in life, Aborigines are just as 'human' as they are, and subject to just as many variations in upward and downward social mobility.

The whole tendency of the modern world is towards integration and standardisation. Increasingly the power of modern technology and communications is changing people into citizens of vast regions or even the world instead of a particular 'sacred area'. It is difficult to see how any native race can stay outside these potent world movements.

Take the worst aspect. Not so long ago, to be a woman *and* an Aborigine meant there was no hope at all of qualifying for a professional career. Now, as several out-standing part-Aboriginal women have shown, it is possible for very determined girls to follow traditional European paths to worldly success. Many young Aboriginal men have similarly been successful in their chosen careers.

They are not to be stigmatised as Aunty and Uncle Toms betraying the interests of their own race. They are people who have come to terms with the dominant culture, have realised why it is dominant, and decided to use it for the benefit of all people.

8. Farewell to Yesterday's Cultural Cringe

From first white settlement, Australian popular culture was dominated by British values in art, writing, theatre, fashion, sport and social behaviour. A temporary victory of Australianism came at the turn of the century when the works of Henry Lawson, 'Banjo' Paterson and C. J. Dennis sold by the tens of thousands, and could often be quoted verbatim by ordinary people. By the 1920s, however, popular culture had again fallen under the sway of overseas publishers and film producers.

One Melbourne critic named Angell Arthur Phillips, descended from a cultured Jewish immigrant family, coined the term 'the cultural cringe' to describe this domination of Australian thinking by the two most powerful English-speaking societies, Britain and America. That domination still exists. But the emergence of a wider nationalism in the 1970s and its continuation in the 1980s gives hope that homegrown culture will become a permanent core of the Australian attitude to life.

Australia's modern artistic renaissance began some years after World War II. Painters like William Dobell (1899–1970), Russell Drysdale (1912–81) and Sidney Nolan (b. 1917), who had continued to work under difficulties during the

Brett Whiteley's stunning painting of an equally stunning architectural masterpiece, **the Sydney Opera House**.

war, suddenly found their productions in great demand. Their uniquely Australian qualities can be seen from examples reproduced in this book. Prices of the best works soared to unprecedented levels, and continue to rise. Many dealers including cultured immigrants opened private galleries which helped to stimulate the interest of collectors and supported many talented younger artists. Immigrant artists such as Louis Kahan and Judy Cassab achieved fame. State governments began to revitalise their arts colleges. New public galleries today attract large crowds.

In 1973 the Whitlam government authorised construction of the Australian National Gallery in Canberra to house the Commonwealth's growing collection of paintings, sculptures and other forms of artistic expression. Unfortunately the gallery became partly sidetracked into the purchase of controversial and expensive works by fashionable overseas modernists. Despite this, and despite its unlovely external architecture, the National Gallery attracts large numbers of tourists to view its entrancing collections of Australian and Pacific art.

In the field of performing arts, one of the most courageous cultural decisions ever taken in Australia was the building of Sydney's astonishing opera house on Bennelong Point. Although funds were badly needed for many other public projects, in 1955 a State Labor government headed by 64-year-old John Joseph Cahill, formerly a fitter in the Railways Department, decided to hold an international contest for a building in which all types of opera, concerts, ballet, drama and public meetings could be held. The winner was a Danish architect, Joern Utzon, 38, whose revolutionary design included unique interlocking concrete shells soaring over the building like sails upon Sydney Harbour.

Constructed by a local company between 1959 and 1972, and financed largely from public lotteries, the $100 million project was recognised as one of the wonders of the world when opened by Queen Elizabeth in 1973. It has since proved of special value in building up permanent audiences for cultural events of all kinds, despite criticism of the level of public funding needed to keep its performing companies in operation. Ticket sales by the Australian Opera and State opera companies now average more than seven million a year.

In 1973 the Whitlam government established the Australia Council in an endeavour to lift community arts and crafts, literature, music, theatre and visual arts into a veritable rebirth of Australian culture. A separate Aboriginal Arts Board was charged with reviving and preserving native culture. Since 1973 Federal governments have spent more than $200 million in subsidising the arts through the Australia Council. Despite some failures, the overall result has been a real interest and participation in all forms of art and culture. One only needs to compare today's widespread artistic sophistication with the bucolic innocence of the 1960s to see what has been achieved.

The worst criticism that can be made of public funding of the arts is that much of the expenditure goes to administrators, organisers and performers; and a comparatively small proportion to originating creative artists—yet the latter are the only people who can interpret the Australian experience as it emerges.

The mass media have generally improved their standards in tune with the general upgrading of public taste and educational standards. Newspapers and radio stations in the 1950s were generally cautious, conservative and unimaginative. Some appalling examples of crassness remain, but today the media cater for a multitude of interests in a much more open manner than ever before.

The modern film industry has become one of Australia's greatest assets, producing with government assistance a remarkable range of quality films acclaimed locally and overseas. During the last decade some 200 feature films written and directed by Australians have won cinema release. Several fine Australian historical series have been produced for television. Documentary and current affairs programmes on all aspects of Australian life are comparable with anything available in other countries, and attract audiences eager to know more about their own nation.

In schools and universities, Australian history and literature courses—once not available anywhere—now attract large numbers of students. As they mature and take new levels of awareness into the general community, we will see the full effects of the Australian cultural renaissance which began not so many years ago.

9. On the Shores of Lake Burley Griffin, a Unique National Capital Arises

Despite fierce controversy over the selection and naming of Canberra, most people hoped that a city worthy of Australia would emerge. At the official opening on the lonely paddocks on 12 March 1913, the Governor-General, Lord Thomas Denman, said:

> To those who criticise the choice of locality, I would recall this phrase: 'There are no points of the compass on the chart of true patriotism.' The time for doubt, misgiving, and criticism, is past. It is always easy to sneer and criticise; but now that a start has been made, it seems to me the duty of patriotic Australians to do all that lies in their power to make this Capital worthy of the Commonwealth. The city that is to be should have a splendid destiny before it, but the making of that destiny lies in your hands, the hands of your children, and those who come after them. Remember that the traditions of this City will be the traditions of Australia. Let us hope that they will be traditions of freedom, of peace, of honour, and of prosperity; that here will be reflected all that is finest and noblest in the national life of the country; that here a city may arise where those responsible for the government of this country in the future may seek and find inspiration in its noble buildings, its broad avenues, its shaded parks, and sheltered gardens—a city bearing perhaps some resemblance to the city beautiful of our dreams.

In 1911 the Fisher government had announced a worldwide competition to find the best design for a city whose optimum population was estimated to be

What Canberra might have been. D. A. Agache's design in the world contest of 1912.

Walter Burley Griffin, the brilliant American architect whose plan for Canberra is now reaching full fruition.

25,000 inhabitants. (Today Canberra has nearly ten times that number.) The contest was promptly boycotted by the Australian and British Architects' Institutes, on the ground that the final decision would be made by Home Affairs Minister King O'Malley instead of trained architects. The result of the boycott was that the first three prizes went to American, Finnish and French architects.

The winning entry, selected personally by O'Malley, was the work of Walter Burley Griffin, a 35-year-old Chicago landscape architect and former associate of the renowned Frank Lloyd Wright. In 1914, the Commonwealth appointed Griffin as Federal Capital Director of Design and Construction.

'I have planned a city not like any other city in the world', said Griffin. 'My idea is to treat architecture as a democratic language of everyday life, not a language of an aristocratic, especially educated cult.' But Griffin was able to achieve little in person. The outbreak of World War I, and continual sabotage by conservative departmental architects, meant that only limited road-building and water supply works could be completed by the time Griffin's appointment expired in 1920. For the first half-century Canberra remained a much-maligned 'bush capital' instead of the noble city originally envisaged.

The most important building erected between the wars was a 'provisional' Parliament House, still in use today. A sprawling white pavilion of no particular architectural style, the building was pushed up quickly to meet the opening date of 9 May 1927, when the Duke of York performed the inauguration ceremony, and Nellie Melba sang 'God Save the King' on the steps outside.

Little more than road-building could be achieved during the depressed 1930s. The next key building to appear was the Australian War Memorial, originally designed in 1927, opened on Armistice Day 1941, and later expanded to commemorate all of Australia's military tradition.

The structure is unique among the world's national monuments, being built around a bronze Roll of Honour which lists without rank or other distinction the 110,000 Australians killed in war, reminding later generations that each person's ultimate sacrifice was equal.

In 1946 the Chifley government established the Australian National University in Canberra. It was designed as a new type of university for this country, in which the emphasis would be on postgraduate training and specialised research.

In 1957 the Menzies government made a fresh attempt to fulfill Walter Burley Griffin's vision for Canberra, by establishing a National Capital Development Commission charged with long-term planning and design. The result has been the steady transformation of the capital from its primitive state into a glowing symbol of Australian national pride.

Griffin's original plan, based on the natural topography of the Molonglo Valley, envisaged five separate areas for specific usages, linked by a sequence of sweeping circuits and radial avenues. The Molonglo River would be dammed to provide a series of connecting lakes, around which the administrative city of the future would rise. A central parliamentary triangle was designated as the 'national area' and symbolic focal point of governmental power.

During the 1960s the Commission dammed the Molonglo as planned and named the waterway Lake Burley Griffin. As a 50th anniversary gift, the British government donated a 53-bell carillon for the lake. On the southern shore, a neoclassical National Library rose, to be joined in the 1980s by a new High Court building, the Australian National Gallery, and a National Archives building.

These and other departures from Griffin's original sites were made necessary by changing circumstances in a world which even Griffin could not fully visualise. For instance, the 195-metre Black Mountain telecommunications tower which has dominated the city since 1980 was originally fought by conservationists, but is necessary to provide the immense flow of inward and outward information needed by a modern national capital. New satellite suburbs joined by freeways have also been added to Griffin's scheme.

The permanent Parliament House now being built above the original Parliament on Capital Hill was chosen from entries in a world competition announced by the Fraser government in 1979. Americans again won first prize, although 36-year-old

Richard Thorp of the winning New York firm of Mitchell, Giurgola and Thorp was born in Sydney.

Their fascinating design, dominated by two giant 'boomerangs', places the Senate and House of Representatives below the normal level of Capital Hill. Vast amounts of earth had to be shifted before building could begin. When the turf is replaced and a high four-legged flagpole erected to tie the two chambers together under the national flag, ordinary citizens will be able to stroll above the lower levels where their representatives are meeting. This concept, almost equalling the Sydney Opera House in architectural originality, won the judges' accolade as 'a building that will become, as it deserves to, a national symbol'. The hoped-for completion date is the Bicentennial Year of 1988.

All of these marvellous projects, carried out at the taxpayers' expense, have tended to magnify the problem of Canberra's existence as an artificially maintained public servants' paradise. As its children mature, many of them automatically enter what is becoming almost an hereditary ruling class, possessing vast power and patronage.

Since the end of World War II, the Commonwealth Public Service has expanded from about 150,000 to more than 400,000, excluding defence forces. Generally the controllers are located in Canberra. They tend to possess diminishing firsthand knowledge of the problems of ordinary Australians, for Canberra's main industry is tourism, and real life is far away.

To ameliorate the serious problem of an inbreeding bureaucracy, the Hawke government proposed in 1983 that applicants outside the Public Service should be able to compete on merit with insiders for all senior positions. Public servants whose performance was unsatisfactory would, for the first time, be dismissed or downgraded. Other staff could be rotated between departments at regular intervals, and even exchanged with private industry. Outside consultants would be hired for specific important tasks. A Polish-born immigrant, Professor Peter Wilenski, well-known for his Labor sympathies, was appointed chairman of the Public Service Board to superintend the reform programme.

If these moves succeed in abolishing the excessive privileges of Commonwealth public servants without subjecting them to direct political control, the suspicion with which most Australians regard bureaucrats should diminish. It would certainly harm the continued growth of a unified Australian outlook if the national capital was looked upon as the luxurious home of a privileged mandarin class.

Yet a strong permanent Public Service with clear ideals of national loyalty remains essential, if only to instruct and restrain the often unsophisticated politicians who come into temporary power from the far reaches of the continent.

Model showing the winning American design for the new Houses of Parliament and central flagpole now being built on Capital Hill, Canberra. Completion is planned for 1988.

The new world-wide confidence in Australia and its future in the great and growing region to which we belong, is itself a reflection of our new self-confidence, our confidence in ourselves and in our future . . .

We can now work together to build an Australia dedicated to fairness, justice and genuine equality of opportunity for all . . . a nation in which all can share fairly in the abundance and all the opportunities offered by this great country of ours, in the great years now within our grasp.

R. J. HAWKE, Prime Minister. Policy speech 1984.

10. To Be An Australian Today . . .

In recent decades Australians have become more conscious of the need to preserve their unique natural environment. **Liffey Falls**, south-west of Launceston, is in one of the beautiful forest areas of Tasmania.

To be an Australian today is to be grateful to the Aborigines and Europeans who pioneered this country, but to realise that a new type of Australian race is rapidly emerging.

To be an Australian today is to be proud of the things that make this country unique, but to be aware that other nations have equally valuable ways of life.

To be an Australian today is to be conscious that the beauty of the natural environment must be preserved for future generations, not destroyed by uncontrolled exploitation for private purposes.

To be an Australian today is to try to be as self-reliant, courageous and full of initiative as the pioneers in success, and as stoical in failure.

To be an Australian today is to believe that all people should have an equal chance to work for a satisfying life, regardless of inherited wealth, race or gender.

To be an Australian today is to applaud those who succeed through unusual talent in commerce, politics, sport and culture, and to applaud them doubly when they achieve something of value for their country.

To be an Australian today is to be determined that the continental integrity of this nation will never be breached by armed invasion, and to make sufficient preparations to deter any such possibility.

To be an Australian today is to help preserve the nuclear stalemate through our alliance with America, while hoping that one day all weapons of mass destruction will be abolished from the earth.

To be an Australian today is to believe in maximum freedom of speech, so that evil and hypocrisy may be exposed wherever they appear.

To be an Australian today is to engage in constant thought and debate about what is best for the country, the region, and the world.

To be an Australian today is to realise that party politics, dispiriting though they occasionally become, are the method by which political freedom is maintained in a few fortunate countries like ours.

To be an Australian today is to support a balanced economic system in which private and government enterprise work in harmony, to avoid the evils of oligarchy on the one hand and totalitarianism on the other hand.

To be an Australian today is to hold that the benefits of new technology should be distributed fairly over the whole population through socially desirable projects.

To be an Australian today is to believe that less fortunate nations should be helped to reach a 'lift-off' point where they can take over their own development.

To be an Australian today is to consider the possibility that some day all mankind might peacefully unite into an homogeneous race, in which the same ideals of equality and social justice can be pursued by all human beings.

The lofty headland of **St Helen's Point**, on the north-east coast of Tasmania, affords magnificent views of the ocean and tide-marked sands. This deserted coastline attracts thousands of tourists during the summer months.

*She is the scroll on which
we are to write
Mythologies our own and
epics new . . .*

BERNARD O'DOWD

A Calendar for Australians

January

1   Commonwealth of Australia proclaimed (1901). Flags should be flown.

1   Edmund Barton first Prime of Australia (1901) to 24 September 1903.

1   Northern Territory transferred to Federal Government (1911).

2   George Bass discovered the most southerly point of Australian mainland—Wilson's Promontory (1798).

2   The name Tasmania adopted, replacing Van Diemen's Land (1856).

3   AIF 6th Division conquered Bardia in World War II (1941).

4   William Dampier sighted north-west coast of 'New Holland' (1688).

5   Bass discovered Westernport Bay, Vic. (1798).

5   New South Wales Constitution proclaimed, granting representative government (1843).

6   J. A. Lyons Prime Minister (1932) to 7 April 1939.

10   Last convicts arrived in Western Australia (1863).

10   J. G. Gorton first Senator to become Prime Minister (1968) to 10 March 1971.

14   Worst bushfires ever in Victoria: seventy-one dead (1939).

15   First issue of Sydney *Bulletin* (1880).

16   First free settlers arrived in Australia on *Bellona* (1793).

16   New South Wales and Queensland railway systems connected at Wallangarra, Qld (1888).

18   Governor Arthur Phillip first entered Botany Bay (1788).

18   Worst train smash in Australian history at Granville, NSW: eighty-three dead, 200 injured (1977).

19   Metric measurements introduced (1970).

20   First parliament opened in Western Australia under responsible government (1891).

21   Governor Phillip first entered Port Jackson and landed at Camp Cove (1788).

21   First road over Blue Mountains completed by Lieutenant William Cox and twenty-eight convicts (1815).

23   Western Australian goldfields water supply opened (1903).

24   French explorer Jean La Perouse arrived at Botany Bay six days after Governor Phillip (1788).

26   Australia Day: celebrates the foundation of Australia (1788). Flags should be flown on 26 January and also on the day observed as a public holiday.

26   NSW Corps deposed Governor William Bligh (1808).

26   H. E. Holt Prime Minister (1966) to 19 December 1967.

February

2   Captain Charles Sturt discovered the Darling River (1829).

3   First tour by a reigning monarch, Queen Elizabeth II, began in Sydney (1954).

3   First church service in Australia conducted by Rev. Richard Johnson at Sydney Cove (1788).

6   Anniversary of Accession of Queen Elizabeth II (1952). Flags should be flown.

7   Colony of New South Wales formally proclaimed and the Governor's Commission read (1788).

9   Charles Sturt reached mouth of the Murray River (1830).

9   S. M. Bruce Prime Minister (1923) to 22 October 1929.

11   Robert O'Hara Burke and William John Wills reached tidal waters of the Gulf of Carpentaria (1861).

12   John Macarthur received grant on which he built Elizabeth Farm House, the oldest building intact in Australia (1793).

12   E. H. Hargraves discovered gold at junction of Summerhill Creek and Lewes Ponds, NSW (1851).

12   Destroyer HMAS *Voyager* sank after collision with aircraft carrier HMAS *Melbourne* off Jervis Bay, NSW: eighty-two killed (1964).

14   Decimal currency introduced (1966).

14   Order of Australia honours system established (1975).

15   Port Phillip entered by Lieutenant John Murray in *Lady Nelson* (1802).

15   Japanese captured Singapore: 15,384 Australian troops imprisoned (1942).

16   Lieutenant-Governor David Collins landed at Risdon Cove, Van Diemen's Land (1804).

16   'Ash Wednesday' bushfires swept southern Australia (1983).

18   Headmaster Stephen Barnes opened first school in Sydney (1793).

19   Darwin bombed by Japanese planes (1942).

22   First Australian land grant issued to James Ruse (1791).

24   Governor Lachlan Macquarie announced establishment of first free school, opened 16 April (1810).

24   Barron Field, first Supreme Court judge, arrived in Sydney (1817).

March

3   First telegraph line opened in Australia: Melbourne to Williamstown, Vic. (1854).

3   Contingent left Sydney for the Sudan War (1885).

5   Irish convicts rebelled at Castle Hill, NSW (1804).

5   R. J. Hawke Prime Minister (1983–).

6   First settlement of Norfolk Island (1788).

10   William McMahon Prime Minister (1971) to 5 December 1972.

12   Canberra inaugurated by Governor-General, Lord Denman (1913).

15   First civil jury in New South Wales Supreme Court began case of Edward Smith Hall of the *Monitor* (1830).

17   Labor Party split over communist influence in trade unions (1955).

17   Australia's first natural gas pipeline opened, Roma to Brisbane (1969).

19   Voting by secret ballot, first in world, became law in Victoria (1856).

19   Edith Cowan, first woman member of any Australian parliament, elected to Western Australian Parliament (1921).

19   Official opening of Sydney Harbour Bridge (1932).

29   Australian cricket team first sent to England (1878).

29   First Federal elections (1901).

31   *Surprise*, first steamboat built in Australia, launched in Sydney (1831).

April

2   Voting by ballot became law in South Australia (1856).

3   Joseph Hawdon and Charley Bonney, first of the 'Overlanders', arrived at Adelaide with stock (1838).

3   Ludwig Leichhardt left Darling Downs and vanished attempting to cross Australia (1848).

3   Soviet spy Vladimir Petrov defected to Australian Security Intelligence Organisation (1954).

4   Queensland government annexed New Guinea: disallowed by British government (1883).

7 Champion racehorse Phar Lap died in USA (1932).

7 Sir Earle Page Prime Minister (1939) to 26 April 1939.

8 Western Australia voted for secession, but move disallowed (1933).

11 Siege of Tobruk began (1941).

11 'Advance Australia Fair' adopted as official National Anthem (1984).

12 First HMAS *Australia* scuttled off Sydney Heads (1924).

17 Police stopped publication of Sydney *Daily Telegraph* at gunpoint in censorship dispute (1944).

20 Lieutenant Zachary Hicks of Cook's ship *Endeavour* sighted first land on Australian eastern seaboard (1770).

21 Stonemasons won eight-hour day in Melbourne (1856).

21 First railway in South Australia, Adelaide to Port Adelaide (1856).

21 Queen's Birthday. Flags should be flown. Flags should also be flown on the day appointed for official celebration of the birthday, usually the second Monday in June.

22 First sitting of South Australian Parliament under responsible government (1857).

22 McDouall Stuart reached geographical centre of Australia (1860).

23 State Savings Bank of New South Wales suspended business due to depression (1931).

24 Australian Natives Association founded (1871).

25 Anzac Day, to commemorate first landing of Anzacs on Gallipoli (1915). Flags should be flown at half-mast until 12 noon, then at masthead until sunset.

26 R. G. Menzies Prime Minister (1939) to 29 August 1941.

27 Mutiny on the *Bounty* (1789).

27 J. C. Watson Prime Minister (1904) to 18 August 1904: formed world's first Federal Labor government.

29 James Cook landed at Kurnell in Botany Bay (1770). Anniversary usually celebrated the nearest Saturday to 29 April. Flags to be flown only on day on which the commemoration ceremony is held.

29 Andrew Fisher Prime Minister (1910) to 24 June 1913.

30 Announcement that Australian troops to fight in Vietnam (1965).

May

1 Forby Sutherland, first British subject to die in Australia (1770).

1 Submarine cable from Victoria to Tasmania opened (1859).

1 Hawkesbury River railway bridge completed (1889).

2 Captain Charles Fremantle took possession of Western Australia (1829).

7 James Cook sailed from Botany Bay and sighted entrance to Port Jackson (1770).

8 First Flying Doctor service began at Cloncurry, Qld (1928).

8 Battle of Coral Sea smashed Japanese invasion force (1942).

9 First Parliament of the Australian Commonwealth opened by Duke of York, later King George V, in Melbourne (1901).

9 First Parliament House at Canberra opened by Duke of York, later King George VI (1927).

9 VE—Victory in Europe—Day (1945).

11 Gregory Blaxland, William Charles Wentworth and William Lawson set out to cross the Blue Mountains (1813).

13 First Fleet sailed from Portsmouth (1787).

13 New South Wales Governor Sir Philip Game dismissed J. T. Lang's government (1932).

14 Henry Parkes formed his first New South Wales ministry (1872).

17 Francis Forbes became first Chief Justice of New South Wales Supreme Court (1824).

19 First issue of the *Monitor*, edited by E. S. Hall (1826).

20 S. J. Goble and I. E. MacIntyre first men to fly around Australia (1924).

22 First fully representative New South Wales Parliament inaugurated (1856).

22 First Queensland Parliament assembled (1860).

24 Sydney first lit with gas (1841).

24 Champion Australian boxer Les Darcy died in USA (1917).

24 Amy Johnson, first woman to fly alone from England, arrived at Darwin (1930).

25 G. W. Evans discovered the Lachlan River (1815).

25 First female suffrage, South Australia (1896).

27 Referendum approved allowing Federal Parliament to legislate for Aborigines (1967).

29 First steam engine started operating in Sydney (1815).

31 Australia's first warship, the steam corvette *Victoria*, arrived in Port Phillip Bay (1856).

June

1 Sir Doug Nicholls, Governor of South Australia, first Aborigine to be knighted (1972).

1 Japanese midget submarines in Sydney Harbour until 8 June (1942).

1 Commonwealth Bank opened for business (1912).

2 E. J. Eyre completed desert crossing from Fowlers Bay, SA, to King George Sound, WA (1841).

2 Alfred Deakin Prime Minister (1909) to 28 April 1910.

3 First Federation referendum: accepted by voters in Victoria, South Australia and Tasmania; rejected in New South Wales (1898).

5 Darling Downs in Queensland discovered by Allan Cunningham (1827).

6 First New South Wales Ministry formed, with S. A. Donaldson as Premier (1856).

6 Queensland granted Separation from New South Wales (1859).

8 John Macarthur arrived in Sydney with first merino sheep (1805).

8 Last convict ship to Sydney, the *Hashemy*, arrived in Port Jackson (1849).

Second Monday   Queen's Birthday weekend holiday.

9 Charles Kingsford Smith and crew completed first Pacific air crossing from USA to Australia (1928).

14 Railway communication Sydney to Melbourne established by opening of Wodonga Bridge (1883).

15 First election of Legislative Councillors in Sydney (1843).

17 Labor Party first entered New South Wales Parliament (1891).

20 Second Federation Referendum succeeded (1899).

20 Arbitration Court accepted principle of equal pay for women (1969).

23 First mail steamship, the *Chusan*, arrived at Melbourne (1852).

24 Joseph Cook Prime Minister (1913) to 17 September 1914.

24 Albert Jacka awarded the Victoria Cross for conspicuous bravery at Gallipoli on 19 May 1915: first Australian VC of World War I (1915).

27 Edward Trickett won Australia's first world sporting title, for sculling (1876).

July

1 Victoria became a separate colony (1851).

1 First Commonwealth old-age pensions paid (1909).

1 Don Bradman established record score in England v. Australia test match (1930).

1 Northern Territory achieved self-government (1978).

1 Franklin River hydro-electric project in Tasmania banned by High Court (1983).

5 Alfred Deakin Prime Minister (1905) to 13 November 1908.

5 E. G. Theodore resigned as Federal Treasurer after political scandal (1930).

6 F. M. Forde Prime Minister (1945) to 13 July 1945.

6 Australia-Japan Trade Agreement signed (1957).

7 Australia's first kidnapping: Graeme Thorne case (1960).

10 Sydney to Melbourne telephone line opened (1907).

10 Sir Thomas Blamey resigned as Victorian Police Commissioner after scandal (1936): later became Australia's leading general of World War II.

13 L. J. Michel discovered first gold in Victoria (1851).

13 J. B. Chifley Prime Minister (1945) to 19 December 1949.

16 William Lane left Sydney for 'New Australia', Paraguay (1893).

16 John Duigan flew first Australian-built aeroplane at Spring Plains, Vic. (1910).

17 Donald Campbell set land speed record of 648·6 kph in Bluebird II on Lake Eyre (1964).

19 Australia's first major engagement on Western Front at Fromelles (1916).

19 Second HMAS *Sydney* sank Italian cruiser *Bartolomeo Colleoni* (1940).

21 Adelaide to Melbourne telegraph service opened (1858).

24 Australia won Davis Cup world tennis championship for first time (1907).

31 Western Australia voted to join the Commonwealth of Australia (1900).

August

1 Transportation to New South Wales ceased (1840).

4 World War I declared (1914).

10 Huge protest meeting in Sydney against proposed Constitution providing for hereditary nobility (1853).

10 Melbourne first lit with gas (1857).

12 Perth founded (1829).

13 First public demonstration of wireless telephony in Sydney (1919).

15 Bill to form settlement in South Australia on Wakefield's principles became law (1834).

15 VJ—Victory over Japan—Day (1945).

16 Matthew Flinders discovered Moreton Bay (1800).

18 Lord Sydney announced Britain's plan to settle Australia (1786).

18 G. H. Reid Prime Minister (1904) to 5 July 1905.

20 American 'Great White Fleet' visited Sydney (1908).

22 James Cook landed on Possession Island and took official possession of the east coast, naming it New South Wales (1770).

22 England connected to Adelaide via Darwin by cable and telegraph lines (1872).

24 First world title fight in Australia—Tommy Burns defeated by Jack Johnson in Sydney (1908).

25 Inaugural meeting of the first New South Wales Legislative Council (1824).

26 First land defeat of Japanese, by Australians at Milne Bay, New Guinea (1942).

27 Explorer John Forrest reached Adelaide from Perth (1870).

28 First meeting of Australasian Association for the Advancement of Science (1888).

29 Australia defeated English test team at the Oval to win the first 'Ashes' (1882).

29 A. W. Fadden Prime Minister (1941) to 7 October 1941.

September

1 Jack Donahoe, bushranger, shot dead by police (1830).

1 ANZUS Treaty signed for mutual defence of Australia, New Zealand and United States of America (1951).

3 Australian flag chosen by public contest (1901).

3 World War II declared (1939).

5 Captain John Lort Stokes discovered Port Darwin (1839).

5 Charles Rasp discovered mineral wealth of Broken Hill (1883).

10 Moreton Bay settlement first called Brisbane (1825).

11 Captain John Hunter became Governor of New South Wales (1795).

12 Lieutenant John Bowen made first permanent occupation of Van Diemen's Land (1803).

12 Railway from Hobson's Bay to Melbourne—the first in Australia—opened (1854).

14 First sod of Transcontinental Railway turned at Port Augusta, SA (1912).

16 First steam tram service opened in Sydney (1879).

16 Royal Australian Navy lost its first submarine off coast of New Britain (1914).

16 Television broadcasts began in Sydney (1956).

17 First International Exhibition opened in Garden Palace, Sydney (1879).

17 Gold discovered at Coolgardie, WA (1892).

17 Andrew Fisher Prime Minister (1914) to 27 October 1915.

19 Coal discovered at Newcastle, NSW (1797).

21 First Victorian gold-mining licence issued (1851).

22 First direct wireless message from England to Australia received at Wahroonga, NSW (1918).

22 Anti-Communist Referendum defeated (1951).

24 Alfred Deakin Prime Minister (1903) to 27 April 1904.

26 Australia won America's Cup yachting contest (1983).

28 Captain Philip Gidley King became third Governor of New South Wales (1800).

28 Captain William Lonsdale arrived at Port Phillip as first Police Magistrate (1836).

28 First Australian troops to Korean War (1950).

October

1 Ludwig Leichhardt set out from Jimbour station in Queensland for Port Essington (1844).

3 Hamilton Hume and William Hovell set out for Westernport, Vic., from Appin, NSW (1824).

3 Australian troops broke through Hindenburg line in World War I (1918).

4 Arrival of first Royal Australian Navy ships in Port Jackson (1913).

7 John Curtin Prime Minister (1941) to 6 July 1945.

8 Yass-Canberra selected as site for Federal capital (1908).

9 Lieutenant-Colonel David Collins formed penal settlement in Port Phillip Bay (1803).

11 Australia's first university inaugurated in Sydney (1852).

11 Boer War declared (1899).

14 First issue of the *Australian*, the first independent newspaper in Australia (1824).

16 Westgate Bridge collapsed in Melbourne: thirty-two dead (1970).

17 Completion of Transcontinental Railway (1917).

17 Snowy River hydro-electric scheme began (1949).

20 US President L. B. Johnson visited Australia (1966).

20 Sydney Opera House opened (1973).

21 Responsible government proclaimed in Western Australia (1890).

21 J. S. T. McGowen became first New South Wales Labor Premier (1910).

22 J. H. Scullin Prime Minister (1929) to 6 January 1932.

24 Sir Henry Parkes delivered his 'Tenterfield' speech on Federation (1889).

24 First responsible ministry in South Australia formed with Boyle T. Finniss as Premier (1856).

24 United Nations Day. United Nations flag should be flown.

27 W. M. Hughes Prime Minister (1915) to 9 February 1923.

28 First Conscription Referendum defeated and Labor Party split (1916).

November

1 World's first stamped envelopes issued in Sydney (1838).

1 First Cabinet under responsible government in Tasmania, with W. T. N. Champ as Premier (1856).

1 World's last great cavalry charge, by Light Horse at Beersheba in Palestine (1917).

First Tuesday Melbourne Cup

2 Battle of Kokoda won in New Guinea (1942).

3 Charles Sturt set out from Sydney on his expedition to the Murrumbidgee (1829).

5 Police strike, Melbourne (1923).

6 Commodore J. E. Erskine proclaimed British protectorate of Papua (1884).

7 First Melbourne Cup race, won by Archer (1861).

The **huge monoliths of Mount Olga** in the Northern Territory provide a spectacular sight. Ernest Giles was the first European to find the mountains, describing them in 1872 as a collection of 'monstrous pink haystacks, leaning for support against one another'.

8 Judge H. B. Higgins announced world's first basic wage (1907).

9 First HMAS *Sydney* defeated German cruiser *Emden* at Cocos Island (1914).

9 Court judgement confirmed award of Archibald Prize to William Dobell for portrait of Joshua Smith (1944).

10 Home of Victorian Premier Sir Stanley Argyle bombed (1931).

11 Remembrance Day (previously Armistice Day). World War I ended at 11 a.m., 11 November 1918. Flags should be flown at masthead from 8 a.m. to 10.30 a.m.; half-mast from 10.30 a.m. to 11.03 a.m.; at masthead from 11.03 a.m. until sunset.

11 Colossal crowds at dedication of Shrine, Melbourne (1934).

11 Ned Kelly hanged at Melbourne Gaol (1880).

11 First cable tram service opened in Melbourne (1885).

11 Australian War Memorial opened in Canberra (1941).

11 Conscription reintroduced by Menzies government (1964).

11 Sir John Kerr, Governor-General, dismissed Whitlam government (1975).

11 J. M. Fraser Prime Minister (1975) to 5 March 1983.

12 Huge iron ore discoveries announced in Pilbara and Hamersley Range, WA (1961).

13 Andrew Fisher Prime Minister (1908) to 2 June 1909.

14 Prince of Wales's Birthday. Flags should be flown.

17 Suez Canal opened, shortening voyage to and from England (1869).

19 Pacifist Egon Kisch defied government to speak at Melbourne Stadium (1934).

20 Douglas Mawson's first Antarctic expedition left Melbourne (1911).

23 First public wireless programmes began, in Sydney (1923).

24 Van Diemen's Land discovered by Abel Tasman (1642).

28 First Cabinet in Victoria under responsible government formed with W. C. Haines as Premier (1855).

29 King George V accepted Sir Isaac Isaacs as first Australian-born Governor-General (1930).

30 Melbourne Olympics began: Australians won thirteen gold medals (1956).

December

2 John Oxley explored Brisbane River (1823).

2 First Parliament met in Tasmania under responsible government (1856).

2 First Australian visit by a Pope, Paul VI: ecumenical service held at Sydney Town Hall (1970).

3 Eureka rebellion suppressed (1854).

3 Separation of Van Diemen's Land from New South Wales (1825).

5 First elected Legislative Council in Western Australia met (1870).

5 Wharf labourers at Port Kembla, NSW, banned loading of pig-iron for Japan (1938).

5 First Australian oil discovered at Exmouth, WA (1953).

5 E. G. Whitlam Prime Minister (1972) to 11 November 1975.

8 War declared on Japan after Pearl Harbour bombed (1941).

10 Queensland proclaimed a separate colony, with R. C. W. Herbert as Premier (1859).

10 Ross and Keith Smith arrived at Darwin to win first Britain-Australia air race (1919).

17 Police shot miners during strike at Rothbury, NSW: one dead, nine wounded (1929).

17 Prime Minister Harold Holt drowned off Portsea, Vic. (1967).

19 R. G. Menzies Prime Minister (1949) to 26 January 1966.

19 John McEwen Prime Minister (1967) to 10 January 1968.

20 Gallipoli evacuated (1915).

23 First visiting English cricket team arrived in Melbourne (1861). First match 1 January 1862.

24 Major Edmund Lockyer arrived at King George Sound, WA, to form a penal settlement (1826).

25 Darwin flattened by cyclone (1974).

27 Prime Minister John Curtin appealed to the USA for help against threatened Japanese invasion (1941).

28 Governor Hindmarsh proclaimed establishment of South Australia (1836).

30 First overland mail left Sydney for Melbourne (1837).

Acknowledgements

THE AUTHOR AND PUBLISHERS would like to express their gratitude to the dozens of librarians, archivists, newspapers, publicity officers, photographers, government departments and private individuals who gave permission for the reproduction of works from their collections. Special thanks go to Debby Cramer for her painstaking efforts in carrying out the picture research for this book. Individual sources and credits are as follows:

Age, Melbourne 200 (right) photo John Lamb

Art Gallery of New South Wales 32 *Whalers off Twofold Bay, 1867* by Oswald Brierly (1817–1894), watercolour, purchased 1901; 84/85 *Without Boundaries* by Sali Herman; 86 (second top) *Banjo Paterson* by Sir John Longstaff; 102 (above left) *Miss Rose Scott* by Sir John Longstaff; 142 *W. M. Hughes* by Augustus John; 144 (top) *Archaeopteryx* by Eric Thake; 162 *The Rt Hon. R. G. Menzies* by William Dobell; 185 (below) *Dame Mary Gilmore* by William Dobell

Art Gallery of South Australia 120 *The Soldier* by Sir Sidney Nolan, oil on board 122 x 122 cm; 184 *Local VDC Parade, 1943* by Russell Drysdale (Australian 1912–1981), oil on three-ply panel 44·4 x 57·1 cm, Elder Bequest Fund, 1943

Australia Post 102 (below); 110 (below); 111 (above); 144 (second and third top and below); 154 (below); 164 (below)

Australian Archives 204; 205 (left) Walkabout series; 209 D. A. Agache's design in 1912 contest, 'Prospect View: Taken on board an aeroplane flying at a hight [*sic*] of 820 feet and at a distance of 6000 feet from The Federal Monument'

Australian Broadcasting Corporation 207 *Sydney Opera House* by Brett Whiteley, reproduced by permission of the artist

Australian Consolidated Press 159 *Australian Women's Weekly* cover, 29 January 1938; 165 *Australian Women's Weekly* cover, 21 October 1939 (painting by Virgil Reilly); 188 *Australian Women's Weekly* cover, 6 January 1951; 192 (above right) *Australian Women's Weekly* cover, 10 March 1954

Australian Information Service 92/93 *Opening of the First Parliament of the Commonwealth of Australia by H.R.H. George, Prince of Wales, 9th May, 1901* by Tom Roberts (RKD 25/8/80/43), reproduced by gracious permission of Her Majesty the Queen; 107 (State and Territory Coats of Arms); 145 (L4504); 189 (L21159); 202; 203 (Australian Bravery Awards)

Australian National Gallery 54 *The Trial* by Sir Sidney Nolan, reproduced by permission of the artist; 59 *Second Class—the Parting* by Abraham Solomon

Australian War Memorial 75 *The Departure of the Australian Contingent for the Sudan 1885* by Arthur Collingridge; 77 *'A' Battery Field Artillery, NSW 1896* by Tom Roberts; 89 *'A' Battery off to war 1899* by W. J. Allam; 116/117 *Emden, beached and done for* by Arthur Burgess; 121 detail from *Anzac—the landing* by George Lambert, 1918–1922; 122 *The man with the donkey* by Leslie Bowles, plaster 1941, bronze 1950; 124 (above) (Neg. No. E2650); 124 (below) *The charge of the Light Horse Brigade at the Nek, 7th August 1915* by George Lambert, 1924; 125 *Wandsworth Hospital, London, in 1915* by George Coates; 127 *Charger and Groom* by George Lambert, 1918, pencil 30 x 22·2 cm (2798); 128 detail from *The charge of the Light Horse at Beersheba, 31st October 1917* by George Lambert; 129 (above) *The incident for which Lieutenant F. H. McNamara was awarded the V.C.* by H. Septimus Power; 129 (below) detail from *Into Damascus* by H. Septimus Power, October 1918; 132/133 *The Anzacs*, bronze by George Lambert; 136 *Over the top* by C. W. Gilbert; 137 (above left) poster by J. S. Watkins (V5632); 137 (above right) poster by Norman Lindsay (V39); 137 (below) poster of Lt Jacka V.C., artist unknown, 119 x 78 cm (V26); 139 (E1480); 140 (above) *The Drover* by George Benson, c. 1918; 140 (below) *Sir John Monash* by Sir John Longstaff; 163 (Neg. No. 1845); 164 (above) (V1101); 167 (Neg. No. 2239/9); 168 *Bomb Dive* by Denis Adams; 169 detail from *HMAS 'Sydney' sinks the Italian cruiser 'Bartolomeo Colleoni'* by Frank Norton, 1949; 170 (Neg. No. 7407); 171 (Neg. No. 5414); 172/173 detail from *Bulimba* by Ivor Hele; 175 (Neg. No. 42769); 176/177 *Raid on Darwin 1942* by K. Swain; 178; 180 (above) *Australian guerrilla fighters in Timor* by Charles Bush; 180 (below) *Emergency landing at night, Perth 1944* by William Dobell; 181 (above) *Taking old Vickers position, Bobduli Ridge, 28 July 1943* by Ivor Hele; 181 (below) *Sir Thomas Blamey* by Sir William Dargie; 182 (Neg. No. 65322); 194 *Taking wounded from Korea to Japan* by Ivor Hele

Ballarat Fine Art Gallery—City of Ballaarat 63 *Subscription Ball*, 1854, by S. T. Gill; 154 (above) *Sydney Bridge 1929* by Francis Derham, colour linocut 17·9 x 25·9 cm

Bay Picture Library, Sydney 206 (below) *The Family 1965* by Russell Drysdale, Collection Mr and Mrs R. C. Crebbin

British Museum, London 18 *Main Settlement on Norfolk Island, 1790* by George Raper (P/717/124), reproduced by courtesy of the Trustees, British Museum (Natural History)

Cornes, D. W. 158 *Sir Donald Bradman* by Alan Fearnley, reproduced by permission of D. W. Cornes and Sir Donald Bradman

Counihan, Noel 196 *Boy 1967*, linocut in the Artist's Collection, Melbourne

Cullen, John and Old, Frank 199 *Sir John Kerr* by Clifton Pugh, 1975, 182·8 x 121·9 cm, photo Ian McKenzie

David Jones (Australia) Pty Ltd 166

Dixson Galleries, Sydney 14 *Sir Joseph Banks* by T. Phillips; 19 (above) *Vice-Admiral John Hunter* by William Mineard Bennett; 20/21 *View of Sydney, Port Jackson, NSW, taken from Rock on the Western side of the Cove, 1803* by J. W. Lancashire (DG 52); 23 *John Macarthur*, artist unknown; 58 (above) *Sir Richard Bourke* by M. Archer Shee

Evan Evans Flags, Melbourne 74 photos Ted Rotherham; 103 (above) photo Ted Rotherham

Geelong Art Gallery 28 *Major Johnston Announcing the Arrest of Governor Bligh* by Raymond Lindsay

Hall, Ken G. 155 *The Exploits of the Emden* souvenir programme, photo David Liddle

Herald and Weekly Times Ltd 157; 160 reproduced by permission of the Australian Broadcasting Corporation; 201 (above and below)

Historic Memorials Committee 33 *William Hovell* by J. Nathan; 38 *Sturt's Reluctant Decision to Return* by Ivor Hele; 110 (above left) *Hon. J. C. Watson* by Sir John Longstaff; 110 (above right) *Rt Hon. Andrew Fisher* by Emanuel Phillips Fox; 146 (left) *Opening of Federal Parliament, Canberra, 9 May 1927* by H. Septimus Power, oil 152 x 245 cm; 146 (right) *Opening of Federal Parliament, Canberra* by W. B. McInnes; 150 (left) *Rt Hon. J. H. Scullin* by W. B. McInnes; 150 (right) *Sir Isaac Isaacs* by Sir John Longstaff; 192 (above left) *Sir William Slim* by Sir William Dargie; 195 (right) *Rt Hon. Sir John Gorton* by June Mendoza; 198 *Rt Hon. E. G. Whitlam* by Clifton Pugh, 1972, oil on hardboard 141·5 x 113·5 cm

Illustrated Melbourne Post (25 May 1865) 52 'Capture and Death of Ben Hall the Bushranger', drawing by Nicholas Chevalier

John Fairfax & Sons Ltd 179

Joint House Department, Parliament House, Canberra 96 (above) *Edmund Barton* by Norman Carter

Joseph Brown Collection 147 *Industrial Landscape 1937* by Russell Drysdale, photo Ian McKenzie

La Trobe Library, Melbourne 34 (below) *John Batman signs treaty with Aborigines* by John Wesley Burtt; 82 (below) *Illustrated London News*, 10 November 1888; 86 (top) *Henry Lawson* by Will Dyson; 148 (above) *The New Australian*, Vol 2, No 1, cover April 1929, reproduced by permission of the Library Council of Victoria, photo Ted Rotherham; 148 (below) *Sydney Mail* 11 November 1925

Library Board of Western Australia, Perth 36 (below) Major Edmund Lockyer, founder of Albany, from a black and white sketch, copied from the Battye Library Pictorial Collection (605P); 41 Sir John Forrest, later Baron, as a young explorer, sketch 1870, copied from the Battye Library Pictorial Collection (5056P)

Melba's Gift Book (Melbourne n.d.) 86 (below) *Melba* by Florence Rodway, location of original painting unknown

Melbourne Cricket Ground Cricket Museum 78/79 *The first international match: England versus the Victorian XVIII on January 1, 2, 3 and 4, 1862*, watercolour by Henry Burn (1809?–1884), photo Ian McKenzie

Mitchell Library, Sydney 30 *Francis Greenway*, probably self-portrait; 31 (below) *John Thomas Bigge*, unsigned portrait, from the portrait on loan to the Mitchell Library; 34 (above) *South Australian Alps as*

Poetry and prose extracts

THE PUBLISHERS wish to thank the following authors, owners of copyright and publishers who have given permission for poetry and prose extracts to appear in this book. While every care has been taken to correctly acknowledge sources, the publishers tender their apologies for any accidental infringement where copyright has proved untraceable.

Geoffrey Dutton for his poem 'Conscripts at the Airport'; Mrs Amy McGrath (née Cumpston) for her poem 'Australia'; Jacaranda Wiley Ltd for the poem 'Let Us Not be Bitter' by Kath Walker; Thomas C. Lothian Pty Ltd for the lines from 'The Southern Call' by Bernard O'Dowd; A. E. Mander for the extract from *The Making of the Australians*; Angus & Robertson Publishers for the extract from *The Moods of Ginger Mick* by C. J. Dennis (copyright Angus & Robertson Publishers); the poems 'The Husband' and 'Anzac Cove' by Leon Gellert, from *Songs of a Campaign* (copyright Mrs C. Gellert); the poems 'Old Botany Bay', 'Old Henry Parkes' and 'No Foe Shall Gather Our Harvest' by Mary Gilmore, from *The Passionate Heart & Other Poems* (copyright Estate of Dame Mary Gilmore); the extracts from *The Desert Column* by Ion L. Idriess (copyright Idriess Enterprises); the lines from the poem 'Said Hanrahan' by John O'Brien (P. J. Hartigan), from *Around the Boree Log* (copyright F. A. Mecham); the poem 'Australia in the Vanguard' by Roderic Quinn, from *Poems* (copyright N. Quinn). The poems by A. B. Paterson, 'The Man from Snowy River', 'On Kiley's Run' and 'Pioneers' from *The Collected Verse of A. B. Paterson* and 'Our Own Flag' from *Singer of the Bush* (Lansdowne) are reprinted with the permission of Angus & Robertson Publishers on behalf of the copyright proprietor, Retusa Pty Ltd. The words of 'Waltzing Matilda' (Queensland version) by A. B. Paterson have been reproduced by arrangement with the copyright proprietors, Retusa Pty Ltd and Allans Music Australia Pty Ltd. The extract from John Manifold's poem 'The Tomb of Lt John Learmonth, A.I.F.' from his *Collected Verse* (1978) is reproduced by permission of University of Queensland Press; Leonard Mann's poem 'To Young Soldiers' is reproduced by permission of Mrs P. Laughlin; Ian Mudie's poem 'New Guinea Campaign' is reproduced by permission of Mrs R. Mudie.

Index